KYLE YOUNGBLOOD
A MAN WITH NOTHING TO LOSE . . .

Big Tony said, "Why do you want Fallon's ass so bad?"

"He had my wife and kids killed," Kyle said.

There was the sound of footsteps. Rich burst into the room, carrying a .12 gauge shotgun.

Kyle dove to the floor and shot Rich with Big Tony's .45. The slug struck Rich with such force that he was driven through the open door onto the patio.

The DOCTOR DEATH series by Herb Fisher from Berkley

DOCTOR DEATH
DOCTOR DEATH: RETRIBUTION

DOCTOR DEATH
RETRIBUTION

HERB
FISHER

BERKLEY BOOKS, NEW YORK

For my wife, Barbara Samantha,
without whom . . . nothing

DOCTOR DEATH: RETRIBUTION

A Berkley Book / published by arrangement with
the author

PRINTING HISTORY
Berkley edition/December 1988

For information address: The Berkley Publishing Group,
200 Madison Avenue, New York, NY 10016.

ISBN: 0-425-11254-3

A BERKLEY BOOK TM 757,375
Berkley Books are published by The Berkley Publishing Group,
200 Madison Avenue, New York, NY 10016.

PRINTED IN THE UNITED STATES OF AMERICA

10 9 8 7 6 5 4 3 2 1

Be comforted
let's make med'cines of our great revenge
to cure this deadly grief.

—Macbeth
Act IV, Scene 3

PROLOGUE

Cuba, 7 January, 1959

The big, dark-haired man could feel the silencer in the muzzle of the pearl-handled .45, stuck in the waistband of his trousers, pressing deeply into the soft, bloated flesh of his huge stomach. He wanted to shift the automatic to make himself more comfortable, but he was afraid the two campesinos digging in the soft earth under his patio might see him and become wary.

He watched without expression as the pit in the rich, dark earth grew deeper. The sharp snick and dull chop of the tools in the campesinos' hands mixed with the monotonous drone of the insects in the black Cuban night as the men toiled in the hole they were digging. The large pile of black earth next to the patio grew by the moment as the hole became deeper.

The big man glanced nervously at the set of double doors that opened onto the patio and led into the living room of the spacious hacienda in which he and his family lived. He turned and looked down at the backs of the two men in the hole. A frown crossed his dark features, wrinkling the deep scar that slashed across his forehead from the hairline to the bridge of his nose. The men in the hole were dressed in the traditional garb of the campesino: loose-fitting white shirts and trousers. The swarthy man could see dark sweat stains on the back of each man as they bent to their labor.

The big man grimaced ever so slightly, then shook his head. He turned and glanced at the padlocked black metal boxes stacked atop each other on the undisturbed slate at the end of the large patio. Soft yellow light streamed through the double doors of the living room, reflecting off the shiny enamel surfaces of the trunklike containers. The man glared hard at the boxes, knowing what had to be done.

Slowly he focused his attention on the men in the hole. He liked them both. They had worked for him and his people all the years he had lived in Cuba. He knew their families, had been invited to their celebrations as well as to their funerals. But he knew that personal feelings could not stand in the way of business, and this was business.

The taller of the campesinos, the one with the coarse black mustache, stopped digging and pulled himself up out of the hole. The other man, shorter and heavier, also stopped and wiped the sweat from his round, brown face with the hem of his loose shirt.

The tall man stood by the pile of loose dirt on the patio and faced his employer.

"The hole . . . it is deep enough, *padron?*" he said in surprisingly good English. The dark man crossed quickly to the hole and looked down into it. Then he looked at the stacked boxes and nodded.

"It's fine," he answered in a harsh whisper that had the sound of a file on an iron bar. "You and Armando can bury the boxes and fill it in." He stepped back from the edge of the pit.

The man known as Armando bellied out of the hole, further soiling his white peasant shirt. He moved to the stacked containers, and gripping the two handles of one, he lifted it effortlessly and set it by the side of the hole. The tall, mustached man took the box underneath and did the same.

"When you bury them, make sure you put a thick layer of dirt between each box," the dark man said raspily.

"*Si, padron.*" The round-faced man nodded and picked up the last box, placing it by the hole.

Within minutes they had set each of the containers deep in the pit and covered them with their own layer of earth. Both of the campesinos then attacked the large pile of dirt with their shovels, quickly filling in the hole.

After the last shovelful had been thrown in, the two men tamped down the low mound of soft earth with their sandal-shod feet. Each of the large black slates was then fitted back into place, so that the patio looked as if it had never been disturbed.

When they had finished, their tired muscles aching, both diggers stood and turned, facing their heavyset, dark employer. They smiled, knowing they had done a good night's work and would be handsomely compensated for it. The large, dark man smiled back, wrinkling his scarred forehead and then, from beneath his loose-fitting yellow Guayabera shirt he produced the pearl-handled .45 automatic, its nickle-plated surface glinting brightly in the soft yellow light from the living room doors. The blue steel cylinder of the silencer protruded obscenely from the muzzle of the weapon.

The eyes of the campesinos showed surprise and then fear as their brains registered what was about to happen. In that short instant between surprise and the recognition of their own deaths, the smiling man squeezed the trigger. There was a sharp, muffled report as the gun jumped in the killer's hand. A red blossom of blood appeared on the front of the tall man's white shirt. He was jerked backward, as if pulled by an invisible wire. His inert body sprawled on the slate of the patio five feet from where he had stood.

The moon-faced man stared back at the body of his friend and then turned beseechingly toward the man holding the gun.

"*Por qué, padron? Por qué?*" he managed to stammer before the dark man squeezed the trigger again. This time the copper-jacketed slug struck high in the pleading man's throat, piercing his trachea and severing his spinal cord. The bullet exited through the nape of his neck, carrying bits of bone and tissue with it.

A stream of blood spurted from the hole in the short man's throat, as well as from his nose and mouth. He crumpled to the patio, a gurgling sound issuing from his gaping wound. Despite his bulk, the big man quickly moved to the two fallen campesinos. He stared down. Both men had dropped on their backs, pain-filled expressions in their open eyes. The eyes stared up dully at the star-filled Cuban night.

Careful not to get any blood on his white-and-black wing-tip shoes, the killer placed the toe of his right shoe under each body and flipped each over on its face. A pool of dark red blood seeped from beneath the corpses. The big man knelt and almost tenderly placed the barrel of the silencer behind each man's right ear and pulled the trigger.

Then he rose quickly and crossed the patio to the double doors. He opened them and entered the house, leaving the two bodies where they had fallen.

Next to the patio, on two four-foot-high pedestals, the statues of two large black cats sat on their haunches, staring down at the two white-clad bodies. The drone of the insects continued unabated, as if nothing had happened.

The cats seemed to be listening . . . waiting for something or someone.

Chapter 1

Tucked away in the northwestern corner of the state, a short drive from the resort of Lake Tahoe, is Carson City, the capital of Nevada. Named after the famed Indian fighter and scout, Kit Carson, the city has been the capital since the Nevada Territory was created in 1861.

At the extreme southern end of Carson City, near the state capitol building, stands the foreboding one-hundred-year-old Nevada State Prison. Built in 1864, the same year Nevada became a state, the maximum-security facility is home to men convicted of capital crimes, and most of the hardened career criminals in the state.

About five miles outside the city limits is another prison. Built in 1964, it is as unlike its older counterpart as a Model-T is to a Ferrari.

The Northern Nevada Correctional Center houses only medium-security prisoners. Built in the shape of a wheel on sixty acres of ground, it is surrounded by two ten-foot-high chain-link fences topped by lethal-looking razor wire. The fences are anchored by four strategically placed guard towers. Two more towers are presently under construction because of the overcrowded conditions at the facility.

The large building that houses the administrative offices, mess hall and gymnasium is at the hub of the wheel. Long, flat-roofed prisoner dorms radiate outward from the hub to form the spokes. Scattered throughout the complex are basketball courts, tennis courts, a baseball diamond and a football field.

Originally built to hold seven hundred inmates, the center is now bulging with nine hundred and ninety-six. There are twelve men in the ten-man rooms, and ten men in the eight-man rooms. The prisoners have to eat in shifts because the mess hall is not large enough to hold the entire prison population.

Dorm B holds prisoners who have been incarcerated for offenses ranging from manslaughter to embezzlement. The majority of the inmates are middle-aged, although an occasional young face shows up in Dorm B from time to time. Most of the prisoners in the dorm are serving sentences that run from two to ten years.

The uniform at the Center is plain white trousers and shirts. Heavy black work shoes complete the prisoner's wardrobe. Each inmate's number, preceded by the letter *N*, is emblazoned across the back of his prison shirt.

In one of the ten-man dorm rooms, a lean, hawk-faced man sat hunkered on his cot, staring through the heavy metal grillwork on the window of his room. The man stared for a long time, not really seeing what he was looking at, just staring into space.

Outside the dorm, on one of the cement basketball courts, four younger convicts were playing a game of two-on-two. One of the players feinted to his right, then quickly dribbled behind his back, cut to his left and executed a nice reverse lay-up with his opposite hand before the man playing him could recover.

The lean, hard-muscled prisoner at the window saw none of this. His mind was focused on the series of events that had led him to this place, where he had spent the past two years away from his wife and children. The lines around the man's mouth were set in bitterness, and the muscles of his jaw twitched involuntarily as his teeth clenched. His dark eyes were clouded with memory. The dark man blinked twice to clear the thoughts from his mind and bring himself back to the present.

A sound in the hall made him turn quickly. An old, silver-haired con, dressed in prison whites, had limped into the room. The old man's face was deeply wrinkled and leathery from years in the strong Nevada sun. He crossed to the cot where the hawk-faced man sat.

"Hey, hero," the old man said, rasping. "The dorm boss told me you got a visitor."

The lean prisoner swung his legs to the floor and stood. He was almost a head taller than the old man.

"Scrappy, I asked you not to call me that," he said slowly, running a hand through his short, straight black hair.

Scrappy dropped onto the cot and massaged his aching left leg before answering.

"Well, for chrissake, Kyle," the old man said with a groan, "you was a hero . . . a Green Beret. You did your duty for this country for twenty years. Two tours in Vietnam . . . won herds of medals, and they shove you in a shithole like this for seven to ten."

"Why don't you get your ornery old butt to the infirmary if that leg is bothering you so much?" said Kyle, ignoring the old con while moving toward the door.

"Why the hell should I?" shouted Scrappy at his back. "All them sumbitches do is rub some kind of hot shit on it. Goddamn horse kicked me twenty years ago, and they're still rubbin' hot shit on my leg." He continued shouting, but by that time Kyle was halfway down the hall.

At the entrance to the visitor's area were two metal double-mesh doors that were opened and closed by a tan-uniformed guard seated at an electronic control panel. One door led to the inmates' dorms. The other door opened into the large, brightly lit room that was used for prisoner visitation at the Center. A floor-to-ceiling wire screen bisected the area. Lined up on each side of the barrier was a row of heavy wooden chairs for the use of the prisoners and their visitors. Behind each row of chairs was a small wooden table where a seated guard watched the meetings with measured indifference.

Kyle Youngblood waited at the second double-mesh door that opened into the screened room. The acne-scarred guard at the control panel glanced at him, yawned and pushed the button. There was a click and the door in front of Kyle popped open. The lean prisoner pushed the gate and stepped into the visitors' room. Behind him the gate clicked shut automatically. The fat guard at the table, on the prisoner's side of the room, looked up and listlessly pointed a finger at the fourth chair in line.

Kyle crossed to the chair and sat down. He turned his head slightly and glanced down the row of chairs. He was the only prisoner in the room. Uneasily he looked across at the mesh door through which the visitors entered their side of the room. Inwardly Kyle hated this setup. There was no privacy. The guards at the tables could watch and listen as prisoner and visitor conversed in low tones. The men were permitted no contact, but every so often some wife or sweetheart would press herself against the unforgiving wire, and the man she had come to visit would try to touch or kiss her through the screen. The guards at the tables would reprimand them in a loud voice. If the couples did not comply, the offending female would be removed forcibly, and the prisoner escorted back to his dorm.

Kyle had witnessed a few of these scenes but never had been involved in one. His wife, Marian, was not given to displays of public affection. He knew she loved him deeply, but her Puritan upbringing had left a deep impression on her behavior.

As Kyle thought about his blond, blue-eyed wife, she appeared in the visitors' door and waited as the guard unlocked the gate. Marian smiled self-consciously as she pushed the gate open and made her way across the room to the screen wall where her husband waited.

Kyle watched her as she moved across the floor. She was wearing the blue print dress he liked . . . the one that perfectly set off her china-blue eyes. The dress clung to the shape of her strong, lithe body as she walked, and the ex–Green Beret felt the stirrings of desire grow.

Marian smiled and slid into the chair opposite him.

"Hello, Kyle, how are you?" she asked in a strained voice. She hated coming to this place . . . to see him like this. Even after two years her face still burned with shame.

"I'm fine, Marian," he answered, keeping his voice low. "How are Seth and Rina?"

"They're doing well. Rina sends her love and says to give her daddy a big kiss." She pressed her hand to her lips and placed it against the screen. The guard in back of her started to rise, but when she removed her hand, he dropped back into his chair with a grunt. "Seth misses you. He keeps asking when you're coming home."

"Tell him I only got a couple months to go to parole, and then we can get on with our lives."

They had opted not to bring the children to the prison to see Kyle. It had been Marian's idea. She had not wanted them to see their father behind bars. When Kyle had been sentenced for killing the men who had tried to kill him and his family at their ranch near Silver Lake, Marian and the children had moved to Carson City to be near the Northern Nevada Correctional Center.

Marian had moved into a small two-bedroom apartment, enrolled the kids in school and gotten a job as a waitress at a diner near the prison. She was able to get by on her wages and Kyle's pension from the army. The children, used to growing up on a ranch, hated living in the city. Marian took them on excursions to the city's green parks and to the sparkling lakes in the area as often as she could. On occasion they had even taken a bus to swim in the clear, cold waters of Lake Tahoe a few miles to the west.

Kyle's dark eyes stared at his wife through the wire as she sat with her hands folded in her lap.

"Two more months, honey," he said softly, "and I'll be outa here."

She looked up at him. "And then what, Kyle? Does it start all over again? Fallon will never give up until either you or he is dead."

Kyle leaned forward in his chair and looked down at the newly painted cement floor. He hated when she got on the subject of Marty Fallon, the crime lord whose son he had killed.

"Hon—" he started to say, but she cut him off.

"I wish to God you had never stopped at Andy's Roadhouse that afternoon. I wish we had never heard of Buddy Fallon. . . ."

"If wishes and buts were candy and nuts, what a wonderful Christmas we'd have," said Kyle softly, looking down at the floor.

"Go on, make fun of me." She was almost sobbing, tears glistening in her blue eyes. "That night those men attacked the ranch . . . we all could have been killed."

"But we weren't." He looked up at her, his dark eyes going hard. "We survived and we're alive. Fallon's three sons are dead. Buddy's death was a mistake. The others were trying to kill us." He stopped and waited for her to look at him. "Marian, I never would let anything happen to you and the kids."

Tears spilled onto her cheeks, and she opened the large canvas handbag she carried, removed a small blue handkerchief and dabbed at her eyes.

"What if you're not there to protect us someday, Kyle? Rina still wakes up with bad dreams from the night those men came after us."

Kyle moved closer to the screen.

"It happened. What do you want me to do?"

"When you get out, let's sell what's left of the ranch and move," she said quickly. "Let's get as far away from Marty Fallon and his guns as we can."

"He's had his revenge, honey," answered the lean rancher. "Fallon pushed *Sheriff* Bookman and that *Prosecutor* Welsh to frame me for defending my family and home against his sons and his hired guns."

The fat guard at the table in back of Kyle looked at his watch and stood.

"Two minutes, Youngblood . . . finish it off," he said in what he felt was his best commanding voice. The fat man sat again and resumed his indifferent pose as he scanned the rest of the room.

Kyle pushed his chair back and stood up. On the other side of the barrier, Marian rose from the chair and wiped her eyes.

"I'm afraid, Kyle," she said, moving closer to the screen. "Fallon knows you're coming out soon. I have a feeling that this thing isn't over yet."

"Just be careful. Keep an eye on the kids. If you notice anything strange, call the police."

Marian was almost touching the screen. The guard in back of her stirred uneasily.

"I'm not afraid for us. Fallon won't hurt us," she said earnestly. "I'm afraid for you . . . what will happen when you get out."

The guard behind Kyle rose stiffly from his table and made his way to where Kyle and Marian stood facing each other.

"I can handle anything that comes our way, Marian. You should know that by now."

"Still *your* code of honor?" she said, taking a step backward. "You'll go on fighting this thing till all of us are dead."

She started to turn toward the gate. His voice made her stop.

"I love you, honey," Kyle said softly. "Kiss the kids for me."

"I love you too," she whispered, blushing. Then she turned and crossed the cement floor to the visitor's gate, her blue dress swirling around her clean, firm legs.

Kyle watched her go as the fat guard tapped his arm. The gate at the far side of the room opened, and Marian passed through it. As she disappeared from view he had a strange sense of foreboding.

Chapter 2

About four hundred miles south of Carson City on the eastern edge of the Mojave Desert and about one hundred and eighteen miles southeast of Las Vegas lay the small town of Silver Lake. The town had gotten its name in the wild days of the late 1800s, when greedy miners, driven by their lust for silver and gold, had swarmed over the earth, digging great holes that never had been filled in.

There was no lake, and surely no silver. There was only a dry lake bed out behind the old graveyard. Legend had it there had been a lake at one time, but it had dried up at the turn of the century during one of the worst droughts in the history of the southwest.

There was one drugstore, one filling station, one bank and a post office next to the general store. The town had a population of eleven hundred souls, not counting the transient prospectors who roamed in off the desert from time to time.

About twenty-five miles due west of Silver Lake, beyond a low range of hills, lay the Three-Bar-F Ranch. The main house was a one-floor white-stucco Spanish hacienda with a red tile roof. Wrought-iron grillwork hung from the hacienda's balconies. A large iron gate guarded the white concrete driveway that led to the oversize double front doors and covered veranda.

Surrounding the hacienda, in contrast to the dusty, arid spreads of the poorer ranches, were lush green lawns with full gardens of native cactus and bushes bearing flaming red flowers. Metal sprinklers showered the lawns, supplied by a huge, ball-shaped steel water tower that rose from behind the ranch like a giant phallus.

Next to the tower was a whitewashed stable area and living quarters for the grooms and stable hands. A small dirt exercise oval stood near the stables. Tucked neatly in back of the large, sprawling hacienda was an Olympic-size swimming pool whose blue waters sparkled in the bright sunlight. Around the pool were a number of small cabanas and three white metal tables, covered by multicolored beach umbrellas. The entire complex was surrounded by an eight-foot-high native rock fence topped by razor-sharp broken glass in a layer of cement.

Marty Fallon glared down at his useless legs and reached for the toggle switch that controlled his motorized steel-and-chrome wheelchair. He pushed the switch, and with a barely audible hum the chair turned slowly around and faced into the room. Marty lifted his head slightly, turning his glare on the three men in his natural-stone and teakwood-paneled library. Behind him, through the double glass patio doors, the early-afternoon sunlight glinted off the blue waters of the Olympic-size pool.

The silver-haired, heavyset man in the wheelchair lifted a large glass tube from the metal tray attached to the front of the chair. He popped the lid off the tube with his thumb and slid a thick brown expensive cigar into his hand. Marty bit off the end of the cigar and spit it into a nearby ashtray. He rolled the end of the tapered brown leaves between his thin lips and sat back in the chair. A tall, muscular man near the bar, in white duck pants and T-shirt, quickly moved to the side of the chair. He picked up a large silver lighter from the leather-topped desk and flicked it. It flamed to life, and he held it to the cigar.

Marty drew in and exhaled a gray cloud of acrid smoke. Then he removed the cigar and frowned at the tip.

"Thanks, Terry," he said to the blond, muscular man in the white pants and T-shirt. "It's like you always read my mind when I want something."

Terry, the houseboy, set the lighter back on the desk.

"I been with you for twelve years, Mr. Fallon." he said, crossing back to the bar. "You kind of get to feel what people want without them asking."

Marty took another drag on the cigar, his cheeks sucking inward, cadaverlike. He let his gaze move slowly around the room, as if he were seeing it for the first time. He loved this room. When he wasn't out by the pool, he spent most of his time in what he called his library.

It was the largest room in the house. A large stone fireplace dominated one wall. Around it, in a square, was a chocolate-brown pit grouping. A bar that would have done justice to any medium-sized watering hole stood along one wall. In another corner was a large-screen television set.

An oil portrait of Marty's dead wife, Maria, hung over the

fireplace. She was dressed as a bride. Near Maria's picture were three smaller portraits of her three sons, Smiley, Junior and Buddy. If one looked closely, one could find a strong resemblance between the woman in the portrait and her now dead sons. Maria was smiling down benevolently into the room. Marty never failed to look at the painting without longing for the sweet Italian girl who had borne him those three strong sons.

The wheelchair-bound man pushed the toggle switch, and the chair hummed to life. It moved smoothly over the thick carpet on rubber-tired wheels. When he was in the center of the room, Marty stopped the chair and wheeled around, facing the two men who sat in the pit group.

One of the men, dressed in light blue slacks and a red polo shirt, was Marty's brother, Manny Fallon. Long a kingpin in the Las Vegas underworld, Manny had come from the same streets in Hell's Kitchen that Marty had and made his "bones" in the Irish Mafia of New York. When his brother had taken the ounce of lead in his spine that left him paralyzed, Manny had brought him to Las Vegas to recuperate. Marty thrived and moved his three sons to the Nevada desert.

The other man in the room was Chick Welsh, the nattily dressed county prosecutor from Silver Lake. It was Welsh who had helped the Fallons frame Kyle Youngblood and send him to prison for a seven- to ten-year sentence.

The tall, slender prosecutor was sunk hip-deep in one of the overstuffed chairs of the pit group. In his hand he held a glass of twelve-year-old Scotch. Welsh raised the glass of amber liquid to his lips and took a sip, letting the fiery alcohol roll over his tongue before swallowing. The room was so still, each man could hear the others breathing.

"Smoothest Scotch in Nevada, Marty," cooed the tall man as he cradled the glass in both hands and held it between his knees.

The man in the wheelchair glanced across the room at Terry, the houseboy, who was leaning against the bar.

"Make sure the prosecutor gets a bottle of the Chivas Regal when he leaves," said Marty, taking another drag on the cigar. Terry nodded, reached behind the ornate bar and came up with a distinctive bottle of amber liquid.

"*Gracias,*" said Welsh, fawning. Fallon pointed the chewed end of the cigar at the prosecutor to acknowledge his thanks.

Manny Fallon pushed his bulk out of the large leather chair and crossed the room to his brother's side. Manny had the same piercing blue eyes as Marty, and even though he was the older of the two, his hair had not yet turned silver.

He placed a hand on Marty's shoulder and squeezed hard.

"Marty, I hate to run, but I got to get back to Vegas," he said, removing his hand. "What are we going to do about this scumbag?"

The man in the wheelchair looked at his brother, then he looked across the room at Chick Welsh before speaking.

"Are you sure he's gettin' out, Chick?" Marty asked in an icy tone. "There's nothin' you can do to keep him in?"

Chick Welsh rose from the pit group with some difficulty. He stared down into his glass before answering.

"I tried everything, Marty." He seemed to groan as he spoke. "I spread money around . . . I tried leaning on people who owed us. Nothing worked."

"You want my advice?" interjected Manny as he crossed to the bar. "I say let the fuckin' son of a bitch get sprung and then . . . hit him."

"Manny, we got a couple months yet." The frightened Chick cringed. "Let me keep trying?"

"Gimme a beer, kid!" Manny fired at Terry, slapping his hand on the bar. The ruddy-faced man turned quickly on Chick. "There's only one way to handle a guy like that: waste him."

Terry reached under the bar and handed Manny a cold can of beer. The heavyset man pulled the tab on the can and drained the contents in three swallows.

Marty Fallon rested his cigar in the plastic ashtray attached to his chair and rubbed his deep blue eyes with both hands.

"I can't believe it," he croaked, dropping his hands to the tray. "This Youngblood kills my three kids, then walks after two years and change."

"Gimme the word, brother," Manny said, punctuating his words with a loud belch, "and he's history."

"It ain't enough to just off this guy." Marty gripped the steel arms of the wheelchair. His eyes bulged, and the blue, wormlike vein on his forehead danced. "He's got to be made to feel what I feel."

"Marty—" Chick began.

"*Shut the fuck up!*" roared the enraged man, slamming his hand down hard on the steel tray. "It's an eye for an eye. He killed my kids."

Chick Welsh's chin dropped to his chest, and his body sagged visibly. He raised the glass of expensive Scotch to his lips and drained it.

"You're sure this is what you want?" asked Manny, moving toward the door.

"I'm *sure,*" Marty answered icily.

Manny reached the door to the library and opened it. He stopped as if he had forgotten something.

"I'm meetin' Big Tony Palermo at the club," Manny rattled off quickly. "He's bein' hassled by some treasury dicks . . . needs a place to stay where he can't be seen. What do ya think?"

"No problem," Marty said absently. "Make the arrangements."

"Thanks. I'll make the *other* arrangements too." He exited swiftly through the door and closed it behind him.

There was no sound in the library for what seemed like a long time. The bright sunlight glinted off the pool outside and speckled the dark walls of the large room.

Chick Welsh crossed to the bar and held his glass out to Terry, who splashed a big dollop of Chivas Regal onto the melting ice cubes.

"I think you're making a big mistake, Marty," said Chick, without turning. "Leave this Youngblood guy alone. He's a killer, a war hero—"

Marty pushed the chair toward the bar.

"Who the fuck asked you, Prosecutor?" the crippled man hissed through clenched teeth. "Besides, I got other plans."

Chapter 3

Marian Youngblood turned over in bed and stared through bleary eyes at the buzzing alarm clock. With a great deal of effort she extended a slender arm and pressed the button on top of the black digital timepiece.

The persistent buzz stopped immediately. Marian rolled over on her back and stared at the ceiling in the dim bedroom. She lay still for a few seconds and then stretched luxuriously, raising both arms above her head. As she lowered them she accidentally bumped her nine-year-old daughter Rina's dark, curly head, propped on a pillow next to her. The little girl moaned softly in her sleep. *God,* thought Marian to herself, *I miss the ranch . . . I miss having the privacy of my own bedroom.* She didn't tell the children, but she missed Kyle terribly. She missed the outdoor style of ranch living, and she hated the evils of the city and what it might do to her children.

Another month, she thought. *Another month and I'll have my husband with me again.* She remembered what it was like to have Kyle's muscular arms around her and having him sleep with his strong, rough hand on her stomach just below her navel.

She felt the desire for him stir deep within her body. It had been more than two years since they had made love. Marian knew she needed him desperately.

With an almost superhuman effort she pushed the thought of Kyle from her mind and turned to the sleeping, curly-haired Rina.

"Rina," she said, nudging the child gently. "Rina, honey, it's time to get up."

The little girl moaned softly, and her soft brown eyes fluttered open. She yawned and rubbed her knuckles into her eyes.

"Do I have to get up, Mom?" she asked, turning her head toward her mother.

"School, young lady . . . and I have to be at work by eight o'clock."

Marian sat up and swung her feet over the side of the bed. The ancient frame squeaked as she moved.

"I had a dream about Daddy," the little girl said, pushing the light quilt from her thin body. "I dreamed all four of us were together and we were playing in the park."

"That's a nice dream, sweetheart," said Marian, slipping into a light blue cotton robe. "Now get your body up and go knock on your brother's door. I know that boy's still in bed."

Rina rolled out of bed and crossed to the light switch by the door. She flicked it, and the bulbs in the fixture attached to the cracked ceiling flared into life. The nine-year-old girl, dressed in her brother's hand-me-down pajamas, opened the bedroom door and paused.

"Mom," she began, looking back at her mother, "how many more days is it until Daddy comes home?"

Marian turned and looked at her. "I don't know exactly, honey. It must only be about thirty days now."

Rina smiled, satisfied by her mother's answer, and padded off on bare feet down the short hall to Seth's room. Behind her, Marian crossed to the small dressing table and looked at herself in the mirror Seth had hung on the wall for her.

The image in the glass looked back at her hauntingly. The face seemed to have aged greatly in the past two years, but her figure was still trim and attractive. It was living in this damned city, she thought, having to work all those hours at the diner . . . avoiding the stares of the hungry-eyed men who seemed to devour her body along with their food.

She turned and looked at the clock. It was almost six-fifty. She still had to shower and make breakfast for the children. Marian hated to be late for work, but her boss was a nice old Greek who understood her problems and looked the other way when she bustled into the diner a few minutes after the other girls.

On this bright May morning, parked on the street near Marian Youngblood's building, two men sat in a light-colored, late-model sedan with Mylar-coated windows. The dark film on the glass made it almost impossible for a passerby to see the interior of the car.

A swarthy, moon-faced man was seated behind the wheel. He was sweating profusely. Occasionally he would peer intently through the darkened windows at the doorway of the apartment building across the street.

His muscular, blond passenger seated next to him drummed

nervously on the dashboard of the car with his well-manicured fingers. Occasionally he, too, sneaked a glance at the doorway of the redbrick building as he repeatedly looked at his watch.

The moon-faced man reached forward and lifted a pack of Marlboros from the top of the dashboard. He shook one out of the pack and punched the lighter in front of him.

"Do you have to smoke?" the blond said curtly. "You been smokin' like a chimney for an hour." He indicated the overflowing ashtray filled with cigarette butts.

"Christ, Terry," Moon-face said, whining. "I don't know about you, but I'm fuckin' nervous."

Terry looked across at him and nodded. The driver placed the cigarette between his thick lips and pressed the now glowing lighter to it. He inhaled deeply, then blew out a cloud of pungent smoke. Terry winced visibly and rubbed at his nose, as if he were trying to wipe it off his square face.

Both men were dressed in the tan uniform of the security guards at the Northern Nevada Correctional Center.

Marian looked across the breakfast table at her fourteen-year-old son. Already Seth was starting to look like his father. The dark, intense look, the high cheekbones, and the close-cropped black hair so reminded her of Kyle that she had mistakenly called the boy by his father's name at times. The both of them had laughed while Rina looked at them with a puzzled expression.

Marian looked at her watch. It was almost seven-thirty. The diner was about four blocks away, in the same direction as the kid's school. In nice weather, like today, they walked it together. When it was damp or cold, they took the bus, which stopped at the corner.

"Hurry up, Seth," she said, getting up from the table. "We'll walk today. It'll do us good."

"Okay, Mom," said the boy, pushing away from the table. "You'd better hustle up Rina. She's been in the bathroom for fifteen minutes."

Marian picked up the dirty dishes and carried them to the sink in the bright, airy kitchen. That was one of the things she had liked about the apartment. It reminded her of her kitchen at the ranch. She had tried to put some light touches around the other rooms so the children could recall what their lives had been like before they had moved to Carson City.

"I'll clean off the table," she said, turning to Seth. "You get your sister."

The boy moved through the doorway. As Marian watched him go she thought, God, he even walks like Kyle. As she placed the remaining dishes in the sink she glanced at her watch again. It was seven thirty-five.

Five minutes later Marian, with Seth and Rina in tow, emerged from the three-story redbrick apartment house and headed east on 5th Street, toward Route 513. It took about fifteen minutes of brisk walking to reach the diner, so she'd be cutting it pretty close. The kids didn't have to be in school till eight-thirty and were in no danger of being late.

There was a slight chill in the morning air, and she was sorry she hadn't worn a sweater over her brown, yellow-trimmed uniform. It probably would be colder when she left work at six o'clock.

"Mrs. Youngblood?" The deep, masculine voice behind her made her stop and turn. The children turned with her. "Are you Marian Youngblood?"

The speaker was a muscular, blond man dressed in the tan uniform of the Northern Nevada Correctional Center. He was wearing a pair of mirrored sunglasses that hid his eyes.

"Yes, I'm Marian Youngblood," she answered, a cold ball forming in the pit of her stomach. "What is it?"

Seth and Rina moved closer to their mother, as if to support her. Marian was unaware of the traffic on the street or the people on the sidewalk passing by. Her attention was riveted on the man in the tan uniform.

"There's been a problem involving your husband at the Center," he said, moving toward her and the children. "They need you out there."

Marian's hand went to her throat in that old gesture of fear.

"Is he hurt?" she asked, finding it hard to swallow.

"I don't know, ma'am," the man said, touching the black visor of his tan cap. "They sent a car for you and the kids. We'd better hurry." He indicated a light-colored sedan with dark windows at the curb.

The man in the uniform stepped to the car. He reached down and opened the door, smiling broadly as Marian and the children came toward him.

Chapter 4

The exercise yard at the Northern Nevada Correctional Center was crowded with inmates enjoying the late-afternoon spring sunshine. A large cluster of men were jammed into a set of temporary metal bleachers that bordered the first-base side of the baseball diamond. Some of the prisoners had removed their shirts, exposing white winter skin to the hot Nevada sun.

The slow-pitch softball game on the field in front of them ground on, but the men in the stands had little interest in its progress or the score of the contest. Most of the men smoked languidly or talked about the world outside the wire. A group standing by the third-base line was comparing tattoos and arguing heatedly about the merits of a nude woman on a fat inmate's stomach. She was drawn so that her pubic area was directly over the man's navel.

Kyle Youngblood sat on a wood-and-concrete bench near the diamond, staring at the players but not seeing them. At the end of the bench was a full-blooded Navajo Indian, who was doing two to four for voluntary manslaughter. He sat with his eyes closed, crooning softly to himself.

The Navajo had mercy-killed his younger brother, who had lost both legs above the knee in a motorcycle/truck crash. The crippled man had begged his kin to kill him. The big Indian obliged his brother by discharging both barrels of a .12-gauge shotgun into the double amputee's chest as he lay in his hospital bed.

One of the softball players hit a long shot into the gap in left center field. There was a shout from some of the men on his team. The Navajo opened his eyes and smiled. He turned and looked at Kyle.

"Nice hit," the Indian said in a low, melodic voice as the outfielders chased down the ball. He shrugged his big shoulders and closed his eyes again when the hawk-faced man at the end of the bench did not reply.

Kyle's mind was elsewhere. Five days ago he had been called to the warden's office and informed that Marian had not reported to work at the diner the previous day. His children had been absent from school as well.

The Greek who owned the diner had notified the police when he had tried to reach Marian at the apartment where there had been no answer. The police had checked at the children's school the next day and found out that Seth and Rina were also missing. A search of the apartment showed that all their possessions and clothing were still on the premises. The authorities had contacted the Center and asked Kyle if Marian had gone on a trip with the children.

That had been on the fourteenth of May. Each day Kyle had checked with the warden's office to see if Marian and the children had turned up. Wild thoughts ran through his mind, but he fought them off, telling himself that Marian must have taken the kids to Silver Lake to visit her family.

He told the police, and they checked with Marian's parents near Silver Lake. They had not seen or heard from their daughter in over a month; that and the fact nothing was missing from the apartment drove Kyle crazy as the days wore on.

It was now almost a week since they had not been seen or heard from, and the ex–Green Beret feared the worst. He knew Marty Fallon wanted his pound of flesh, but he never thought the crime lord would take out his revenge on an innocent woman and her children.

Kyle kicked at a dirt patch worn in the grass under his feet by the black, high-topped work shoes of the countless men who had used the bench before him. He tilted his head toward the cloudless sky. In his mind he saw Marian's smiling face in the kitchen of their ranch, then he was with Seth, shooting clay pigeons on the butte and cuddling the brown-eyed Rina to his chest at bedtime.

He felt helpless, trapped in here behind the wire, where he could not protect them. All his life he had defended others, and now he could not help his own when they needed him most. A wave of guilt swept over Kyle, and his head dropped into his hands.

There was a light touch on his back. Kyle lifted his head and swiveled around to see who was behind him.

"Youngblood?" A tall correctional officer with a fierce, black mustache faced him. There were dark sweat stains in the armpits of the man's tan uniform shirt.

"Yes," said Kyle, standing. He noted that the guard looked very nervous.

"Warden Bates wants to see you in his office." The man

continued, not looking Kyle directly in the eye as he spoke.

"Is it about my family?" asked Kyle evenly, stepping around the bench.

"I don't know." The guard shuffled his feet self-consciously. "They just told me to come and get you."

The glass-paneled door was gilt-lettered with the sign:

JUSTIN R. BATES
WARDEN
NORTHERN NEVADA
CORRECTIONAL CENTER

Kyle stood outside the glass door looking in at the balding, red-faced warden, who was talking animatedly to a tall, gray-haired man with a soft, almost feminine face. Father White, a Catholic priest, had been the prison chaplain for the past three months. Kyle had seen him on occasion but never had spoken to the clergyman.

There was another man in Bates's spare, austere office. He was seated in one of the leather chairs with his back to the door. The seated man was dressed in civilian clothes. From Kyle's angle he could not see the man's face.

The ex–Green Beret watched intently through the glass door for the wave that would beckon him into the office. He saw Bates wipe his glistening pate with the palm of his hand, turn away from Father White, and speak to the man seated in the leather chair.

Kyle stared at the red-faced warden like a hungry animal watching his prey in the forest. He was looking for some sign that would give him a hint as to why he had been summoned.

The warden looked through the door at Kyle and grimaced slightly. His face turned a brighter red, and he waved a stubby-fingered hand at Kyle, beckoning him toward the door.

With a sense of dread the lean rancher pushed open the glass door and entered the office. He paused and closed the door behind him.

"Come in, Kyle . . . come in," said Bates, attempting a smile.

Kyle came farther into the room and approached the warden's desk.

"Do you have any word about my family?" asked Kyle hoarsely. Waiting for an answer, he glanced from the warden to the tall, gray-haired man standing near the desk.

"Kyle"—Warden Bates rose from behind his desk—"you know Father White?"

The lean inmate focused his attention on the tall chaplain, who extended his hand.

"How are you, Mr. Youngblood?" The priest smiled, but his eyes betrayed his sadness.

Kyle took the offered hand.

"Is something wrong?" the rancher asked, looking hard into each man's face.

"Kyle," Bates said with a grimace, "this is Detective Nero of the Hawthorne Police Department." The warden waved his hand at the large man seated in the leather chair.

The ex–Green Beret turned slowly and faced the detective, who remained seated. Nero was dressed in a rumpled three-piece tan suit with several food stains on the front of the jacket. The big man's coal-black eyes peered out of a puffy, dough-white face, topped off by a gray crew cut. Kyle felt a strong sense of foreboding as he looked into the cold black eyes of the thick-bodied detective.

There was movement behind him, and the rancher felt an arm placed around his shoulders.

"Son," Father White said, squeezing Kyle's sinewy deltoid with surprising strength. "In our lives the Lord sometimes gives us terrible trials to overcome."

The rancher pulled his eyes from the riveting stare of the detective. He turned slowly and looked at Bates.

"It's Marian and the kids . . .?" Kyle's question hung in the still air of the room like stale smoke at a poker game.

"I'm afraid so." Bates's head dropped. His reddish-pink pate glistened with sweat as he studied the desktop.

"What happened?" Kyle's voice gained in pitch. "What the *hell* happened to them?"

There was no answer to his question. Kyle's dark eyes turned from one man's face to the other. He felt Father White relax his grip.

"Courage, son . . . courage," the tall priest whispered.

"What happened?" the rancher asked again.

Warden Bates looked at the lumpy detective, who rose slowly from the leather chair. Standing, the man seemed even more rumpled than when he was seated. He reached inside his stained suit jacket and withdrew a small three-ring, black-leather notebook. Nero opened it and thumbed the pages till he came to the one he wanted.

"Mr. Youngblood," he said with a drawl, "a couple of campers found three bodies down by Walker Lake, off Interstate 95." The detective thumbed another page. "One was an adult female—

blonde hair, blue eyes, in her late thirties. The other two victims were male and female children. The boy was in his early teens, the girl about ten."

Kyle stared at Nero's puffy lips as the detective droned on. He read from the notebook as if he were quoting a laundry list. The rancher heard the words, but they didn't register. It was as if the man were speaking under water.

"They're not sure it was *your* family," Father White said, placing his hand on Kyle's shoulder again. He could feel the ex–Green Beret's wire-tight body tense, and he removed his hand.

"They were found about halfway up Cory Peak." Nero's drone continued. "Each victim was shot twice in the back of the head with a 9-mm Beretta automatic. None of the bodies showed any signs of sexual molestation."

There was a slight smile on the detective's puffy face as he finished reading his notes. He closed the black notebook and slipped it back in his inside pocket.

The rancher stared at the man's smirking mouth. A guttural moan formed in Kyle's throat, and he started to drop into a fighting crouch. The dark, frightening look clouded his hawk-featured face as he took on the appearance of an animal ready to spring.

Kyle wanted to smash the offending lips . . . to crush the man's face till it was a bloody pulp. He took a step forward. Fear showed in Nero's coal-black eyes, and he involuntarily took a step backward, almost falling over the leather chair.

"Youngblood!" Warden Bates's nervous rasp broke the deadly stillness of the room. Kyle stopped and slowly came out of his crouch. "They're not certain who they are. There was no identification on the bodies," continued Bates. He looked at the chaplain, hoping the clergyman would say something.

"I know who they are," said Kyle hoarsely. "I *know* who they are. . . ."

"We think they may be the missing woman and children. We'll need a positive ID, Warden Bates." Nero moved to the side of the leather chair, keeping it between himself and Kyle. "The bodies are in the morgue in Hawthorne. We'd like your prisoner to come down and take a look at them."

Kyle turned slowly and stared at the red-faced warden, who averted his eyes to look at a picture on his desk. The lean rancher's head followed Bates's gaze to the photograph. In the plain wooden frame, a smiling, dark-haired woman stood on a sunny, faraway beach with three smiling children clustered around her.

• • •

The old Silver Lake Cemetery lay baking in the hot desert sun. Out behind the rows of weather-beaten crosses and headstones sat the dry lake bed that had given the town its name. Dust devils and dried mesquite danced across the flat, arid surface of the dead lake, giving it an eerie, unearthly appearance.

In a remote section of the cemetery, near a small, gnarled cottonwood tree, three different-sized caskets lay within a rectangle of chrome rails. The three boxes rested on rolled cloth tapes that would soon take them to their final resting place. The smallest casket was snow-white in color. A single red rose lay atop its lid like a drop of blood. The other two coffins, made of stained light wood, also held a solitary red rose.

Kyle Youngblood, dressed in an ill-fitting blue suit, stood stoically at the foot of the graves. The rancher was flanked by two tan-uniformed correctional officers from the Center. One of the guards was linked to Kyle by a pair of chrome-plated handcuffs that encircled both mens' wrists.

There were few mourners at the graveside service. Marian's parents and two of her blond-haired, blue-eyed sisters, joined by their husbands, stood in dark-clothed silence, perspiring in the noonday heat. Grace Cooper, the widow of a sheriff's deputy with whom Kyle had served in Vietnam, stood off to one side dabbing at her eyes with a tissue.

As the gray-suited minister intoned the last words of the funeral service from a white-jacketed Bible, he made the sign of the cross and stepped back from the head of the three graves. As if on signal, two men in dirty overalls and soiled T-shirts detached themselves from the shade of the small cottonwood tree and stepped onto the burial plot. Each man, in turn, released the catch on the tape rolls that held the coffins over the open graves. The boxes containing the remains of Marian, Rina, and Seth Youngblood descended slowly into the earth.

Kyle watched with head bowed as each casket disappeared over the edge of the artificial grass carpet. Though he mourned his wife and children, his mind burned with one thought: retribution.

From the moment he had stood next to Detective Nero in the Hawthorne morgue and looked down at the ravaged faces of his slaughtered family, only one man's face had dominated his thoughts: Marty Fallon.

Nero had told him there were no leads, although witnesses in Carson City had seen Marian and the children get into a tan sedan with a man in a Correctional Center uniform. A check of the car's license plate revealed it had been stolen the previous day.

The killings had all the earmarks of a gang hit: a payback execution. Marty Fallon had been questioned, but he was visiting his brother, Manny, in Las Vegas the week of the abduction and murders. Marty had told the investigators to send his condolences to Kyle.

Now Kyle Youngblood stood staring into the three open maws that held his family. He had seen death before . . . as a soldier he had faced it many times.

This was different. When two men met in combat and one died, there was a certain code of honor, a sense of ethics about the killing. Each man knew why he was there, and if one died, so be it. They were all soldiers sharing the same danger, the same experience. The murder of innocents he could not abide, whether it was his family or someone else's.

Kyle felt the black rage rising in his soul, like a gorge from the very depths of his being. He could hear the strains of martial airs drifting in his mind, as he had at his epic battle for the hamlet of Kontum in Vietnam where he had single-handedly killed one hundred and sixty-four North Vietnamese regulars.

Unconsciously he started to crouch, and the same guttural moan formed in his throat. Both guards looked at him uneasily. The one with the cuffs glanced down to see if the restraints were secure.

The minister closed his Bible and smiled benignly, as if he were very satisfied with himself. He paused, looking down, gathering his thoughts. As he raised his head he found himself looking into Kyle's dark, threatening countenance.

Flustered, the clergyman nodded to the other mourners and beat a hasty retreat down the asphalt path to his car. Kyle, lost deep in his thoughts, was unaware that the man had left. A sharp tug on the circle of metal around his wrist jolted him back to the present.

"Let's go, buddy," the smooth-shaven guard said, tugging at the cuffs again. "We got a long ride to the airport."

Kyle's body straightened. Using his free hand, he wiped at his eyes, which were stinging a bit. Throughout his entire ordeal—at the morgue, making funeral arrangements for his family—he had been a rock, steeling himself by using the self-discipline of his years of training in the military.

Now he felt the hard edge of his defensive perimeter starting to erode. Thoughts of Marian and the children were seeping through cracks in the thorny wall his subconscious had erected.

The guard to whom he was cuffed started down the black asphalt path winding between the neat rows of marble headstones and crosses that sprouted in the old cemetery like stone growths in a farmer's field.

Kyle looked back at the three open graves as the other guard fell in behind. He saw the two men, in dirty overalls, lift shovels from behind the carpeted mound of loose earth.

"I warned her," came the harsh, shrill sound of the woman's voice. "I warned her not to marry *you.*"

Marian's white-faced mother blocked their path. Behind the anguished woman, Marian's father stood in stony silence. Kyle stared at the raging woman as if he did not recognize her.

"Ma'am, step aside . . . please." The smooth-shaven officer motioned with his free hand.

"Doctor Death!" She screamed, pointing an accusing finger at the shackled man. *"Doctor Death . . . They named you right. You are death.* You bring nothin' but death. . . ."

Kyle turned a cold, icy stare on the thin woman in the plain black dress. She was right, he thought. *I am death. I will bring death to those who brought death to my wife and children . . . no matter what the cost. No matter how long it takes.*

Chapter 5

Kyle zipped up the fly of his worn jeans. He picked a clean white T-shirt off his cot and slipped it on over his lean, hard-muscled torso. As Kyle tucked the shirt in his Levi's, he glanced around the Spartan dorm room that had been his home for the past thirty months.

The room was empty at this time of the morning. The nine other inmates he shared it with were off at work or out in the exercise yard.

A little less than a month had passed since Marian and the children had been laid to rest in the small cemetery at Silver Lake. Memories of what had happened to them haunted Kyle like scenes in an out-of-control movie. No matter how hard he tried to concentrate, his mind kept slipping back to the morgue and the cemetery and the imagined killers of his family.

Justin Bates, the warden, had contacted the governor of Nevada and informed him of the circumstances surrounding Kyle's imprisonment and the ensuing deaths of his family. The governor had responded with a quick pardon for the ex–Green Beret, with no probationary period.

The Hawthorne Sheriff's Department had run an investigation and thoroughly searched the scene of the executions. They had come up empty. Because the victims had been kidnapped, the FBI had become involved. They had fared no better.

Kyle knew, deep in his soul, that Marty Fallon had ordered the revenge murders of Marian and the children. When he mentally pictured the wheelchair-bound crime lord, he knew that his intuition about the killings was dead on target.

Two and a half years ago Fallon had sent hired killers to ambush Kyle on the small access road to his ranch. The mob chieftan hadn't given a thought to the fact that Seth and Rina might be killed or injured. All Fallon wanted was revenge against Kyle for killing his youngest son, Buddy, in a parking-lot fight at a local roadhouse.

The pieces of the puzzle fit neatly together in Kyle's mind, yet he knew the law would never convict Marty Fallon. The man was too powerful. His connections were too high and too strong. Kyle knew whatever there was to be done, he would have to do himself.

The lean rancher scooped up what was left of his clothing and possessions and dropped them into the open canvas duffel bag at his feet. He drew the rope tight on the bag, looked around the room once more, and headed for the door.

Scrappy was seated on a patch of grass with his back against one of the dorm buildings. He sat with his eyes closed, letting the warm morning sunshine bathe his grizzled face.

"You'd never have made it in 'Nam, old man," quipped Kyle, who had squatted next to him.

The old con's red-rimmed eyes snapped open, and his close-cropped silver head turned toward the familiar voice.

"Christ, Kyle," he said, croaking, "you're slicker'n duck shit. I never heard you come up on me."

"You shouldn't be sleepin' on guard duty." Kyle laughed. "They might put you in the stockade."

Scrappy's bright eyes took in Kyle's jeans and T-shirt, as well as the tightly stuffed canvas duffel bag on the grass in front of him.

"They got me already, hero." The old man chortled. "That would be addin' insult to injury."

"I think they got us all, Scrappy." Kyle sighed, stretching his large, strong hands out in front of him.

"Looks like you're fixin' on leavin' the old Scrapper." The old con nodded his gray head at the canvas bag.

"I'm on my way to see Bates," said Kyle slowly. "Probably wants to give me some fatherly advice."

Scrappy pulled a green, fuzzy-tipped weed from among the blades of grass at his side. He snapped off the fuzzy end and placed the stem between his dry lips.

"You goin' after Fallon?" the old man said raspily, looking straight ahead.

"Do you really want to know?" Kyle said, answering Scrappy's question with one of his own. "They may *talk* to you . . . if something happens."

Scrappy removed the stem and spit into the dirt at his feet.

"Son, you know me better'n that." He replaced the weed. "Them fuckers could put a hot poker on my nuts, and I wouldn't give them directions to the shithouse."

Kyle laughed at the old man's speech. He liked Scrappy and trusted him. The old con was one of the few men Kyle had taken to when he'd entered the Center to serve his time.

"I want *him*, Scrappy," said the rancher, his face hardening. "I want that son of a bitch so bad . . ." His voice trailed off. "That's all I can think about."

"It's gonna take a lot of doin' and a lot of bucks, Kyle." The old con scratched his head and spit again. "Guys like Fallon got lots of power. They feed on power."

Kyle rose from his hunkered-down position and held out his hand to the old man. Scrappy took the offered hand and pulled himself to his feet.

"I'm gonna try it my way first," said the ex–Green Beret. "I have enough hate in my gut to handle anything he's got."

"Yer still goin' to need money for livin'," said Scrappy, holding on to Kyle's hand. "Let me help ya."

Kyle felt the old man squeeze his hand.

"You don't have any cash," said Kyle, releasing Scrappy's hand. "Besides, I don't know when I could pay you back."

"Let me worry about that. I got some money put away. A lady friend of mine, in Carson City, is holdin' it for me. I want you to take what you need."

"Scrappy, I . . ." Kyle started to protest.

"I don't want to hear no more about it. You'll pay me back when you got it." He placed an arm around Kyle's shoulders. "Lean over here and I'll give you the name and address."

Kyle bent his head, and Scrappy whispered the information in his ear. Then the rancher straightened up and extended his hand.

"Thanks, Scrappy," he said emotionally. "I won't forget you for this."

"Shit, hero," the old man said, "you goin' to make me blubber. Just do me one favor . . . get that son of a bitch that did in your wife and kids."

He took Kyle's hand and pumped it a couple times. Then he let go and dropped back down to his position against the wall.

Kyle picked up the duffel bag and headed across the compound toward the administration building. As Scrappy watched him go, the old man's eyes became bright with moisture, and he wiped them with the back of his hand.

When Kyle entered the glass-enclosed office, Bates rose from behind his desk and extended his hand. Kyle took it and gave him a firm shake.

"Big day for you, eh?" said the red-faced warden, dropping back in his seat.

Kyle nodded.

"I wanted to thank you, Warden . . . for gettin' me out," said the rancher. "I appreciate it."

"Have a seat, Kyle." Bates indicated one of the leather chairs. "I wanted to talk to you before you left. That's why I sent for you."

Kyle eased into the stiff-backed chair and looked at the warden over the bare desktop.

"Any new developments?" asked Kyle, leaning forward.

"Nope. The FBI and the people in Hawthorne have run into a dead end."

"I'm not surprised," said Kyle coldly. "Most times, if you want something done, you have to do it yourself."

Bates leaned forward across the desk and stared into Kyle's dark eyes.

"Youngblood . . . don't take the law into your own hands. I know you're bitter and I can't blame you"—he paused for breath—"but use the system. It's not perfect, but it's the only one we have."

Kyle stared back into Bates's earnest face, half hearing what the warden was saying. The drone of the man's voice did not even penetrate Kyle's consciousness, for the lean, hawk-faced rancher's mind was pondering how long it would take him to reach Silver Lake by bus.

Chapter 6

A day later a dust-covered Greyhound bus rolled down Silver Lake's wide main street. It turned left at the intersection of Fremont and Sutter, continued on until it reached the run-down bus station in the middle of the block.

The bus's air brakes hissed loudly, scaring an emaciated stray dog that bolted from under the station's rusted marquee into the street, where it was nearly struck by a passing pickup truck. Two old men, dressed in Western shirts and Levi's, sat on some empty wooden boxes set against the depot wall. On their heads were battered, straw cowboy hats pulled down low over their eyes. One of the men constantly spit into a rusted coffee can at his feet, while the other eyeballed the dusty Greyhound that had started to discharge its passengers.

Kyle moved down the cramped aisle of the bus, feeling a sense of nervous tension run through his body like an electric current. As he approached the open doors at the front of the bus, the rancher looked through one of the dirty windows, trying to catch a glimpse of the town he had left two and a half years before.

A young Marine, directly in front of Kyle, reached up and pulled a yellow-and-red gym bag with the letters U.S.M.C. stenciled on the side from the luggage rack over his head. He grasped the chrome rail with his free hand and swung down the steps onto the sidewalk.

Kyle took the two steps to the pavement slowly. He glanced at the young Marine moving off down the street. There was something vaguely familiar about the boy.

As the rancher exited the bus one of the old men seated on the boxes looked up sharply. His hat brim shaded the top half of his face, but his squinted eyes missed nothing as Kyle moved to the side of the Greyhound to wait for the sweating driver to remove his duffel bag from the luggage bay.

The old man got up quickly from the box, shot a furtive glance at his partner, and hustled off down the street toward the Silver Lake Sheriff's Office. In his haste he kicked over the rusted coffee can half full of tobacco juice. The brown contents of the can spilled onto the sidewalk and spread toward the curb.

Kyle took the canvas bag from the driver and hoisted it to his shoulder. Then he followed the old man down the street, carefully stepping over the brown puddle as it ran over the curb and into the gutter.

The Greek's diner had been remodeled in the thirty months Kyle had spent in the Northern Nevada Correctional Center. As he sat at the counter sipping an early-morning cup of black coffee, he glanced at the new booths and fixtures. Kyle missed the old, uncomfortable wooden tables and chairs, the white tile floor, and the cracked, vinyl-topped swivel stools at the counter. There was something missing. The place was too clean . . . too antiseptic-looking.

The rancher had brought his wife there for dinner on their tenth anniversary. The booth he and Marian had eaten in was gone. In its place was one of molded fiberglass. Kyle recalled the bottle of wine they had shared, and the warm, sensuous lovemaking in the big brass bed later that night at the ranch. His eyes started to sting, and he had to pinch the bridge of his nose with his thumb and forefinger to make the watering stop.

Kyle dropped his left hand to his thigh as he took another sip from the brightly colored plastic cup. Even the old white porcelain mugs were gone. With his hand he could feel the wad of bills in the left-hand pocket of his jeans.

Scrappy's friend, in Carson City, had turned out to be a dumpy, bleached-out blond in her late fifties who owned seven cats that meowed constantly. Through her heavy makeup she had oozed maudlin amounts of pity about Marian and the children, which had embarrassed Kyle and made him uneasy.

He borrowed two thousand dollars. She had wanted to press another five hundred on him, but he had turned it down, thanking her for her generosity. The blond, whose name was Verna, had asked Kyle to stay the night, winking lewdly at him. The rancher thanked her again to a chorus of meows and beat a hasty retreat through the front door.

Kyle sipped the last of his coffee, dropped a dollar bill on the new countertop, and stood. On a stool at the end of the counter he noticed the young Marine from the bus staring his way. As Kyle focused on him the young man, in a fresh tan uniform, averted his gaze.

The hawk-faced man looked closely at the profile of the close-cropped recruit. A glimmer of recognition slowly dawned on him as he realized who the young Marine was.

As the rancher made his way to the door the youngster glanced up furtively from the counter, catching Kyle's eye once again. Kyle nodded. The boy smiled self-consciously, then looked away again.

Kyle turned from the door and crossed to where the boy sat. He stood behind him for a beat before speaking.

"How are you doin', Matt?" said Kyle softly. "I didn't know you were in the service."

Matt Harvey swiveled slowly around on the stool and looked up into Kyle's face.

"Hi, Kyle," the young recruit answered. "I got liberty for thirty days. I just finished boot camp at Pendelton."

"How's your mother and father doin'?" asked Kyle, referring to Sam and Belle Harvey, who had owned the adjoining ranch.

"They're okay, I guess," answered the handsome young man. "I haven't seen 'em in a while."

"Tell 'em I said hello," said Kyle, rising from the stool. "You take care of yourself." The rancher started for the door.

"Kyle"—the boy's voice stopped him—"my pa wanted to help you that night." The boy's head dropped. "He really did . . . he wasn't scared . . ."

"I know," said the ex–Green Beret coldly, without turning. "I know he *wanted* to help."

Kyle started toward the door again. The youngest of Sam Harvey's three sons watched as the lean man moved down the aisle. The boy felt he had to say something else.

"How's your family doin', Kyle?" he said to the rancher's retreating back.

"They're dead," answered Kyle as he pushed out the diner door.

The rental truck was a semi-new Ford pickup. There were some dents and the covers on the seats were split, but it was a lot nicer than the old Chevy truck Kyle had owned when he'd had the ranch. The Ford handled well and had good acceleration, which was all he could ask of it.

He'd had to pay a week's rental up front, one hundred and forty dollars, because he didn't have any credit cards. The pretty rental agent behind the counter at the agency had given him an odd look when he told her he had never owned or used plastic money.

Kyle eased the truck down the wide main street of Silver Lake. The town hadn't changed at all in the past thirty months. Cooper's Service Station was still at the corner next to the bank. Clayton's General Store occupied the double storefront in the middle of the block.

The rancher took the left fork at the end of Fremont and headed toward the old cemetery. The truck ate up the four blocks quickly and made the left turn past the battered iron gates into the graveyard.

Following the winding asphalt road, Kyle used the lone cottonwood on the small knoll for a landmark to find the freshly dug plots of his family. He parked the truck and crossed the sparsely grassed earth to the graves.

Kyle looked down at the three rectangles of raw brown dirt. Grass had not yet started to sprout through the loose clumps of earth. Instead of a tombstone, the head of each grave was marked by a bronze tablet bearing the name of the person resting there.

As Kyle stared down at the names of his wife and children, inscribed on the markers, the sound of a car door slamming made him turn. What he saw made the muscles of his jaw tighten.

Big John Bookman, Silver Lake's sheriff, had exited his tan police car and was making his way across the scattered graves toward him. The massive lawman was sweating profusely in the early-afternoon desert heat. His tan shirt had large, dark stains under the arms and near the bulging waistband of his trousers.

Big John had been Silver Lake's elected sheriff since 1947, when he had beaten his predecessor, Sheriff Alfie McVey, in a landslide victory. The landslide vote had been caused by a leaked story that Sheriff McVey had humped a drunken female prisoner in one of the jail's holding cells. No one knew where the story had come from, but Deputy John Bookman had been on duty the night in question.

During his first few years on the job, the big sheriff had played it reasonably straight. He was not above fixing a parking ticket or "cutting some slack" for a local rancher's son who had gotten into a minor hassle with the law.

As time went on, Big John found it easier and easier to take the graft money that was offered to him. He'd paid for his children's college education and built up a hefty retirement nest egg. By now he was in the "pocket" of every two-bit hoodlum in the county.

Marty Fallon and his sons had been Bookman's biggest benefactors over the years. It was this fact of life that had kept the sheriff from coming to Kyle's aid on the night of the attack on the

Youngblood ranch some three years ago.

Bookman had sent Deputy Del Cooper, Kyle's friend, on a false errand to pick up a prisoner in a town four hundred miles away. Del had made the redheaded Grace Cooper a widow that night when he skidded off the road and into a telephone pole to avoid an oncoming truck.

Kyle watched as the big man stepped gingerly over another fresh grave and made his way toward him. Big John stopped a couple paces away. He doffed his wide-brimmed summer straw hat and nervously wiped the sweatband with a wrinkled blue kerchief that he took out of his rear pocket.

"Howdy, Kyle," Bookman said, puffing, obviously out of breath from his walk up the knoll.

"Sheriff." Kyle nodded coldly, his lips drawn into a thin, scarlike line.

"I read in the paper where the governor gave you a pardon," said the sheriff, putting the straw hat back on his head.

"*Bad* news travels fast," said Kyle sarcastically. He started to turn his back on Bookman.

"Kyle, I don't want no trouble in my town." The big man was almost whining. "Why don't you let it go? Let the dead lie."

The lean rancher took a step toward Bookman, causing the sheriff to retreat and almost lose his balance.

"You sorry son of a bitch," Kyle said with a growl, a dark, menacing look starting to take over his features. "You want to see trouble, you want to see the dead . . . look behind me."

The ex–Green Beret started to crouch, like an animal about to spring. Bookman retreated further, stepping into the soft earth of the plot he had crossed over on his way up the knoll. Big John toppled backward, sprawling full-length across the grave.

With fear in his eyes the big sheriff scrambled to his feet and ran the remaining distance to his car. He glanced back once to see if Kyle was following him. Big John opened the door of his car and climbed in without bothering to slap the dirt stains from his uniform.

Kyle watched Bookman start the car and drive hastily out of the cemetery. Slowly he turned back to the graves of his family as the sheriff's tan vehicle careened through the battered gates and up the highway back to Silver Lake.

As the lean rancher looked down at the bronze markers, he knew he could not "let it go," as Bookman had said. He would seek revenge until he, or the ones responsible, were dead.

At the foot of Rina's grave he dropped to one knee and bowed his head. Something yellow caught his eye among the brown clods of earth. He reached out and plucked a yellow buttercup from the grave.

Kyle held the fragile blossom in his hand and stared at it for a long time before rising and walking down the knoll to his truck.

Chapter 7

It was about three-thirty that afternoon when Kyle eased the rented pickup into an empty parking space in front of Clayton's General Store. He turned off the engine and sat for a long moment staring vacantly through the dusty windshield.

Had it only been three years? He wondered what would have happened if he had not stopped at Andy's Roadhouse for a beer on the way home from Silver Lake that day. Kyle regretted few things in his life, but that moment at Andy's was one he would now like to have back.

He remembered something that Scrappy, the old con, had said to him before he'd left the Center. They were on a bench in the exercise yard, and Kyle had voiced his feelings about the deaths of Marian and the children. Scrappy had closed his eyes, leaned back on the bench, and said, "You can't look back. You can't have regrets in this life. You'll drive yourself nuts."

Kyle had looked at the old man and realized that what he said was true, but he still flailed himself for having stopped at the roadhouse. It was a burden he would carry for the rest of his life.

The rancher sighed deeply and extracted the ignition key from the lock. He opened the door of the truck and slid to the street, searching in his jeans pocket for a quarter to feed the parking meter.

The bell on Clayton's door tinkled merrily as Kyle entered. As he looked around he noted that the store hadn't changed much. The gun rack and ammunition case were still behind the front counter by the cash register. Pipe racks of ranch-style clothing filled the back of the store. The hardware and food sections were still located in a large section on the left.

As Kyle looked around he realized he was the only customer. There was a creak, an accordion-pleated fiber door behind the register was pushed back, and a small balding man stepped to the counter. It was Clayton Peters, the owner of the store.

The man's eyes widened with surprise as he saw Kyle standing in front of him. He tried to smile, but it came off more as a smirk.

"Hi, Kyle," he said, leaning on the countertop with both hands. "I heard you were in town."

Kyle looked at him coldly and moved closer to the counter.

"Seems like nobody can keep a secret anymore," Kyle said softly. Peters didn't know what to make out of Kyle's comment. He smiled again, this time showing a set of tobacco-stained teeth.

"I was sorry to hear about your wife and kids, Kyle." The storekeeper looked uncomfortable. "They got any idea who done it?"

Kyle stared at Clayton Peters for a long moment. To the balding man it seemed as though the rancher's eyes had changed to a darker color.

"The police are workin' on it." Kyle's voice was almost inaudible.

"That's good, Kyle . . . that's good," said Peters, rubbing his sweating palms together. "What can I get you today?"

Kyle looked past him at the display of hunting knives hanging on a pegboard against the wall.

"I need a knife, Clayton," said Kyle, leaning forward. "That Ka-Bar style will do fine." He pointed at the Marine Corps replica pinned on the board.

"Are you allowed to buy a knife?" asked Peters tentatively.

"I'm not on probation. I've been *pardoned* by the governor." Kyle's face took on the dark, menacing look again. "While you're at it, I need some black shoe polish and a pair of light gloves."

"Sure thing, Kyle," said the storekeeper as he turned and started to unhook the bluish-black, leather-handled knife from the pegboard. "I was just concerned. We ain't supposed to sell weapons to—"

"Don't worry yourself, Clayton." Kyle smiled. "I just need the knife to do some carvin'."

The sun was starting to drop low, just topping the range of blue hills on the western rim of the desert, when Kyle turned up the small access road that led to his old ranch. He maneuvered the pickup around the sharp curve and past the gnarled trunk of the cottonwood, where he and his children had been ambushed by Marty Fallon's hired killers.

The sight of the old stable and the burned-out skeleton of his ranch house made him start. In his mind he had pictured the house to be standing against the desert sky as it once had been. Most of the posts and barbed wire he and Seth had used to shorten the defensive perimeter on the night of the attack were still upright. Some of the posts had rotted at the base and dropped into the reddish dust of the ranch yard or were hanging by their grotesque strands of rusted wire.

Kyle pulled the rented Ford up to the twisted hulk of his old truck, which sat in the ranch yard like a rusting war memorial on some remote Pacific island. He cut the engine, opened the door, and stepped down into reddish dust.

To his left stood the stable where he had kept his quarter horses and other stock. Directly in front of him were the remnants of his one-story ranch house. The stone chimney rose starkly out of the charred timbers like a black finger pointing to heaven.

Kyle moved toward what had been the back porch. He stepped on the warped boards and peered into what had been the kitchen. The refrigerator and stove were blackened, rusted hunks of metal twisted by the intense heat. All the wood in the room had been burned away by the flames.

He had made himself come back to this place of death . . . this charnel house. Twelve men had been sent to kill him that night, and he had killed them all. It was as if he *needed* to see this killing ground once again, to draw a kind of sustenance from it, like a warrior king of old, looking across the bodies of his fallen foes after a day-long battle.

As Kyle stared into the blackened embers of the room, a piece of faded olive-drab cloth, sticking out from under a charred timber, caught his eye. He stepped through what was left of the door frame and reached for the piece of material. Kyle caught it between his thumb and forefinger and pulled it free.

It was a piece of cloth from the flak jacket his comrades in 'Nam had given him to commemorate what he'd done at Kontum. They had inscribed the nickname Doctor Death on the back in large white block letters. It had saved Kyle's life the night of the attack at the ranch.

The edges were charred, but there was a foot-square piece still intact. Kyle turned the olive-drab section over in his fingers. On the back, in white block letters, he could still make out one word:

DEATH

Chapter 8

The headlamps of the Ford pickup bore into the thick blackness of the desert night. Kyle Youngblood hit the high-beam button with his left foot and dimmed the brights as a car approached from the opposite direction. The driver blinked his lights twice, thanking Kyle for the courtesy.

The rancher looked down at his left wrist, trying to catch a glimpse of the luminescent dial on his watch. It was the same one he had worn through two tours of duty in Vietnam. The light from the dash made the greenish numbers glow enough to show him it was 10:05 P.M.

On the seat next to Kyle lay the purchases he had made at Clayton's. A small coil of brown lamp cord lay on top of the dash. A closet knob, from Kyle's motel room, was knotted at each end of the cord.

His mind was carefully, almost surgically, going over the plan of attack on the Three-Bar-F. Kyle had driven by the ranch in the late afternoon, on his way back to the motel. He had seen the stone wall surrounding the main house and stable area. He had also seen the armed men patrolling the manicured grounds.

The rancher felt the best way to get at Marty Fallon was through the back of the complex, where the horses were stabled. He could gain entrance next to the pool, then find a back door into the house.

The wheelchair-bound man was sure to have a bodyguard, but the element of surprise would be on Kyle's side.

The ex–Green Beret had chosen a knife as a quiet, efficient means of extracting his revenge on the crimelord. The Ka-Bar would be swift, deadly, and silent. In his mind Kyle felt a firearm could attract too much attention and would have been too easy a death for a man who had caused so much grief.

His instincts told him he had to move in and out of the

Three-Bar-F complex quickly. Kyle had counted four men with guns inside the wall, and one guarding the gate, on his drive-by in the afternoon. There were probably more men inside the house, but he'd take care of that problem when he came to it.

The crossroad to the Fallon spread came up quickly in the darkness. He cut the wheel sharply to the left. The truck's tires squealed in complaint as the vehicle swerved wildly on the asphalt and hit the shoulder. It fishtailed sideways on the dirt, then righted itself as Kyle turned the truck into the skid and came back on the highway.

The rancher squeezed the wheel with both hands and breathed a sigh of relief.

"Pay attention to what you're doin', Kyle," he said aloud. "You don't want to do Fallon no favors by killin' yourself."

The eight-foot-high natural-stone wall and front gate of the Fallon ranch was set back a short way from the road on which Kyle was traveling. As he came around a slow curve the lights of his rented truck picked up the black, glossy metal of the closed gate.

"Oh, shit," said Kyle through clenched teeth. "They got the son of a bitch lit up like a Christmas tree."

Floodlights, mounted on the white-stucco hacienda's red-tiled roof, bathed the lush green grounds of the Three-Bar-F in bright yellow light. As the rented Ford pickup cruised slowly past, Kyle again counted four men with shotguns.

Two men, dressed like ranch hands, were seated on the covered veranda talking. They had their weapons draped across their knees. The other two stood in the driveway smoking. The guard at the front gate was carrying what looked like an M16 cradled in his left arm.

Kyle's mind was racing as the truck rolled by the gate and moved past the natural-stone wall. He cursed himself softly for not seeing the mounted lights earlier that afternoon. There was no way he could go over the wall with the place lit up like the Strip in Las Vegas.

Somehow he had to blow those lights. He only needed the darkness to cover him for a few minutes. If they were able to get them back on and "wasted" him after he was finished with Fallon, so be it.

As he came to the end of the stone wall he saw a small dirt access road that led away from the ranch and into the desert. Kyle cut his lights and steered the truck slowly onto the rutted road.

He peered into the blackness, trying hard to discern the contour and perimeters of the road he was on. The truck jounced and rocked as it continued on into the desert for about a hundred yards.

Kyle stopped the pickup and reached under the seat for the flashlight the rental agency had provided. He snapped it on, pointed it out the window, and swept it over the nearby terrain. A large brown rabbit sat frozen in the glare of the light. The red reflection of its eyes glinted back at Kyle from the darkness. He moved the shaft of light to the left and found what he was looking for: a large stand of cactus that rose from the desert floor like a spiny, multiarmed creature.

Kyle snapped off the light and dropped it on the seat next to him. He turned the key in the ignition, and the truck's motor coughed twice and started. The rancher dropped the shift lever into drive and moved the truck off the small road till it was hidden behind the stand of tall cactus.

As the glow of the Three-Bar-F's floodlights reflected against the night sky behind him, Kyle opened the door of the rented truck and stepped to the ground. He had been careful to take the small bulb out of the dome fixture in the cab so that it would not light when he opened the truck's door.

The dirt crunched eerily beneath Kyle's boots as the drone of thousands of insects rose and fell like a pulse in the chill night air of the desert. He paused by the side of the truck. He listened closely to the sounds in the darkness.

Kyle heard a scurrying sound off to his left. He smiled softly to himself as he remembered the brown rabbit and slid his hand across the vinyl seat of the truck.

The Ka-Bar knife, gloves, and shoe polish were in a bag on his right. Slowly he reached down on the floor, where he'd stashed a heavy, dark woolen blanket that he had taken from the motel. The rancher lifted it and placed it on the seat.

Kyle took the flat jar of black shoe polish from the bag and unscrewed the lid. He rubbed the fingers of his right hand across the surface of the slick material in the jar, then smeared it on the exposed skin of his face. He worked the polish around the nape of his neck and under his chin, making sure to get down under the edge of the black turtleneck sweater he was wearing.

When he had finished covering his face and neck, Kyle wiped his fingers on the motel blanket, picked up the Ka-Bar, and slipped the leather scabbard onto his belt. Then he took the light cord and attached closet knobs from the dash and stuffed the homemade garrote into his hip pocket so that it would not rattle.

Next he slipped the light work gloves on, picked up the blanket from the seat, and threw it over his shoulder. Finally he softly closed the door of the truck and turned toward the ranch.

Crouching behind the cactus, Kyle could see the armed guard at the front gate now talking to one of the other men. From his vantage point he could see he was about a football field away from the road that the Three-Bar-F fronted on.

The rancher could also see the short wooden power poles, spaced about thirty yards apart, running off into the darkness on his side of the road. Two high-voltage lines were strung from crossbars on the poles. The lines were attached to removable rings on the pot-shaped transformers about fourteen feet up each pole.

Kyle knew there was no way he could get over the wall and into the floodlit complex without blowing the lights. He looked off to the left and saw the pole and wires that supplied the power to the house.

Years before, at the Special Forces Training Center in Fort Bragg, North Carolina, he had been taught to disable energy sources as part of a Destabilization/Counterinsurgency course. In Bragg he'd had the proper tools, and there hadn't been the added hazard of armed men firing at him.

Kyle started to trot forward at a crouch. He bent low at the waist, even though he knew the men in the brightly lit yard could not spot him in the darkness. Luckily the power poles were on his side of the road. As he reached his objective he dropped facedown in the dirt. The lights of an approaching car were coming up the road toward the ranch.

Kyle dug into the earth and started to inch back from the pole as the blue sedan sped past. He glanced up for an instant, in time to see the car's headlamps pick up what looked like a pile of trash just beyond the left extremity of the wall, where Fallon's horses were stabled.

As the taillights of the speeding car disappeared in the darkness, Kyle rose to his feet and sprinted across the road toward the pile of refuse. The guard at the gate was engrossed in conversation with his comrade and didn't look up as the figure in black darted toward the far edge of the wall.

Breathing hard, the rancher ran the final few feet to the trash pile and once again dropped facedown in the dust. Even though he was now out of view of the men at the gate, he stayed down and crawled around the back of the pile.

Some of the light from inside the yard spilled over the wall and dimly lit the area where Kyle lay. He could make out some of the objects in the pile. Some of the junk looked like pieces of equipment the stable hands and grooms had discarded.

He saw the remnants of broken saddles and an assortment of sun-dried leather reins and harnesses. Under the tack there was something else. Kyle reached into the pile and moved some of the refuse aside. He jumped as a small green lizard scurried from beneath a pile of rusted beer cans and disappeared into the darkness.

Kyle extended his right arm and moved a couple of torn green trash bags. The end of the tack pole protruded from the middle of another pile of green bags. Kyle gripped the end of the pole with his gloved hand and slowly drew it out of the heap.

The wooden pole was about twelve feet long and had a deep crack near the top. He examined it carefully and was able to pry it apart with his fingers.

He lay the shaft next to his blanket and returned to searching his treasure of odds and ends. The rancher knew what he was looking for would be in the pile. Any trash heap near a stable would hold one or more.

Kyle moved the junk around with his gloved hands till his fingers closed on the object he was looking for: a piece of a broken bit. Kyle held the hooked metal object up to the light. It was just what he needed.

The rancher pried the split end of the tack pole apart and wedged the broken bit deeply into the crack. Satisfied, he rummaged in the pile until he came up with a piece of leather harness strap he could use to tie the metal hook tightly into place. Kyle wrapped the strap around the end of the pole. When he finished, he snugged the end into the split in order to secure it.

The rancher stood in the dark and hefted the pole in both hands. He decided to leave his blanket by the pile of refuse as he started to trot toward the road and the pole that carried the power into the Three-Bar-F.

When he reached the base of the wooden pole, he crouched and peered up into the darkness. The rancher could barely make out the ringlike plugs in the transformer.

Kyle scanned the highway to make sure there were no cars coming. Then he rose slowly, with his jury-rigged pole hook in both hands. He knew that once he pulled the plugs on the transformer and cut the power to the house, he would have to get over the wall before the men inside could get the lights back on again.

He lifted the tack pole till it was level with one of the plugs.

Carefully he moved the homemade hook toward the ring that held the high-voltage wire. As the metal bit touched the ring a shower of sparks lit up the night. The lights in the ranch complex flickered sporadically as he inserted the hook and pulled hard.

There was a loud pop, and another shower of sparks rained down on him. The floodlit ranch yard behind him went dark, as if some unseen giant hand had pulled a master switch. Kyle heard shouts as the men behind the wall called to each other trying to find out the cause of the power failure.

Once more he inserted the hook in the other plug and pulled. There was a pop, and another shower of sparks issued forth at the point of contact.

Kyle dropped the pole and headed in a direct line for the trash pile, where he had left the heavy blanket. He heard more shouts, and the sound of running feet thudding on the grass of Fallon's yard.

Kyle scooped up the blanket and ran the short distance to the stone wall. As he reached the barrier he laid the blanket on the ground and folded it to double thickness. Then he rose and flipped it over the razor-sharp glass on top of the wall.

Kyle leapt, catching the top edge of the stone. He could feel the imbedded glass bite beneath the blanket, but he hoisted himself to the top of the wall and dropped over into the ranch yard.

Immediately he could sense men running past him in the covering darkness. As he started to move toward the rear of the hacienda, one of the moving figures near him stopped.

"Hey, Rich," the man called out, "what the fuck is it with the lights?"

Kyle froze and grunted some unintelligible words as the man came toward him. He slipped the Ka-Bar out of its scabbard and watched warily as the figure approached.

"Hey, what the fuck is it with you?" the guard called mockingly. "You got marbles in your mouth?"

He was almost on top of Kyle now. The rancher could barely make out the silhouette of the shotgun cradled in his left arm.

As the guard stepped next to him Kyle moved to his right, cupped his left hand over the man's mouth, and deftly slit his throat with the keen edge of the blue-black blade.

Despite the glove, Kyle's right hand felt hot and wet as blood from the severed jugular poured from the gaping wound in the guard's throat. The man struggled for an instant, his body rigid and his mouth biting hard against Kyle's gloved left hand. Then he sighed and limply dropped to the ground.

The man had made no sound, but Kyle quickly swiveled his head around in the darkness, trying to see if any of the other men were near him. There was no movement in the immediate area.

Once again he started toward the back part of the house, stepping as softly as he could. Off to his right, a flashlight suddenly flicked on. It was not aimed directly at him, but he could see one man standing in the beam of the torch. They were about fifty feet from him.

"What the hell do you think happened, Rich?" the man with the light asked gruffly.

"Probably some asshole ran his car into a power pole," the man named Rich answered. "An' get that fuckin' light out of my eyes." The man holding the flashlight lowered it, and both men walked toward the front gate.

As they moved off, Kyle started to breathe. He watched the white beam dance away down the broad driveway. Only then did he start to cross the yard toward the patio at the back of the house.

As he slipped through the darkness Kyle wiped the Ka-Bar on the leg of his jeans and slipped it back into its scabbard.

The large Olympic-size pool behind the house shimmered softly as a light breeze blew across its surface. Kyle stepped carefully onto the flagstone patio. He made his way past the cabanas and the round metal tables with their brightly colored umbrellas.

He was working his way toward the double glass doors that opened onto the patio when he saw the dark shape of a man. A guard was standing by the sliding doors with his back turned.

Kyle slipped the electric cord out of his back pocket and gripped the closet knobs in each hand as he inched toward the unsuspecting man. The drone of the insects seemed to grow more incessant as Kyle came up behind him.

In an instant the rancher crossed his arms at the wrists and looped the cord around the guard's neck. He yanked the knobs hard, tightening the wire, at the same time jamming his right knee into the small of the man's back. It was a classic garrote technique.

As the cord tightened on the man's windpipe Kyle increased the pressure on his back with the knee. The guard emitted a short, strangled cry and collapsed as the vertebrae in his back ruptured, severing his spinal cord.

Kyle pulled the wire even tighter to make sure the man was dead, then he gently lowered the body to the patio. As he looked up, he glanced through the sliding doors into Marty Fallon's library.

Someone had lit a large candle and placed it on the desk. Its warm glow flickered eerily on the dark-paneled walls. Kyle could barely see if anyone was in the room.

He placed a gloved hand on the metal door handle and pulled on it softly. Almost silently it slid back on well-oiled runners, and Kyle stepped onto the heavy pile of the expensive carpet.

Chapter 9

In the flickering light of the candle, Kyle could make out a platinum frame on top of the large leather-topped desk in front of him. In the frame he recognized a younger, smiling Marty Fallon and three young boys, who Kyle guessed were his now dead sons.

A slight sound at the heavy door across the room made him look up sharply and slide the Ka-Bar out of its scabbard. Kyle glided silently into the shadows near the doorway. The ornate knob turned, and the heavy door was noiselessly pushed inward.

A big man in an expensive white Palm Beach suit, stepped cautiously into the room as if he were afraid of bumping into something in the dark. He took a couple of hesitant sliding steps, his hands held out in front of him.

"Fuckin' lights," the man growled. "Fuckin' hicks . . . don't know how to run nothin'."

At that instant Kyle was beside the bulky figure, pressing the point of the blue-black blade against the fleshy folds of the man's throat.

"Don't move," Kyle snapped. "Don't make a sound or you're dead."

Kyle knew this wasn't Marty Fallon he had at the end of his knife . . . unless there had been some miraculous cure that had lifted him out of his wheelchair. But whoever it was could lead him to the man he wanted.

"What . . . !" the big man exclaimed. "C'mon, Nick, stop screwin' around. I ain't in the mood." The man in the white suit tried to turn, but Kyle pressed the point of the Ka-Bar deeper, stopping him.

"Nick's dead," Kyle snapped again. "Now turn around real slow and don't try nothin', or you'll be joinin' him."

The big man turned slowly. In the semidarkness of the room Kyle could make out his features. A large, prominent nose dominated the man's face. A pair of close-set, hungry black eyes stared from under thick, dark brows. A deep scar ran vertically up his forehead, from the bridge of his large nose to his hairline.

"What the fuck are you made up for . . . a minstrel show?" the man asked, his eyes widening in surprise when he saw Kyle's blackened face for the first time.

"Where's Fallon?" Kyle asked tersely, ignoring the man's question.

"He's on vacation," the man flipped back. "Who the hell are you?"

Kyle reached out with his left hand and patted the man under the arms and around the waist. His hand stopped when it came in contact with the butt of a nickle-plated .45. Kyle drew the automatic out of the man's belt and stuck it in the waistband of his own jeans.

"That's not important, mister," said Kyle. "What's important is that you've got about ten seconds to live if you don't tell me where Fallon is?"

"Look, pal," the big man said, an edge of fear coming into his voice, "he's gone to some island off the coast of Mexico. I'm only usin' the house. I got some Treasury assholes breathin' down my neck."

"Shit!" Kyle snarled, his mind racing. Fallon was gone. He should have known and checked it out more thoroughly before making his move.

"Look, pal," the big man said softly, "why don't you take that shiv out of my neck and we can talk. You don't want to kill me. I'm Big Tony Palermo. I can make it worth your while."

Kyle kept the knife point pressed hard into the soft flesh. A thin line of blood ran down Big Tony's neck, staining the collar of his silk shirt.

The rancher grabbed the big man's belt and pulled him to the leather chair across from the bar. He pushed the mobster in the chest, and Palermo dropped heavily onto the cushioned seat.

"If you shout for help, I'll kill you," said Kyle removing the Ka-Bar.

Big Tony sighed heavily and placed his fingers on his throat. He brought his hand away and looked at it.

"Jesus Christ! You asshole!" He whined. "You cut me."

"I want Fallon's exact location. If I don't get it, you are going to die."

Big Tony tried to rise, but Kyle motioned him back with the point of his knife.

"Christ! You must be the soldier boy Marty was goin' nuts over," the mobster said. "You're the one who croaked his sons."

"Where is he?" Kyle's voice was like ice.

Big Tony again touched the small knife wound on his neck, then turned his black stare on the rancher. The deep scar on his forehead wrinkled as he spoke.

"I told you, he's on his private island off the west coast of Mexico." He ran his fingers through the thick mass of iron-gray hair before continuing. "I think it's named Santa Maria. The place is a fuckin' fort. He's got a hundred men, and machine guns, choppers, boats, and radar. You can't get near him without an army."

"I don't have an army," said Kyle coldly.

"Buy one," Big Tony quipped, laughing. "Why do you want his ass so bad?"

Kyle looked at the big man in the white suit. He didn't know why, but he felt compelled to tell him.

"He had my wife and kids kidnapped and murdered," Kyle said softly.

"No shit!" Big Tony blurted out. "Probably 'cause you hit his sons. That's a tough way to go." He leaned forward in his chair. "You want to get a guy who has money and power, you've got to have money *and* power."

There was the sound of footsteps in the hall beyond the heavy door. Kyle raised the Ka-Bar and pointed it at Palermo's throat.

"Quiet!" he whispered.

"They won't bother me." Big Tony said softly. "They're probably tryin' to get the emergency generator runnin'. You blow the lights?"

"Yeah," Kyle said, nodding.

"Pretty slick, soldier boy." The big man grinned. "You need money to buy an army, I got the money."

"And you're goin' to *give* it to me," said Kyle sarcastically.

"No, I'm going to *share* it with you. I got thirty million dollars buried in Cuba that I can't get at. Somebody with your know-how and moxie could maybe bring it out."

Kyle's eyes widened. He looked at the big man in the leather chair suspiciously.

"Thirty million?" Kyle said, rasping incredulously.

"Yeah, casino money," answered Big Tony, smiling. "Its been there since 1959. That bearded son of a bitch, Castro, screwed me. I couldn't take it with me when he threw us out, so I buried it on my ranch . . . you interested?"

In the distance there was the sound of a heavy motor starting up. The lights in the library started to flicker, then came on.

Kyle heard the thud of running feet on the patio. He turned in the direction of the double glass doors as one of them slid open and the man named Rich burst into the room. In his hands he carried a Remington .12-gauge automatic shotgun. Behind Kyle, Big Tony got to his feet and held up his hands to stop Rich.

It was too late. As Kyle dived to the floor Rich squeezed the trigger of the .12-gauge twice. One load struck the big man in the chest and neck. The large lead pellets tore into his lungs and aorta, causing an immediate hemorrhage that started to drown his insides with blood. His neck and the lower half of his face were also peppered with the heavy shot, but his windpipe was still intact, allowing him to breathe.

The second load struck Big Tony in the right shoulder. Some of the shot carried on and struck bottles and glasses behind the bar, shattering them. Despite his bulk, the big mobster was knocked backward over a leather chair. He fell heavily to the floor, his white tropical suit covered with blood.

On the floor, Kyle already had Big Tony's .45 out and cocked. He snapped off a shot at the man in the patio doorway. The slug struck Rich in the pit of the stomach with such force that he was driven through the open glass door and onto the patio, where he fell across the body of the unfortunate Nick.

Immediately a short, swarthy man took Rich's place in the doorway. He raised his .12-gauge and got off a shot before Kyle could fire. The shot pattern peppered the teak walls, shattering a lamp and some pictures.

From his prone position on the floor Kyle aimed the .45 and squeezed the trigger. The automatic bucked in his hand as the slug tore into the stocky man's chest, killing him instantly. The guard was blown backward into the glass door and fell forward, leaving a smear of blood on the pane.

Suddenly, behind Kyle, there was a pounding on the heavy door to the library.

"Mr. Palermo!" a voice shouted. "Mr. Palermo, are you okay?" The door popped open, and a tall man in a blue jogging suit entered the room. His right hand held a 9-mm Browning automatic.

Kyle was too close to the man to bring his own weapon to bear. No more than three feet separated them.

With a catlike move Kyle spun onto his back and lashed out with his left foot. He caught the man in the jogging suit flush in the groin. The tall man screamed in agony as his stomach seemed to drop to the floor. Through his pain he tried to aim his automatic at Kyle, who had gotten to his knees and, with a swift lunge, drove the Ka-Bar into the guard's abdomen. Kyle ripped upward, the blade feeling the flesh give way to its keen edge. The man's eyes glazed, and he toppled forward onto Big Tony, who was lying on his back with his feet and the backs of his knees on the toppled leather chair.

Kyle crawled over to the dead man and retrieved his combat knife. Then he pulled the man off the fatally wounded mobster.

Big Tony looked bad. His dark eyes had taken on a glassy look. The man's bloody lips moved as if he were trying to say something. Kyle placed his ear near the stricken man's shattered mouth.

"El Gato Negro . . . patio," he said, gurgling. "El Gato Negro . . . patio." Bloody spittle foamed on his lips. There was a kind of rattle in his throat. "My daughter Denise . . . Miami . . . she knows . . ." There was a long sigh, like air escaping from a punctured tire. The big man's eyes rolled up, and he was gone.

Kyle rose to his feet and looked quietly around Marty Fallon's bloodstained library. He took a deep breath and looked at the blasted portrait of Marty on the wall.

"It's not over yet, you old bastard. It's not over yet."

He stepped over the body of the dead man in the blue jogging suit and made his way to the patio door. The swarthy man lay on his face behind the desk. Kyle glanced at him. There was a gaping wound in the middle of his back. He looked at Big Tony's automatic in his hand.

"The son of a bitch must be using hollow points," Kyle said softly to the dead men in the room.

The cool night air felt good on his face as he made his way across the patio to the wall, where his blanket still hung. As he reached the barrier and prepared to scale it, he heard a sound behind him in the floodlit yard. It was the unmistakable snick of an M16 being cocked.

"Okay, asshole," the voice behind him growled. "Turn around, real slow."

The guard who had been stationed at the gate had heard the gunfire and started for the back of the house to investigate. He had seen Kyle come off the patio and make his way to the wall.

Kyle turned to stare into the muzzle of the man's M16.

"Drop your weapon," said Kyle calmly, "or I'll kill you."

"You got it all wrong, mister." The guard said incredulously. "I'm going to kill *you*." As he spoke, he made the mistake of stepping closer to the ex–Green Beret.

With a swift movement Kyle knocked aside the barrel of the M16 with his left hand and drew the Ka-Bar with his right. Before the surprised man could cry out, the point of the blade had pierced his windpipe. He dropped the weapon and grasped his throat with both hands. Blood spurted from between his fingers as he fell heavily to the ground.

Kyle wiped his knife on the dead man's trouser leg, slipped it back into its scabbard and scrambled over the wall. He ripped the blanket down from where it had been held by the glass shards at the top of the wall and sprinted toward his truck, which was parked on the other side of the road.

The pickup was where he had left it. Kyle opened the door, climbed in and started the engine. He drove slowly back down the rutted access road to the highway. When he felt the asphalt under his tires, he reached out and turned on his headlights.

As the rented truck moved off into the darkness a dark blue sedan parked a short distance up the highway from the Three-Bar-F came to life and sped off after Kyle's pickup. In the front seat were two stern-faced men dressed in three-piece suits.

As the sedan passed Marty Fallon's floodlit complex the man in the passenger seat glanced through the ranch gate, but he did not see the seven dead men who lay scattered throughout the beautiful hacienda and lush grounds.

Chapter 10

Kyle worked the small cake of soap into a foamy lather with his strong hands. He raised his still-blackened face from the rust-stained basin of the motel sink and stared hard at his image in the steamy mirror.

Some of the black shoe polish had become streaky because of the sweat on his forehead and high cheekbones. White lines of flesh showed through the blackness, making him look like a grotesque caricature of some long dead Indian brave.

Kyle raised his soapy hands to his face and started to wash the shoe polish away. The water in the sink turned black as he rinsed his face and hands again and again.

The rancher glanced at the yellowing face of his watch, lying on top of the white porcelain toilet tank to his left. It was 11:55 P.M. He had called McCarran International in Las Vegas and made reservations on the 3:30 A.M. red-eye to Miami.

As Kyle worked the lather into the nape of his neck, his mind raced wildly around the events of the past two hours. He felt he had to leave Silver Lake before daylight. The bodies at the Three-Bar-F would be discovered, and Big John Bookman would get a call. Kyle knew the big sheriff would immediately suspect him, although he'd left no physical evidence at the ranch to point directly to him.

The drive to McCarran would take about two and a half hours. He would have to turn in the truck at the rental agency, which was another fifteen minutes. From that point the flight to Miami would take at least four and a half hours. He calculated that if he left Vegas on time, it would be only 12:30 A.M. in Miami and his plane would touch down at Miami International at 5:00 A.M.

Rafe Phillips would still be asleep when he got there. Kyle had tried to call his old comrade in arms from a roadside phone booth, but the number he had in his old unit directory had been disconnected.

Kyle needed Rafe. He needed the man who had been closest to him in Vietnam. He thought about the amiable black man whose ready laugh had brightened many of the countless patrols the two had been on.

Rafe had not been with him at Kontum. The black soldier had taken some pieces of shrapnel in his back and legs in a predawn mortar attack the week before. He had been sent back to the "world," as the combat troops, in country, were fond of calling anywhere on earth outside Vietnam.

Kyle had missed him like family, the same way he had missed some of the other men who had become casualties or were "short-timers" and rotated home from the hell of Southeast Asia to the real world.

He had kept in touch with Rafe Phillips over the years, exchanging letters and phone calls at Christmas and other holidays. They had made plans to meet in Miami once, but it had fallen through when Seth and Rina had both come down with the chicken pox. As the years stretched on, the letters and calls became less frequent and then had stopped, but Kyle knew that the bond of men who had been in combat together could never be torn apart by the distance that separated them now.

The shoe polish was gone from his face, neck and ears. Kyle took the towel from the the rack on his right and dried his face and hands. As he turned from the mirror he glanced at the reflection of his lean-musculed torso. There were numerous scars, mementos of the wounds caused by the small fragments of hot metal that had pierced his flesh. Each mark had a story . . . each scar a price he had paid in twenty years of service to his country.

Kyle crossed into the drab motel room, where he had clean jeans and a fresh shirt laid out on the bed. His mind drifted back to Big Tony's last words as he started to pull on his jeans.

The man had been right: If Kyle wanted revenge, he would need money and power to get it. Right now he had neither. The money that would help him reach his goal lay buried on some ranch in Cuba, thousands of miles away. His first step had to be Miami and Rafe.

Kyle hoped, with his friend's help, that he would be able to find Denise Palermo. He knew she was the key that would open the door to the treasure room.

The rancher slipped into the fresh shirt, buttoned it and stuffed the tails into his jeans. Then he picked up the duffel bag and crossed to the door, his keen eyes making a sweep of the small room to see if he had missed anything.

Satisfied, Kyle snapped off the light, opened the door and stepped out into the early-morning desert chill. The stars were beginning to fade as he climbed into the truck and started the engine.

As the rented pickup eased out of the motel parking lot, the headlights on a dark blue sedan flickered on. The crew-cut man behind the wheel put the car in gear and stepped on the accelerator. As the sedan rolled forward the driver turned to the man next to him.

"What do you think, Chet?" asked the driver softly. "You think Palermo told him?"

The man in the passenger seat turned and looked at the driver.

"Yeah, I think he's dirty," said the passenger. "I think we've got to stick to this guy like white on rice."

Chapter 11

Miami, from the air, looked like the Magic City its Chamber of Commerce proclaimed it to be. The tall pink-and-white skyscrapers resembled a child's set of pastel-colored building blocks. To the west, the taller structures gave way to the boxlike bedroom communities of Miami Springs and Sweetwater. Then the lush, verdant green of the Everglades took over and ran off toward the Gulf of Mexico. To the east, the translucent Atlantic showed varying shades of emerald green in the waters that lapped the once opulent hotels of Miami Beach's shopworn gold coast. Farther out, beyond the green shallows, the water was a darker blue as the sea bed fell away toward the islands of the Bahamas.

As the huge jet banked for its final approach Kyle caught another glimpse of the Magic City. Somewhere down there, he thought, Rafe would be leaving for work. The rancher glanced at his watch. It was 8:45 A.M. His flight had been delayed close to four hours in Las Vegas, causing him to keep looking over his shoulder, expecting to see Big John Bookman come striding through the glass doors of McCarran Airport.

His ears popped a bit as the airliner dropped swiftly toward Miami International's runway. Kyle felt a slight bump as the plane's wheels touched down. He unfastened his seat belt as the big jet taxied toward the group of white buildings that served as the airport's terminal.

Kyle rose as the plane came to a stop, and the other passengers crowded into the aisle, moving quietly toward the exit doors. Four seats behind him, two men, dressed in similar three-piece suits, stood and retrieved brown leather attaché cases from the floor of the cabin.

The Treasury men, Chet Allen and Phil McGregor, glanced at each other and eased into the aisle in front of an elderly Cuban couple that was returning from a visit with their son, who was a dealer at Caesar's Palace.

The Cuban cabdriver kept looking at his fare in the rearview mirror as he moved his vehicle through the trash-strewn streets of the Liberty section of Miami. The cabbie had looked at the rancher oddly when Kyle had given him Rafe's address in all-black Liberty. The driver had even asked Kyle twice, in broken English, if he was sure he had the right address.

It was still morning, but Kyle could feel south Florida's summer heat baking through the roof of the cab. They made a right turn off the palm-lined, garbage-littered boulevard and almost struck a mangy dog, who was gnawing at the bones of a chicken carcass in the middle of the street. The dog skittered off down a urine-soaked alley as the cab's brakes screeched loudly.

A group of middle-aged black men, lounging in front of a shuttered bar, glanced curiously at the cab and its white occupant. One of the men pointed and said something to the others, who turned and glared at the passenger in the backseat.

Kyle's driver stepped on the accelerator, but before the cab had gone ten feet, a beer bottle, thrown by one of the loungers, crashed onto the hood of the vehicle. The cabbie jammed his foot down hard on the gas, and the taxi left a trail of rubber as it jackrabbited down the street.

"Friendly group," said Kyle, smiling at the driver in the mirror.

"I try to tell you, man"—the cabbie waved his arm—"this ees a bad part of town for you whiteys."

"Seems pretty rough," Kyle offered, shaking his head at the squalor.

His mind had focused on one thing since he'd boarded the plane at McCarran: Denise Palermo. Big Tony's daughter had to be somewhere in Miami. He didn't know what she looked like or where she lived, but he had to find her and El Gato Negro.

The cab suddenly jolted to a stop. "This is it, boss." The driver turned and faced Kyle. "Number 124 Palmetto."

Kyle looked through the window of the cab at 124 Palmetto. It was a low, white wooden frame house set back from the street. A small scraggly lawn lay between the street and the house. A forlorn palm tree grew in the center of the lawn. There was a cement walk leading to a screened porch. The whole structure was badly in need of paint.

A child's red bike lay on its side on the lawn. Some other toys were scattered about the driveway and walk. Two empty trash-littered lots lay on either side of the house.

"What do I owe you?" Kyle asked the Cuban, pulling the roll of bills from his pocket.

The man glanced at the meter, then turned a gap-toothed grin on Kyle.

"Five and a quarter, *hombre,*" he said. "You want me to wait? It's hard to get a cab to stop down here."

"Maybe you'd better," Kyle said, handing the man a five and a one, "till I see if someone's home."

He opened the door of the cab and climbed out. Almost immediately his nostrils were assailed by the odor of rotting garbage.

As Kyle walked up the path toward the porch a heavyset black woman in a red-and-blue tube top, barely covering her huge bosom, opened the front door of a house down the street. She came out on her step and stared at Kyle as if he had just exited a spaceship instead of a taxi.

Kyle reached the porch and knocked. He waited a few seconds and knocked again. There was movement inside the house. The front door opened, and an attractive but haggard-looking black woman in her late thirties appeared in the doorway.

Betty Phillips looked at the white man standing on her step, and despite the early-morning heat she felt a chill that made her pull her ratty yellow terry-cloth robe tightly around her. Betty's mind could not conceive why the dark, hawk-faced man had come to her door, but there was something familiar about his face.

She crossed the porch and looked at Kyle through the screen door.

"Can I help you?" asked Betty in a thin voice that barely disguised her fear.

"Betty, I'm Kyle Youngblood." He smiled. "Rafe and I served together in Vietnam."

The tired-looking black woman stared at Kyle through the torn screen. So this was the man her husband idolized, she thought, the one he constantly talked about. Although she had never met him, Rafe had showed her pictures of Kyle from 'Nam . . . that's why his face had looked so familiar.

Rafe had filled her with stories about Kyle, till she felt she knew him better than she did her own husband. More than once Rafe had told her how Kyle had saved his life by keeping their unit from going on a suicidal patrol.

Now he was here, at the threshold of her home, the man who had caused Rafe to go back for that second tour in Vietnam, the man who ironically had saved his life but had exposed him to death and danger for another year.

"Rafe's not here," she said without opening the screen door. "He's at work."

Kyle sighed deeply. "Do you know where I can find him, Betty? It's real important. I tried to call, but your phone was out of order."

Betty Phillips looked at Kyle's drawn face. She hesitated and tightened the belt on her robe once more. She was ashamed to tell him the phone company had shut it off because they couldn't pay the bill.

"He's workin' on the new condos on Key Biscayne," she said almost inaudibly. "It's all the way down at the tip, past Crandon Park."

"Do you know the name of the condos?"

"I think they're called the Cape Towers."

"Thanks, Betty," he said, stepping back. "It was good meeting you. Rafe talked about you a lot in 'Nam."

He turned and started for the cab, which was still waiting at the curb. Betty watched the slim-hipped man move down the walk.

"Youngblood!" she called out. He turned back to her. "You're not going to take him away from me again, are you? We got two kids."

Kyle looked at her for a beat, then he shrugged his shoulders. He turned back to the waiting cab, opened the rear door, and climbed in.

Betty Phillips watched apprehensively as the taxi drove off down Palmetto. A cold hand of fear scraped her innards as the vehicle turned the corner at the end of the block.

Chapter 12

Key Biscayne was the largest of the three keys that lay just south of Miami Beach. If one looked at it on a map, it resembled a finger pointing the way to the rest of the Florida keys.

Because of its size, the island had a large golf course located at its northern end. Most of the southern end, where Cape Florida lay, was taken up by the Bill Baggs State Park. To the west, across the short span of the Intracoastal Waterway, was the college community of Coral Gables. To the east lay the vast stretch of the Atlantic.

Kyle's cab rolled east on the Tamiami Trail, crossed 27th Avenue S.W., where the famed Orange Bowl was located and took the cloverleaf south onto Interstate 95. The Cape Towers were rising on a small spit of land on the western side of Key Biscayne. The spot formed the lower half of a little cove, where the developers planned to incorporate a large marina to package with their condominiums.

The cabbie made a right onto the sandy construction road just past the lush tropical beauty of Crandon Park. The cab bounced along the pitted road and slid to a stop on the sand in front of the skeletal steel frames of the buildings.

Kyle stepped out of the cab into the oppressive heat of Miami's mid-morning. Around him, hard-hatted, bare-chested construction workers in cutoff jeans and shorts stared curiously as the cabdriver retrieved Kyle's duffel bag from the trunk.

The cab fare came to fifteen dollars. Kyle handed the driver a twenty and thanked him. The cabbie gave the rancher a gap-toothed grin, saluted and hopped back into the cab.

As the taxi sped off, spewing sand and pieces of broken cement from its rear tires, Kyle turned and looked at the men who were still staring at him. Kyle hefted the canvas bag onto his shoulder and made his way toward a light blue construction trailer that carried a sign emblazoned with large white letters that read:

GOODMAN BROS. INC.
CONSTRUCTION CO.
OFFICE

Kyle pulled open the metal door of the trailer and was surprised to feel a blast of cool air bathe him. A short, stocky man sat behind a gray metal desk that was strewn with blueprints and copies of work orders. A number of empty cardboard coffee containers completed the office's decor.

The stocky man saw the surprise register on Kyle's face. He removed the stub of a cigar from his clenched teeth.

"Thank God for air-conditioning, eh?" he said, pointing to an open vent in the roof of the trailer. "You from the inspector's office . . . I'm Irv Goodman." The man came around the messy desk and offered his stubby-fingered hand.

Kyle dropped his duffel bag and took Goodman's hand. The palm was sweaty and cold. Goodman was obviously a very nervous man.

"No, I'm not from the inspector's office," said Kyle, shaking the stocky man's clammy hand. "My name's Youngblood. I'm looking for an old army buddy."

Goodman seemed to relax. He jammed the cigar stub back in his thick lips.

"Army buddy, eh? What's his name?"

"Rafe Phillips," answered Kyle as Goodman moved back behind his desk.

"Phillips, Phillips . . ." The stocky builder scratched his head. "Don't ring a bell."

"He's black, about six foot, 185, has a deep scar on his right cheek."

Goodman scratched his head again before he spoke.

"I got three hundred guys working here. Half of them are blacks with scars, and they *all* look alike." He snickered and spit into a trash can near his desk.

"We served together in 'Nam," said Kyle impassively. A muscle twitched in his jaw as he clenched his teeth. "I haven't seen him for ten years."

"Check with my foreman," said Goodman, turning back to the blueprints. "He may be able to tell you something. All I do is sign checks."

The stocky man did not look up as Kyle left the air-conditioned trailer. The bright sunshine and oppressive heat hit him like a blast furnace as he crunched across the broken pieces of concrete and the fine sand.

Near one of the three construction elevators that climbed the steel frames of the half-finished buildings, a group of workmen were clustered around a fat, bearded man in clean khakis. The fat man was wearing a yellow fiberglass hard hat bearing the inscription, THE MAN.

As Kyle came toward them the men dispersed and went to the various duties that had been assigned to them. The Man eyed the approaching stranger warily from under the short visor of his hard hat.

"If you're lookin' for work, pal," he said in a surprisingly high-pitched voice, "you're too late. We hired a full crew just yesterday."

Kyle dropped his bag on the sand.

"I'm lookin' for an old army buddy," he said, starting to feel the sweat running down his ribs and back. "He's a black guy, late thirties . . . name's Rafe Phillips."

The fat foreman massaged his bearded chin with the thumb and forefinger of his right hand before answering.

"I know the dude. He's a mason . . . been working here since we started. You ain't lookin' to cause trouble?"

"No," said Kyle in a tired voice. "I just want to talk to him."

The bearded man looked at Kyle for a long moment before deciding he was all right.

"Rafe's workin' in the second building, tenth floor. Take the elevator."

"Thanks," said Kyle, picking up his bag.

"Make sure you put on a hard hat," the foreman called after him. "There's a couple in the elevator. Our insurance won't cover you if you don't."

Kyle found a hard hat and put it on as the wire cage ground slowly upward on complaining cables. The two other men in the elevator, obviously construction workers, eyeballed him curiously before they got off at the sixth floor.

The steel cage jolted to a stop as it reached the tenth floor. Kyle pushed down on the wire-mesh grate, and it opened like the jaws of a trap, allowing him to step out on the raw cement floor to look around.

There were about fifteen workmen on the floor. One man was applying a welding torch to a stand of copper tubing rising out of the concrete. Sparks showered from the end of the torch in a fiery display.

The entire level had not been enclosed yet. The only barrier that separated the men on the floor and the ten-story drop to the sandy surface of Key Biscayne was a yellow ribbon that stretched around the outside of the building.

Bare electric light bulbs were strung from the ceiling, but the level was still dimly lit, and Kyle had to strain into the murky setting, trying to find Rafe.

He edged a bit farther out toward the center of the floor and stopped. A group of four men were laying cinder block at the edge of the floor facing the mainland. One of them was Rafe.

Kyle dropped his bag and crossed the littered concrete toward Rafe, who was "buttering" the top of a block with mortar so that he could set it in place.

Rafe lifted the block and was about to place it when Kyle came up behind him. The black man was shirtless, and Kyle could see the shiny shrapnel scars that marked his strong, muscular back.

"Make sure you do a good job, Rafe," Kyle said softly. "I wouldn't want this place to collapse when it's finished."

Rafe Phillips dropped the block haphazardly on the line of blocks and turned.

"Jesus H. Christ!" he shouted, grinning from ear to ear. "Blood! Is it really you? Where the hell did you come from?"

Before Kyle could answer, he was wrapped in two strong black arms and lifted off the floor. The three other masons stopped work and stared at the two men as Rafe returned Kyle to the floor.

"It's good to see you, Rafe," Kyle said, smiling. "It's been a long time."

"Long time, my ass, Kyle," Rafe said loudly. "It's been forever."

"Too long." Kyle nodded.

Rafe embraced Kyle in a bear hug again. Then he turned to the other three men. "You see this guy?" he said, pointing to Kyle. "He's the *toughest* sumbitch whoever lived. Took out one hundred and sixty-four NVA in one fight and saved my ass more than once."

"Rafe," said Kyle in an embarrassed tone.

The other men smiled and made friendly gestures. Rafe took Kyle by the arm and pulled him away from the work area.

"Christ, I can't believe you're here," he said, bubbling, taking off his hard hat and wiping his forehead and the bridge of his flattened nose.

The nose was a memento of his teens when he'd been an amateur boxer in the hot, muggy gyms around Miami. Rafe had been good, so good that a couple of sharp Miami shysters had been after him to turn pro.

His father, an inveterate wino, had died around that time in a dirty, garbage-filled alley behind a south Miami bar. He had been beaten to death by two other winos who were after his bottle of cheap muscatel.

Malcolm Phillips left behind a sick wife, six minor children and not enough money to bury him. Rafe, being the oldest, quit high school and took on two jobs to help his mother support the family.

Because Rafe had had to work, he couldn't train properly, and his boxing skills soon eroded. Rafe Phillips became just another tough, talented black kid from the streets who *could* have made it, except for some bad breaks.

Rafe's mother, Leona, had been killed two years later in an accident going to work as a domestic in Miami Beach. After that the young black fighter went a little crazy. He joined one of the many street gangs that roamed the city, and because of his flashing fists he rose quickly in the gang's hierarchy, until he became one of its warlords.

One night, in a fight with a rival gang, Rafe was stabbed in the face and back and left for dead. He survived his wounds and gave up the streets for an apprentice job with a friend's father, who was a mason. He had met Betty Williams while working on a job at her house. They dated for a while and married a short time later.

"Rafe, I've got to talk to you," Kyle said quietly.

"Sure thing, Blood. What's up?"

Kyle took him by the arm and led Rafe over to the side of the building facing the Atlantic. Both men sat down on the edge of the floor with their legs dangling in space.

"I stopped by your place," Kyle said. "Betty told me you were out here. Seems like she's still bitter about me gettin' you to re-up."

"Yeah, would you believe she's still bustin' my balls about that?" He picked up a broken piece of concrete and threw it far out, away from the men who were working below. "Speakin' of wives . . . how's Marian and the kids?"

Kyle stared out at the serene beauty of the ocean as he spoke.

"They're dead," he answered softly. It was as if someone else had said the words. He watched a small sailboat glide slowly past the Cape. A freighter trailing a plume of black smoke steamed steadily south on the horizon.

"What . . . how . . . ?" Rafe stammered, staring at Kyle in wide-eyed amazement.

In the next fifteen minutes Kyle told his story quietly to Rafe, who sat shaking his close-cropped head in utter disbelief. When Kyle had finished, Rafe sat with his head drooped, looking at his worn work shoes hanging in space.

"There's more, Rafe," said Kyle. "There's another part to this story."

"Oh, man!" The black man sighed. There were tears in Rafe's eyes. "They killed your wife and babies while you were in the joint?"

"There was nothing I could do," said Kyle, nodding. "They never had a chance."

"An' you *know* who these mothafuckers are?" Rafe was in a rage, wiping at his eyes.

"Yeah," said Kyle, putting his hand on Rafe's arm. "That's the other part of the story. Last night I went to Fallon's ranch to kill him, but he had skipped to some island."

"I don't care where he is, Blood. You got to get that sumbitch."

Kyle looked at Rafe's tear-streaked face for a beat. Then he turned and looked around the floor to see if anyone was near them.

"I want that more than anything, but I need money to get at him," said Kyle softly.

"Brother, I'll follow you into the jaws of hell and back," said Rafe, wiping at his eyes again with the back of his hand. "You can have anything I got, but I'm tapped. I'm drivin' a cab weekends to put food on the table."

"I know where we can get all the money we'll ever need," Kyle said, lowering his voice even more.

"Yeah, in Fort Knox." Rafe laughed ironically.

"No . . . in Cuba," said Kyle, jerking his thumb toward the southern tip of the Cape.

"Same thing, Blood!" Rafe flipped back.

"Rafe, I know there's thirty million dollars buried in Cuba at a place called El Gato Negro."

Rafe looked off at the freighter, which was now hull down on the southern horizon.

"The black cat?" He turned and looked at Kyle and shook his head. "Who tol' you about this thirty million?"

"You ever hear of Big Tony Palermo?" asked Kyle, swiveling his head around again.

"The Mafia dude?" Rafe's head snapped up. "How'd you get to him?"

"He was at Fallon's ranch," said Kyle. "He was going to make a deal with me to bring the money out just before he died."

"You off him?"

"Nah," answered Kyle, shaking his head. "One of his own people did it."

Rafe got to his feet, kicking some of the loose concrete into space. He put a hand out. Kyle took it and pulled himself to his feet with a grunt.

"Goddamn, thirty million . . . that's some heavy shit," said Rafe with a whistle. "That would really get Betty off my ass."

"This'll get me what *I* want, and get *you* out of hock," Kyle said earnestly. "Share and share alike."

"That's good, Blood . . . 'cause my ass has been in hock ever since 'Nam. Where do we start?"

"Palermo said he had a daughter, Denise, who was livin' in Miami," Kyle offered. "We've got to find her first."

"She's probably connected . . . *if* she's his daughter. I know a dude who might know where she is." Rafe started toward the elevator. "Just one thing, Blood—" Rafe stopped and turned toward Kyle.

"What's that?" asked Kyle, looking at his friend curiously.

"I hate black cats!"

Chapter 13

On the ride back to Palmetto Drive, Kyle filled Rafe in on the rest of what had happened to him and his family over the past three years. Rafe had gripped the steering wheel of his battered pickup as if he were trying to squeeze juice from it.

Now Kyle sat on the worn, secondhand couch in Rafe's sparsely furnished hurricane room, watching his friend's two children play with their toys on the linoleum-covered floor. The seven-year-old, Alicia, rocked a small doll in her arms while pretending to give it a bottle.

Rafe's bright-eyed five-year-old son, Tony, kept lining up a row of tiny cars, making believe he was jumping them with another car. Occasionally he would sneak a shy look at Kyle, who would wink at the boy, making him turn away.

Even though the kitchen was two rooms away, at the back of the house, Kyle could still hear Rafe and Betty arguing loudly. At times their voices were low and hushed, and then they would erupt in a paroxysm of shouting.

Kyle felt disturbed that he had come here and disrupted Rafe's life like this, but he needed him. Kyle justified the thought in his mind by telling himself that their mission was good for Rafe and his family . . . whatever the risk.

"Betty, honey, I got to give it a shot. This could be the thing we been waitin' for." Rafe's deep voice sifted into the hurricane room. It was almost as if Kyle were in his head. "Look around you . . . you think I like to see you and the kids livin' like this?"

"Rafe. I don't like it," she said. "Every time you get involved with this man, somethin' bad happens."

"Sweetheart, I owe him." Rafe's voice was a bit softer. "He took a lot of shit because he kept that sorry-ass captain from sendin' us on that suicide mission."

In the other room Kyle shifted uneasily on the couch as he heard

Rafe's words. Both of the children turned and looked at him.

"So you're going to keep payin' him back your whole life 'cause he saved *your* sorry ass." Betty's voice was louder than before.

"The team that took our place was wiped out to a man," shouted Rafe. "I wouldn't be sittin' here now if it wasn't for Kyle."

As he listened, Kyle wondered if he should intervene and tell Betty what was waiting in Cuba for her and the children. He started to get to his feet, but the voices from the kitchen stopped him again.

"Man waves his little finger," Betty said acidly, "an' here comes Uncle Tom to do his beck and call."

"Come on, Betty," Rafe said. "He'll hear you. Don't talk like that. I'm only goin' for you and the kids."

Kyle heard a chair scrape and the scuffling of feet. The children seemed to pay no attention; apparently they were used to the shouting.

"You big fool!" she almost screamed. "Can't you see *we* want you? I don't want nothin' to happen to you."

"Ain't nothin' goin' to happen to this ol' Florida boy. I come back from two tours in 'Nam, didn't I?"

"Yeah, that second tour was his doin' too," she railed back. "I got a bad feelin' about this, Rafe."

Later that afternoon Rafe maneuvered his old truck into a parking space in front of a three-story pink-stucco apartment building. The name, painted in black, over the dirty front glass doors read: FLAMINGO.

The place surely had seen better days. There were a number of broken windows, and paint was chipping off the stucco. The glass in one of the front doors was broken and had been replaced by a piece of plywood. There was some obscene graffiti that had been spray-painted on the front of the building by a few local artists.

The Flamingo had been a hotel until its conversion into an apartment building that housed thirty-four black families in units that had been built to hold twenty-five.

Rafe and Kyle exited the truck and made their way toward the front of the building. A group of black teenagers, lounging on the corner, looked at the two curiously as they entered the seedy apartment house.

"You think this guy'll know where we can find her?" Kyle asked, looking at the trash thrown on the floor of the large room.

"I used to run with this dude," said Rafe, pushing the button by the elevator doors. "He's still into a lot of shit. He may know somethin'."

An elderly black woman came down the stairs. She walked with a cane and carried an empty shopping bag. The woman stopped and looked at Kyle and Rafe.

"You boys can push that button till yore balls fall off," she said, smiling. "That damn thing ain't worked since 1973."

"Thanks," said Rafe as the woman limped toward the front doors. "Lonnie Saunders still on the third floor?"

"He a bad boy," the fat woman said without turning around. "He up there, but I wouldn't bother them motherfuckers."

She pushed open the lobby door and limped out into the bright sunshine.

"That's somebody's grandmother, Blood." Rafe laughed.

He led Kyle up the dark stairway. On the second floor landing they had to step over a teenage heroin junkie lying facedown in a pool of his own vomit.

Kyle bent to look at the boy.

"Let 'em be," said Rafe, taking the rancher's arm. "He'll be okay . . . his *friends* will take care of him."

They moved up the dark stairwell to the third floor. Rafe walked down the dark hall, squinting at the numbers on the doors. The sound of a baby crying came from one of the apartments. Kyle turned his head toward it as a woman's harsh voice cut off the infant's wailing.

Rafe stopped before a paint-peeled door at the end of the hall and knocked. Kyle stood off to one side as Rafe knocked again. There was movement inside the apartment, and the door opened a crack.

A black face wearing thick, wire-framed glasses appeared at the opening. The face looked at Rafe questioningly.

"Hey, brother!" said Rafe loudly. "Don'tcha know me?" The door opened wider to reveal a short black man wearing a green, black and red flowered dashiki.

"Damn . . . Rafe Phillips." The man's face split into a wide grin. "Where the hell you been, man?"

"I been around Lonnie, I been around."

"Hey, come on in, man," said Lonnie, opening the door wide enough to admit Rafe. "Come on in."

Rafe stepped inside the door, and Lonnie embraced him warmly.

"Hey, man, it's good to see you." The man in the dashiki started to pull Rafe into the room. "What brings you here . . . slummin'?"

"Brother, this is *all* slums. We can't get away from 'em." Rafe turned back and reached for Kyle. He grasped his arm and pulled him into the room. "Lonnie, I brought a friend with me. This here is Kyle Youngblood."

The black man in the thick glasses watched as Kyle entered the room. The friendly grin turned sour, and hatred reflected through the lenses of his thick glasses.

"Man," Lonnie said, seething, "you got a lot of guts bringin' a honkie mothafucker to my pad."

Rafe had taken a long shot by bringing Kyle to see Lonnie. Now he had to convince Lonnie to help them.

"Hey, man . . . cool it." Rafe directed at the man in the dashiki. "This man is a brother. He saved my life."

"That don' mean jack-shit to me." Lonnie turned his back on them and moved farther into the murky room.

Rafe followed him, but Kyle hung by the open door. The rancher squinted into the dark corners of the filthy apartment. He saw the end of a cigarette glow in one of the corners as the man who held it drew the smoke into his lungs.

Two other men sat at a wooden table sucking on two short hoses attached to an oddly shaped bong. A fourth man, with a shaved head, sat on the floor by a shuttered window, using a whetstone to hone a sharp edge on a wicked-looking machete.

The entire room was permeated by the telltale, sickeningly sweet odor of marijuana.

"Lonnie, I come to ask you a question, man . . . for old times' sake," said Rafe, coming farther into the room. The bald man honing the machete stopped and got to his feet, swinging the sharpened blade slowly at his side.

"What is it you want from me, Rafe?" Lonnie asked coldly.

Rafe stepped toward him.

"We're lookin' for a girl," said Rafe, "a white girl. Her name is Denise Palermo. She's connected . . . very high up." Lonnie turned and glared at Rafe before answering. The men at the bong stopped smoking and looked up.

"Why you think I got a line on an ofay woman?" The black man's voice dripped with ice.

"I know you're cool, brother." Rafe smiled. "You know what's comin' down on the street. If she's into anything dirty, you're the one to ask."

Lonnie gave Rafe a cold-eyed stare. Then he turned and spoke to the man who sat smoking in the far corner.

"Abdullah," he said to him, "you ever hear of a white woman—Denise Palermo—workin' the street?"

The man known as Abdullah took a deep drag on his cigarette and exhaled the smoke in a long, slow column from his broad nose. He rose from his chair and came toward the center of the room. His huge head was covered with filthy dreadlocks that looked like hairy black snakes.

Kyle could not believe the size of the man. Abdullah was wearing a dirty tank top with a picture of Mickey Mouse silk-screened on the front. He was about six feet eight inches tall and weighed between three and three hundred and twenty pounds. The massive development of his deltoids and arms signaled the fact that he was heavily into weight training.

"Man!" Rafe whistled. "You one big mothafucker, Abdullah."

The big man looked at Rafe and smiled, showing a mouthful of gold teeth.

"She may be in the city," the giant rumbled in a voice that sounded like a boot scraping a wooden floor. "She may be a hooker . . . lots of white women is hookers." He paused and smiled tauntingly at Kyle. "She could be workin' in one of them porno houses. I can remember seein' an ofay woman they said was *connected* in one of them topless go-go bars."

The big man stood next to Lonnie, staring at the two intruders. His hamlike fists clenched and unclenched as if waiting to smash something. The gold-toothed smile was still painted on his blue-black face.

"Is that what you wanted to know, *brother*?" asked the black man in the dashiki, a sinister edge creeping into his voice.

"Yeah," said Rafe, starting to ease toward the door. "Thanks for your help, man." He turned to Kyle, who was now next to his elbow. "We better get movin', Blood. We got some places to check out."

As Rafe and Kyle turned to leave, they found their exit blocked by the bald man who had eased in behind them. He held the razor-sharp machete poised across his chest in both hands. The sunlight that squeezed between the warped pieces of plywood in the window glinted off the long blade.

The two men who had been using the bong dropped the hoses and stood up. The dead air in the dimly lit room hung heavy, as if it were waiting for something to happen.

Lonnie's hand shot out, grabbing Kyle by the arm and spinning him around.

"Listen, honkie." The black man spat the words into Kyle's face. "I don't give a shit about you, but a brother like Rafe could get his ass shot off lookin' for white meat in this town."

Kyle ripped his arm out of Lonnie's grasp and dropped into his fighting crouch as a fierce, dark look overtook his features. Lonnie stepped forward and threw a looping right at Kyle's head. The rancher blocked it easily and caught the black man flush in the face with the heel of his hand.

Kyle felt the crunch of bone under his palm as the bone around Lonnie's left eye fractured. The black man screamed as the lens of his thick glasses was squashed into his cheek and eyelid. He hurtled backward with stunning force into the giant Abdullah, nearly toppling the big man.

Abdullah regained his balance and stepped over the fallen Lonnie as the bald man with the sharpened machete swung it at Rafe's head. As the long knife descended toward him the black vet grasped the man's wrist with both hands and pulled hard, twisting at the same time. At that instant he brought his right knee up into the man's stomach.

The machete wielder grunted and dropped his weapon to the floor. Rafe nailed him with two quick punches to the side of the head as he fell heavily to the floor.

As Rafe disposed of his man the giant Abdullah launched his three-hundred-pound bulk at Kyle with a howl of anger. As he did, Kyle lashed out with his booted right foot, catching the huge man flush in the crotch.

As Abdullah felt the pit of his stomach drop into his shoes, he screamed and doubled over. Kyle stepped to the side and fired his right elbow one . . . two . . . three . . . four times into the side of the giant's temple. He moaned once and fell to the floor like a felled ox.

Rafe stepped to Kyle's side as the two bong smokers at the table stared in wide-eyed fear.

"We don' want no trouble, man," one of them pleaded as Lonnie groaned from the floor.

"Damn, Kyle," said Rafe, his voice full of admiration. "You are still quicker'n a fuckin' snake."

Kyle turned to him, ignoring the two other men.

"You ain't half bad your own self, son," he replied. "Now let's get the hell out of this place and find Big Tony's daughter."

Chapter 14

It was about five-thirty in the afternoon when Rafe's old pickup pulled out of the parking lot of the Pick-A-Dilly, a sleazy go-go bar in the South Beach section, at the southern tip of Miami Beach.

Rafe turned right on Ocean Drive and moved north, riding adjacent to the old hotels and their stone verandas, full of elderly people. On the beach some sun worshipers still lay on the sand trying to catch the last of the late-afternoon rays.

A couple vehicles behind, a nondescript tan sedan kept pace with Rafe's truck. The occupants of the car, Chet Allen and Phil McGregor, peered intently through the windshield of the sedan, not wanting to lose sight of the pickup.

Allen, in the passenger seat, reached forward and turned off the car's air-conditioner.

"Too cold, Chief?" said the driver, his thin lips pulling back in a smirk.

"Phil, to answer your question," said the T-man, "I've an icicle hanging from each of my testicles."

Phil McGregor cackled, his thin lips again pulling back to reveal a set of uneven, tobacco-stained teeth. He repeated the high, shrill laugh and cast a glance at his boss in the passenger seat.

"What the hell do you think they're on to, Chief?" he asked. "They've hit five of them shithole go-go bars since they left that sleazy hotel in Miami."

"They've got some kind of lead, Phil," said Allen softly, rubbing his chin. "We've got to be patient. Just keep following the rainbow, and the pot of gold will be waiting for us at the end."

The pickup made a left, and then a quick right on Collins, where it crossed Lincoln Road. It then headed north along the lavish hotels of Miami Beach's once fabulous gold coast.

Kyle looked out at the crowded sidewalks and the slow-moving line of cars and buses in front of them.

"Christ, Rafe," he mused. "I ain't sure I like bein' around all these people. Back in Nevada you could fire a howitzer and not hit a person for a hundred miles."

Rafe laughed as the line of vehicles stopped for a red light.

"You country boys are all alike—gotta get back to the ranch," said Rafe. Kyle looked at him and smiled. Rafe was right: He missed the outdoors and life on the ranch. There was something about the city and its people that made him feel unclean. It was as if he had just worked on a dung heap and felt like he needed to take a shower.

"Partner," he said as Rafe put the truck in gear and it lurched forward. "We're at a dead end. There's too many of these go-go places down here . . . an' we're not even sure she works in one."

"It's the only lead we got," said Rafe, looking at him. "She may not even be in Miami—there was no listing in the phone book."

Kyle scratched the stubble on his craggy jaw. He was frustrated. With no money and no way to get any, they had run into a wall.

"If we only had somebody on the street," mused Kyle absentmindedly. "A guy we could trust."

"Vinnie Troiano!" shouted Rafe, slamming the steering wheel with the flat of his palm. *"Hot damn! Vinnie Troiano!"*

Kyle turned and stared at Rafe as if he had gone over the edge.

"Vinnie Troiano . . . what the hell are you . . . ?"

"Blood! You remember him. Dark, nice-lookin' Italian kid in our outfit. . . ."

Kyle's mind raced backward, sorting out memories and faces like slides on a screen. Finally he put together a face and a name.

"Christ! Yes, I remember him," said Kyle. "Short, good-lookin' kid. Wild as hell . . . his older brother was a Marine grunt . . . bought it at Khe San."

"That's him, Blood." Rafe smiled. "He was into all kinds of shit when he was a civilian—pimpin', burglary . . ."

"What's that got to do with our problem?" Kyle asked, marveling again at the crowd milling along the sidewalk in front of one of the big hotels.

"He was from *Miami,* Blood," cooed the black man, smiling broadly. "He was from Miami."

The Cast-a-Ways wasn't really a hotel, it was more of a boatel. Built in North Miami Beach in the 1950s, it had become known as *the* place to see, more of a curiosity than a class hotel. The main building, with its distinctive Oriental, pagodalike styling, looked like the entire structure had been taken from downtown Peking. A charter boat dock ran the length of the block in front of the boatel; its gleaming white occupants rode their moorings gently as they rocked in their sidewalk slips.

Rafe and Kyle walked slowly along the row of boats, peering intently into each cockpit, trying to see if Vinnie Troiano was aboard any of the boats. Although it was six o'clock, many of the captains and boat boys were out on the sidewalk soliciting parties for the next day's charters.

"Rafe, we gotta be crazy," said Kyle as they moved from boat to boat. "We could be barkin' up the same wrong tree with Vinnie as we are with Denise Palermo: He may not even be in Miami."

Rafe stopped at the slip holding a beautifully appointed forty-five-foot Hatteras, with the name *Neptune's Choice* painted on the transom. The captain, shirtless and deeply tanned with a shock of unruly blond hair sticking out from under a white, black-visored hat, sat in one of the chairs set up in the cockpit. He eyed Rafe and Kyle, sizing them up as a potential charter.

"Kyle," said Rafe earnestly, "I got a feelin' our man is here. He loved boats . . . worked around them all his life. He hung around here before 'Nam, ain't no reason he wouldn't come back."

"If he's alive. We don't even know if he made it back to the 'world'," Kyle said, shaking his head.

"Kin I help you gents?" The voice came from behind them. Both men turned to see the blond captain climb over the transom of his boat and step onto the sidewalk. "Name's Captain Ted. If you're lookin' for a boat, the *Neptune's Choice* is the best on the street."

"We're lookin' for—" Rafe started to say, but Captain Ted cut him off.

"Take you and your friend out for a half-day . . . two hundred dollars. Full day I can do for three-fifty."

Rafe looked at Kyle and then back to the captain.

"Captain, we're lookin' for—" Rafe started again.

"Nothin' like deep-sea fishin'," said Captain Ted. "Make a man of ya'. Sail . . . 'cuda . . . marlin . . . shark. They're all out there." He jerked his thumb in the direction of the ocean.

"Captain," Kyle said, cutting in, "we're lookin' for an old friend who might be workin' on one of these boats. His name's Vinnie Troiano."

The blond man wrinkled his nose and looked off down the row of boats.

"Whyn't you say so in the first place, instead of makin' me go through all that shit?'' the fisherman said angrily. ''He's on the *Linda C.''*

Captain Ted jerked his thumb at a boat a few slips down from where they stood. Rafe shot a furtive glance at Kyle as the blond man stepped back onto his boat.

Rafe skipped happily as they hustled the few feet down the dock to the slip where the *Linda C.* was moored.

''I told you he was here, Blood!'' the black man said, gushing. ''I told you.''

They stood on the sidewalk looking into the pilothouse of the sleek forty-five-foot Bertram. A short, well-built man in his late twenties was storing fishing tackle in a locker under the gunwale. He was wearing a pair of cutoff jeans and a T-shirt. The back of the shirt was emblazoned with the logo of the WRECK BAR that was located inside the Cast-a-Ways.

''Hey, wop!'' Rafe called down to the man in the cockpit. ''Is this tub for rent?''

Vinnie Troiano turned quickly, a flush of anger on his handsome, stubbly face.

''Who the hell are you callin' a—'' he blurted out, and then a look of recognition appeared in his bright brown eyes. ''Rafe . . . Kyle,'' he said, stammering.

''Hey, Vincent,'' said Kyle, nodding at the speechless man who stood staring at them. ''How've you been?''

Vinnie looked at his former comrades in arms as if he were looking at two apparitions.

''Hey, asshole, say somethin','' Rafe said. ''Pussy got yo' tongue?''

Vinnie took the few steps across the cockpit and extended both deeply tanned arms to Kyle and Rafe.

''What the hell are you two doin' here?'' he gushed as he dropped a short gangplank across the aft gunwale onto the sidewalk.

''We ain't lookin' to go fishin', man,'' said Rafe, laughing.

''Goddamn . . . this is great,'' said the curly-haired man, jumping onto the gunwale. ''Come on, get your sorry asses down here.''

He took each of them by the arm and pulled them onto the short board, and from there they dropped into the cockpit. The *Linda C.* bobbed slightly with the sudden increase in weight. As the boat steadied, the three men embraced hungrily, causing some of the passersby on the sidewalk to look at them curiously.

''Hey, Cherry,'' said Rafe, finally breaking out of Vinnie's bear hug. "Is this your boat?"

The short mate looked at him and laughed. He looked around the cockpit before answering.

"Don't I wish." He sighed. "I'm bustin' my ass to put food in my belly. I'm a mate . . . it don't pay shit."

"There're other jobs," Kyle said softly.

Vinnie looked at him and shrugged.

"The only other thing I know how to do is kill. 'Nam did a good job of training me for that."

"We all got good at that, brother." Rafe nodded.

"Hey, don't get me wrong," he said, sitting on the edge of the gunwale. "I love what I'm doin'. It gives me time to shoot pool, play a little golf . . . it just don't pay no bread. I walk the beach early every morning lookin' for bales of pot."

"Pot?" asked Kyle, a surprised look on his dark face.

"Pot . . . marijuana. The drug runners dump their cargoes whenever the Coast Guard gets near them," said Vinnie. "Sometimes a bale'll wash up on the beach."

"No shit!" exclaimed Rafe.

"Yeah, a cabana boy across the street at the Newport found a bale one morning and put himself through law school." Vinnie smiled wryly. Rafe clapped him on the back and laughed.

"Man, I may be comin' over here and doin' some beachcombin' with you."

"Vincent," Kyle said, breaking in, "we've got something that could be a little more substantial than lookin' for drugs on a beach."

Vinnie looked at his former group leader, a man he hadn't seen for over ten years. Kyle looked older. The lines in his face appeared deeper, but his body still looked taut and hard. When Kyle spoke, his dark eyes pinpointed the other person's and seemed to penetrate the soul.

Vinnie had been born and raised in Miami. He had graduated from Miami-Dade High School in 1967 and immediately joined the Army.

The young Vinnie was tough and agile, and he needed a challenge to enhance his machismo image, so he volunteered to become an Airborne Ranger and was sent to jump school at Fort Benning, Georgia. While at Benning he became friendly with some Special Forces cadre, who were taking some extra jump training. One night, over some beers at a local slop chute, they told him about their Green Beret training at the John F. Kennedy Center in Fort Bragg, North Carolina.

It was not long afterward that Trooper Vincent Troiano was enrolled at the Center, where he completed the rugged training course it took to wear the silver wings and green beret. He graduated in October 1968, and was shipped to Vietnam the following month.

The fresh-faced soldier, in highly polished jump boots and brand-new beret, landed in-country at the sprawling Bien Hoa air base on November 10, 1968. After a quick indoctrination he was choppered to the Special Forces camp at Lang Vei, where he met Kyle Youngblood and Rafe Phillips. Both men were nearing the end of their first tour of duty in 'Nam.

Although he was a "cherry," Vinnie held his own among the veterans and short-timers. After a few patrols and operations he became a respected and reliable member of Kyle's team.

In the spring of 1969, he had been hospitalized with a severe case of immersion foot, which came from slogging ankle-deep through the water-laden jungle floor of one of the thickest rain forests in the world. Rafe had been wounded by mortar fire the week before, so neither of them had been with Kyle at the epic battle of Kontum.

Late in 1969, the young Green Beret took a round in the thigh while on patrol. The bullet severed an artery, and he'd almost bled to death on the medevac chopper. Vinnie survived because of a quick-thinking corpsman who pinched off the hemorrhaging artery.

Vinnie was airlifted back to the "world," and a V.A. hospital at Valley Forge near Philadelphia. He was discharged and returned to the Miami area and the Cast-a-Ways in the summer of 1970.

It was starting to get dark when Kyle and Rafe finished telling Vinnie why they had come to see him. The string of Japanese lanterns hanging over the slips in front of the Cast-a-Ways had been lit, making the sleek boats look even more beautiful.

Vinnie ran a hand through his thick, curly hair and shook his head. He looked up at the overhead in the *Linda C.*'s cabin and whistled.

"Thirty million . . . and you'll cut me in?" He whistled again. "Christ, Kyle, are you sure?"

The rancher took a long swig of the cold can of beer in his hand and nodded.

"That's what the big man said, Vinnie," Kyle shot back at him. "It's buried ninety miles from here on his old ranch."

"It may as well be nine thousand," Vinnie said dejectedly. "That's Castro country."

Kyle drank the last of the beer and squashed the can in his hand.

"We can get in there, kid," he said, throwing the aluminum can into a plastic trash container. "With some guts and the right equipment, we can get in and out without Castro knowin'. I *need* the money."

"I know Kyle, but—"

"We think Big Tony's daughter is somewhere in Miami," Kyle said, cutting him off. "She knows where the money is."

"I don't know any broads named Palermo," Vinnie shot back.

Kyle reached out and picked a *Penthouse* magazine off a stack of girlie magazines lying on the dinette table.

"Vinnie," said Kyle, opening the magazine to a nude spread, "I know these aren't your boss's *Playboys* and *Penthouses*."

"Come on, man," interjected Rafe. "You got to know a broad named Denise who's into this porno shit. She knows where the bread is."

"I heard of a chick," Vinnie said, rubbing his temples vigorously, "an exotic dancer, but her name ain't Denise, it's Kristel."

"Is she *connected*, man?" said Rafe excitedly, grabbing Vinnie's shoulder. "My friend said this broad he heard of was connected."

Vinnie stood up and looked at Kyle and Rafe. He put both hands on the dinette table and leaned forward.

"Guys, let's go find Kristel," he said slowly as the *Linda C*. rocked gently. "I'm tired of bein' poor."

Chapter 15

The Caribe A-Go-Go was a run-down, one-story bar out on U.S. 1. It had been a fertilizer warehouse at one time. Now, lithe teenage girls with firm, round breasts did bumps and grinds in sequined and lame G-strings to raucous rock and roll. Their older, heavier counterparts at the Caribe danced a little slower and used copious amounts of body makeup to cover the stretch marks on their distended stomachs and sagging breasts.

For twenty-four hours day and night they gyrated to the beat of the music on a small circular stage behind the bar. Their audiences consisted mostly of lonely truckers who stopped in for a cold beer, and if they got lucky, they might get in a quick hump with one of the dancers for twenty bucks in the dirty trailer behind the Caribe.

Once in a while a local biker gang would drop in to drink the cheap beer and taunt the go-go girls. Mostly the patrons were sad, bored men who sought a brief moment of fantasy.

Some of the plastic facing in the marquee set over the Caribe's front doors was broken, and the light bulbs inside the sign were visible. The names of the dancers had been hung on the black lines that ran across the dirty, cracked plastic.

One name, Kristel, topped the list in letters that were larger than the others. The sign also announced COLD BEER and 24-HOUR TOPLESS GO-GO.

There were two large, sixteen-wheel rigs parked in back near the "meat wagon," which is what the girls called the trailer. A row of five chopped cycles, all of them big Harleys, were parked alongside the building facing U.S. 1. There were a couple old pickups and three or four sun-bleached cars sitting in the parking lot in front of the bar.

Rafe spun the wheel of his truck to the left and cut across the highway in the face of oncoming traffic. There was a blare of horns, and one of the drivers blinked his lights and gave the men in the truck the finger through the windshield of his vehicle.

Rafe's truck missed the driveway and bumped over the curb into the parking lot. He cut the wheel to the right, narrowly missing one of the Harleys.

"Jesus Christ, Rafe," Vinnie said with a moan. "I know you're in a hurry to see some white pussy, but you don't have to go through the wall."

"I had it all the way, my man." Rafe laughed, bringing the truck to a stop by one of the rigs. "You got to have confidence."

Vinnie looked at Kyle, who rolled his eyes toward the roof of the cab. Rafe opened the driver's door and slid out while Kyle and Vinnie exited the other side.

They walked around the front of the truck and headed toward the entrance to the bar. As they passed between the rig and the "meat wagon," the door of the trailer opened and a smiling trucker emerged. He took the two steps to the parking lot and adjusted the zipper on his jeans as he eyeballed the three men.

"Best twenty bucks I ever spent," he said to them while reaching back and slamming the door of the trailer. The cheap lock didn't catch, and the metal door popped open, revealing a tired-looking blonde wearing only a pair of leopard-print bikini panties.

"Hey, cowboy!" she yelled. "Shut the door. Where were you brought up . . . in a fuckin' barn?"

The trucker looked at the three men and laughed. Then he pushed the trailer door tight, but not before Kyle and the others had gotten a good look at the girl's melonlike breasts.

"Hot, damn!" said Vinnie. "I think I'm goin' to like this."

"Business before pleasure, bro," Rafe chided. "Just remember why we're here."

The trucker climbed into his rig and fired up the engine as the three men rounded the side of the bar and passed the row of bikes. The back fender of one of the choppers had a plate that read:

COBRA M.C.
PUSSY POSSE
MIAMI FLA.

The interior of the low-ceilinged Caribe A-Go-Go was smoke-filled and noisy. The circular bar took up most of the room. In the center of the bar was a raised stage, where a haggard-looking blonde was bumping and grinding herself into an early grave to the beat of a Buddy Holly tune.

The lights in the place were dim except for the gelled spotlights on the stage that kept switching from red to blue to red with each bump and grind. There was only one bartender, a partially bald fat man in Elvis Presley sideburns. He had a dirty white apron wrapped around his bulging waist. His white formal shirt matched the apron. A forty-five-year-old waitress wearing retainers worked the tables for minimum wage and tips.

Around the bar sat four or five bored-looking men nursing shots and beers. Their eyes were glued to the gyrating pelvis and the wobbling globes of the dancer's bare breasts.

There were some tables scattered around the big room. Most of them were empty. At a table in the corner one of the girls had her hand inside the fly of an elderly tourist who had wandered in looking for a little action.

The five bikers were seated at a table near the bar. To a man, they wore sleeveless denim vests over dirty T-shirts. On the back of the vests were emblazoned their symbol: a hooded cobra about to strike. The snake's eyes were red-and-green motorcycle wheels. Around the perimeter of the encircled cobra was printed: COBRA M.C. MIAMI, FLORIDA.

All five of the men wore an assortment of leather, chains, and dog collars studded with evil-looking metal spikes. The fronts of their vests were decorated with various Nazi and American military decorations, and an occasional obscene phrase.

On the whole they were big, muscular men with long, greasy hair and beards. As the music played, they stomped the wooden floor with hobnailed engineer boots and pounded on the table with their beer bottles.

One biker, with a head of thick, red hair and a full beard, appeared to be larger than the others. By his actions it was obvious the redhead was the leader of the group. As the music pounded out its orgasmic beat the bearded biker jumped out of his chair with a howl and grabbed his crotch with both hands. At the same time he jerked upward with his hands, thrusting his lower body at the girl onstage.

As Vinnie led Kyle and Rafe across the dirty floor to the bar, the red-haired biker put both hands up to his mouth and cupped them.

"Hey, sister," he shouted. *"I seen cows with better-lookin' tits!"*

The bikers at the table howled with laughter and pounded each other on the back. One of the others, with a mask tattooed across the bridge of his nose and his eyes, got to his feet and cupped his hands around his bearded mouth.

"Hell," he yelled, *"I seen* bulls *with better-lookin' tits!"*

Again they howled and stomped the floor. The dancer yawned tiredly and flipped them the finger, which brought on another paroxysm of laughter.

Kyle pulled out a bar stool and sat down. Rafe and Vinnie took one on either side of him.

"What'll it be, gents?" the fat bartender said loudly, trying to make himself heard over the music and noise.

"Three Millers" said Kyle, holding up three fingers.

"You got it." The barman winked. He turned and walked a few feet to the cold chest and took out three bottles.

The dancer, seeing three new faces at the bar, turned her attention toward them. She aligned herself directly in front of Vinnie and started to go through a series of squats and pelvic thrusts that started the young vet groaning. He stuck his tongue out and rolled it around his lips. The girl took the tip of her finger, stuck it in her G-string, took it out, and licked it with a big smile.

"Hey!" yelled Redbeard. *"Leave them faggots alone, honey. The real men are over here."*

Kyle and Rafe didn't turn, but Vinnie did as the bartender returned with their beers.

"What are you lookin' at, faggot?" the redhead called out derisively.

Vinnie started to rise, but Kyle's viselike grip on his arm held him fast.

"Take it easy," Kyle said softly. "We don't want no trouble."

"Don't fuck with them," the fat barman rasped at Kyle, setting the beers down. "They're bad news."

Kyle threw a ten-dollar bill on the bar. The fat man took it and punched the sale into the cash register behind him. Then he turned and slapped the change on the wet surface.

"When does Kristel go on?" asked Kyle as he pushed a couple dollar bills toward the man.

"She's on next." The fat man winked lewdly.

As if in answer to Kyle's question, the Buddy Holly song faded and the tired dancer heaved a sigh and started down the steps at the side of the stage.

Kyle picked up the frosted brown bottle in front of him and took a long swallow of the cold brew. At the rear of the room a curtain was pulled aside, and an attractive brunette with flashing dark eyes made her way to the steps leading to the stage. She was wearing a short green robe, which covered her shapely legs to the top of her thighs.

She stopped and removed the wrap, revealing a trim, lithe body and a pair of high, firm breasts. Her olive skin was tanned to a glowing bronze. A silver lamé G-string flashed sweet promise as she dropped the robe on the top step and mounted the stage.

The bartender picked up the hand mike that was on a short stand next to the register. He flicked the switch and held it up to his mouth.

"Ladies and gentlemen," he intoned in his best show-business voice. "Brought back by popular demand, the Caribe A-Go-Go, Miami's distinctive showplace, is proud to present the one and only . . . Kristel."

There was a smattering of applause from the men seated at the bar. The elderly tourist was too involved with what was going on inside his pants to look up. The bikers howled and stomped. They pounded on their table, causing some of the empty bottles to fall and break on the wooden floor.

Suddenly a wild, almost junglelike beat drowned out the howling bikers. The colored lights started bleeding again, from red to blue, reflecting off the haze of stale cigarette smoke that hung over the stage.

Kristel stood on the small, bare stage with her head bowed and her arms crossed at the wrists, covering her G-string. She paused for a beat, as if listening to the music, and then she started to dance. As the lithe brunette moved around the stage it was obvious, even to this audience, that she'd had years of dance training. Each of the woman's movements blended into the other, so that there was no hesitation in the flow of her body, which paralleled the beat of the music.

There *had* been many years of ballet training in the woman's early years. Her mother had encouraged it. Her father had paid for it. In fact, she had yearned for the discipline of the metronome and the instructor's baton that tapped out the relentless beat. The young dancer had been good, but not good enough. It seemed there was always the shadow of her past and her father's reputation that choked her talent.

Now, as she danced seminude in a sleazy bar for groups of sex-starved morons, she fantasized that she was performing on the New York stage for beautifully gowned women and tuxedoed men who covered her stage with flowers and shouted accolades at her. Night after night this was her ballet, her triumph . . . until each dance ended and she opened her eyes.

Rafe and Vinnie could not take their eyes from the graceful dancer. Their heads followed her undulating body around the stage, as if they expected the thirty million to fall out of her G-string. Kyle watched the woman with veiled eyes and quietly sipped his beer, showing no outward sign of emotion.

As Kristel's music faded and stopped, she seemed to come out of her trancelike state and stare around the room. It was almost as if she did not know where she was. She left the stage to another smattering of applause and calls for an encore from some of the men who had not drunk themselves into a stupor.

As she shrugged into the short green robe the fat bartender came up behind her and tried to slip his pudgy hand inside her wrap. Kristel jerked violently away from him and headed for the curtained doorway, while the fat man shook his head.

With a deep sigh the barman turned from her retreating figure to see Kyle beckoning him from the front of the bar. He shambled over to where the three vets sat.

"Another round, gents?" he asked, leaning both his fat hands on the bar.

"Yeah," said Kyle softly. He took a five off the bar and stuffed it in the man's shirt pocket. "An' tell Kristel there are three *gentlemen* out here who would like very much to meet her."

"I get your drift." The bartender winked broadly. "I'll get her as soon as I set up the next act. Whyn't you grab that empty table? She don't like to meet clients at the bar."

The next act, a young Cuban girl who danced with a stuffed monkey wrapped around her leg, was on about ten minutes when the curtains across the rear doorway parted and Kristel made her way through the smoky bar to where Rafe, Kyle and Vinnie sat nursing their second round of beers. She had changed into a pair of skintight Levi's and a white tank top that had the inscription "Dancers do it on their toes" silk-screened across the front.

"Fatso said you guys wanted to see me," she said in a husky voice. Kyle started to rise, but she pulled out a chair and sat before he could get to his feet. Rafe and Vinnie did not move.

"I'm Kyle Youngblood, and this is Rafe Phillips and Vinnie Troiano." Kyle dropped back into his chair as the music from the speakers on either side of the stage blared on. "Would you like a drink?"

"Before we go any further," she said, shaking her head, "I don't go for no three-on-one parties."

"We ain't lookin' for no action, lady," said Rafe, smiling

broadly. "We'd just like a little information from you."

"That's a switch." She snickered, looking around the table at the three men.

Kyle had been wondering how to approach the woman about Big Tony and her identity. He decided a frontal assault was best.

"Denise," he started, leaning closer so he would not have to raise his voice, "we'd like to talk to you about your father."

He saw the startled look flare in her bright brown eyes, then disappear as she regained control.

"Denise?" she said, a nervous edge creeping into her voice. "You got the wrong lady, mister. My name is Kristel."

"Look," Kyle said, pressing on, "we know you're Denise Palermo and that your father was Big Tony."

The pretty brunette's face showed shock as she closed her eyes.

"You said *was?*" She struggled for control. "Has something happened to him?"

"You're Denise Palermo?" said Kyle, shooting furtive glances at Rafe and Vinnie.

"Yeah," she said, nodding her head. "Has something happened to my father?"

"He's dead," Kyle said softly. "I was with him when he died. He left you a message."

Her face blanched, and her full lips drew into a tight line.

"How do you know all this?" she asked, her voice going a little shrill. "Are you cops?"

"Do we look like cops?" Vinnie asked, leaning back on his chair. Denise turned toward him.

"Anybody can look like a cop." she shot at him. "Two weeks ago I was busted by a guy dressed like a priest."

"Shows to go ya"—Rafe laughed—"you can't trust anybody these days."

The young Cuban girl finished her stint by rubbing the stuffed monkey's hairy face violently into her crotch while gyrating her hips wildly and moaning in Spanish. Denise Palermo looked from one man to another at the table.

"I got a couple questions for you guys," she said slowly, back in control again. "How did he die, and what kind of message did he leave?"

Kyle's dark eyes peered intently into Denise's face as he spoke.

"He was shot by one of his bodyguards at a ranch in Nevada." Kyle said softly, looking for some kind of reaction from her. There was none.

"It figures," she said ironically. "What was the message?"

"What does El Gato Negro mean to you?"

"El Gato Negro . . . the black cat?" She looked at him, a puzzled expression on her face.

Before Kyle could answer, a huge, freckled hand clamped on Rafe's shoulder and spun him out of his chair onto the dirty floor.

"Hey, nigger"—the big, red-haired biker had come up behind Rafe at the table—"lookin' for a little white poontang?"

"Get lost, asshole," said Vinnie, getting to his feet. His right hand was wrapped around the neck of his beer bottle.

"You talkin' to me, nigger lover?" roared the big biker. "'Cause that's what you are for settin' this here *boy* up with a white woman."

He came around the table to where Vinnie was standing as Rafe got to his feet. Denise stood up, her chair making a scraping noise in the strangely quiet room.

Kyle had not moved. He sat very still, his hands resting on the table. He never took his eyes off the red-haired biker, who was towering over Vinnie.

"Hey, Swindell," the Cobra with the mask tattoo yelled from the other table. "If you don't hit that little fucker, you're chickenshit!" The other men at the table laughed derisively.

The big redhead looked back at his friend and smiled. It was then that Vinnie hit him on the side of the head with the beer bottle. The biker named Swindell howled in pain. He grabbed the side of his face with both hands and staggered backward. Blood started to seep from between his fingers and trickle down his massive forearm.

Denise gave a short cry and moved against the bar. The other bikers leapt to their feet shouting and charged across the open space between the two tables to aid their stricken leader.

Swindell recovered his balance and dropped his hands from his ruined face, revealing a jagged wound that ran from the corner of his eye to his jawbone. With a snort of rage he went for Vinnie, who had assumed a karate stance with both hands extended . . . palms down in front of him.

Rafe plunged headlong into the four Cobras charging at the table as Kyle got to his feet. The black man hit two of the bikers with a block that sent them sprawling. He was on the two men before they could recover, kicking and punching them with a series of well-aimed blows.

Kyle had sized up the situation as Vinnie's hand had descended with the bottle. He knew they were outnumbered five-to-three, but he counted on Rafe's and Vinnie's superior training and fighting instincts to help carry the day.

As Rafe pummeled the two men on the floor, the biker with the tattoo mask and his companion had gotten to Vinnie and pinioned his arms to his sides. Swindell positioned himself in front of the helpless vet and prepared to deliver a crushing blow that would rearrange his handsome Italian face.

At that moment Kyle came up behind the men who were holding Vinnie and drove a speared fist into the kidney of the man who was holding his right arm. The biker grunted and let go. He crumpled to the floor, writhing in pain.

With one arm free, Vinnie managed to avoid the big redhead's swing as he ducked under it and brought his knee up into the biker's groin. Swindell doubled over slightly, but to Vinnie's surprise he did not go down. This is one tough son of a bitch. The thought flashed in the vet's mind as the tattooed biker let go of his left arm.

Kyle saw the masked man drop Vinnie's arm and turn toward him. Something metallic flashed across the fingers of the man's right hand . . . he was wearing a pair of deadly, spiked brass knuckles.

The Cobra aimed a roundhouse punch at Kyle's face, but the ex–Green Beret blocked it and stepped in, driving his speared fist into the man's throat so hard that it ruptured his trachea. The biker's eyes bulged, and both hands reached for his throat as blood gushed from his mouth and nostrils. Kyle finished him off with a side kick to the knee that dropped the man to the floor.

The heat of battle was on Kyle now. He could feel the hot blood coursing through his veins, driving him . . . quickening his movements. He could hear the martial airs as they played in his head. Somewhere on a distant plain a bagpipe skirled.

Kyle dropped low into his fighting crouch. *I am Doctor Death,* his mind seemed to whisper to him. *Come to me and die.*

Now Kyle was face-to-face with the red-haired leader of the Cobras. The entire left side of the man's face was covered with blood. He stared hard into Kyle's darkening face, and what he saw there drove a spear of doubt into Swindell's mind.

In that instant of hesitation Kyle struck with the speed of the deadly snake for which the cycle gang was named. He drove four lightning-quick kicks and punches into the big man's mutilated face, forcing him backward. Finally Kyle spun and delivered a savage kick with his heel to Swindell's face. The blow broke the biker's nose and jaw, knocking him unconscious. He fell to the floor like a huge tree that had been felled by a chain saw.

Rafe and the other two men were still rolling on the floor, trying to get the best of each other, sending tables and chairs flying in the process. Kyle and Vinnie stood off to one side, watching as the black man attempted to subdue the two Cobras. Out of the corner of his eye Rafe saw his two friends smiling down at him.

"If it wouldn't be too much trouble," he said, gasping, "would one of you jack-offs give me a hand?"

Kyle looked at Vinnie, who grinned wickedly. Then he reached down and picked up an overturned chair. He raised it over his head and brought it down heavily on the head and shoulders of the biker who had just rolled over on top of Rafe. The man grunted and went limp.

Rafe pushed him off and sent a well-aimed elbow into the other man's temple. The biker's eyes rolled up, and he collapsed in a heap at the feet of his companion. The black man got to his knees, breathing heavily. He wiped his forehead and looked around the Caribe A-Go-Go.

The fat bartender was on the phone, frantically trying to contact the Miami Police Department. Two of the regulars were sound asleep on the bar, their heads resting on their arms. The others had cut out when the fight had started.

The five Cobras were scattered over the floor and smashed fixtures. Two of the bikers were semiconscious and groaning softly.

Rafe looked at Kyle, whose dark eyes were also panning the room. Youngblood turned and gave the black vet an appalled look: Denise Palermo was gone.

Chapter 16

It was 11:25 P.M. when Rafe's old pickup pulled into the parking lot of the Coconut Grove, a garden-style living complex on N.W. 135th Street in Opa Locka. Vinnie's modest studio apartment was about three blocks west of the abandoned Opa Locka Naval Airfield, which lay across the street from Grantigny Park.

Rafe eased the truck into a vacant parking space and cut the engine. He punched the light switch into the dash and sat back with a sigh.

"Goddamn!" He laughed, looking at Vinnie, who was sitting next to him. "You white boys cry poor . . . an' live rich."

"Rich," Vinnie said with a snort. "This place is only two hundred and ten a month, and I'm two months behind right now."

Rafe made a clucking sound with his tongue and tried to pat Vinnie on the head. The short Italian brushed away his hand with another snort.

"If you two'll stop bustin' on each other," Kyle said hoarsely, "we got a problem that needs solvin'."

Rafe took the key out of the ignition and turned to Kyle.

"Sorry, Blood." The black man said softly. "We was only joshin'."

"Damn biker assholes," Vinnie said through clenched teeth. "We had her. We had the answer right in our damn hands."

"Maybe we can pick up on her again." Rafe said hopefully.

Kyle put both hands on top of the dashboard and stretched his hard-muscled frame.

"I don't think so," he said softly as he opened the truck door. "Did you see that look on her face? She was scared to death."

Vinnie's apartment was up one flight of metal stairs. It was joined to another apartment by a shared balcony that overlooked a small, brackish swimming pool. The room had a tiny kitchenette and a cubbyhole for a bathroom. The studio bed, which doubled as a couch, was badly in need of re-covering. The toilet in the small bathroom kept running until someone jiggled its handle.

Stacks of girlie magazines lay strewn about the small apartment. Vinnie had torn out some of the centerfolds and thumbtacked them to the walls. The girls in the pictures smiled invitingly into the room, their vuluptuous bodies exuding sensual pleasure but never fulfilling their paper promise.

Vinnie crossed into the kitchenette and opened thc small refrigerator as Kyle and Rafe flopped on the worn couch. He took out three bottles of beer and popped them open with the palm of his hand on the edge of the Formica countertop. Some of the bitter liquid foamed to the top as he picked them up and returned to the others.

"Here's a cold one for ya, Doc," Vinnie said, handing one of the bottles to Kyle. "An' one for the *darkie*." He shoved the other bottle at Rafe, who smiled wryly.

Vinnie dropped into a small chair by the television set and took a long draught of his beer.

"Can't we go another route on this thing, man?" asked Rafe. "There's got to be somebody in this town, besides Denise Palermo, who knows where this El Gato Negro is."

"All we got is fuckin' Cubans all over the place." Vinnie laughed. "We may as well be livin' in Havana."

Kyle and Rafe laughed and looked at Vinnie.

"Out of the mouths of babes . . ." Rafe said admiringly.

"Vincent," Kyle said, putting the beer bottle down and standing up. "El Gato Negro *is* in Cuba. Some of these displaced Cubans could know where it is."

Rafe drained the bottle and rose to his feet with a grunt.

"Where's the best place to look?" he asked, hitching up his pants.

"Little Havana," Vinnie said, picking up the empty bottles. "That's as good a place as any. If there's anyone who's into Cubano shit, we can find 'em in Little Havana."

"It's after twelve," said Kyle, looking at his watch. "Are we goin' to find anybody awake?"

Vinnie dropped the empty bottles into a white plastic trash container and started for the door.

"Believe me, Doc," Vinnie said, turning the knob, "I used to run with this little *muchacha* down there. Nobody in Little Havana ever sleeps."

He opened the door and held it as Rafe and Kyle exited the apartment.

"Oh shit!" exclaimed Rafe as he stepped onto the modest balcony. "Betty's goin' to ream my ass for not gettin' in touch with her."

"Call her," Vinnie said, closing the door.

"I can't," Rafe said, lying. "Our phone's out."

About five miles northeast of Opa Locka, in the plush beach community of Hallandale, the Three Islands Condominiums rose into the clear night sky like the spires of a castle in a child's fairy tale. Built in the early 1970s along a picturesque causeway, the complex stood on three small islets that were connected by short concrete bridges. The condominium complex was a self-contained community, with its own shopping center and medical facility.

In a luxurious seventh-floor apartment Denise Palermo, still dressed in the skintight Levi's and tank top, sat blindfolded with her hands cuffed behind her back. Mascara-streaked tears stained her cheeks under the folded dinner napkin knotted across her eyes.

A coatless Chet Allen straddled a hard-backed kitchen chair set in front of the attractive brunette. His chin rested on his arms, which were folded across the top of the chair back. As the crew-cut T-man eyed the shackled dancer, his grim-faced partner, Phil McGregor, paced back and forth behind him in the deep-piled carpet. He seemed like a scavanger waiting to feed upon a carcass after the predators had finished with it. McGregor was also coatless, but he had rolled up his shirt sleeves. The straps of a tan leather holster braced his thick shoulders, and the blue-black butt of a .45-caliber automatic was visible under his left armpit.

Allen took a deep breath and slowly exhaled. He looked around the expensively furnished apartment. The place reeked of money. These Miami agents go first-class, he mused silently, as his gaze took in the high-priced lamps, paintings, and mirrored walls. It would be very nice to live like this, he thought.

The T-man turned his gaze on the woman shackled to the chair. Allen knew she was the one who could help him attain his goal.

"Now, Kristel . . . or is it Denise?" he said smoothly. "We know you spoke to this Youngblood fellow and his friends. We followed them to your club."

Denise strained against the handcuffs. She turned her head from side to side, as if listening for something.

"What the hell is this, you bastards?" she said hysterically. "I told you everything I know."

"Denise . . . Denise . . ." Allen said softly, taking a small red notebook out of his vest pocket. He opened the book and thumbed through it, finding the page he wanted. "Who is this Vincent Troiano? We had your friend Youngblood and the black man tailed to his apartment—"

"I told you . . . I met them tonight for the first time," she said, cutting him off.

Allen nodded to the crew-cut McGregor, who quickly stepped in front of Denise and slapped her hard across the face. Her head snapped back, then dropped to her chest. The big T-man reached out, grabbed a handful of dark, curly hair and jerked her head back. He raised his hand to slap her again, but Allen rose from his chair and grabbed his partner's upraised arm. Denise's head dropped as McGregor let go. She sobbed uncontrollably.

"It doesn't pay to be dishonest with us, sweetheart," Allen said, smiling. "There's a lot of money involved here."

The T-man moved behind her and untied the blindfold. Denise blinked several times, trying to accustom her eyes to the brightly lit room. There was some swelling and a large blue bruise on her left cheek.

Slowly she lifted her head as Allen came around in front of her. She glared at the two men with hatred in her dark eyes.

"I told you," she said slowly, between sobs. "The guy didn't say anything. I don't know what money you're talking about."

The crew-cut McGregor stepped in front of his boss and grabbed her roughly by the shoulders.

"The money your old man took out of Cuba twenty years ago!" The T-man snarled viciously, shaking her violently. His face was so close, the manacled woman could see his uneven, tobacco-stained teeth and smell the stale cigarette smoke on his breath.

Allen tapped the big man on the arm twice.

"Now, Phil"—his voice was syrupy sweet—"we don't want to browbeat the young lady. We want her help."

He slipped the key to the handcuffs out of his vest pocket and gave it to his partner. McGregor moved around behind Denise. There was a slight click as he unlocked the manacles.

The dancer's arms dropped to her sides. There was a red circle of raw flesh around the base of each hand. In turn, Denise grabbed each wrist with the opposite hand and kneaded them vigorously, trying to restore the circulation in her hands and fingers.

"I told you the truth," she said, keeping some control. "I was ten years old. I don't remember my father having any money when we left Cuba."

As she spoke, her mind raced backward to the lush green grounds of the ranch in Cuba. She remembered the night they were forced to leave: the confusion, the shouting, the bearded men in the dark green fatigue uniforms brandishing their guns . . .

The Fidelistas had pulled up to the ranch in jeeps and trucks, firing their weapons in the air, frightening the Cuban servants. Her father was pushed into a jeep, and she and her mother were placed in a small canvas-topped truck. They were driven to an airfield near Havana and placed aboard a two-engine plane with nothing but the clothing on their backs.

Now she wanted to know what these men wanted from her. Christ, she thought, if she had money, would she be working those scumbag bars, showing her tits and ass to a bunch of horny creeps with dirty fingernails?

When these two men had forced her into their car in the parking lot of the Caribe A-Go-Go as she fled the fight, she had assumed she would be raped. Denise had mentally prepared herself to give in to her abductors without a struggle if it would save her life.

Instead they had taken her to this apartment, handcuffed her to a chair and slapped her around, firing questions at her for which she had no answers.

"Denise, we trust you," Allen said, taking her by the hands and pulling her out of the chair. "I'm sure if you knew where your father had *misplaced* thirty million dollars of the government's money, you'd want to tell us where it is."

Allen studied her face as he mentioned the thirty-million-dollar figure. A flash of excitement flared for an instant in her dark eyes, then died as she suppressed it.

"Thirty million dollars?" Denise said hoarsely as Allen put his arm around her shoulders. "You think I'd be bustin' my ass if I had thirty million dollars?"

"I didn't say you had it, darling," the T-man almost whispered. "I thought you might help us find it, so we could share it with you."

Big Tony's daughter looked at the seamed face in front of her. The cold blue eyes were emotionless. The skin across the man's cheekbones was so tightly stretched, he had the strained look of a lighthouse keeper staring out at the vast expanse of the sea.

"What is it you want me to do?" the attractive brunette asked softly as she looked out of the window at the headlights of a car moving slowly across the causeway.

Chapter 17

Even though it was after midnight, the streets of the Little Havana section of Miami were still populated with some of its pleasure-seeking inhabitants. They roamed the seamy streets seeking food, sex, drugs, or any other kind of recreation that might cross their nocturnal paths.

Most of them had fled Cuba when Castro had come to power in 1959, and even though they had been in the United States for twenty years, they still clung to the culture of their homeland. The signs over the small shops and cantinas were all written in Spanish. There were sidewalk cafés with gaily colored tableclothes and awnings set up for the patrons, who lounged quietly picking at a late dinner or sipping a rum-laced drink.

Kyle, Rafe and Vinnie sat dejectedly at one of the sidewalk tables in front of a small café, which was wedged between a produce store and a barbershop on the main thoroughfare of the Cuban community. Rafe sat glumly with his feet crossed at the ankles and his legs stretched out in front of him. The black man stared at the frosted brown bottle of beer in front of him. He reached for it and picked it up. The cold, bitter liquid trickled down his throat, and he returned the bottle to the plastic, red-checked tablecloth.

The other two men at the table watched as Rafe made small wet interlocking rings with the bottle on the plastic.

"What do we do now?" said Rafe, putting all their unanswered questions in one sentence. "We done hit ten cantinas and restaurants in the last hour, and none of these people got the slightest notion what the fuck we're talkin' about."

"I'm sorry," Vinnie said softly. "I thought comin' down here would give us a good shot at findin' an answer." He looked across at Kyle, who appeared to be deep in thought.

A group of Cuban teenagers passed close to them on the

sidewalk. They gave the three men at the table a hard look. One of the teens, taller than the others, stumbled over Rafe's outstretched feet. He stopped and turned to stare angrily at the black vet.

"Watch you fuggin' feet, man," the brown-skinned youth snapped through clenched teeth.

"Hey, sorry, *amigo*." Rafe smiled at the boy and waved.

"I ain't you fuggin' *amigo,* man," the youth said growling menacingly and clenching his fists. A dark-skinned, curly-haired teenager at his side took his arm and pulled him away.

As the group moved down the street the tall boy whom Rafe had tripped shrugged off the curly-haired youth who was holding his arm. Scowling, he turned and gave the black man at the table the finger. Rafe smiled and waved the beer bottle in salute to the youth's crass gesture.

"Mothafuckers are hostile down here, man," Rafe said to no one in particular. "I need some black folks to make me feel at home."

"Yeah," said Kyle, "like your buddy Lonnie." Both he and Rafe laughed, and Vinnie gave them a puzzled look.

A waiter wearing a yellow guayabera made his way to their table.

"You want some more beer, *hombres?*" he said with a trace of a heavy accent. Kyle reached in his jeans pocket and threw a ten-dollar bill on the table.

"No, I think we've had it, pal," the rancher said, pushing his chair back from the table. The waiter scooped up the ten and dropped it on the cork-lined, brown plastic tray.

"I bring your change, señor," said the man, starting to turn.

"Keep it." Kyle stood and stopped the waiter with his hand. "I'd like to ask you a question."

Rafe and Vinnie sat watching Kyle and the heavyset server with the tray.

"*Si,* what is it you want to know?"

"We're lookin' for somebody who can tell us where we might find a ranch in Cuba." Kyle spoke slowly, evenly, looking the man in the eye.

"Cuba?" The waiter's brown eyes widened in surprise. "A *ranch* in Cuba?"

Kyle took the man's arm and pulled him closer.

"Yeah," he said softly. "It's got something to do with a place named El Gato Negro. You ever hear of it?"

The heavyset waiter looked from Kyle to the other two men seated at the table. He jerked his arm out of Kyle's grasp and stepped back.

"No, señor, I have never heard of a ranch by this name."

"Maybe you know somebody who has. We've tried every place on the street," interjected Rafe, leaning forward in his chair.

"There is a pool room . . . Rivera's, around the corner," the waiter said as he started to walk away. "They may have the information you want."

He turned and walked into the café, leaving the three men to stare blankly at his back.

"Maybe we should give it a shot, Blood," Rafe said, rising from his chair.

Rivera's combination cantina and pool hall was not exactly around the corner, as the heavyset waiter had directed them. The three vets found the seedy establishment three blocks south, after they had turned left off the main street.

The streets leading to Rivera's were dark and foreboding compared to the brightly lit wide boulevard they had just left. There were few streetlights, and they had not seen any of the local residents for the last two blocks. A number of trash-strewn vacant lots and dark alleyways dotted the landscape, making it look more like a battle zone than a residential Miami neighborhood.

Rivera's sat in the middle of the next block adjacent to an empty lot. It had been a cigar store at one time. The wide plate-glass window was still in evidence. It had been painted a bilious green color that was starting to flake. Streamers of yellow light seeped through the chipped paint and shed small beams on the dirty sidewalk. A crudely lettered sign had been hand-painted across the window. The words *billiard* and *academy* had been misspelled, and some of the letters in *cantina* were chipped away.

The small bell over the door tinkled merrily as Kyle, followed by Rafe and Vinnie, entered the dingy, smoke-filled pool hall. There was a surprisingly new bar set along the right hand-wall, which did not fit in with the worn look of the place. Four plain wooden tables surrounded by worn chairs took up the open area in front of the bar.

At the rear of the cantina were four medium-size pool tables lit by green-shaded lamps hanging on chains, which were suspended from the wooden ceiling. All the tables were being used by an assortment of young Cubans, most of whom were smoking or talking softly while watching the games unfold across the green-topped tables.

At the sound of the bell the players, as well as the observers, sitting on high-backed chairs or clustered in the tight corners, lifted their heads. It was as if a signal had been given to look at the trio of strangers who had entered the cantina. Their eyeballs seemed to click as they zeroed in on the three men.

The door at the rear of the pool area opened, and a swarthy man with a heavy, black moustache and wire-framed aviator glasses entered the still room. He was carrying a cardboard case of bottled beer. He stopped for an instant, eyeing the three men standing near the bar, then he continued toward them.

"You *gentlemen* lost?" he asked, heaving the case onto the bar. The men around the pool tables still eyed them sullenly.

"No," answered Kyle slowly as the man ducked under the cutaway and stepped behind the bar. "I think we found what we wanted."

"What could that be?" the owner shot back sarcastically, taking a sidelong glance at the group of hostile men at the pool tables who were watching them closely.

"We would like some information, *compadre,*" Rafe said. "We're lookin' for somethin'."

Alberto Rivera opened the case of beer he had set on the surface of the bar. He started to remove the bottles and place them in an old metal Coca Cola box that served as an ice chest. He had imbedded about twelve bottles in the cracked ice when he looked up.

"You vice, man?" Rivera said coldly. "We got no drugs. No numbers here, man."

The men around the tables stirred uneasily and started to drift silently into the area near the bar.

"We ain't cops, brother," Rafe said quickly as the owner dipped into the case of beer again. "We just want to ask a couple questions."

Rivera looked at Rafe coldly. He removed the last four bottles from the case and shoved them into the ice. As he looked up, most of the men from the pool area were now surrounding the Americans at the bar, cutting off the only exit from the cantina.

"Look, why don't you go while you can?" The owner said uneasily, looking at the menacing faces of his regulars.

"You ever hear of a place called El Gato Negro?" asked Kyle, leaning across the bar.

"El Gato Negro?" The owner's eyes widened with surprise. "You know what this means? The Black Cat."

"Yeah, we know what it means, brother," Rafe interjected. "We just want to know where it is."

By now the pool players and their friends had closed into a loose circle around the three Americans. Some of the men held their pool cues clubbed and slid them nervously along their wet palms. The three vets looked around the circle of dark faces.

"Eh, *muchachos! El Yanquis quienes . . . El Gato Negro,*" said Rivera to the grim group. One of the men, taller than the rest, wearing a hot pink shirt, stepped toward Kyle and the others. He took a wide stance and placed his hands on his hips.

"Hey, Yankee boy," Pink Shirt intoned mockingly. "Don't you know what that means? It means 'the black pussy.'" He took a couple steps toward Rafe so that he was face-to-face with the black man. "You want some black pussy, *man?*" The men behind him snickered loudly, and he turned to acknowledge their approval.

"No thanks, *amigo,*" said Rafe, stepping back. A thin sheen of sweat had appeared on his high forehead, making it glisten. "I got all the black pussy I can handle."

On either side of him, Kyle and Vinnie scanned the circle of Cubans for any overt signs of sudden movement. The men stirred uneasily, glaring at the three strangers. Rafe and the tall man in the pink shirt had locked eyes as the clank of the rickety fan droned on.

Kyle reached into his pocket and withdrew what was left of his two thousand dollars. He peeled a twenty from the middle and threw it on the bar.

"Give the boys a round on us, buddy," he directed the tense Rivera without taking his eyes from the hostile group in front of him.

Rivera snatched up the twenty and held it above his head.

"Eh, *muchachos!*" the owner shouted. "*Mucho cervesa . . . mucho cervesa . . .*" Some of the faces in the circle brightened, and two of them started toward the bar.

"No!" Pink Shirt said with a snarl. "I don't want no fuggin' Yankee beer."

He reached into his back pocket and withdrew a pearl-handled stiletto, which he waved above his head. The enraged man pressed the button on the white handle, and a razor-sharp, six-inch blade snapped out of the hilt into the dim light of the cantina.

There were grunts of encouragement from some of the men, but on the whole they were silent, like a pack waiting for a signal . . . for something to trigger them into action.

Kyle stepped quickly to Rafe's side while Vinnie warily covered their backs against any kind of flanking movement by the Cubans. Pink Shirt waved the sharp point of the knife in front of him in a deadly, mesmerizing circle. Rafe crouched, extending his arms, never taking his eyes from the gleaming blade.

The tall man suddenly lunged forward, aiming the stiletto at the black man's stomach. Rafe sidestepped and grasped the arm holding the knife at the wrist and above the elbow with both hands. At the same time he brought his right leg across in a sweeping motion, kicking the man's feet out from under him. As the Cuban fell heavily to the floor Rafe brought his knee up sharply into the man's elbow, breaking it with a loud crack.

Pink Shirt screamed in pain as the knife clattered to the dirty wooden floor. As the tall man lay writhing in agony, holding his broken arm with his good hand, the black vet stepped forward and kicked him solidly in the throat with his steel-toed work boot. An ugly, rasping sound issued from the stricken man's mouth, and he rolled onto his face as fresh blood seeped from his nose and shattered larynx.

"Would any of you mothafuckers like some of the same?" cooed Rafe in a deadly tone to the circle of stunned men as they looked down at their motionless comrade.

"Why don't you boys have a cold one on us, and we'll let bygones be bygones," said Kyle as he bent down and picked the stiletto up from the floor. He closed the deadly blade against his thigh and slipped it in his pocket. Then he motioned to Vinnie with a nod of his head.

As the three Americans started for the door the men in front of the hostile circle parted and let them pass. The only sound in the dingy room was the clanking of the old fan.

Outside the cantina, the muggy, tropical air of the Miami night seemed to close in on the three men as they stood on the sidewalk by the vacant lot. An old school bus, its side windows painted over, was parked alongside the wall belonging to Rivera's.

As Kyle looked at the bus an odd feeling crept along the base of his skull. He did not recall the bus being there when they'd entered the cantina.

Rafe looked at his two companions and laughed.

"Like I said, Blood . . . these are some hostile mothafuckers."

"They hate us," Vinnie said, " 'cause they feel we been shittin' on 'em."

"Bullshit, man." Rafe said angrily. "They coulda stayed with Fidel . . . woulda been more jobs for the brothers."

Vinnie sat down dejectedly on the curb and hung his arms over his knees. Kyle and Rafe joined him.

"Christ," he said. "If you guys plan on gettin' in any more fights tonight, count me out. I feel like I'm back in 'Nam."

"It's gotta be Rafe, Vincent," said Kyle, laughing. "He even stirred up some of his blood brothers earlier today."

Rafe reached into the gutter and picked up an empty wine bottle that one of the local residents had discarded earlier that night.

"Where do we go from here, my man?" said Rafe, looking at the label on the bottle. He was about to drop it back into the street when he felt the unmistakable steel circle of a gun barrel poking into the right side of his neck.

"Don't be a litterbug, my friend," a disembodied voice behind them said softly. "The three of you stand up slowly, and you'll live a little while longer."

Chapter 18

They had been taken by surprise. As he lay blindfolded, bound hand and foot, on the floor of the old bus, Kyle's mind flailed at itself. How the hell could he let that happen? The voice in his head chastised him as his face pressed into the stale-smelling mattress on which he was lying.

The four Cubans had silently exited the school bus parked on the vacant lot, and come up behind them with drawn guns. The three vets had been hustled quickly into the vehicle with opaque windows where they had been bound, gagged, and blindfolded.

Now the former school transport careened along the darkened streets of the city, taking its trio of captives to an unknown destination. The men who had taken them remained silent as the old bus swayed from side to side.

Kyle's mind raced wildly, trying to guess why they had been taken. Who were these men? He decided that whoever they were, they had been damn good professionals. His mind tried to formulate an escape plan. Vinnie and Rafe were lying on either side of him. He could feel their bodies jostle his every time the bus hit a bump or made a turn. Kyle wondered what thoughts were going through the minds of his two comrades.

The ex–Green Beret knew they could do nothing with their hands tied behind their backs. They would have to look for an opening when they got the chance . . . if they got the chance.

From somewhere in the rear of the bus he heard a metallic snick as the slide on a .45-caliber automatic was pulled back and snapped into place.

The old houseboat had been berthed at its mooring along the bank of the Black Creek Canal in South Miami for five years. Its windows had long ago been covered by thick sheets of marine plywood. A slimy, greenish mold clung to the vessel's hull, working its way upward toward the short deck that circled the large boxlike cabin that made up the run-down boat's upper superstructure. Paint was chipping and peeling from the bulkheads and what could be seen of the hull.

A hand-painted FOR SALE sign had been nailed to a piling next to a rotting board that served as a gangplank. The name of the owner and the telephone number on the sign was barely visible because the paint had faded so badly.

Inside the houseboat's large cabin, Kyle, Rafe and Vinnie sat on three wooden crates with their hands tied behind their backs. The blindfolds were still in place, but their gags had been removed. Around them, also seated on crates, were eleven dour-looking men, their handguns drawn.

A twelfth man, with coarse, straight hair and a fierce black mustache, stood in front of the three captives, directing a powerful electric lantern at the bound men. His name was Luis Carreras.

The large cabin they were in was bare except for the crates on which the men were seated. A replica of a fringed flag hung on one of the bulkheads. The words *Brigada Asalto* and the picture of a charging soldier with a fixed bayonette were emblazoned on it.

Carreras held the lantern at his waist so that it cast eerie shadows on the faces of the captives and the men seated in the circle.

"Well, *muchachos,* what is it going to be, eh?" said the man with the lantern, flicking the bright light across the faces of the bound men. "Are you Fidelistas . . . or CIA?"

"Hey, *amigo,*" said Rafe lightly. "We don't even know what that means."

Carreras stepped quickly in front of Rafe and with his free hand slipped a .357 Magnum from the waistband of his trousers and placed it against the black man's temple.

"Don't try to bullshit me," the Cuban said harshly, cocking the pistol. Some of the men on the crates shifted uneasily. "You three come into my town with a cock-and-bull story, asking questions, and we're supposed to believe you?"

"We were only tryin' to get a little info, brother," said Rafe quickly, shifting his head away from the muzzle of the Magnum.

"Señor," said Kyle softly, "untie us, take off these blindfolds, and we'll tell you what we're after."

Carreras hesitated for a beat. Then he motioned to one of the men seated in the circle.

"We'll remove the blindfolds, but your hands will remain tied." The man Carreras had singled out stepped behind each of the bound men and slipped the dirty white cloths off their eyes. Then he moved quickly back to his crate.

Carreras held the bright light directly in the eyes of the three men in the center of the circle, making them squint and drop their heads.

"Thanks for nothin'," said Vinnie bitterly, looking at the deck.

"*De nada,*" answered the Cuban, laughing. "Now I want answers . . . *rapido.*"

"We're not CIA," said Kyle. "We're tryin' to find anybody that's heard of a place called El Gato Negro or knew Big Tony Palermo."

"You can't be Fidelistas." Carreras laughed. "That story is too dumb. You must be CIA."

Outside the circle of light made by the bright lantern, one of the men slipped his pistol into his belt and stood. He was stocky, with a thin mustache. A wreath of shiny black hair encircled his bald pate.

"*Si,*" said Manny Lopez, stepping forward into the circle. He walked with a slight limp. "I knew Señor Palermo. My father and I worked for him at the Villa de Capri in Havana . . . twenty years ago."

"*Ciudado,*" Carreras said sharply to Lopez, holding up his hand.

"It is all right, Jefe." The stocky man answered. "They're not going anywhere."

Kyle got a good look at the man who had spoken as Carreras lowered the light.

"You worked for him?" Kyle asked Lopez, excitement brimming in his voice like a stream overrunning its bank.

"*Si,* I also worked for him at his ranch, El Gato Negro. I was a groom there before Fidel."

"Hot, damn!" exclaimed Rafe. "El Gato Negro *is* the ranch."

Kyle's mind was now like a kaleidoscope. Thoughts rushed at him with lightning speed. He registered them quickly and filed them in their proper place.

To Kyle their situation was like the telling of a good news/bad news joke. The good news was that they had found this man who knew Palermo and knew exactly where the ranch was located. The bad news was, they were still prisoners.

Kyle knew he had to do something to free them. They were now on the verge of reaching their goal.

"Señor," he said to Carreras. "I'd like to speak to this man alone for five minutes. He'll understand everything."

"How do I know you won't try to escape?" the chief said.

"You've got my friends. I'm not goin' anyplace without them."

• • •

The roof of the dilapidated houseboat was partially rotted through. Pieces of tin sheething had been nailed over the soft places, but it still felt as if the entire roof would give way under the weight of anyone who walked on it.

Kyle, his hands still bound behind his back, sat on the edge of the solid railing that rimmed the roof. Lopez stood in front of him, his right hand on the pistol in his belt.

"Well, my friend," said the stocky Cuban, eyeing Kyle suspiciously. "You had better talk fast. El Jefe only gave us five minutes."

For an instant Kyle strained at the rough rope cutting into his wrists. The thought flashed in his head that he might be able to work his hands free and overpower the man who stood over him. Then what? If he did manage it, the stocky Cuban would never trust him and reveal what they wanted to know. Rafe and Vinnie might be killed if the men below suspected anything.

"We're after money," said Kyle, deciding against that plan of attack. "A lot of money. We think it may be buried somewhere in Cuba."

"Do you have any idea where?"

"Yeah," said Kyle, nodding. "By the way, what the hell is the Villa de Capri?"

"The Capri was one of the biggest gambling casinos in Cuba." Lopez laughed. "People came from all over the world. Lots of . . . how you say, high rollers from the States? And lots of movie stars."

"What was Palermo's connection?"

"He was the big boss, the manager," answered Lopez.

"Tell me about El Gato Negro," said Kyle, trying to keep the eagerness out of his voice.

"It was very beautiful," the bald man said wistfully. "There were many horses and some cattle . . ."

"Was there a patio?"

Lopez gave him an odd look before answering.

"Patio . . . *si*—by the pool. A big one." He paused. "Señor . . . ?"

"Youngblood, Kyle Youngblood," Kyle answered.

"Señor Youngblood, I am Manny Lopez." Both men nodded as Lopez continued. "I have answered your questions, but I can only suspect what you want."

Kyle knew the man in front of him held the key to the future. Without the money his plan of getting at Marty Fallon on his fortified island was doomed to failure.

"Cards on the table, Manny?" Kyle said, looking the squat Cuban in the eye.

"*Si,*" the bald man answered, nodding.

The sound of an engine running at low speed made Kyle turn and look behind him. A beautifully trimmed cabin cruiser was making its way down the dark canal. The boat's running lights reflected eerily off the still water.

"We want to go to the ranch in Cuba," Kyle said as the cruiser slid farther down the canal, leaving a slight V-shaped wake that rippled the dark water. The houseboat rocked lazily in the whitecapped wavelets.

"Señor, you are *loco,*" Lopez whispered incredulously in the darkness. "Fidel has the island sewn up tight . . . like a drum. A fish cannot swim in or out without him knowing it. Why is it you want to go?"

Kyle took a deep breath before answering.

"For thirty million dollars."

It was a half hour later when Manny Lopez maneuvered the old bus through the deserted streets of South Miami. He thought of what the hawk-faced Yankee had said to him on the roof of the Brigade's headquarters. A share of thirty million dollars would buy a great many tacos for his long-suffering wife and four *niños*.

The Yankee had said an equal portion of the money for all those who shared the danger. He would be able to get rid of his night job at the stinking cantina, but he would never give up the other job at the racetrack.

He loved the graceful beauty of the animals he cared for. It was worth getting up early in the morning, swamping out the stalls just to be near the high-strung thoroughbreds. He even liked the pungent smell of the horse manure, but his wife, Clara, couldn't stand the odor. She always made him take off his soiled boots whenever he came home from his job as an assistant trainer.

Manny was held in high esteem by the other veterans of the Bay of Pigs, Brigada Asalto. In 1961, he and his father and older brother had been among the first to enlist in the Brigade, which would attempt to return to the Cuban motherland and free it from Castro's communist rule.

They had gone ashore at the red beach and fought their way inland. Three days later they were taken prisoner, along with hundreds of others, in the Zapata Swamp. The Brigade members were interrogated for a week, then paraded before the national television cameras in a mass trial that turned into a political coup for the Castro regime.

A month later Manny, his father and old brother were interned in the infamous circular buildings of the Model Prison on the Isle of Pines. The elder Lopez, already gravely ill with cancer, died after six weeks in the cruel environment of the prison. Manny's brother, Gerardo, was beaten to death by a sadistic sergeant in the prison's punishment pavilion for striking a trustee who had been trying to steal his sandals.

Manny, himself, was kicked and severely beaten by a group of guards with bayonets and rubber hoses during one of the "inspections" at the prison. He was knocked down a flight of stone steps which caused a compound fracture of his right leg that had never been set properly and left him with a permanent limp.

He was finally repatriated, along with the rest of the Brigade survivors, for a shopping list of food and drugs worth fifty-three million dollars that was negotiated by Castro as a ransom. When he stepped from the plane at Homestead Air Force base in December of 1962, Manny's hatred of the communists and his desire to drive them from his homeland was still simmering in him like a banked fire.

"Hey, Lopez." Rafe's voice broke into Manny's thoughts. "What the hell did you tell the guy with the Magnum that sprung us?"

"I told him the truth," answered the squat Cuban, stopping the bus behind Rafe's truck. "I told him you wanted to go to Cuba to hunt for buried treasure."

"Christ!" exclaimed Vinnie. "What did he say?"

Lopez pulled the lever and opened the door of the bus.

"He thought you were all *loco* but harmless. So he let you go. Sometimes it is best to tell the truth."

Kyle rose from the foul-smelling mattress lying on the floor of the bus. He made his way forward to where Manny Lopez sat behind the wheel.

"What do you say, *amigo*?" said Kyle. "Can we count on you?"

"Thirty million dollars," Lopez whispered.

"You could lead us to it," said Kyle earnestly.

Manny Lopez gripped the chipped black steering wheel of the bus with both hands and sighed deeply before answering.

"I went back to Cuba once . . . at the Bahia de Cochinos. How you say . . . Bay of Pigs? We were taken prisoner. My father and my brother died in prison on the Islo de Pinos."

"That was a long time ago," said Kyle.

"On the Red Beach we called for help," Lopez said in a sad voice. "The Yankee ships and planes stood off the beach and did nothing while we died."

Rafe reached up and put a hand on Manny's shoulder.

"Like the man said, Lopez . . . that was a long time ago." The black man squeezed the Cuban's shoulder.

"Do you put a time limit on a promise to a friend?" asked Manny, turning to Rafe.

"You help us find the money, *amigo,*" Kyle interjected, "an' you'll cure a lot of hurts."

"Go back to Cuba again?" Lopez smiled slowly. "Back to the homeland? Aieee! That would be good." He reached out and offered his hand to Kyle. "Where do you want me to meet with you?"

Chapter 19

The reddish-orange ball of the Miami sun was halfway up the eastern horizon when Manny Lopez knocked on the door of Vinnie Troiano's studio apartment in Opa Locka. Across the street from the converted motel, unseen by the stocky Cuban, a tan sedan sat parked in the shimmering, early-morning heat. From inside the car two men and a woman stared silently at the small balcony where Manny Lopez waited.

The door finally opened, and a yawning Vinnie Troiano, wearing nothing but a pair of white jockey shorts, admitted the bald Cuban. As the door to the apartment closed, the man in the passenger seat of the sedan turned and said something to the attractive, dark-haired girl in the backseat.

As Manny entered the apartment Kyle rose from the small table in the kitchenette, where he had been sipping a cup of strong black coffee. Kyle came around the edge of the Formica-topped island that separated the kitchen area from the living room and extended his hand.

"I'm glad you could make it, Manny." The two men shook hands. "How about a cup of coffee?"

"*Nada* . . . nothing, thank you. I had an early breakfast."

"Sit down," said Kyle, rubbing at his nose. "Rafe'll be out of the bathroom in a couple minutes."

"I think he fell in." Vinnie laughed. "Either that or he has a copy of *Playboy* in there."

Kyle rubbed at his nose again. Ever since the stocky Cuban had entered the apartment, Kyle's nostrils had picked up a faint stable smell. The odor triggered a mental image of his ranch in Nevada and his murdered wife and children. He fought it down, but tears stung his eyes and he had to pinch the bridge of his nose to keep them from spilling down his cheeks.

Manny Lopez stared at Kyle's lean, hawklike face. He saw the tears glisten in the man's dark eyes and the muscles of his jaw and neck tighten.

"Are you all right, señor?" Manny asked, the concern evident in his voice. "Is anything wrong?"

Before Kyle could answer, the door to the bathroom opened and Rafe stepped into the room. He had a copy of *Penthouse* in his hand.

"Hey, Vinnie," he said to the good-looking Italian. "How come they never have any 'sisters' in these magazines?"

"Too ugly!" said Vinnie, laughing as he dropped onto the worn couch.

"Up yours, wop," retorted Rafe. He raised the middle finger of his right hand in a derisive salute.

"Gentlemen," the stocky Cuban said, breaking in. "Can we get down to . . . how you say . . . brass tacks? I have to get to my other job shortly. There are four little ones with hungry mouths at home."

"I know what you mean, *amigo,*" said Rafe. "My wife was all over my ass for not goin' to work this mornin'."

Kyle gestured at the couch, and Lopez crossed to it and sat down.

"Friends," Kyle Youngblood said firmly, "if we can pull this off, none of you will ever have to work again."

"What is it you need to know?" the bald man asked.

"You know exactly where the ranch is?" said Kyle, looking intently into Manny's face.

"*Si,* I have not been there for many years, but I could find it easily."

Rafe crossed to the couch and sat on the frayed arm.

"We got to come up with some kind of plan, Blood," he said, propping himself up with his elbow on Vinnie's shoulder.

"We're goin' to have to rely on Manny to give us the best route to the island and the ranch," Kyle answered.

"I will do my best," Lopez said softly. "But we will need maps and charts."

Later that afternoon, as a line of tourists gawked along the sidewalk in front of the Cast-a-Ways, four anxious men sat around a table in the cabin of the fishing boat, the *Linda C*. Vinnie's boss, Captain Russ, had long since gone home, disgusted because he hadn't been able to book a deep-sea charter for that day.

On the table lay an unfurled chart of the Florida Straits and the coastal waters of Cuba. Each curled end of the heavy paper was held down by a full bottle of beer.

Manny Lopez leaned forward and pointed a finger at a place on the chart.

"There are many coves on the southern coast," Lopez said. "A small force could slip in undetected at night."

Kyle leaned away from the table and laced his fingers behind his head.

"Problem is, we need a boat big enough and fast enough to get us in and out in one piece." The rancher took a long drink from one of the bottles of beer.

"We got one, Blood," chirped Rafe, clapping Vinnie on the back with one big hand.

"Forget it. My boss is in hock up to his ass," said Vinnie, shaking his head. "Besides, he's scared shitless."

"Even for thirty million?" said Rafe.

"Even for thirty million." Vinnie nodded.

"We need more than a boat," said Kyle, leaning forward again. "We need front money for weapons and supplies."

Lopez looked at Kyle and shook his head. "How much money are we talking about, Señor Kyle?"

"I don't know," Kyle answered, standing up. "I don't have any idea what the cost of ordnance is today."

"Plus the price of the boat," chimed in Vinnie, who had been silent up to that point.

Kyle crossed to one of the bunks that was forward of the table and sat down.

"What we need," he said slowly, "is a guy who is willing to risk his money for a percentage of what we get."

The four men looked at each other and fell silent. The air in the small cabin was heavy with disappointment. Slowly Manny Lopez lifted his head from the charts.

"I may know of such a man," he said evenly. "His name is Clifford Ordile. I met him when we were training for the Bay of Pigs in Guatemala. He was CIA."

Kyle looked up from the bunk as Vinnie's and Rafe's heads snapped to attention.

"Hey, *hermano*." The black man beamed. "Where do we find this dude?"

"The last I heard of him, he had quit the Agency and was running a charter-boat business in Key West."

"Well, what in hell are we waitin' for?" exclaimed Rafe, jumping to his feet. "Let's go for it!"

Chapter 20

The Overseas Highway is a miraculous ribbon of concrete suspended on cement pilings above the azure-blue water of the Atlantic Ocean and Florida Bay. The road runs for 106 miles, from Key Largo to the quaint, bizzare town of Key West. The keys run an actual distance of 180 miles, from Biscayne Bay in the north, to the Dry Tortugas at their southern tip.

Manny Lopez's multicolored Ford van, carrying Kyle, Rafe and Vinnie, had just passed Mile Marker 80 on the lower half of Matacumbe Key when Manny took his hand off the wheel and glanced at his watch. It was nearly twelve o'clock. He calculated mentally that at this rate they would be in Key West by 2:00 P.M. at the latest.

The stocky Cuban peered through the bug-spattered windshield of the old van and tapped his fingers on the steering wheel to the rythmn of a soft, Latin beat. High white clouds drifted slowly overhead in the clear blue sky. Off to the left, in the shimmering stretch of the Atlantic, a flash of silver caught his eye as a fish broke the surface of the sea and disappeared.

Lopez looked across at Kyle, who was seated next to him in the passenger seat. He looked as if he were deep in thought. The round-faced Cuban read a deep sadness in the man's face and eyes, as if something very tragic had happened to mar his life.

Manny glanced over his shoulder into the back of the van. The black man and the short one called Vinnie were sleeping soundly on the blue air mattress he had bought for the children to rest on when he and Clara took them on vacations.

Manny drove steadily southward, crossing the small fragments of twisted and tortured coral reef and limestone the original Spanish settlers had named Los Matires—The Martyrs—because of their appearance. His mind wandered back to the previous night, when he had told his little Clarita he was going on an expedition to Cuba with three strangers. He told her that the trip would make them rich beyond their wildest dreams. The tiny raven-haired woman had blanched and then cried, fearing she would never see him again.

Manny assured her that it was not to be another Bay of Pigs but a private enterprise that would make them wealthy. He told her he would be gone about a week, and if she did not hear from him during that time, not to worry.

In the morning he kissed her and the four *niños* good-bye. The only thing he really regretted was that he would be away from his job at the track and his beloved horses.

"Not much grazin' land on these little islands." Kyle's voice broke into Manny's thoughts.

"No, I'm afraid not." Manny laughed. "But the early ones did some farming."

"Farming?" Kyle said incredulously.

"*Si,*" the Cuban answered. "They grew limes, pineapples, fruits . . . till the hurricanes wiped them out."

Kyle looked out at the great expanse of water surrounding him and shook his head.

"I sure as hell would hate to be around here in a hurricane."

"You see that key we just crossed, *hombre*? That's Matacumbe," said Lopez, jerking his thumb toward the rear of the van. "Eight hundred men . . . railroad workers drowned in the big storm of 1935. They built a monument for them on Islamorada."

"Like I said, no way I would want to be on these little pieces of rock when that wind starts to blow."

Lopez laughed and went back to drumming on the steering wheel. He gave Kyle a sidelong glance and grinned.

"Thirty million dollars . . . aieee!" He sighed loudly and decided he liked this grim-faced Yankee more and more.

Ninety minutes and sixty miles farther south, the van rolled past Mile Marker 20 in the lower keys. Here the little islands were lower and darker, with a heavier covering of mangrove trees. On some of these swampy islands, dangerous-looking dirt roads ran off into the thickets of mangrove, promising lethal adventure to those who might want to explore them.

The multicolored van moved down U.S. 1, across Sugarloaf Key and Saddlebush. It rolled over the bridge and onto Boca Chica Key. Rafe and Vinnie were now awake and sat quietly with their backs resting against the panneled interior of the truck. It was 1:30 P.M.

Kyle looked at one of the dirt roads leading into the mangroves.

"Where do those roads go, *amigo*?" he asked matter-of-factly.

"They'll lead you to trouble," said Lopez. "At the end of each is an inlet or a bay used by the drug runners. They are good places to stay away from."

"Just checkin'," Kyle said lightly. "I was wonderin' if we might use one of the inlets comin' back from Cuba."

Lopez shook his head violently.

"Uh-uh . . . almost all of them are inhabited by *hombres malos* . . . bad guys. They kill you for what you have in your pockets."

"That ain't much," chimed in Rafe from the rear of the van.

All four of them laughed as the van crossed Boca Chica Channel and rolled onto Stock Island.

"Tell me some more about this guy Ordile we're tryin' to find," said Kyle.

"Cliff had too much . . . how you say? . . . conscience," said Lopez. "After the Bay of Pigs he resigned the CIA and came down here to fish."

"Christ, Manny," Rafe said, breaking in, "that's eighteen years ago. This guy could be history."

"No, my friend," Lopez shot back. "I know this man. He lived with us. He trained us . . . he is a good man. Cliff quit because of what his government promised but didn't do for us."

"How do you know he'll be at this Land's End Marina?" asked Kyle.

"The Brigade, *mi amigo*, has ways of finding old friends . . . and old enemies."

High above their heads in the cloud-tufted sky, a small blue-and-white chopper was keeping pace with the van as it headed toward Key West. In the front passenger seat, next to the pilot, a stone-faced Chet Allen, still nattily dressed in a tan three-piece suit, watched the oddly painted vehicle through mirrored sunglasses.

Directly behind him sat Phil McGregor, who looked a bit pale under his newly acquired Florida sunburn. The crew-cut T-man had a dread of flying that was evident in his pallor, as well as in the beads of perspiration glistening on his forehead.

The seat next to him was occupied by a smiling Denise Palermo.

Chapter 21

There is a mystery about Key West. It is a town founded by wreckers, smugglers, and Conchs, Bahamians who came over from Eleuthera in the early 1800s in order to continue their "wrecking" industry. Along with these Conchs, blacks and Cubans helped make up the early population of Key West.

It is a city of unexpected contrasts . . . of fine houses and shacks, painted primly white or weathered down to the silvery bone. Tropical flowers and trees bloom everywhere . . . jacaranda, bougainvillea, poinciana and frangipani. The leaves and petals of these beautiful plants vainly try to cover the burned-out, trash-littered lots and seedy trappings of this eccentric town built in the middle of an ocean.

As Manny Lopez's van made a sharp right turn onto Roosevelt Boulevard and passed the garish Searstown shopping center, the small blue-and-white chopper veered to the left and set down at the Key West International Airport, which lay at the southeastern end of the island.

The van continued on Roosevelt, tracking the northern end of the key. It crossed Kennedy Drive, then hit the southern tip of Garrison Bight, where the masts and tuna towers of hundreds of sailboats and power cruisers lined the sky.

"This is not Cliff's marina," said Manny before any of them could ask the question.

"Christ!" Vinnie croaked, looking out of the small, heart-shaped window cut in the rear panel of the van. "I thought we had a lot of boats at the Cast-a-Ways. There must be two thousand of those mothers out there."

Manny drove slowly along the bight, giving his passengers a chance to eyeball the massed vessels.

"We were told Cliff's boat is in a small marina near Old Town," Lopez said, speeding up a bit. "We should be there shortly."

The van continued right onto Palm Avenue, then left onto Eaton, and right again on William, which took them to the smaller Key West Bight. The Land's End Marina was located at the eastern end of the bight. Here the boats were not as numerous or as rich-looking.

As Manny's van passed under the LAND'S END sign, one of the links in the chain holding it gave way, and the loose end swung down, nearly hitting the van.

"Classy place," said Kyle sarcastically as he looked past the bone-white, ramshackle shed that served as an office.

Most of the slips were vacant, and the rickety dock, set on rotting pilings, looked as though it might collapse at any second. At the end of the long pier Kyle could make out a fat blond man in a red tank top and denim cutoffs. He was dangling a hand line in the water.

Lopez stopped the van in front of the office and cut the engine.

"Wait here till I see if he is at his slip," the squat Cuban said as he exited the van.

Manny opened the torn screen door and entered the shack. A rough, boxlike counter with some papers and a silver desk bell from a hotel took up about half the small room. On the wall behind the counter, a seminude girl, wearing a wet, cut-off T-shirt and the bottom half of a string bikini, smiled at him from a calendar that advertised a local dive shop.

The round-faced Cuban reached out and tapped the bell with the palm of his hand, although he knew no one was in the small building. He tapped it again, and the small tinkle of the bell rang through the empty shack.

"Hello!" Manny called out. "Hello! Is anyone here?"

As he turned to go, he guiltily sneaked a look at the girl on the calendar and rolled his eyes toward the ceiling. A pang of conscience quickly stabbed at him as he thought of his Clarita waiting at home.

Outside in the van, Kyle was watching the fat man in the red tank top pull a flopping fish out of the water on his hand line as Manny exited the shack. The Cuban made his way to the passenger side of the truck.

"There is no one inside, *amigo,*" Lopez said dejectedly.

"Shit!" Vinnie howled from the back of the van. "We ride all the way down here, and nobody's fuckin' home. Besides that . . . I'm starvin'."

"You think you're hungry," Rafe chimed in. "When I told

Betty where I was goin', she threw me out of the house without breakfast.''

Kyle looked at Manny, then peered out again at the fat blond man, who was just getting his wriggling fish off the hook and dropping it into a bushel basket.

''Let's try that guy at the end of the dock, then we can get somethin' to eat.''

The blond man seemed to pay no attention as Kyle and Manny made their way toward him down the long dock. As they stopped a few feet from him he looked up to acknowledge their presence. Kyle could see the flabby white flesh as it fought to get out of the red tank top. He was surprised the man's skin hadn't tanned or turned red in the uncompromising tropical sun.

''Can I help ya?'' the man said as he forced some bait on a wicked-looking hook. Kyle rubbed his nose as the overwhelming stench of fish that had been too long in the sun rolled over him.

Manny removed his straw hat, took out a handkerchief, and wiped his glistening pate.

''We are looking for a charter-boat captain,'' said Manny. ''Clifford Ordile.''

''Ain't here,'' the fat man said without looking up.

''Is his boat out?'' Manny asked, taking a step closer.

''Nope.'' The fisherman looked up quickly and stopped the Cuban with his eyes. ''His boat is down. He ran it onto a coral head about two months ago.''

''You mean, the boat sunk?'' asked Kyle, noting the trace of an English accent in the man's speech.

''Quicker'n a gull can shit,'' the fat man said, scratching mightily at the area around his crotch with his free hand. ''No insurance, either. The company thought he did it on purpose.''

''Where is he now?'' Manny smiled. ''We are old friends of his from Miami.''

The fat man dropped his line in the water and scratched again before answering.

''When he's on the beach, he usually hangs out at the Green Parrot. It's on Southard, just off Duval.''

''Thank you,'' said Manny, putting his straw hat back on his bare, burning scalp as he and Kyle turned to go.

''If you see Cliff''—the fat man's voice echoed behind them—''he still owes me two months' rent for the slip.''

The Green Parrot was a funky, down-home bar in the middle of Key West's Old Town. As Manny Lopez and Kyle entered the dim bar, their eyes adjusted slowly to the gloom.

The room itself was long and narrow, with the bar along one wall and a row of booths along the other. There were a trio of empty pool tables in the rear, and only two of the stools along the bar were occupied. A young couple sat in a booth near the door, nuzzling each other like a pair of puppies in a litter.

After Kyle and the others had left the Land's End Marina at Key West Bight, they had eaten a late lunch at a place called Shorty's, on Duval. Then Kyle and Manny had dropped Rafe and Vinnie at the South Beach Motel, a cheap place on the ocean side of the island, and told them to get a couple rooms for the night.

The daytime bartender at the Green Parrot was a huge man with a shaved head. He sported a pitch-black goatee and mustache. There was a large gold hoop hanging from his left earlobe.

Manny stepped to the bar and leaned toward the man.

"Excuse me, friend," the squat Cuban said quietly. "We are looking for someone . . . Clifford Ordile?"

The big bartender gave Manny a look as if he had picked his pocket and jerked his thumb at the booths that faded into the gloom at the rear of the bar. The Cuban's eyes followed the man's thumb. He could barely make out a form in the darkness in the last booth at the end of the row.

Manny glanced back at Kyle, and the two men moved toward the booth that had been indicated by the big bartender. As they approached, Kyle could make out a short, wiry man with a square face and a gray crew cut.

The former CIA man had both hands on the table in front of him. His left hand was wrapped around a cold bottle of Budweiser. A white napkin covered his right hand. Both men could see the snub-nosed snout of a .38 Police Special poking from under the napkin.

"Have a seat, gentlemen," said Ordile softly. "Keep your hands where I can scc them."

"Why the gun, Cliff?" Manny asked in a surprised voice. "Don't you recognize me?" He slid into the booth opposite the ex-CIA man. Kyle eased in beside him

"I *do* recognize you, Manny," Ordile answered. "That's the reason for the gun."

"*Por que?*" Manny looked at his old friend with a hurt expression in his eyes.

Ordile sat back and raised the muzzle of the .38 so that it was pointed directly at Manny's chest. Kyle could make out two puckered bullet-wound scars on the man's right forearm.

"You came here to kill me," Cliff said almost inaudibly. "Because of what happened to the Brigade."

The squat Cuban's face broke into a wide grin, showing his two gold inlays. He slapped the table with the palm of his hand, causing the crew-cut man to menace him with the pistol. Kyle sat stock-still, waiting for Ordile to squeeze the trigger. A regular seated at the bar near them turned his head at the sound of the slap and stared at the three men disinterestedly for a moment. Then he turned back to his beer.

"No . . . no, my friend," Manny said, smiling. "You couldn't be more wrong."

"We're unarmed, Ordile," Kyle interjected. "If we had come to kill you, we'd both be carryin' weapons."

Kyle held his hands out, palms up, to illustrate his point.

"This is Kyle Youngblood," said Lopez. "We have come with a proposition that can make you wealthy."

A gleam appeared in Ordile's piercing blue eyes as he lowered the .38. There was a tiny metallic click as he uncocked the weapon and slipped it in his waistband under his T-shirt.

"Sorry about the gun, fellas," he said apologetically. "I'm still a little touchy. What kind of deal you got?"

Kyle leaned forward and fixed the crew-cut man with a dark, intense stare as he spoke.

"We need a boat . . . big and fast."

"I'm on the beach—my boat's under thirty feet of water."

"We know." Lopez nodded.

Ordile picked up the Budweiser and drained half the bottle.

"We thought you might know somebody who'd be interested," Kyle continued.

"I doubt it," the wiry man said. "I owe everybody. I couldn't get a gallon of gas, let alone a boat. I even got thrown out of my apartment. Been sleepin' on the beach . . ."

Ordile paused, finishing the bottle, and Kyle cut in.

"With a boat and weapons, there's a lot of money waitin' for the right guys."

"Weapons?" the former CIA man said, the surprise evident in his voice. "I thought you were talkin' about treasure. Where do you want to go?"

"Cuba!" Lopez said evenly.

Ordile leaned back against the booth's padded interior. He held his hand to his forehead as he spoke.

"Holy shit! Not again."

Manny Lopez reached out and put a work-hardened hand on the wiry man's arm.

"It is different this time, *amigo,*" said Manny. "This time we are going after thirty million dollars."

Ordile's eyes became two gleaming points of blue steel as the amount of money registered in his brain.

"Thirty million?" he said, and swallowed hard. A burn scar near his Adam's apple moved slightly as he swallowed again.

"Buried on a ranch near Havana," said Kyle softly.

"The man I worked for," Manny said, breaking in, "hid it when Fidel took over."

Cliff sat stunned, looking at them. Then he leaned forward and bowed his head.

"Thirty million," he repeated. "Are you sure? Shit. I don't know."

Kyle leaned over and put his mouth near Ordile's ear.

"We're in a bind. We need a boat. We need weapons . . ."

"Guns are no problem," Ordile said, raising his head. "I can get any weapon you want for the right price."

Kyle looked him in the eye and shook his close-cropped head.

"Yeah," he said, sighing. "For the right price."

The regular at the bar stood and walked over to the garish 1950s jukebox that rested between two empty booths. The man dropped some coins in the slot and punched a couple of buttons. There was a pause, and then the happy sounds of The Beach Boys pulsed through the dim bar like an unwanted party guest.

Chapter 22

An hour later Kyle and Manny Lopez were seated on a double bed in one of the rooms Rafe had taken for them at the South Beach Motel. The room was fairly spacious, with two double beds, a color television set and a balcony that opened onto the beach.

Kyle told them what Cliff Ordile had said, as Rafe and Vinnie sat shaking their heads. Ordile had hinted that if they came up with a boat and the money, they could count on him to get the ordnance they needed. Cliff said he would stop by the South Beach later that night to check with them.

"I'm a little shaky on this, Blood," said Rafe, looking at Kyle. "We don' know nothin' about this dude."

Before Kyle could answer, Manny Lopez cut in.

"Cliff is a good man. I know a great deal about him. We shared a great many Cuba Libres together in the old days."

"That don' mean jack-shit, Manny . . . when you got all this money on the line," the black man said, his shiny face showing the emotion with which he spoke.

"I *know* the man," Manny continued. "He is honorable. He is a graduate of the Citadel, and served in Vietnam as an officer after the Bay of Pigs."

"That's two strikes against him right now." Vinnie laughed.

Lopez continued, ignoring the remark. "His brother was an officer in the Marines. He was killed in Vietnam during the Tet Offensive. His father is a retired army officer, and another brother is an Air Force colonel—"

"Whoa, hold on," said Kyle, holding up his hand. "We believe you. We don't need a family history."

"I resent that you are not taking my word," he directed at Rafe. "Cliff has a sense of honor. If he says he will do something, he does it. That is the reason he quit the Agency . . . because they did not keep their word to us."

"It don't make any difference whether we trust the man or not." Vinnie sighed heavily. "We ain't got enough capital to finance ourselves into a pay toilet."

"Jesus H. Christ," Rafe said with a moan. "Where the fuck are we goin' to come up with that kind of bread?"

Before Kyle could answer, there was a light tapping on the motel door. The four men in the room looked at each other.

"You expectin' anybody?" Kyle asked, looking at Rafe.

"Could be Ordile," Rafe said softly.

"Too early," Kyle shot back.

The black man shook his head and started to rise.

"Maybe Manny's boys followed us," suggested Vinnie.

"They would have no need to," said Manny. "What we are after means nothing to them."

Kyle rose and slipped his hand into his jeans pocket. He fingered the compact stiletto he had retrieved from the floor of the cantina the night before.

"You'd better answer it." He nodded to Vinnie, who rose from the other bed and crossed the room. Vinnie grasped the knob and pulled the door open.

Framed in the doorway, haloed by the late-afternoon sunlight of the keys, was Denise Palermo. Vinnie stepped back, a startled expression on his face.

"Are you going to keep me standing out here all day?" she said sarcastically.

Vinnie moved aside, and Denise entered the room. The attractive brunette stood just inside the door, her hands on her well-rounded hips. She was wearing a pink camisole top and a pair of tight jeans. The men in the room stared at her silently.

"How'd you find us?" Kyle finally asked as Vinnie closed the door.

She looked around at the suspicious faces and laughed.

"Just dumb luck," the attractive brunette said. "I'm down here on vacation this week. I spotted you on Duval and followed you here."

"You're a regular detective," Rafe said, flashing a sarcastic smile.

Denise ignored the remark and came straight at Kyle.

"Why were you asking about my father?" she said, stopping a foot from him. "And what's this shit about El Gato Negro?"

Before Kyle could answer, Manny Lopez rose and moved to Denise's side. He touched her elbow, and she turned toward him abruptly.

"Señorita Denny," he said softly, "you don't remember me?"

Denise looked into his broad face.

"I'm sorry . . . I . . . I . . ." she said, stammering.

"I am Manny. I worked at your father's ranch in Cuba," the stocky Cuban said almost wistfully.

Denise looked startled, her hard shell beginning to crack.

"God," she said with a rasp. "I was only ten years old."

"It's a damn family reunion," Rafe joked, turning to Vinnie.

Manny Lopez reached out and took Denise's hand.

"It has been twenty years," he said almost inaudibly. "You were such a little girl."

"That time is a blur to me." She pulled her hand away. "We left quickly, my mother crying . . . my father angry, shouting . . ."

"It was a crazy time when Fidel took over." Manny nodded. "My family escaped in a small fishing boat."

There was a long pause in the still room as the stocky Cuban and the lithe dancer faced each other.

"You both lived at the ranch?" Kyle's voice broke the spell.

"A long time ago." The dark-eyed woman nodded. She stared at Kyle, who looked deeply into her eyes. "What is it you want?" she said suddenly. "What else did my father say before he died?"

"Kristel . . . Denise . . . thanks for stopping by," said Kyle, taking her arm and guiding her toward the door.

"Okay," she said angrily. "I can take a hint. I know you bastards are into something big, and I'll haunt you till I find out what it is."

She turned quickly and crossed to the door. Vinnie tried to open it for her, but she pushed him out of the way and threw the door open, exiting into the warm tropical sunlight.

Vinnie whistled softly and closed the door.

"She's full of shit," he said quietly. "She followed us down here."

"I don't like it," Kyle interjected. "She's got to be workin' with somebody. We'd better keep our eyes open."

"Why did you not tell her about the money, señor?" Lopez said to Kyle.

"It's plain and simple, Manny," Kyle answered. "I don't trust her."

"It is her father's money, *amigo*."

"The money belongs to whoever gets it first," said Rafe, putting his arm around Manny's shoulder.

Chapter 23

After her confrontation with Kyle and the others, Denise left the South Beach Motel and went directly to the Reflexions on Duval at the ocean. She passed through the huge parking garage at its base and took the elevator to the second floor where Chet Allen and Phil McGregor awaited her.

She knocked softly on the door and waited. There was a slight movement inside the room, and the lock clicked. A beat later the door opened, and Phil McGregor, still dressed in his three-piece suit ushered her inside.

Chet Allen was seated on the balcony of the plushly furnished suite. He had a glass of orange juice in his hand and was staring out at the beach and the languid Gulf of Mexico, with its myriad sunbathers, swimmers and boats.

The T-man glanced up as Denise came through the sliding glass doors. He indicated a piece of white metal furniture, and she dropped into the chair. Denise noted the T-man had taken off his suit jacket in deference to the tropical heat.

"Would you like a glass of orange juice?" Allen said, indicating a pitcher and a glass on a small table near him.

"No thanks." The dancer shook her head as McGregor slid back the doors and entered the balcony.

"So how did it go with our friends?" said Allen, leaning back and taking a sip of juice from the tall glass.

"Nothing," she spat out, "I got nothing. They practically threw me out of the place. I don't think they bought my story about the vacation, either."

Allen rolled the glass of juice between his hands and continued. "You've got to try harder, darling," he said sweetly. "You've got to gain their confidence."

"It'll be tough," said Denise. "They're suspicious and they

picked up this new guy. He knew me when I lived at the ranch in Cuba."

"That'd be Lopez, boss," McGregor interjected. "The spick that joined them in Miami."

Allen took another sip of the orange juice and smiled, his thin lips curving back slightly, revealing small, sharp teeth. The thought that he looked like a large white rat popped into Denise's head.

"Yes." He nodded at McGregor. Then he turned back to Denise. "We are going to try harder . . . aren't we, girl? We know what's at stake here. We need you on the inside."

The lithe dancer looked from Allen to McGregor, then out toward the shimmering gulf, where the red-orange ball of the sun reflected off the aquamarine water.

Later that night, after the tourists and some of the more romantic inhabitants of Key West had watched the fantastic sunset from Fort Taylor Beach, Kyle and the others lay across the beds in the South Beach Motel. In a corner of the unit the color television droned on meaninglessly, airing a ludicrous prime-time sitcom.

The remnants of the three orders of nachos in silver foil plates and four or five nearly empty Chinese food containers lay scattered on the bed and floor of the room. Empty and half-empty bottles of beer were also scattered around the room.

A fifth man had joined the others. He sat sprawled in a soft brown easy chair with a half-empty bottle of beer in his hand. Morosely he raised the bottle to his lips while taking a perfunctory glance at the ignored television set.

Cliff Ordile had dropped in, as he had promised. Manny had introduced the ex-CIA man to the wary Rafe and Vinnie. At first the two vets had been a little cool to the wiry, crew-cut charter captain, but after sharing a takeout Mexican/Chinese dinner and four or five beers, they had mellowed and accepted him into their midst.

Now the five men sat in various poses of disappointment, longing for something that lay across ninety miles of open water . . . something that could change all of their lives forever.

"Cliff," Kyle said, shifting a pillow under his head. "Did you try any of the people you know who own a boat?"

"We're better off not tellin' some of those sleazeballs," he said, turning to Kyle. "They could cause us no end of grief."

"We might be smart involving Señorita Denny," said Lopez. "She lived on the ranch. She may know exactly where her father hid the money."

"That may not be a bad idea," said Ordile to no one in particular. "She may know some people . . . have some contacts . . ."

"Could be a good idea to talk to her, Blood," Rafe said to Kyle. "We was goin' to talk to her in Miami. Maybe we could find out if her old man was bullshittin' or not."

Kyle swung his feet over the edge of the bed and sat up.

"You know that if we talk to her, we have to cut her in," Kyle said, rummaging through one of the tinfoil plates for some nacho chips.

"There is plenty for all of us," said Manny. "*If* the money is there."

Kyle stood up and sighed. He crossed to the center of the room.

"I'm willin' to try anything at this point," he said to the others. "See if we can locate her."

Suddenly Rafe jumped to his feet and spread his hands for silence. His eyes were fixed on the television, where the image of a well-dressed middle-aged man and woman filled the screen.

"Turn up the fuckin' sound!" he screamed at Ordile, who was closest to the set. *"Turn up the fuckin' sound!"*

The wiry boat captain leaned forward and twisted the small knob. Almost immediately the trained voice of the announcer filled the room.

"T. Carl Palmer, millionaire sportsman, and his lovely wife, Pet, daughter of a prominent Florida chain-store owner, have decided to spend a fabulous two-week vacation in and around the beautiful waters of Key West. The Palmers will be making the Garrison Bight Marina the home for their fifty-three-foot Hatteras, *The Pet-o-Gold,* for the next two weeks."

Rafe stood transfixed by the two figures on the screen. The set faded to black, and another news story about a fishing tournament took its place.

Rafe turned to Kyle, who stood near the bed, looking like a man who had seen a horrific vision of the past. The muscles of the rancher's jaw tightened as he clenched his teeth. Ordile reached out and turned off the television as Vinnie sat up.

"That guy on the TV," he said excitedly. "That was Captain—"

"Yeah, that was the mothafucker," Rafe said, cutting him off.

"What is it?" Manny Lopez asked, looking from one man to the other. "Who was that man and woman?"

Kyle stood like a stone, looking neither right or left. His fists were clenched tightly at his sides.

"That guy was an officer we served with in 'Nam," Rafe said bitterly. "He was always lookin' for body counts . . . pushin' us over the edge . . . suicide missions . . ."

"The guy was a rotten prick," said Vinnie, sitting up.

Rafe crossed to where Kyle was standing.

"Christ!" he said to the rigid man. "Remember the time at Dak To? He dropped into a hot L.Z. and took off when we took some incomin' fire. You nearly killed him when—"

"Cut it, Rafe," Kyle shot at the black man. "Nobody wants to hear it."

"Youngblood," said Cliff Ordile, getting out of the overstuffed chair. "How well do you know this guy?"

"No way," snapped Kyle. "No goddamn way."

"Hold on, man." The ex-CIA man came toward Kyle. "This guy may be sent from heaven."

"I'd like to send him to hell," said Vinnie.

Ordile was almost in Kyle's face. He put out a hand and touched the ex–Green Beret's rigid shoulder.

"We need a boat . . . we need money," Ordile said, looking into Kyle's dark face.

"This man has both, *hombre,*" Manny said earnestly.

Kyle seemed to drop into a crouch. The look on his hawk-featured face was terrifying.

"No way," he said with a snarl.

Cliff Ordile noted the physical change in the man he was talking to. A chill moved from the base of his skull to the small of his back, and he shuddered involuntarily. To his credit he didn't back off.

"Youngblood," the crew-cut man said, "be reasonable. It's all wrapped up in a neat little bundle. Sometimes we got to wade through a ton of shit to get to the brass ring."

With a sudden lurch Kyle lunged past the man and hit the double doors to the low balcony. He vaulted the metal railing and dropped to the beach about five feet below.

The other four men in the room were stunned. Rafe moved first, heading toward the open doors to the balcony. As he went through them Cliff Ordile called after him.

"Try to talk some sense into him, Rafe. This is the only shot we got."

Rafe disappeared into the night as Vinnie said softly to the crew-cut man, "You don't understand, Cliff. Kyle hated this guy enough to kill him."

"Don't give me that shit, sonny," he said harshly. "I was *there.* I know what it was like." He took a deep breath. "I was an officer.

One night I came back from the boonies with less than half the men in my command. I wanted to frag the asshole that sent us out myself."

Vinnie's eyes widened in surprise as Lopez looked at him and smiled.

It took Rafe about ten minutes to find Kyle on the dark beach. He was sitting by the water's edge staring out at the silvery surface of the dark ocean. Little waves of foam rippled toward the shore and stopped just short of where Kyle sat with his arms folded across his knees.

"Hey, Blood," said Rafe, hunkering down in the sand beside him. "You okay? I had a hard time findin' ya."

"I ain't goin' to talk to him, Rafe," Kyle said raspily, sighing deeply. "Palermo's daughter is a whole different ball of wax, but Palmer . . ."

"I dig where you're comin' from, Blood," the black man said, tossing a seashell into the sea. It made a plopping noise, and then there was nothing but the hum of insects and the whisper of the small waves. "You're like my brother. You know I hate that mothafucker as much as you do. . . ."

Kyle sat, head down, shaking it from side to side.

"I can't," he said from somewhere deep down inside his body. "He is one evil bastard. I don't even know how he got on our side."

"Blood, this is *the* chance to get the money you need to get at Fallon for what he did to you." Rafe moved closer. "You may not get another."

Kyle's head came up slowly. Even in the darkness his black eyes glinted with that strange inner fire.

"I guess we're between a rock and a hard place," he said bitterly. "If I want Fallon, I got to ask the *man*."

"You been there before, brother," said Rafe, rising with a grunt. "All we can do is talk to the dude."

Kyle rose and stood beside the black man, feeling the strong kindred spirit that men who have shared danger and survived feel for each other. He looked out to sea for an instant, thinking how much Marian and the children would have enjoyed this place. Then he heaved a heavy sigh and turned to follow Rafe up the beach.

Chapter 24

It was early the next morning when Kyle and Rafe pulled up to the Garrison Bight Marina in Manny Lopez's multicolored van. As they exited the old truck the two men got some odd looks from the wealthier boat owners, who were parking their exotic automobiles in the marina parking lot.

Kyle entered the office, staring down a handsomely dressed older couple who were glaring at him. Rafe smiled and winked at the blue-haired matron. She flushed and turned quickly away from him.

The bleached blond man behind the counter in the marina office was dressed in a pair of short shorts and a brightly colored Hawaiian shirt. He gave Kyle directions to the slip where the Palmers had docked the *Pet-o-Gold*.

Kyle led the way down the wooden planking of the dock to where the sparkling fifty-three-foot Hatteras rocked gently at her moorings. He read the name printed in gilt letters on the varnished transom of the sleek cruiser:

PET-O-GOLD
WEST PALM BEACH,
FLORIDA.

The rancher's unpracticed eye took in the beauty of the immaculate boat. Even tied up in the slip, she looked fast. Vinnie and Ordile had told them what to look for. She had a pulpit attached to the foredeck, and a tuna tower rose high above the flying bridge. A set of outriggers spiked the air on her starboard and port sides. The boat looked as if she had just come out of the showroom.

Both men looked around. Luckily most of the slips on this side of the marina were vacant, their occupants taking full advantage of the abundant fishing waters around the lower keys. Kyle moved closer and peered over the aluminum rails and into the cockpit. Two fighting chairs had been removed from their bases and lay on their backs on the deck. The cockpit itself was empty.

From inside the cabin both men could hear the sounds of music and a woman singing softly to herself. Before Kyle could stop him, Rafe had climbed the short ladder from the dock and scrambled down it into the empty cockpit. Kyle shrugged and followed him.

Rafe bent forward and looked down the companionway into the cabin. He turned to Kyle and placed a finger to his lips. Then he motioned to him with the palm of his hand. The rancher moved next to the black man and followed his gaze into the main cabin.

In the middle of the spacious salon a well-built blonde wearing nothing but a pair of red bikini panties and white tennis shoes was exercising to music that was coming from a small portable radio lying on a bunk. From their vantage point they could see she was in excellent condition as she went through a series of alternate toe touches in time to the music. Her tan, lithe body rippled with muscle as she went through some more gyrations. Rafe noted that her small, defined breasts hardly bobbed as she exercised.

He was about to say something to Kyle when he heard a footstep and the sound of an automatic pistol being cocked. A smooth voice that both men had burned into their memories floated almost gently into their consciousness.

"Enjoying the *view,* gentlemen?"

Kyle and Rafe knew immediately who it was. Kyle seemed frozen to the spot, his face contorted with emotion.

"Look . . ." Rafe started to turn.

"No . . . *you* look," the voice ordered, harsher now. "Raise your hands and don't turn around." They could hear the owner of the voice step toward them.

"Look, we just—" Rafe began.

"Why don't we all step into the cabin." The voice was gentle and smooth again. "The *view* is so much better."

As Kyle and Rafe entered the large, plushly furnished cabin with their hands in the air, the seminude woman stopped exercising and turned, and her light green eyes widened with surprise as she saw her husband usher two strangers down the ladder at gunpoint.

Pet Palmer made no move to cover her nakedness. Her face and eyes shone with a peculiar brightness as she felt the eyes of the two men play over her body.

"Seems we have some uninvited guests, Pet," the disembodied voice said softly. "Maybe you had better put on your wrap."

Slowly the attractive blond retrieved a short Japanese kimono from an unmade berth on her left. Sensuously she drew it on as Kyle and Rafe waited with their hands raised.

"Should I call the Harbor Police, Carl?" she asked, reaching for a white phone on the bulkhead as she turned off the stereo next to it.

"For two Peeping Toms?" Palmer answered. "I think I'll just shoot them out of hand."

Both Kyle and Rafe turned at the man's words. They knew Palmer's reputation as a killer from their experiences in Southeast Asia. Neither of them wanted to take a bullet in the back. Rafe was first to speak.

"Hold on, Captain Palmer," he said to the tall, distinguished ex-officer aiming the 9-mm Browning automatic at his head. "Don' go pullin' that trigger. We got an offer you can't refuse."

Palmer's cold blue eyes registered a look of mild surprise, but his gun hand never wavered.

"Captain Palmer?" He peered intently into the black man's sweaty face. "How did you . . . ?" A look of recognition flared in the deadly blue eyes. "Phillips! I thought you were dead."

"Nah, they tried, Captain," Rafe said lightly. "But me and Kyle . . ."

As Rafe spoke, Kyle turned to face the man holding the gun. He appraised Palmer with his dark eyes, feeling the anger boil within his soul.

The years had been kind to Palmer. Despite being past fifty, he still had a ramrod-straight posture and a trim athletic look. He was wearing a pair of white duck pants and an expensive yellow polo shirt that showed off his tan.

"Youngblood," he said as a look of hatred flickered across his face. He swung the Browning toward Kyle.

"Captain Palmer," Kyle said bitterly. His eyes looked like two pieces of coal as he glared at the millionaire's handsome face.

"Pet, my love," Carl Palmer said, averting his eyes for an instant. "These two *gentlemen* were in my command in Vietnam. I'm afraid there was some bad blood between—or is it among?—us?"

"That's too bad," purred the attractive woman sitting on the berth and crossing her strong legs. "I had hoped they came aboard to see me."

"Not really," Palmer said with a grunt. "I think they came with murderous intent. Am I correct, gentlemen?"

"Captain," said Rafe, "we ain't even armed."

"There are other ways to kill," countered the man holding the gun. "You and Youngblood have been trained in them all."

Kyle could stand it no longer. He did not want to be on this boat, in the presence of this man he hated and for whom he had no respect.

"Let's cut through the bullshit, Palmer," Kyle said abruptly. "We came here to make you rich."

The tall silver-haired man laughed, showing a set of evenly capped white teeth. The 9-mm wavered slightly in his grasp.

"That doesn't wash, Youngblood. I'm already rich." He looked past them to his attractive wife, who sat on the edge of the berth with her kimono carelessly hanging open. "Isn't that right, my love?"

Pet Palmer picked up a pack of cigarettes from a small shelf near the berth. She tapped one out before answering.

"Just as long as my daddy has his department-store chain." She picked up a butane lighter, flicked the wheel and held the blue flame to the tip of the cigarette as she inhaled. "You are very rich, my love."

Pet giggled and took a long drag on the cigarette.

"The both of you have so much money that thirty million, tax-free dollars doesn't mean a thing to you?" Kyle said evenly.

"If you're talking about a sunken treasure hunt," Palmer said, laughing again, "we've been that route already—"

"Captain, this is American greenbacks . . . buried in Cuba," Rafe said, breaking in.

Palmer again looked at his attractive wife, then back to Kyle and Rafe.

"Lower your hands, gentlemen," he said, tucking the Browning in the waistband of his white pants. "You've bought yourself some time."

Chapter 25

It was after eleven o'clock when Kyle and Rafe returned to the South Beach Motel. The oppressive early-morning heat of the lower keys was making both men perspire heavily as they made their way to the door of the motel room.

Rafe was bubbling with good humor, but Kyle was deep in thought. He had mixed emotions about dealing with a man like Carl Palmer. The rancher's spirit soared because his former captain had provided the boat and the money needed to get to Cuba. Yet deep in his soul he knew Palmer was a man who loved to kill and had loyalty to no one except, possibly, his rich wife.

He knew the ex-officer's background: graduate of Dartmouth; big game hunter; connections high up in the Pentagon, where his father had served as a colonel for many years.

Palmer had probably used his father's influence to get a commission, then enrolled in the Special Forces school at Fort Bragg. He served one tour in Vietnam, rising to the rank of captain before he returned home.

In 'Nam he had been a vicious, demanding leader, caring nothing for the men who served under him. He wanted body counts and didn't care how he got them. The only problem was . . . sometimes the bodies were men in his own command.

In those days Palmer had political aspirations and felt a military record was a sure path to the governor's mansion. Kyle had lost track of him when the captain was rotated back to the "world," but he still carried the hatred he felt for the man deep in his heart.

Rafe was already banging on the door of the room when Kyle reached it. The door opened, revealing a smiling Vinnie.

"Well, did he go for it?" the stocky Italian asked eagerly, pulling Rafe inside the room. Kyle followed and closed the door.

Ordile was sitting in the same chair in front of the television set, which was turned off. Lopez was lying on one of the beds in his shorts and a white T-shirt, his head propped up on a pillow.

As Kyle and Rafe entered, he sat up and swung his feet over the edge of the bed.

"Well, what is it, *amigos*?" Manny said, standing up. "Do we go to Cuba . . . or do we go home?"

Rafe looked at the three men dejectedly. He glanced at Kyle, who stood behind him, and then his broad face split in a wide grin.

"The mothafucker went for it!" he howled, jumping in the air with his fist raised.

"What about the boat and the money?" asked Ordile, pushing himself out of the chair.

"Everything," said Kyle, closing the door. "We use the boat, and he'll stake us for the weapons and supplies."

Vinnie wrapped his suntanned arms around Rafe and hugged him. The two vets whirled each other around in the center of the room.

"What do we give him?" said Ordile, rising from the chair and facing Kyle.

The rancher dropped on the bed and sighed.

"One third of whatever we bring out."

"One third . . . shit!" the crew-cut man said, exploding. "We take all the risk, and he takes all the gravy."

"Not so, my man," said Rafe, breathing heavily from his celebrating with Vinnie. "Palmer and his wife are goin' with us."

"What?" said Ordile. "We're takin' them too?"

Kyle looked at him, then turned to Lopez and Vinnie.

"That's the only way he would make the deal," said Kyle resignedly. "He and his wife go—and get one third."

"He felt we needed him more than he needed us," said Rafe, flopping on the bed next to Kyle.

"I still don't like it." The ex-CIA man dropped back in the chair.

Manny Lopez crossed to where Ordile sat staring at the blank television screen.

"Cliff," he said softly, placing a hand on the man's shoulder. "Two thirds of something is better than a whole of nothing."

Ordile snorted and looked at Manny, who patted him on the shoulder. There was a dead stillness in the room as the five men weighed their desires and dreams against the risks and dangers of the expedition.

"Cliff . . ." It was Kyle's voice that broke the spell. "You said you could get us any kind of ordnance we needed. How much time do you need?"

"About a week," Ordile said with a grunt, still unhappy. "Depends on what you want."

"Get started on it," Kyle answered. "I'll make you a *wish* list."

"Amigo," said Manny Lopez, crossing to the desk. "In the excitement I almost forgot to tell you . . . we found Señorita Denny."

Kyle gave the Cuban an agonized look.

"That's great!" he said sarcastically.

"She's stayin' at the Pier House on the gulf side," Vinnie volunteered. "We told her we'd call when you and Rafe got back."

"The Pier House?" Kyle shot back.

"It don't figure," Cliff said, pushing himself out of the chair and crossing to the phone on the night table. "The tab there is a little heavy for a bimbo who says she's a go-go dancer."

Chet Allen and Phil McGregor had used their connections to get Denise a room at the posh Pier House Resort. They did not want her staying at the Ocean Key House for fear that Kyle and the others might discover the liaison between them and the attractive brunette.

Now Denise Palmer sat at a round, glass-topped table on the wooden deck at the rear of the Pier House. An empty salt-rimmed margarita glass stood on the table in front of her. She played with it nervously as she glanced at her watch for what seemed like the twentieth time.

The call had surprised her. She thought she would have to make the first move and con her way into the midst. But the call had come like a surprise invitation to a party. It had been from one of them she had not met. He identified himself as Cliff and said they wanted to speak with her.

Her first thought was that they wanted to kill her, so she opted for a public place at her hotel where they would be surrounded by witnesses. Now she was not so sure. The man had sounded sincere, almost friendly, on the phone. Still, she would take no chances.

Denise looked at her watch again. It was a little after five. She glanced around for the waiter to order another drink and saw Kyle Youngblood, Rafe and Manny Lopez coming toward her through the maze of crowded tables.

The Cuban was the first to reach her table. He held out his hand, and Denise took it. Rafe and Kyle joined him and took seats without any amenities.

"Señorita Denny," said Lopez, sitting next to her.

Before she could speak, a very thin waiter in a green Pier House shirt and white shorts appeared at her elbow.

"Happy Hour ends in ten minutes, folks," the man said in a thin, reedy voice. "Can I get you a round?"

"Margarita," Denise said softly as the thin man picked up her empty glass. Kyle and the others ordered beers.

Denise looked at the three men. Then she sat back and crossed her shapely legs, revealing quite a bit of tanned thigh under the short denim skirt.

"Okay, boys," she said harshly, "let's cut the bullshit. Where's that guy Cliff, and why did he call me?"

"Cliff's busy," Kyle said matter-of-factly. "He's doin' some shoppin'."

Rafe giggled and put his hand over his mouth as he looked at Kyle. It wasn't a lie. Cliff and Vinnie had taken Kyle's "wish" list and had gone to visit a couple of Cliff's "friends." Manny leaned forward and placed a hand on Denise's arm.

"We still need some answers from you, señorita," the Cuban said in a low voice. "There are many unanswered questions."

She avoided Manny's eyes and looked directly at Kyle.

"You left Miami like a bunch of theives," she said, her dark eyes flashing. "I couldn't have found you if I knew where to look."

"You're talkin' like we owe you somethin'," shot back Kyle. "We don't owe you a thing."

"What the hell do you mean?" Denise uncrossed her legs and leaned forward. Her husky voice got a little shrill. "It's my old man's money."

A couple at the next table turned and looked at her. Rafe gave Kyle a knowing glance.

The second she uttered the words, Denise Palermo knew she had screwed up. Alarm bells went off in her head and in her stomach. Still, she held her poise and veiled her dark eyes so that the men she faced would not know how frightened she was. The only telltale clue was a thin trickle of sweat that ran down her neck and between the cleavage of her ample breasts.

"How'd you know it was money we were after?" Kyle asked slowly.

She sat back, in control again.

"I knew it all along," she said, crossing her legs. "I played you like a fish."

"Then you must know where your old man hid the loot," Rafe said as the skinny waiter returned with the drinks.

"Beers for the boys!" he piped up in his reedy voice. He set the bottles and glasses down in front of them, using his best Playboy Bunny dip. "A margarita for the lady." He slipped the check off his silver tray and slapped it on the table in front of Kyle. Then he moved off toward a man who was waving at him from a table near the rail.

"Yeah, I know where he hid it," Denise said, smiling. "What's in it for me?"

"When your father came home from the casino," Kyle asked, ignoring her question, "was he ever carrying any kind of bag?"

She uncrossed her legs again and sat forward, her elbows on the table. The deep cleavage between her breasts was centered in the low-cut vee of her blouse.

"You ain't gettin' nothin' from me until I know what my cut is," Denise Palermo said harshly. "You wanna play, you gotta pay."

Kyle looked across at the woman, then at Rafe and Manny.

"Full share of whatever we bring out." He sighed, looking out at the red ball of the setting sun.

"Can I trust you guys?" the dancer asked.

"Señorita"—Manny Lopez took her hand and looked directly into her eyes—"I swear to you on the lives of my wife and children."

The crowd on the deck buzzed with conversation as the sun dipped toward the distant horizon. Denise took a sip from the salt-rimmed glass. On the far end of the deck a three-man steel band in colorful Hawaiian shirts started to play "Yellow Bird."

"On certain nights he would bring home a large black bag." she said, as if she were watching Big Tony do it in front of her. "It looked like the ones doctors used to carry."

"*Si, si!*" said Manny in an excited tone. "I remember it too. He would not let any of us touch it."

"I wonder why," Rafe said sarcastically.

"What was in those black bags?" she asked, looking at them intently.

"A shitload of money, baby," the black man cooed, taking a sip of his beer. "A shitload of money."

"I want to go with you," Denise said quickly.

"Too dangerous," Kyle shot back, pushing his chair away from the table. "Besides, we already got one woman aboard the boat."

Denise knew that Allen and McGregor would want her with them to protect their interests. Her mind whirled as she tried to come up with an answer.

Kyle stood and threw a twenty-dollar bill on the table.

"Let's go," he said curtly. "I want to see how Cliff and Vinnie made out." He turned to Denise. "When you remember where your father buried the cash, let us know."

"Take me with you and I'll tell you anything you want to know," she said weakly.

Kyle turned and started to move toward the large double doors that opened onto the deck. Denise looked after him and turned back to the table. "Is he always that bitchy?" she asked Rafe.

"Nah, he's a good guy who just went through a load of bad bullshit." The black man stood and patted her shoulder. Manny Lopez rose and smiled at her.

"His wife and two children were killed just a short time ago," he said. "It's affected him deeply."

She stood up and grabbed Rafe's arm.

"Rafe, please," she said, "talk him into letting me go. He's your friend. You can do it. I won't be any trouble. . . ."

At a table on the other side of the deck, two men, distinctly out of place in their three-piece wash-and-wear suits, were attacking a pair of large lobsters with nutcrackers and small forks. Each was wearing a white plastic bib imprinted with a picture of a large red lobster.

As they ate, the two men had looked up occasionally and peered intently at the table where Denise Palermo was sitting with her newfound partners.

Chapter 26

At about the same time the meeting on the deck at the Pier House was taking place, Cliff Ordile and Vinnie Troiano were bouncing along in Manny Lopez's van on one of the dirt roads that cut through the mangroves on one of the lower keys. The van creaked and groaned as it rolled slowly over the ruts and holes in the sandy gravel.

After what seemed like an eternity the truck broke out of the thick tangle of mangroves into a clearing that surrounded a small inlet. A wooden shack, bleached bone-white by the relentless sun, sat up on stilts built halfway into the waters of the gulf. Next to it, a short rickety dock extended out into the serene body of water.

Cliff parked the van in front of the shack and cut the engine. There was no sign of life, either around the ramshackle building or in the nearby mangrove thicket. Both Vinnie and the ex-CIA man looked at each other and shrugged. They both had the feeling they were being watched.

Cliff Ordile knew the men he was about to deal with. Both Squint and Powell had been running guns and drugs in South Florida for over twenty years. They had been caught a couple of times and spent some years in federal prisons. At times they had killed indiscriminately to cover their tracks.

Cliff Ordile exited the van and looked around. Unconsciously he fingered the .38 Police Special in the waistband of his trousers. The back of his neck prickled as he felt a set of unseen eyes boring into his back. On the porch of the shack an old rattan rocking chair tipped slowly back and forth, as if someone had just left it.

Vinnie climbed out of the other side of the truck and closed the door quickly. He was unarmed, but he, too, felt as if they were being observed.

Cliff came around the front of the van and froze. Slowly he raised his hands in the air. Vinnie saw him and followed his eyes.

The ugly muzzle of an AK-47 assault rifle was pointing at them from between two split boards in the wall of the shack. Vinnie raised his hands.

"Tha's right, Slick," drawled a whiny voice from inside the old building. "Jes' get them hands up nice and high where we can see 'em."

There was a noise behind them, and the tangle of mangroves and brush at the edge of the clearing moved slightly. A wrinkled older man, his stringy hair tied in a loose ponytail at the nape of his neck, stepped into the clearing. The man was dressed in greasy olive-drab fatigues. He was aiming a Winchester .12-gauge shotgun at them. One hand was on the slide action of the piece, the other wrapped in the pistol grip.

The muzzle of the AK-47 disappeared, and the door of the shack opened. A tall man with matted red hair and a beard stepped out on the porch, the Russian-made weapon hanging loosely in his hands. His right eye was almost entirely closed by a scar caused by a beer bottle that had been thrown in a bar fight when he was a teenager. He was wearing a sleeveless T-shirt and a pair of cutoff camos.

"Hello, Squint," said Cliff easily. "Good to see ya again."

The man came down the steps and hawked a mouthful of spit into the dirt at his feet.

"What say, Slick?" the red-haired man said, fixing Cliff with his one good eye. "Why you haulin' your ex-government ass out here?"

"Not to look at your ugly, fuckin' face," Ordile said lightly, lowering his hands. Vinnie followed his lead. The one-eyed man put his head back and guffawed loudly.

"You hear that, Pop?" he yelled at the older man with the ponytail. "This sumbitch still got some balls."

"Yeah," the man with the shotgun said without humor. "Maybe we oughta cut 'em off and shove 'em in his big mouth."

The man named Squint laughed again, a high-pitched hyenalike laugh that had an edge of hysteria to it.

"Mebbe he come here to buy some good shit?" the redhead said, cradling the AK-47 in the crook of his arm. He moved his free hand to his nose and made a sniffing noise.

"No drugs, Squint!" Cliff said, reaching in his pocket. The one-eyed man whipped the assault rifle into firing position with surprising speed. Ordile pulled Kyle's ordnance list from his pocket. "We need some guns."

He held out the piece of motel stationery to the one-eyed man, who lowered his weapon and took it grudgingly.

"Guns, huh?" He held the list up within range of his good eye. "Les see what you got."

Squint looked at the piece of paper for what seemed like an eternity. Then he whistled softly.

"Anything wrong?" asked Cliff.

"Sheee-it, Slick," the redhead said, almost crooning. "You plannin' to invade Cuba again. This is some heavy shit."

"Can you fill it?" Vinnie spoke for the first time.

Squint swung his one-eyed gaze toward Vinnie. He looked at him appraisingly.

"Hold your water, junior," the redhead said harshly. "I'm dealin' with my main man here."

Squint held the list up again. His sun-blistered lips moved as he ticked off the list with his finger. Then he whistled again.

"The 9-mm Browning Hi-Power automatics are no problem. Two M-203, combo M16 and M-79 grenade launchers are no problem. Four Uzis, okay." The one-eyed man went down the page as if he were reading off a grocery list. "Two M-60 machine guns, Claymoors, LAWs rockets . . . most of this shit is no problem, Slick."

"Anything that is?" said Ordile.

Squint scratched at his beard with the hand holding the paper.

"The M-40 106 Recoilless Rifle could be. All this rocket shit made them obsolete . . . hard to get."

"The guy I'm buyin' this stuff for said we gotta have everything on the list."

"Gonna cost you," the redhead said, smiling slowly and showing uneven, tobacco-stained teeth. The man with the ponytail laughed loudly.

"How much?" Ordile asked, flashing a look at Vinnie.

"Thirty thousand!"

"Thirty thousand?" Ordile gasped. "That's a lot of money."

"Inflation, my man," said Squint. "This ain't 1961. When you need this shit?"

Cliff looked at Vinnie again.

"A week. But I gotta get the price approved. I'll be in touch, tell you where we want it delivered and how."

"Okay, remember, cash only. No credit cards, no checks." The redhead laughed that high, squealing, hyenalike laugh again. "You fucker," he said seriously. "Ah still think you and the beaners are goin' to hit the Bay of Pigs again."

Cliff stole a furtive look at Vinnie, and the both of them smiled weakly.

• • •

An hour later Denise Palermo was in her plush suite at the Pier House. Phil McGregor was staring out the window at the red glow of the setting sun. Chet Allen sat facing the lithe dancer as she told them about her meeting with Kyle and the others.

"You think they're going to take you with them?" Allen asked, tapping the ends of his fingers together. "I would want that very much."

"This Kyle guy . . . he's runnin' the whole show," said Denise. "So far he's said no, but I got a couple of the others workin' on him."

Allen rose stiffly from his chair.

"I know you'll do well, my dear. Phil and I are counting on you," he said with a sinister smile that showed his needlelike rat's teeth.

"They must have the money they needed," she volunteered. "They were acting pretty cocky . . . said something about a boat."

"Yes, an old army comrade, T. Carl Palmer, and his wife came to the rescue. They have everything they need to mount the expedition."

"Christ!" Denise exclaimed. "You people know everything."

"We're the government, Denise. It's our job to know," said Allen, stepping to her and placing a hand on her shoulder. He smiled his ratlike smile again. "For your cooperation, Uncle Sam is going to make sure you get *everything* that's coming to you."

Behind her, Phil McGregor turned from the window and gave his boss a knowing look.

It was noon the following day when Kyle and Rafe sat in the spacious *Pet-o-Gold*. Palmer sat across from them, scanning the list of weapons and supplies Kyle had drawn up.

Pet Palmer, her tanned, well-toned body, covered only by the triangular patches of a knitted string bikini, sat next to her husband, sipping a Bloody Mary. She seemed disinterested in the conversation, content to sip her drink and occasionally run her manicured fingers through her long, blond hair.

"You're not planning to start World War III, are you, Youngblood?" said Palmer, looking up from the list. "M-60s . . . LAWs rockets . . . grenades . . ."

"Captain, I was trained to be ready for any possibility," answered Kyle. "I don't want to start a job and find out I don't have a tool that I need."

"I understand that, but a six-man raft . . . mopeds . . . ?"

"The raft is for an emergency. The mopeds are for transport on the island. The ranch is about twelve miles from the coast."

"What's all this going to cost me?" asked Palmer, sitting back in the plush kapok-filled cushions.

"It's a little heavy, Captain," chimed in Rafe. "Forty thousand sound like a lot?"

Palmer laughed and turned to Pet, who looked up, amused.

"That's about what it costs to train one of Carl's thoroughbreds for a year," she said, and finished off the Bloody Mary.

"It'll all be delivered here Friday morning," said Kyle. "We need the money before then."

"No problem." Palmer looked at Pet again. "You can pick up the cash here in two days."

Rafe and Kyle stood up. Palmer made a motion as if to shake hands, but neither man acknowledged the other's gesture. Palmer dropped his hand to his side after an awkward pause.

"This is a fine-lookin' boat, Captain," said Rafe. "How many knots she do?"

Pet stood up and stretched.

"She's a fifty-three-foot Hatteras, equipped with high-performance 12 TIs," Pet intoned, as if she were reading a textbook. "At top speed she'll do thirty-two knots. Her range is over a thousand miles, with both auxiliary tanks in use. She sleeps eight and has a full galley."

"As you can see, gentlemen," said Palmer, "my wife will not be excess baggage on this voyage."

Kyle put a foot up on the ladder that led to the dock. He stopped and turned.

"I've got Lopez out looking for an old fishing boat," Kyle said matter-of-factly. "The cost is figured in the forty thousand."

"Why the old boat?" Palmer looked surprised.

"We'll need it to beat their radar," said Kyle. "We're goin' to be dressed as Cuban fisherman." He turned to Pet. "Any problem towing another boat, Mrs. Palmer?"

"No . . . we can make it through the Windward Passage or around Pinar Del Rio with plenty to spare." She paused and gave Kyle a feline smile. "Please call me Pet."

"Okay, that's it," said Kyle. "We'll see you in two days to pick up the money."

He was up and over the gunwale before Palmer or Pet could answer him. Rafe touched his forehead in a light salute and followed Kyle.

As the two men disappeared down the row of empty slips, Carl

Palmer turned to his sleek, tanned wife and smiled.

"Call me Pet," he said, mimicking the tone she had used to Kyle. "Nice touch, my love."

"I couldn't think of anything else to say to the man," she answered, pouring a Bloody Mary from the blue-and-white thermos on the deck. "I didn't want him calling me Mrs. Palmer all the way to Cuba and back."

Chapter 27

By Friday morning the *Pet-o-Gold* had been fueled, and her water tanks filled. The lockers in the galley were filled to capacity. The mopeds and the six-man raft had been stowed neatly under a tarpaulin on the spacious foredeck.

The old clothes that would serve to disguise them as Cuban fisherman had been placed below, along with old hats and shoes that had been purchased at a secondhand thrift shop in Old Town. The clothing, which Kyle would not allow to be washed, still held a distinctive odor from the previous owners.

Other supplies, like flashlights, rope, waterproof duffel bags, two-way radios, machetes and rucksacks had been purchased clandestinely during the week and stored forward of the main cabin.

Kyle, Rafe and Ordile lounged in the cockpit of the large cabin cruiser. Palmer and his wife were below in the main salon, making a last-minute check on the charts they would need to make the run around Pinar Del Rio at the western end of Cuba.

Rafe stood and shaded his eyes, looking toward the end of the dock and the entrance to the marina.

"I hope them two scumbags you're dealin' with don't fuck us over, Cliff," Rafe said, dropping back on the padded bench.

"You never know," Ordile said. "I dealt with assholes like that when I was with the Company. Sometimes you eat the bear . . . sometimes the bear eats you."

Rafe looked unhappy. He nudged Kyle with his elbow.

"Yeah," the black man barked. "Well, the fuckin' bear got fifteen thousand dollars of our stake money."

"I had to give them half the total price," explained Ordile. "Or they wouldn't go for the deal."

"Relax," Kyle said easily to Rafe. He glanced at his watch. "They'll be here. It's only ten after ten. They're only forty minutes late."

Rafe stood up again and crossed the large cockpit. He shaded his eyes and scanned the open entrance to the bight.

"Where the hell are Manny and Vinnie?" Rafe asked, turning around. "I thought he found the fishin' boat yesterday . . . mothafucker's so old, it probably sank."

"Will you take it easy?" Kyle stood and crossed to Rafe. He rubbed the black man's back between the shoulder blades. "We're goin' to meet them outside the bight. There ain't as many eyes watchin'."

"I'm sorry, Blood," Rafe said, crossing back to his seat. "I jes' don' want nothin' to go wrong."

Ordile leaned back and laced his fingers behind his head.

"Talkin' about goin' wrong," the ex-CIA man said, closing his eyes, "what happened to that broad, Denise?"

"I told her to be here at nine," answered Kyle.

"I still think it's a mistake cuttin' her in, but it's your gig," Cliff said, concern evident in his voice.

Kyle glanced at the open companionway door, where down in the cabin the Palmers were still poring over their charts.

"Our friends Manny and Rafe talked me into lettin' her go with us."

"Hey, wait a minute, Blood." Rafe got up quickly. "You're the one who tol' her she could go if she remembered where her old man buried the money."

Kyle glanced back at the cabin again.

"She came up with somethin'," Kyle said, moving closer to Rafe and Ordile. "The night before they left Cuba, she heard the sound of diggin' behind the house where the patio was located. She said somethin' to her mother, and the woman acted scared and told her to go back to sleep."

Before either man could answer him, the sound of a heavy engine and the grinding of gears drifted toward them across the empty marina. Ordile was the first to swing his head in the direction of the sound.

A two-and-a-half-ton army truck with a tattered, olive-drab canvas top had pulled through the marina gate and was heading toward the end of the dock. As it passed the office the door opened and the bleached-blond manager rushed out. He had an annoyed look on his made-up face.

Rafe was up the short ladder and on the dock like a singed cat. Kyle and Ordile were close behind. By the time the three men had reached the end of the dock where the truck was parked, Squint and Pop Powell had gotten out and were dropping the tailgate.

The red-haired Squint hopped up onto the back of the truck and started to walk one of the heavy crates toward the tailgate. Pop Powell eyed Rafe and Kyle as they neared the rear of the deuce-and-a-half.

"Thought you guys were jerkin' us off," Ordile said to the man with the ponytail. "You were supposed to be here at nine-thirty."

"Deal's a deal," the wrinkled man said, spitting in the dirt. "Got stuck in traffic."

The one-eyed man had wrestled a large wooden crate onto the tailgate of the truck. Kyle and Rafe stepped forward to help Powell lift it off.

"Were you able to get all the goods?" asked Cliff, looking at the side of the crate. There was a large red cross and the words MEDICAL SUPPLIES stenciled on the rough wood.

"We had a little problem with the Recoilless, but we got one," Squint said, and moved back into the truck.

"The M-60s are in this crate," Powell said, tapping the box with a dirty hand. As he turned slightly they could see the butt end of a .45 stuck in the waistband of his fatigue pants.

"Mind if I take a look?" said Kyle, stepping to the tailgate and picking up a short crowbar that was lying on the truck bed.

Kyle placed the flat end of the metal bar under the heavy wooden lid of the crate and applied pressure. There was a cracking sound as the nails lifted out of the pine boards. The rancher moved the bar to the other end and did the same thing. The lid came away, and he and Ordile placed their fingers under it and pulled it back.

Squint came out on the tailgate and set down a square wooden box with rope handles that was marked PRIDE OF PORTUGAL . . . ANCHOVIES. It was filled with smoke grenades.

"What'samatter, Slick?" he said to Ordile. "Don't trust us?"

"No, as a matter of fact, I don't," said Ordile as he lifted the case of "anchovies" off the truck and set it next to the "medical supplies." The redheaded man whinnied his high-pitched hyenalike laugh and went back into the truck as Kyle peered into the large crate. He could make out two M-60 machine guns and two extra barrels. The weapons were packed in white chips of Styrofoam to keep them from being damaged in shipment.

Although the guns had been well-greased with cosmoline, Kyle could tell they had been used.

"These guns ain't new," he said to Powell as Squint brought another case of "anchovies" out of the truck.

"You didn't say you wanted new shit, Slick," the one-eyed

man said to Ordile. "You only said you wanted M-60s."

Rafe had been strangely silent during the unloading. The black man's whole body pulsed with excitement from being so close to the tools of war he had used in Vietnam. It was as if he were welcoming home old friends.

"Who gives a rat-fuck," the black man said, exhilarated, "as long as these fuckers shoot straight." Rafe looked at Kyle and grinned, showing his even white teeth.

In his own way Kyle felt the same exhilaration that came from being near the weapons. He felt like a child on Christmas morning about to open his presents.

Squint dropped some smaller cases and crates on the tailgate, and the men stacked them near the back of the deuce-and-a-half. When they finished, all of them were sweating profusely in the mid-morning heat.

The redhead dropped to the ground and slammed the tailgate into place. Then he put in the pins.

"You got twenty thousand rounds for each of the M-60s . . . five hundred rounds for the 9-mms . . . a thousand each for the M16s . . ."

"What about the Uzis?" said Ordile, hefting one of the smaller boxes onto his shoulder.

"I got you ten thousand rounds for the Uzis," Squint said, wiping his ruined face with a dirty handkerchief. "I could only find twenty-five rounds for the Recoilless. That shit is tough to get." He walked over to a case marked ENGINE PARTS and patted it with his hand. "These are your MAs . . . Claymoors. Everything's in there: det cord, C-4, clackers, remote switches."

Rafe picked up the case and set it on his shoulder. He and Cliff started down the dock toward the *Pet-o-Gold*.

"Store everything in the hold," said Kyle, reaching into the rear pocket of his jeans.

"Nobody's storin' any-fuckin'-thing anywhere," Squint said in a surly voice, "until I get the rest of my money."

Kyle pulled a manila envelope out of his rear pocket and handed it to the one-eyed man. "Never thought you'd ask," Kyle said as the redhead tore open the envelope.

Squint took out the money as Rafe and Ordile set down the cases on the dock and watched the gunrunner count the crisp hundred-dollar bills.

Squint counted out fifteen thousand and held the money out to Kyle. "I thought this felt a little light. You're short ten thousand."

Ordile came at him, a furious look on his face.

"What the hell are you tryin' to pull?" he said angrily. "The price was thirty thousand."

As Kyle closed in on him the one-eyed man snapped a razor-edge fishing knife from a scabbard at his back. He menaced Cliff with it. His partner slipped the Colt .45 out of his belt and pointed it at Ordile and the others.

Kyle was in the best spot, which was about two feet from the ponytailed man holding the automatic. He lashed out with his left foot and caught Pop Powell on the outside of his right knee, which buckled inward. As the man started to topple, Kyle struck with the speed of a deadly snake. He brought his speared right fist down hard on the wrinkled man's gun hand, breaking his wrist. Pop screamed, dropped the .45 and continued his fall onto his damaged right knee and wrist.

At the same instant Squint made a lunge at Cliff Ordile with the lethal fishing knife. The ex-CIA man sidestepped the sharp point and grabbed the redhead's wrist. He brought the arm up behind his back in a hammerlock, careful to avoid the knife. Then he drove the one-eyed man into the raised tailgate of the truck, stunning him. He pushed Squint's face up against the back of the truck.

"Like your partner said, Squint," Cliff grunted in the man's ear, "a deal's a deal." Then he slipped the sharp knife out of the man's hand, released him and dropped back. Squint turned around slowly and glared at the three men with his one good eye. There was a smear of blood on his forehead, and a trickle ran from his nose.

"Right," he said. "A deal's a deal." He stooped and picked up the manila envelope from where he had dropped it during the attack. Unsteadily he crossed to where Pop Powell lay on his back in the dirt, groaning and holding his shattered wrist.

Rafe lifted the case he had been carrying and hefted it to his shoulder.

"If you boys move out peaceful like, we won't report your asses to the Better Business Bureau."

As Squint helped Powell into the cab of the truck, a sun-bleached Key West taxi came through the gates of the marina. The cab rolled past the marina office and took the turn toward the dock where the deuce-and-a-half was parked. As it pulled up to the stacked crates and cases, Squint threw the truck into gear and roared up the drive toward the gate of the marina.

The rear door of the cab opened, and Denise Palermo stepped out. She was wearing a pair of snug-fitting white shorts and a white halter top that showed off her dark tan. The cabdriver got out and opened the trunk of the taxi. He removed a small, square cosmetic case and a matching medium-size valise. He set them on the ground by Denise's feet.

She reached into her shoulder bag and paid the driver with a five-dollar bill as Kyle and Cliff watched her. The driver started to climb back into his cab and paused a beat longer than he had to as he observed the stack of wooden crates and boxes. Then he slid in behind the wheel of the cab and sped off.

Kyle noted the more than casual interest in the cache of weapons. He shrugged and filed it in the back of his mind as he knelt in the dirt and picked up the .45 Pop Powell had dropped. The rancher stuck the automatic in his jeans at the base of his spine as the lithe brunette approached him with a smile on her attractive face.

By noon, the weapons crates had been loaded into the hold of the big Hatteras. Cliff and Rafe, shirts off and perspiring heavily, lay atop a couple of the bigger boxes sipping a couple of cold Budweisers.

In the main cabin of the *Pet-o-Gold,* Kyle and Denise were seated at a round table with Carl and Pet Palmer. Palmer had a glass of milk in front of him. Pet and Denise sipped at Bloody Marys. Kyle's strong hand was wrapped around a brown bottle of Budweiser.

"I must say"—Palmer raised his glass of milk toward Denise—"this is a very attractive addition to our crew."

He raised the glass to his lips and took a long drink. Denise smiled self-consciously and looked at Kyle.

"When we're ashore, Denise and your wife will stay with the boat," said Kyle. "They can cruise around and fish till we get back."

"I'm curious, Youngblood," the ex-captain said, looking directly at Denise. "Why did you cut another person in on the deal?"

"She lived at the ranch," Kyle answered, "and she remembered where the money was buried. You can never have too much good intelligence before a mission, Captain."

Pet lifted her Bloody Mary and sipped at it.

"I am a little miffed at you, dear," she said to Denise. "I rather liked being the only female on board with all these men."

"I'll try to stay out of your way, *dear.*" Denise replied, smiling sarcastically. Pet gave her a sour look and turned away.

Palmer stood up and looked at his watch.

"We'd better get under way. We have to rendezvous with your

man Lopez at three o'clock.'' He raised his glass of milk. ''To a successful voyage.''

Palmer drained the glass. Denise and Pet both lifted their Bloody Marys and drank the toast. Kyle did not move. Instead, he held the beer bottle in his hand and stared at it as if seeing a distant time in a distant place.

Chapter 28

It was after one P.M. when the *Pet-o-Gold* eased out of Garrison Bight into the Gulf of Mexico. Pet Palmer was at the wheel as the big boat headed west, hugging the shoreline. The fifty-three-foot Hatteras rounded the edge of Old Town and turned south past Fort Taylor and into the Florida Straits.

As the sleek boat passed the ruins of the old fort at the tip of Key West, Chet Allen and Phil McGregor followed her progress from the stony beach with a pair of high-powered field glasses. Not until the boat was out of sight did the crew-cut T-man put the glasses down and favor his partner with a thin, rodentlike smile.

The *Pet* rendezvoused with Lopez and Vinnie Troiano in the Straits at three forty-five that afternoon, about fifty miles south of Key West. Rafe had been standing watch on the flying bridge when he picked up the old twenty-foot fishing boat slogging its way through the light seas.

Lopez had picked wisely. The tired old fisherman was an open boat that had seen better days. Its sails were patched and it was badly in need of paint, but it was seaworthy and had the look they needed to fool the Cuban coastal patrol.

Manny was seated at the tiller, and Vinnie had stationed himself at the bow of the old boat. When the *Pet* hove into view, the stocky Italian took off his T-shirt and waved it wildly over his head.

Rafe pointed out the twenty-footer to Pet, who turned the big boat toward the wallowing fisherman. The black man then called down into the cockpit and alerted the others, who rushed to the gunwales to see what Lopez had purchased.

As the big Hatteras closed on the old boat, Pet Palmer expertly throttled back the engines so that the big boat's wash would not swamp the smaller one. Despite Pet's efforts, the twenty-footer pitched violently as the big boat came alongside.

Cliff Ordile jumped into the rocking boat and helped Vinnie furl the sails as Manny Lopez caught a coil of line thrown to him by Rafe, who had come down the ladder into the cockpit. Rafe lashed the end of the heavy line to a cleat set in the stern rail of the big powerboat as Manny handed his end to Vinnie, who tied it off to a metal ring on the bow.

Carl Palmer came up the ladder and into the cockpit of the *Pet* as Kyle and Rafe were helping swing the fishing boat alongside. He watched the two men struggle with the line but made no effort to help.

The stern of the old boat started to swing around, and the men aboard it were able to read the crude white letters Manny Lopez had painted on the transom:

EL GATO NEGRO
JUCARO
ISLO DE PINOS.

Later that night, as the *Pet-o-Gold* cruised southwesterly at ten knots, toward the Yucatan channel off the western tip of Cuba, Kyle, Manny Lopez and the rest of the small expeditionary force was gathered around the table in the large cabin. Maps and charts were scattered across the highly polished wooden surface. Pet Palmer and Denise were on the bridge. The intercom had been left open so the women could hear the briefing.

Palmer leaned over and scanned the chart Manny had placed on top of the others.

"How close do we have to go in, Lopez?" he asked. "I don't want to lose the boat."

"Not too close," answered Manny. "I would not worry, Señor Palmer."

Kyle shouldered in and hunched over the chart. A lamp, a replica of an old oil lantern, swung back and forth, casting eerie shadows on the men's faces.

"Cuban radar range is thirty-two miles," Kyle said. "Their boats patrol up to five."

"What about air surveillance?" asked Cliff Ordile.

Kyle leaned back and looked at him.

"We'll go in at night in the old boat," he said. "Even if they pick us up, we'll look local."

Manny Lopez traced a line with his finger along the southern coast of Cuba.

"Where we land—Punta Mora—is a very deserted area," the

stocky Cuban said. "There is good cover . . . mangrove swamps. My father took me fishing there many times when I was a boy."

"What about coast guard patrols?" interjected Palmer.

Manny looked around at him.

"Not often . . . this is the southern coast."

"What kind of boats are they using?" asked Cliff.

Lopez took out a handkerchief and wiped his sweaty face.

"My people tell me they are like the American PT boats of World War II."

"What kind of armament?" asked Rafe, speaking for the first time.

"They have twin 25-mm antiaircraft guns and two .50-caliber machine guns. There is also a 76-mm cannon."

"Great!" croaked Palmer.

"How about the crew?" Kyle asked, looking around at the others.

"They are Komar class boats. They usually carry eleven men . . . top speed forty knots."

There was silence in the cabin. Kyle scanned the faces of the men as the swinging lamp continued to cast its eerie shadows.

"Go ahead, Manny," he said to Lopez. "Give us the rest of it."

The round-faced Cuban pulled a large map of Cuba from under the chart and placed it on top.

"As we come around Pinar del Rio, we have to cross between the Islo de Pinos—the Isle of Pines—and the coast of Cuba. That is a very dangerous passage."

"Why?" Palmer asked.

"There is a great deal of traffic. We will have to be careful," answered Lopez. "When we cross into the Gulf of Batabano, we will have a short run to our embarcation point."

Vinnie leaned in and looked at the spot Lopez indicated on the map with his finger.

"I hope that old boat makes it to the coast and back," he said softly.

"There is a small lagoon," said Manny, ignoring him. "Once we land, it is a mile from there to the road." He indicated an open area between two towns. "The ranch lies on this road, between Melesa del Sur and Guines."

"Anything else?" said Kyle, looking around.

Rafe stood up and steadied himself on the table.

"Jes' one thing," he said, smiling. "Les' hope them mothafuckers are asleep when we make our move."

"Amen!" Ordile intoned, crossing himself.

Chapter 29

By mid-morning of the second day the *Pet-o-Gold* had reached a point in the Yucatan channel about one hundred miles off the Cuban coast. The big boat moved along at a leisurely pace, the old fishing boat bouncing along behind her like a dutiful puppy.

In the spacious cabin, Kyle and the rest of the party had already started opening the crates and cases of weapons. They had the lid off the large crate marked MEDICAL SUPPLIES. Rafe and Vinnie were each cleaning cosmoline off the M-60s with some rags they had found in the galley.

"Christ," said Vinnie, "does this bring back memories?"

"You ain't shittin', bro," said Rafe, wiping down the barrel and the gas cylinder of the weapon. "Feels good to have one of these babies in my hands again."

"When you finish up," said Kyle, reaching into an open case at his feet, "take those 'pigs' up on the bridge . . . set one up on either side. Make sure to stack the belts next to the gun."

"Yowsah, yowsah, boss," Rafe joked as he carried the M-60 up the ladder. "C'mon, wop," he shouted back at Vinnie, who was just putting the finishing touches on his weapon. He stood and hefted it against his hip and aimed it toward the open sea.

Kyle withdrew two 9-mm Browing automatics from the case as Vinnie scrambled up the ladder after Rafe. The rancher handed the two automatics to Lopez and Ordile, who sat facing him in the cockpit. Before he could speak, he heard Palmer's voice shouting from the flying bridge.

"Be careful with that goddamn M-60, Phillips . . . that decking is made of imported Burmese teak." Suddenly Palmer's tanned face appeared over the safety rail. "Will you tell your two clowns to be careful? They're making holes in my boat," he shouted down at Kyle.

Manny Lopez smiled up at him as he spoke. "Señor Palmer,

soon you will have enough money to buy ten boats like this."

Kyle laughed and reached into the case. He removed another Browning High-Power and three tubular silencers. He handed two of the black metal tubes to Lopez and Ordile.

"Test-fire these when you get a chance," he said, inserting a silencer into one of the muzzles.

Cliff stood and held his automatic in his right hand. He extended his right arm and steadied it with his left hand in the classic firing position. The ex-CIA man sighted on an imaginary target off the starboard side.

"I feel like I'm back in the 'business' again," he said to Manny, squeezing the trigger on an empty firing chamber.

"I hope this is better than our last visit," the Cuban replied, turning the automatic over in his hands.

Rafe and Vinnie came sliding down the rails of the ladder. Both of them dived into the pistol case and removed the 9-mms. Rafe sighted his weapon upward at the bridge and closed one eye.

"I still like a .45 for knockin' people down," Rafe said, pulling the trigger.

"You got more firepower with this weapon," said Kyle, holding up his 9-mm. "This gun holds thirteen rounds in the magazine and one in the chamber. Colt .45 got seven in the mag, one in the chamber. *This* Browning design is forty years old . . . got no history of malfunctions."

"I thought you said we was gettin' Uzis and M-203s too." Rafe tucked the automatic in the waistband of his olive-drab pants. He was shirtless, as was Vinnie. Perspiration ran down his sinewy, black body in little rivulets.

"I think the Uzis are in the crate under the one marked anchovies," said Kyle, pointing to a stack of boxes resting against the after bulkhead.

Rafe crossed to the boxes and lifted one off. He picked up a clawhammer and started attacking the lid of the second box with it.

"Better watch it, Rafe," Vinnie said chidingly. "You may be bangin' on those Claymoors."

"Man, takes a lot for that C-4 to go up," said Rafe, tearing the lid off the box with the claw end of the hammer. "I knew a dude used to eat that shit . . . jes' so he'd get sick on patrol. One night he set up an M.A. on a red ball . . . Charlie come by an' tripped the wire. The sumbitch never went off cause the mothafucker ate the C-4."

"He must have wanted to get out of Vietnam badly to eat the explosives," said Manny, shaking his head.

"Guess so," Rafe said, reaching into the box and retrieving an olive-drab tube about three feet long. There was a black handle on the underside, and a flip sight on top.

"Jesus H. Christ, Blood," Rafe exclaimed. "You got LAWs rockets . . . these mothafuckers are bad . . . blow open a goddamn bank vault."

Lopez rose from his padded seat against the coaming. He took the LAWs rocket from Rafe.

"This is a fine weapon," he said, hefting it. "I wish we had such things in the assault."

"You think that's bad," said Rafe, rummaging among the other boxes. "Wait'll I show you an M-203."

"What is that?" asked Manny, putting down the olive-drab tube.

Ordile sat forward, his elbows on his knees, the Browning dangling from one hand.

"It's a marraige of a 40-mm grenade launcher with an M16 rifle fitted to it," the ex-CIA man recited. "They were introduced in 'Nam in 1969. They can hit point targets at one hundred fifty meters, and area targets up to three hundred fifty meters."

The men in the cabin turned and looked at him. Cliff stood up, smiled wryly and bowed from the waist.

"You think we're goin' to need heavy stuff like this?" asked Vinnie, looking at Kyle.

"I don't know, Vincent," Kyle answered, and turned to Manny, who had dropped back in his seat. "Manny'll know more than me about that."

"In the southern part of the island they mostly rely on local militia," said the bald man, taking off his straw hat and wiping his reddened pate with a kerchief. "They have jeeps with .50-caliber machine guns and AK-47 assault rifles. I don't think there's heavy equipment."

Kyle sat on the edge of a large crate.

"I don't want to run into any surprises when we get there," Kyle said, looking at the stocky Cuban. "Manny, get together with Denise and draw a floor plan of the ranch based on what you two can remember."

"*Si,*" said Manny. "Where is Señorita Denny?"

"I think she's below makin' sandwiches," said Rafe, pulling a case of smoke grenades out of the stack and starting to open them.

"Rafe, Vinnie," said Kyle tersely. "Later this afternoon I want to mount the Recoilless on the foredeck."

"You got it, Blood," replied Rafe, ripping the lid off the box.

"Manny, I need that floor plan for the final briefing tonight."

"You will have it, *compadre*."

Kyle turned and looked out at the strong sunlight shimmering off the blue water. He felt an excitement pulse through him as he welcomed the confrontation with death. He had felt the same exhilaration before impending attacks in Vietnam and the night of the Fallons' assault on his ranch. Never had he felt so close to life as when he faced death.

He knew he wanted this. His mind and his body longed for it. This is what he had been groomed for; as doctors and lawyers are trained in their professions, he had been trained in his.

Chapter 30

That night Denise and Pet were on the flying bridge guiding the *Pet-o-Gold* southward, seemingly headed for Honduras and Nicaragua. When the time came, the big Hatteras would do a 180-degree turn and make a swift run for the Channel of the Indians that lay between the Isle of Pines and the coast of Cuba.

Below, in the big cabin, six grim-faced men sat around the large table. The oil lamp replica swung as it had before, casting the same eerie glow. On the table, instead of maps and charts, was the floor plan of the ranch house Manny Lopez had drawn with Denise Palermo's help.

Kyle eyed it thoughtfully, then sat back in his chair.

"We're gettin' close," he said earnestly. "I want to make a few points before we go over the operation."

"Shoot," said Vinnie, sucking on a cold can of Coke.

"When we're ashore," Kyle continued, "only one guy gives orders." He looked at the faces of the men around the table, letting his gaze linger a bit longer on Palmer. There was no reply. "Okay," Kyle went on, "our objective is to get in and get out *alive* . . . with the *money*."

Rafe stood up and leaned across the table, almost getting hit by the swinging lamp. He high-fived with Vinnie.

"Right on, brother!"

Kyle looked at the black man, who sat down a bit sheepishly.

"Next," Kyle said in a cold, even tone, "this may not go down well with some of you, but it has got to be." He hit the table with his fist for emphasis. "Any wounded will be left behind. We'll be movin' fast . . . wounded slow us down."

"Even *you*?" It was Palmer who spoke.

He looked at Kyle with those malevolent blue eyes, the swinging lamp casting vivid shadows on his tan face.

"Even me," the hawk-faced man answered after a beat in a voice that left no doubt as to his meaning.

Kyle nodded to Manny Lopez, who leaned over the crudely drawn map of the area and the floor plan of the house.

"The house is set on a small knoll overlooking the road. It is surrounded on all sides by fenced fields." Lopez indicated the places on the map. "There is a small, heavily wooded area near the road where we can hide the mopeds."

"How far is it from the woods to the house?" asked Ordile, pointing at the spots on the map.

"It's about half a mile," the Cuban answered. "The lagoon I picked for the landing is about twelve miles from the ranch on this back road."

Kyle reached under the table and held up a pair of dirty white cotton trousers and a matching loose-fitting shirt. He took a wide-brimmed straw hat from a shelf and dropped it on Rafe's head.

"We'll be wearin' these to disguise ourselves as fisherman," he said as Rafe clowned with the hat.

"What about our weapons?" Ordile asked.

"Rucksacks," Kyle said quickly. "All the ammo, Uzis and other gear will fit in them. We'll wrap the 203s in burlap."

"The whole trip from the lagoon to the ranch," continued Manny, "should take two hours . . . if there is no trouble."

Pet Palmer and Denise sat at the dimly lit control panel on the flying bridge as the men below went over the operational plan that would take place the next day. The engines of the big boat throbbed with a dull beat as the sleek craft's bow creamed the sea, pushing her southward.

Denise sighed heavily and looked out over the rail at the dark water.

"There's something about the sea at night," the attractive brunette said wistfully.

"You read my mind," said Pet, leaning on the chrome wheel. "Are you sweet on any of those guys?"

"Why?" the dancer asked in a surprised voice.

Pet peered into the inky blackness in front of the Venturi windshield before answering.

"Just curious. You're not wearing any rings. I was wondering what your connection was."

"Strictly money, Mrs. Palmer." Denise replied. "I could go for a guy like Kyle, but it would never work."

"Why not?" said Pet, turning toward her.

Denise looked at the wealthy, well-groomed woman's profile in the dim glow of the console.

"Because I'm a whore," she said softly. "Some women are forced into it . . . some women are *born* to it."

Down in the cabin, Manny was pointing to a rectangular area on the floor plan at the rear of the house.

"This is the swimming pool," he said, then moved his finger. "And this is the patio. It is the only one. It must be where the money is buried."

"What room is this?" said Palmer, pointing to an area just off the patio.

"That is the living room," said Manny. "There are large French doors that open onto the patio."

"How accurate is this floor plan?" asked Palmer nervously.

"I drew this from memory," answered Manny. "I have not seen it for a long time."

Cliff Ordile leaned forward and stared at the crudely drawn map and floor plan.

"Anyone living there now?"

"I do not know." Lopez shrugged.

"What if someone *is* living at the ranch?" Palmer directed the question at the broad-faced Cuban.

Kyle stood and looked down at the five men around the table.

"We'll cross that bridge when we come to it," he said. The tense sound of his voice hung in the air of the cabin as the men turned their faces toward him.

Chapter 31

By 9:45 P.M., the *Pet* had negotiated the treacherous Channel of the Indians and was deep into the Gulf of Batabano off the southern Cuban coast. Palmer had turned northeastward when it had gotten dark and made for the channel. The big Hatteras made the passage without running lights, risking a possible collision but cutting down their chances of being discovered.

Now the *Pet-o-Gold* was hove to some twenty miles south of Punta Mora. The old fisherman had been lashed along the port side. She was loaded hull-down in the water with equipment and weapons that would be needed ashore. A small but powerful outboard motor had been clamped to the transom of the old boat.

Kyle Youngblood, dressed in the white pants and shirt of a *campesino,* lifted the six-man raft and tossed it to Rafe, who had been covering the gear in the *El Gato Negro* with a waterproof tarp.

"Make sure you secure this, Rafe," he said to the black man, who was dressed in the same fashion. Kyle turned and slipped down the ladder into the large cabin. The curtains on the windows and portholes had been drawn, and red bulbs had been placed in all the light fixtures to lessen their chance of discovery.

Vinnie was seated on one of the bunks scanning a copy of *Playboy* in the dim light. Lopez and Ordile were putting some last-minute items in their rucksacks. Pet and Denise were seated at the table with Carl Palmer.

The scene was bizzare enough to bring an unaccustomed smile to Kyle's face. All of the men in the plush cabin were dressed in *campesino* costume. Everyone but Lopez and Rafe had used the brown stain on their hands and faces. The two women were wearing shorts and halter tops. In the reddish hue of the bulbs their skin took on the same appearance as the men's.

"Boat's ready," Kyle said tersely. "Get your gear assembled. I want to shove off by ten."

Vinnie stood up and tucked the copy of *Playboy* into his waistband and pulled his loose shirt over it. He hefted his rucksack onto his shoulder. The burlap-wrapped M-203 dangled from the crook of his arm as he headed for the ladder.

Lopez and Ordile stood and lifted their rucksacks from the deck of the cabin.

"*Si*, Jefe," Lopez said to Kyle. Then he turned to Denise. "*Adios*, Señorita Denny," he said softly. "Hopefully we go to find the gift your *padre* left for us twenty years ago."

Both men climbed the ladder to the cockpit. Kyle turned toward the three people at the table. Before he could speak, Denise rose from her seat.

"Watch yourself," she said to the rancher. "I want to be rich."

"If your father was tellin' the truth," Kyle replied, "you won't have to worry for the rest of your life."

Palmer pushed his chair back and stood.

"We'd better get moving, Youngblood," he said, lifting his rucksack to the table. "If you want to stay on schedule."

"You're right." Kyle nodded. "Ladies, if it all goes the way we planned it, we should be back at these coordinates by ten tomorrow morning."

Pet squashed a cigarette in the ashtray and looked at Kyle.

"We'll be here," she said coolly. "I want to cruise around outside their radar range."

"Good idea," said Kyle. "Keep your lights off. If you're approached by any kind of boat, make like your fishin' and head south."

Palmer leaned over and kissed Pet on the cheek.

"We're off for fame and fortune, my love," he said. "Keep her steady."

Both men climbed the ladder and emerged into the hot, humid night air. Even though they were twenty miles off the coast, the dank smell of rotting vegetation wafted to them on the strong breeze.

The rest of the party was already aboard the old fishing boat. Manny Lopez was in the stern next to the outboard motor. Cliff Ordile was huddled near him, his back against the tarp-covered mopeds. Vinnie and Rafe had made a little tent out of the tarpaulin that covered the rest of the equipment and were lying beneath it.

There was space in the bow. Palmer dropped his rucksack first, then carefully jumped into the gently pitching boat. Kyle threw his rucksack to Palmer, then went over the rail into the remaining space in the bow of the boat.

Pet Palmer and Denise stood at the rail in the cockpit and looked down into the *El Gato Negro*. The women were both amazed—the men actually looked like Cuban fisherman.

As Manny Lopez cast off the stern line and Kyle unlashed the bow, Denise Palermo did something she had not done since her early years in Catholic school . . . she prayed, asking God to protect the men and help them find her father's money.

Then a thought entered her mind . . . like the shaft of an arrow. It was something she had tried to push away over the last two days on the *Pet-o-Gold*.

Manny Lopez started the powerful outboard, and the buzz-saw sound jolted her subconscious, underlining the feeling she was having. As she watched the twenty-footer fade into the blackness of the Cuban night, she wondered if she had done the right thing in making her deal with Chet Allen and Phil McGregor.

Chapter 32

As the old fishing boat wallowed toward the distant shore, the blackness of the tropical night closed around it. The only sound was the persistent buzz of the outboard motor as it pushed the twenty-footer through the dark water.

In the cramped boat, each man sat with his own thoughts, wondering what fate had planned for him when he reached the now invisible shore. Some dreamed of the riches that awaited them; others of the dangers they might encounter in seeking the wealth.

Manny Lopez sat impassively at the steering handle, peering into the blackness, trying to see if he could pick out a light ashore that might guide them in. Cliff Ordile lay near him, his eyes closed and his head propped against the mopeds. He appeared to be asleep.

In the middle of the boat, Rafe and Vinnie lay under the tentlike structure they had rigged out of the tarp. Both men lay on their backs with their eyes open, feeling the vibration of the motor as it shuddered through the hull.

T. Carl Palmer sat next to Kyle in the bow of the boat. Slowly, steadily, he wiped the Browning 9-mm with an oily rag. He kept turning the automatic over in his hands.

Kyle looked at his former captain's shadowy face in the darkness.

"Why'd you decide to come along?" Kyle asked softly.

"I wanted to protect my investment," said Palmer, looking up. He continued to wipe the Browning.

"You could have done that from your boat," said Kyle, trying to see the man's face in the dark.

"That's true," Palmer replied almost inaudibly.

Kyle leaned closer to him.

"I think I know the real reason, Palmer," the hawk-faced man rasped at him. "You like to use that little *toy* in your hand." Kyle's voice raised an octave. "You're hopin' you'll get a chance to kill some people."

The ex–Green Beret captain slowly raised the 9-mm and pointed it in the direction of Kyle's voice.

"My life has been extremely boring lately, Youngblood." The sound of Palmer's voice was full of dire meaning.

Kyle glanced at the yellowed crystal of his watch. He felt an uneasy sensation running down the back of his neck into his spine.

The luminescent dial on Kyle's watch read ten thirty-five.

A short distance from where the old fisherman continued to labor toward Punta Mora, a twenty-seven-foot coastal patrol boat, the 176, slid through the darkness. Most of her crew of eleven lined the rails straining into the pitch-black night, trying to locate the direction of the drone they were hearing. On the bridge, Captain Enrique Fernandez, tall and with a fierce black mustache, looked tensely at his second in command, who stood at the helm. The elusive, monotonus whine was like a mosquito in a dark bedroom in the middle of the night.

"The lookouts report no contact, Captain," the man at the wheel said tersely. "Do you want to use the searchlight?"

"Not yet," said Fernandez. "Is there nothing on the radar?"

"No contact, sir." He turned toward the captain. "Perhaps we had better use the light?"

Fernandez sighed deeply and wiped his brow with the sleeve of his olive-drab uniform.

"*Si,*" he said, and turned to a sailor who stood on a small metal platform above the bridge. "Manolo, turn on the light."

The short seaman threw the switch, and a strong finger of white light sliced through the darkness and danced across the sea some distance away. The men at the rails followed the beam with their eyes as it moved slowly back and forth.

Less than a quarter of a mile to the north, Kyle and the rest of the party aboard the *El Gato Negro* saw the white beam the instant it flicked on.

"Lopez, kill the motor," Kyle whispered hoarsely as he scrambled over Palmer, collapsing Vinnie and Rafe's tent in the process.

By the time he reached the stern, Manny had killed the outboard.

"What do you think it is?" Ordile said, slipping the Uzi out of his rucksack.

"Patrol boat," Kyle said. "I think they heard us." He turned to

Manny. "Get the motor out of the water."

Manny quickly loosened the clamps and pulled the small outboard into the boat. He handed it to Ordile, who slipped it under the tarpaulin.

"Hey, what the fuck is goin' on?" whispered Rafe, poking his head out from under the makeshift tent.

"Cuban patrol boat," said Ordile. "Stay under the tarp."

Lopez moved closer to Kyle, who was staring at the oncoming patrol boat.

"What do you want to do, *amigo*?" he whispered to Kyle.

"You do the talking," Kyle replied. "Tell them we're fisherman. We got lost in the dark."

"*Si,*" Lopez answered, watching the oncoming patrol boat. "What if it does not work?"

'Let's try to talk our way out," said Kyle, loud enough for all of them to hear. "Don't fire unless they fire first."

The 176 moved inexorably toward the old fishing boat and its tense crew. The shaft of its light scanned the sea in front of the bow like the single eye of a Cyclops. Suddenly the white beam transfixed the old boat and held it.

The excited Cuban sailors lined the rails, pointing and jabbering in Spanish. Because of the harmless appearance of the *El Gato Negro,* no one had manned the .50-caliber machine guns or the 76-mm cannon on the foredeck.

Captain Fernandez reached down and lifted a gunmetal-gray bullhorn to his lips as the 176 drew alongside the old vessel. It looked like a fishing boat and the men were dressed like fishermen, yet there was something that did not seem quite right.

He pressed the button on the battery-operated megaphone.

"*Aboard the fishing boat,*" the metallic voice boomed in Spanish. "*Heave to and identify yourself.*"

Two of the sailors at the rail reached down with metal boat hooks and fastened them under the gunwale of the twenty-footer. The searchlight held the men in the fisherman in its brassy glare.

Ordile had his hand covered by the tarp. His finger was on the trigger of the Uzi. Under the collapsed tent, Rafe and Vinnie had both taken the burlap off the M-203s at their sides and held them ready.

Palmer sat in the bow of the boat, his straw hat shading his brown-stained face and the glassy stare of his blue eyes. His sweating right hand rested on the thick butt of the 9-mm under his loose-fitting white shirt.

"*Captain*!" Lopez shouted, looking up at the bridge. "*We are only poor fishermen from Jucaro. We are lost in the dark. Can you give us some help?"*

The men at the rail laughed and directed some derogatory remarks to the men in the fishing boat.

"*What happened to your motor?*" Fernandez said, still using the bullhorn.

Manny looked at Kyle before answering. The rancher met his eyes and gestured to continue talking.

"*What motor?*" said Manny, turning his face toward the bridge. "*We are only poor fisherman. We have no motor.*"

"*We heard a motor . . . hold fast!*" the captain called out. "*I am sending two men aboard to check you over.*" He turned to the men at the rail. "Pepe, Carlos, see what they have."

The two sailors, both bearing side arms, climbed nimbly over the rail and dropped into the spot near the bow that Kyle had vacated. The men turned toward the center of the craft. One of them started to lift the tarp that covered Rafe and Vinnie when the Browning High-Power suddenly appeared in Palmer's fist. He squeezed the trigger, and the report echoed over the water. Flame spurted from the muzzle of the weapon as it discharged.

The young Cuban sailor was only three feet from Palmer when he fired. The slug struck the man in the base of the neck and continued upward, taking off the front of the man's skull.

The other sailor, who was about a foot in front of his stricken comrade, started to turn but was hit in the face by pieces of bloody bone and brain tissue. The second sailor had only a second to react to the horror of what he had seen.

Palmer squeezed the trigger again. This time the round struck the second seaman in the center of his chest, killing him instantly and driving him backward onto the tarpaulin-covered Vinnie and Rafe.

The men on the 176 were stunned by what they had seen. Before any of them could react, Cliff Ordile pulled the Uzi from under the tarp and fired at the five men standing by the rail. They were driven into the superstructure of the cabin by the fusillade of lead. Four were killed in the volley . . . the other was mortally wounded, taking two rounds in the stomach.

Rafe and Vinnie threw back the tarp and opened up with their M16s. A slug from Rafe's weapon caught the lookout as he was starting to pull his side arm. A gout of blood appeared on the front of the man's shirt, and he crumpled over the metal railing onto the deck below.

Kyle hadn't fired, but he had drawn his 9-mm when Palmer's first round had killed the young Cuban seaman. Now he leapt to the deck of the patrol boat, looking upward at the bridge, where Fernandez and his second in command stood frozen in horror.

The mate, a short man in olive drab, started to react. He reached for the butt of a pistol he was carrying in a shoulder holster under his left arm. Kyle dropped the man with a deft shot before he could withdraw the weapon. The mate toppled backward into Fernandez, who clamored down the port-side ladder attached to the bridge's superstructure.

The tall captain came around the side of the deck housing and was slipping into the ring that accompanied one of the .50-caliber machine guns when Rafe came over the rail and saw him. The black vet swung the muzzle of the M16 toward Fernandez and squeezed the trigger.

The weapon jumped in his hand, and the staccato bursts rang in his ears. He could see blossoms of blood appear on the man's olive-drab uniform. Fernandez's body jerked and shuddered as the rounds struck home.

Rafe released the trigger, and the tall captain's body slumped over the gun ring. The entire patrol boat was now clothed in a deadly silence. In the melee the only man who had not fired a shot was Manny Lopez. The squat Cuban sat in the stern of the *El Gato Negro* with his head bowed. The sequence of events in which ten died had taken less than three minutes.

Kyle and Rafe scrambled quietly over the deck of the 176 as Vinnie and Ordile lashed the fishing boat to the rail so the two vessels would not drift apart. Kyle motioned to the black man with his Browning to check the below-deck area. Rafe found the ladder and softly started to descend a step at a time.

Kyle counted five bodies along the rail. The sailor with the abdominal wound groaned. Kyle knelt by his side and felt for a pulse in the man's neck with his fingers. It was very weak.

As the rancher rose, the sailor looked at him with glazed dark eyes.

"*Madre de Dios!*" The man gasped. "*Quien es?*" Then he gave a long, rattling sigh and stared into the black night with sightless eyes.

The ladder Rafe was on led directly into a large cabin. In front of him, toward the bow, was a smaller cabin with its hatch slightly ajar.

As Rafe stepped off the ladder onto the deck he could see a man in an olive-drab uniform hunched in front of a radio. He was jabbering excitedly in Spanish.

The black vet quickly closed the distance to the hatch and pushed it open with the muzzle of the M16. The radioman heard Rafe behind him. He turned quickly and went for the .45 lying by the radio. Rafe squeezed the trigger, and the rifle erupted in the small cabin. The slugs tore into the man's body at point-blank range. Some of the high-powered rounds went completely through the sailor and smashed into the radio behind him.

There was a shower of sparks and a loud squawk. The instrument buzzed, then died. The radioman was hurled backward into his radio. His face contorted in pain, and then he pitched forward, a dark red stain spreading on the back of his uniform.

Back on deck, Palmer and Vinnie had boarded the patrol boat as Kyle helped Lopez and Ordile over the rail. They looked at the bodies of the dead Cubans and turned to Kyle.

"What now?" said Ordile hoarsely.

"First things first," Kyle replied. "Vinnie, kill that spotlight. We don't want to attract any more attention than we already have."

Without a word Vinnie scrambled up the starboard ladder and onto the lookout platform as Rafe came back on deck. The short Italian hit the switch on the light and once again threw the two boats into darkness.

"There was a guy at the radio," Rafe reported to Kyle. "I had to waste him. He might have sent out a Mayday."

"Shit!" said Ordile. "What the hell do we do now?"

Kyle looked toward the ex-CIA man's shadowy form standing near him on the deck.

"Kill the engines, Cliff," Kyle ordered. "They've been idling since we've been aboard."

"Aye aye, sir," said Ordile as he moved to the ladder and climbed to the bridge. A moment later the three diesels stopped their dull but powerful murmur.

Manny Lopez turned to Palmer, who was standing next to him on the dark deck, slippery with blood.

"Why did you have to shoot?" he said savagely to the handsome man. "This could have been avoided."

"I had no alternative." Palmer answered matter-of-factly. "They would have found our weapons."

"We might have been able to take them prisoner," said Manny bitterly as Vinnie and Ordile joined them on the deck.

"We got more important things to worry about," Kyle said curtly. "Rafe killed a radioman below . . . sounded like he was gettin' off a message."

"Could you tell who he was talking to?" Manny Lopez said tentatively.

Rafe popped the empty magazine from the M16 and slapped in a full one.

"Didn't have time to ask," he shot back at Manny.

"This may change our plans," Ordile said seriously. "We have to assume he got off his message. A couple of patrol boats could be bearing down on us right now."

"I ain't assumin' nothin'," Kyle said angrily. "The whole damn Cuban Navy could be bearin' down on us." He slammed his fist against the bulkhead. "We've come too far to turn back."

"I'm with you, Blood," said Rafe, stepping to Kyle's side.

"Count me in, Rafe," Vinnie said as he joined them.

Kyle looked at the shadowy form of the other three men.

"What about the rest of you?" he asked in a cold voice.

Manny Lopez and Cliff Ordile hung back for a beat, then joined the others.

Palmer stood against the rail, a lone figure against the dark sea.

"What's your plan, Youngblood?" he said finally.

Kyle stepped to one side and knelt on the deck.

"Runnin' into this patrol boat could be a hell of a break," said Kyle, "if we could make whoever is lookin' for us think this was done by refugees tryin' to escape."

"How do you propose to do that, my friend?" asked Manny.

Kyle's mind was racing, visualizing his plan as if he were watching it on a television screen.

"We take all our gear off the old boat," he said quickly. "Then weight the bodies and dump 'em in the ocean, shoot up the old fishing boat and . . ."

". . . whoever finds it will think it was full of refugees who were taken prisoner or killed by the patrol boat, which we ride to Punta Mora," interjected Ordile.

"Hopefully the other boats'll ride out to sea lookin' for us," Kyle finished. "At least it may buy us some time."

Rafe moved closer to Kyle and patted him on the back.

"Pure fuckin' genius, baby," he said, chuckling. "Pure fuckin' genius."

It was almost eleven-thirty when Kyle and the others had finished taking their gear off the old boat and stowed it aboard the 176. The bodies of the eleven Cuban sailors had been hastily weighted with whatever heavy objects could be found and dropped over the side of the patrol boat.

Kyle looked at his watch, then slipped his Ka-Bar from its

scabbard at his waist. He then cut the lines that were holding the two boats together.

Kyle turned to Rafe, who standing on the foredeck by one of the .50-caliber machine guns.

"Rafe," he said to the black man, "you still think you can handle that fifty?"

"Can a dawg piss on a tree?" said Rafe, laughing.

"Why don't you put some holes in the fishin' boat?" Kyle said. "Not too many . . . I want it to float awhile."

Rafe gave Kyle a high salute and climbed into the firing ring. He pulled the cocking lever on the .50-caliber and swung the gun toward the old fisherman that was starting to float free.

He squeezed the trigger, and the big gun chattered into life. Chips of wood flew from the shattered hull of the *El Gato Negro*, and she began to settle in the dark water.

Cliff Ordile and Vinnie watched from the bridge. Manny stood sadly by the rail.

"Manny," the ex-CIA man called down to the saddened Cuban, "why don't you monitor the radio and see if they're looking for us?"

"Forget it," said Vinnie, punching the starter. "When Rafe blew the radioman away, the slug smashed the set. Palmer's below tryin' to get it workin'."

Vinnie punched the starter button again and the big diesels on the 176 roared to life. He spun the wheel hard, and the sleek gunboat sped toward Punta Mora, five miles away across the stretch of dark ocean.

In the patrol boat's frothy wake the *El Gato Negro* settled up to its gunwales, rocking gently in the whitecapped waves as the bullet-riddled pieces of debris floated to the surface.

Chapter 33

A short time later Cliff Ordile nosed the comandeered Cuban patrol boat through a mass of overhanging mangroves and marsh grass. The incessant drone of thousands of insects issued from the shoreline as the 176 found the opening and eased through it into a small lagoon.

Manny Lopez was now on the bridge next to Cliff as the others lined the rails, peering into the darkness, nervous fingers on the triggers of their weapons.

"There was a small dock we used to fish from when I was a boy," Manny said softly. "I don't know if it is still here."

"I sure hope so," Ordile said with a growl. "It's blacker than the inside of a coal miner's shithouse."

He eased the big boat toward the silhouetted trees on the dark, ominous shoreline.

"I think I see it," Manny whispered hoarsely, gripping Cliff's arm. "The dock is still there."

While Kyle and the others nosed slowly through the dark lagoon aboard the 176, another Komar class Cuban patrol craft was crisscrossing the Gulf of Batabano five miles south of Punta Mora.

The radio operator on the 181 had intercepted a garbled message from the 176 boat. The man's words had lacked coherence, then the radio had gone dead. The sailor had reported the transmission to his captain, Guillermo Ortega, a very thorough, seasoned officer whose family were high-ranking members of Cuba's Communist Party. Ortega listened to the young operator and ordered the helmsman to steer a course to the area where he knew his sister ship was patrolling.

The big gunboat cut through the water, its powerful searchlight making great sweeping arcs over the sea. Its crew, like the men on the ill-fated 176, lined the rails following the white shaft of light with their eyes.

On the metal platform above the bridge, the lookout strained into the night, looking for anything that might give them a clue to the whereabouts of the 176.

Suddenly the bearded sailor's eye caught sight of a floating object.

"*Captain!*" the man shouted. "*Off the starboard bow. There is something in the water.*" He pinpointed the object with the searchlight.

"Head toward it," Ortega told the helmsman.

The man turned the wheel slightly, and the big boat veered toward the floating object. As they closed in on the wrecked hull of the *El Gato Negro,* two of the sailors at the starboard rail reached out and secured the submerged hull with their boat hooks while the helmsman throttled back the 181's engines.

"What is it?" the tall bearded Ortega called out to his men.

"*An old fishing boat, Captain!*" one of the seamen yelled back.

Ortega scanned the wreckage as the lookout held the light on it.

"It looks like Captain Fernandez did a good job," Ortega said proudly. "Are there any survivors?"

"No . . . no bodies, either!" one of the men holding the boat hooks called back.

"They must have taken them aboard," the bearded captain said to the man at the helm. Then he turned to the men at the rail. "Cast her adrift and we'll sink her."

As the men at the rail started to disengage their hooks, a bloody, white face appeared in the water from under the shattered hull of the old fishing boat. One of the men with a boat hook snared the body and dragged it toward him.

"*Cuidado!*" the sailor shouted.

Ortega leaned over the retaining shield of the bridge, trying to get a better look.

"*Quien es?*" he called out.

"It is Capitan Fernandez from the 176," the crewman shouted up to him.

Ortega struck the bridge railing hard with his hand.

"Check the wreck closer!" he said angrily. "Something is wrong here."

Two sailors went over the starboard railing and dropped into the half-sunken shell of the old boat. They thrashed around in the thigh-deep water as the other crewman watched from the deck.

Suddenly one of the men in the shattered boat reached into the water and held up a dripping copy of the *Playboy* magazine Vinnie had hidden.

"*Yankees?*" the man screamed.

"Yankees?" repeated Ortega. "Make for shore . . . top speed."

It had taken twenty minutes for Kyle and the others to unload their weapons and equipment onto the rickety wooden dock that jutted a short distance into the lagoon. The superstructure of the patrol boat loomed large against the backdrop of the dark mangroves and star-laden sky.

They gathered on the marshy ground next to the old dock, a bizarre band dressed in white *campesino* outfits and wide-brimmed straw hats. Each man carried an olive-drab rucksack on his back filled with the equipment they would need to make the operation successful.

Six shiny, black Puch mopeds stood lined up on the watery ground facing the men. Strange calls and exotic noises mixed with the drone of mosquitoes and other insects that inhabited the mangrove forest around them. Above all, the fetid, rank smell of rotting vegetation permeated the lagoon and small clearing like a fog.

"Makes me feel like I was back in-country, humpin' this mothafuckin' ruck again," said Rafe, adjusting the straps on his burden.

"Fuckin' bugs are as bad," Vinnie said angrily, slapping at his neck.

Kyle hefted the six-man raft and set it on the handlebars of his Puch. He lifted the small outboard motor and handed it to Vinnie.

"Hook this on to the back of your bike," he said. "Use a couple bungi cords."

"Why the hell are you dragging that damn raft with us?" Palmer asked, a hint of irritation in his voice.

"Boy Scout training," Kyle shot back sarcastically. "Be prepared."

"We'd better get movin'," said Cliff, "if we want to reach the ranch before daylight."

"Right," said Kyle. He turned to Manny. "Which way?"

The squat Cuban moved to his moped and took it off the kickstand.

"Through there." He pointed to an opening in the mangroves. "It is about a mile. We will have to push the bikes till we get to the road. The ground is too soft, and the jungle too thick."

"Okay, Manny . . . let's move out," said Kyle. "You take the point."

Manny Lopez pushed his moped into the opening in the thick mangrove forest. The others followed suit, in single file. As they moved, their boots made a squishing sound in the moist earth. The heavy forest closed in around them till there was no trace of the clearing and the lagoon they had just left.

After a few minutes of slogging through the heavy undergrowth, Kyle stopped the small column by the base of a tall tree. He took a long length of nylon rope he had hanging from his belt and threw it over a branch high in the tree.

Next he took the six-man raft and the outboard motor and tied them to the end of the line as the others watched. The rancher pulled on the free end of the rope until the two pieces of gear were up against the branch. Then he tied the end of the line off around the tree trunk, leaving the raft and motor high off the ground.

"Okay," he said, breathing heavily from his exertions. "Show's over . . . let's move out."

Chapter 34

As they neared the fringe of the mangrove forest and the road, the ground became firmer and the going much easier. Each man had been badly bitten by the swarms of mosquitoes that inhabited the area. The one thing they had forgotten to bring was insect repellent.

Finally the mangrove and heavy undergrowth thinned out, and Lopez raised his hand, signaling a halt. Kyle put his Puch on its kickstand and hustled up to him.

"What's up?" he whispered hoarsely to Manny, hunkering down beside him.

"Nothing," the squat Cuban answered, pointing ahead in the darkness. "We have reached the road."

"How do you know?" Kyle asked, his eyes following Manny's finger.

As if in answer to his question, there was the roar of a big engine, and a set of powerful headlamps flashed by, no more than ten yards from where they had stopped.

"Good work, Manny," Kyle said, patting him on the back. "I didn't expect any traffic this time of night."

"Some trucks with farm products," Manny said softly, "that's all we should encounter."

"Good," whispered Kyle, turning to Ordile, who was directly behind him. "Cliff, bring it up . . . tell the others."

In a matter of seconds they had all hunkered down around Kyle, listening, waiting expectantly for his orders.

"We'll travel in pairs," Kyle said. "I don't like to split the force, but a big group might attract attention. Five-minute intervals." He rose in the darkness. "Manny and I will go first, then Vinnie and Rafe. Cliff, you and Palmer can be the rear guard."

"How will we know when we hit the turnoff for the ranch?" asked Cliff, standing up and shaking his legs.

"There is a huge tree," said Manny. "I will give you three short blinks on my flashlight."

Kyle walked back, retrieved his bike and pushed it toward the road. Manny Lopez moved in behind him. The rancher mounted the Puch. He pushed in the clutch and pedaled out onto the asphalt. The bike's motor caught with a high-pitched buzzing sound. He waited as Manny started his bike, and then the two men took off down the dark road.

"Goddamn!" Rafe chuckled. "Manny looked like a hunch-backed gorilla trying to hump a football." The others snickered in the darkness of the forest, then settled back to wait their turn on the road.

Ortega's boat had reached the swampy mangrove forest of Punta Mora. The 181 nosed along the thickly forested shoreline, its powerful searchlight scanning the jungle, seeking an opening in the seeming impenetrable wall of foliage. Crewmen stood in the firing rings of the .50-caliber machine guns, firing short bursts of tracer rounds into the trees, trying to flush their prey.

During the half-hour ride on the two-lane blacktop road, Kyle and Manny had seen two flatbed trucks. Each had blinked its lights, and the men on the mopeds had waved back in greeting.

When they reached the big tree the squat Cuban had referred to, they turned off, skirting the huge trunk and bringing their bikes to a halt behind it. Both men cut their motors and switched off the single lamps on the bikes.

"Vinnie and Rafe should be here in a couple minutes," Kyle said, getting off the Puch and setting it up on its kickstand. "You'd better get your light out. They may miss the tree."

"*Si,*" said Lopez. He dismounted and set his bike next to Kyle's.

Manny moved toward the road and knelt down. He scooped up a handful of earth and put it to his nose.

"Cuba!" he said softly.

"What's that?" Kyle asked, turning toward him.

"This is my land," Manny said fervently. "I love this country. In America I feel I am a stranger." He smelled the handful of earth again. "Even now, for this short time, I feel I am home."

"I know what you mean," said Kyle, placing a hand on his shoulder. "I felt like that when I came home from Vietnam and went back to my ranch."

Each man looked at the other as they stood at the edge of the road. In the distance they could hear a low buzz, like the sound a fly makes when it is trapped against a screen.

Manny Lopez stepped onto the road. He could barely see the reflection of the headlamps of Vinnie and Rafe's mopeds. The Cuban lifted the hooded flashlight in his hand and blinked it three times.

The white finger of bright light slowly edged along the shoreline. It passed an opening in the thick mass of mangroves and stopped. Then it eased slowly back and rested on the opening. The bearded lookout on the metal platform above the bridge pointed and jabbered excitedly in Spanish. The helmsman pushed the throttle forward. The 181 slowly nosed its sleek gray bow into the slight gap in the trees that led to the small lagoon, where at a dilapidated dock the missing 176 boat rode at its mooring lines.

Back at the huge tree, Kyle and the others had hidden their mopeds in the thick undergrowth. The Uzis had been brought out of the rucksacks, and the burlap had been stripped from the M-203s. Each man had also inserted a tubular silencer into the muzzle of his Browning 9-mm.

Manny moved out to the point, holding the Uzi in one hand.

"The ranch house is a mile through these trees," he said. "This trail will take us to it."

He moved quickly onto the barely discernible trail and disappeared into the darkness as Kyle and the others fell in behind him.

As Manny Lopez led the small column through the small patch of forest toward the ranch house, Ortega's patrol boat slid slowly into the small lagoon. The men in the gun rings peered intently into the darkness, trying to pick up some sign of the missing boat.

On the foredeck three of the crewmen readied the 76-mm cannon. Overhead, the lookout panned the thick rain forest that rimmed the small clearing around the lagoon with the searchlight.

Suddenly there was a cry from one of the sailors as the powerful light picked up the gray hull and superstructure of the 176, tied to a forlorn wooden dock that jutted into the brackish waters of the small lagoon.

The men on the .50's swung their guns in the direction of the missing boat expecting a fight. The crew at the 76-mm cranked the cannon into position and slammed the breach on the belt-fed gun closed.

The white light from the metal platform bathed over the 176 as her counterpart edged closer. Each man aboard the 181 had his finger on the trigger of his weapon. They ached for revenge against the Yankees who had killed their comrades.

It had taken twenty minutes to reach the perimeter of the wood-fenced pastures that surrounded El Gato Negro. Lopez halted them in a small clump of trees that bordered one of the fences. He pointed to a low silhouette that stood outlined against the dark sky.

"That is the ranch house," he said softly, pointing to the bulky shape. "The path from the front door leads to the road."

The entire house was dark, except for a lighted window near the entrance.

"I guess that answers your question, Palmer," Kyle said sarcastically. "Somebody's in the house."

"I could have told you that," Palmer shot back, speaking for the first time since they had left the road.

"Who the hell is in there?" Ordile said angrily.

"I don't give a shit. They could have the whole fuckin' Cuban army in there," Rafe exploded. "They ain't keepin' us from this money."

Kyle turned and faced them. He hunkered down on his haunches, an old habit he had acquired from years in the service.

"Rafe's right . . . this don't change a thing," said Kyle. "It's the same plan I gave you on the boat. We go in three teams. Manny, you and Cliff take the right." He turned to Rafe. "Rafe, you and Vinnie take the back of the house. . . ."

"What about me, *sir*?" cut in Palmer, an edge to his voice.

Kyle stood and turned slowly toward the former officer.

"You and I will take the left, *Captain*," he said, his voice icy cold. "I am goin' to stick to you like white on rice."

The rest of the men stood and checked their gear.

"I'll be happy for the company," Palmer said through the darkness as he quietly slipped the safety off his Uzi.

"Okay, let's move out," Kyle ordered, ignoring him. "You've got ten minutes to get to your position, then get into the house any way you can."

Rafe and Vinnie slipped through the three-rail wooden fence and ran across the open pasture in that half-crouch men in combat are accustomed to using. They veered to their left and then ran straight up toward the rear of the big house.

Ordile and Lopez were next through the fence. The two men went straight up the knoll toward the ranch, running a few yards and dropping to the ground. They rose, covered a few more yards and dropped again.

Kyle tapped Palmer's shoulder and pointed to the left and the rear of the house. They would have to skirt Rafe and Vinnie's route in order to come up on the left side of the big building.

Kyle knew the man he was with was unstable. As he moved forward the rancher's adrenaline was pumping blood through his veins at a fever pitch. All his senses were honed to a fine edge. The dark, warlike visage had taken over his features, and he could once again hear the strains of martial music in his ears.

The one negative that nagged at the back of his mind, like a small rodent worrying a sack of grain, was the man at his back.

Farther up the knoll, to Kyle's right, Manny and Cliff were making good progress toward the house. The familiar odor of horse manure in the large pasture had lulled Manny into dreams of the thoroughbreds he loved.

He and Cliff were about twenty-five yards from the house and about to rise for the final sprint when a dark figure suddenly loomed up in front of them.

"Halto! Quien es?" a voice shouted in a strange, guttural Spanish.

Cliff Ordile's reactions were quicker than Manny's. He rolled onto his side, at the same time drawing his Browning 9-mm and aiming it in one motion. He squeezed off one round. There was a flat, zipping sound as the silencer did its work. The dark figure grunted as the slug struck him in the chest, and he crumpled to the ground.

The quiet lagoon rang with the angry shouts of Ortega's crew as they swarmed over the 176, looking for clues as to what had happened to their countrymen. The captain stood on the bridge of his patrol boat with his arms folded across his chest.

"Damn Yankees!" The words exploded from his lips. "I will make them pay dearly for this."

One of his crewman raised his head above the windshield of the 176's bridge.

"No one is aboard, sir," he called out to Ortega.

"This has gone far enough," the captain of the 181 said to his mate. "Radio the base and tell them what has happened. We're awaiting their orders."

Chapter 35

Rafe and Vinnie had negotiated the pasture without encountering any opposition. Now they were at the rear of the large ranch house. Seven minutes had elapsed.

They had skirted a large swimming pool and stepped onto the black-slate patio. Two huge cat statues sat on pedestals overlooking the pool and patio.

"Will you look at them suckers?" Rafe whispered, glancing up at them. "It's a good thing they're statues. I'd like to shit myself."

Vinnie seemed to be paying no attention to what the black vet was saying. He stared down at the slate beneath his feet.

"Rafe," he said softly, "you think the money is under us now? I'm so excited, I feel like I'm goin' to piss in my pants."

The two men laughed softly and moved to the set of large French doors that opened onto the patio. Rafe reached out and tried the handle. It turned grudgingly, and the door swung inward.

He looked at Vinnie and gave him a thumbs-up sign, then led the way into the darkened living room.

On the other side of the house, Kyle and Carl Palmer had found an open window and had quickly climbed through it into the kitchen. Palmer's rucksack had struck the lower part of the window and made a slight noise. The rancher turned and glared at him in the darkness. They both froze in position, waiting to see if anyone responded to the noise.

On the other side of the house, Manny Lopez and Cliff Ordile were still at the body of the sentry Cliff had shot. The ex-CIA man ran his hands over the man's uniform in the blackness, trying to find out his identity.

"Who is he?" Manny said anxiously.

"I can't tell," Cliff said. "I'm not goin' to use my light to find out."

"Leave him," said Manny. "We have to get to the house."

Not far from where Manny and Cliff had shot the sentry, Vinnie and Rafe were walking cautiously through the large Spanish-style living room.

"This is how I made my livin' before I joined the Army," whispered Vinnie.

"Jes' don' make no noise, you jive-ass honkie," said Rafe softly. He smiled in the darkness as they edged toward a hall at the far end of the room.

Kyle and Palmer moved through the kitchen toward an open door that led to a long, dark hall. Kyle had taken the safety off his Uzi and now held the weapon in the ready position. Palmer's machine gun was slung, but he carried the Browning High-Power in his right hand.

They moved through the open door into the hall, each man covering the other in the classic move-and-cover combat technique used in house-to-house fighting.

Kyle slipped down the hall, flattened himself against the rough stucco wall then waved Palmer on with his left hand. The ex-captain moved a few feet past Kyle, flattened himself against the opposite wall then waved Kyle on with his 9-mm.

There was a slight movement in one of the rooms that led off the long hall. Kyle moved past Palmer and slipped his Ka-Bar out of its scabbard. He held it ready as the muzzle of Rafe's M-203 poked into the long hall.

As the black man stepped in front of him Kyle slipped his hand over Rafe's mouth and held his knife hand to his own lips, signaling silence. Vinnie joined them a beat later, and the three men gathered behind Kyle in the dark hall.

At the end of the hall a small wooden door leaked white light at its bottom. As Kyle and the others inched closer, they could make out the muted sound of several masculine voices speaking in an unknown guttural tongue.

Manny and Cliff had reached the south wall of the ranch house, where they found an open window that had an old-fashioned sliding screen in it. They crouched beneath the casement for a short time, listening for movement from within, trying to pinpoint if there was anyone inside.

After a short time Cliff rose, slid the screen back and quietly removed it from the window. Then he slipped out of his rucksack, eased it through the opening and gently placed it on the floor of the room.

The ex-CIA man handed Manny his Uzi and then bellied over the windowsill into the darkened room. The squat Cuban handed Cliff both automatic weapons, then he, too, slipped out of his rucksack and pushed it through the window to his crew-cut partner. Then he eased over the sill and into the room.

They were in a large bedroom, dominated by a huge brass bed. In the bed were two forms covered by a white sheet. The remains of a large, round candle flickered gently in a glass dish on a long, wooden dresser.

In the dim, flickering light the two intruders could see that the forms in the bed were those of a man and woman. Ordile slid his 9-mm out of his white, loose-fitting trousers and cocked it. Manny followed suit and removed his flashlight from one of the straps on the rucksack.

As he snapped on the hooded torch the man in the bed sat upright, blinking in the light's glare.

"What . . . who . . . ?" he said sleepily, trying to stare beyond the light. The man was well-built and in his late forties. The woman, who was lying next to the bald man, emitted a little scream and sat up beside him, staring into the glare of the light. She had long, dark hair and bright black eyes that were cloudy with sleep. The large, round globes of her voluptuous breasts, with their dark nipples and areolas, were plainly visible. When she realized what was happening, she grasped wildly for the sheet that covered her legs and tried to conceal her nakedness with it.

Manny Lopez stepped forward with the light.

"Quien es?" he asked. *"Como se llama?"*

"Who the hell are you?" the man in the bed demanded in broken, guttural English. "What are you doing here? I am *tovarich*!"

"Holy shit!" blurted Ordile. "A Russian!"

The man swung his legs out of the bed and stood up. He was completely nude. Slowly he stepped to a chair by the side of the bed and picked up a lightweight dressing gown. He slipped into it as the dark-haired girl on the bed stared at the two strangers in wide-eyed terror.

"Da," the man said, tying the robe. "I am Major Pieter Kuznetsov of the Soviet Army . . . and who might you two *gentlemen* be?"

Chapter 36

Kyle stood at the door of the room at the end of the long corridor. He listened intently, trying to count the number of men in the room. As near as he could count, he could pick out three distinct voices speaking in a language he could not understand.

Finally he turned to the men gathered behind him.

"Rafe, you and Vinnie use your M16s," he whispered. "Palmer and I will cover you with the Uzis. I'm goin' to kick in the door at the count of three." He looked directly at Palmer. "Don't fire unless they fire first."

Rafe and Vinnie stepped to the side to give Kyle room. They both held their M-203s chest high, in the ready position, as Kyle raised his right leg and drove the heel of his boot into the closed door about three inches from the knob.

The splintered door flew inward with a crash. Kyle stepped to his left as Rafe and Vinnie slipped quickly into the room with leveled weapons. Kyle and Palmer followed them and spread out on either side, fingers on the triggers of their Uzis.

Seated around a table in the small room were four men. They obviously had been playing cards when Kyle had smashed through the door. Money and loose cards lay scattered across the inlaid wooden table in the center of the room. Stale smoke from the rich Cuban cigars the men were smoking hung in the air.

The card players, dressed in T-shirts and jodhpurlike trousers and boots, sat in a state of shock and stared at the four armed men who had interrupted their game. A matching tunic-type jacket hung from the back of each man's chair. One of them, a square-faced man was wearing a garrison cap with a small red star centered over the black bill. Four AK-47 assault rifles were stacked on a small leather couch under a window.

"Holy shit!" exclaimed Rafe. "Russians!"

• • •

Ten miles to the west, at a Cuban Army base named for Che Guevara, Colonel Ramon Macias had just received Captain Ortega's urgent transmission. The tall, bearded colonel removed a large cigar from his thin lips and smiled. This could not be another invasion . . . one boatload of imperialist Yankees. More likely it was a CIA assassination attempt on Fidel's life.

Whoever they are, he thought as he reached for the phone, *my men and I will make short work of them.* Most of the men in his company were tough, hardened veterans of campaigns in Africa, where they had served as advisers to rebel forces.

Macias knew the area well. He had fished the region with Fidel many times before the revolution in 1959. There were many inlets and coves in the swampy area . . . good places to make a secret landing such as this. According to Ortega's message, the Yankee bastards had found one.

A sudden thought struck the tall colonel as his orderly rang the barracks. El Gato Negro ranch was a short distance from where Ortega had found the missing 176 boat. The ranch was where the Russian pig, Kuznetsov, the missile adviser, and his mistress were billeted. He wondered if the Yankees could be after him.

No . . . He laughed and shrugged off the thought. The major was small cheese in the international game. There was no way the Americans would want the bald-headed bastard.

A short time later a jeep carrying Macias, his driver and a gunner for the mounted .50-caliber machine gun rolled through the barbed-wire gates of Base Che Guevara. They headed southeast on the road that led to the small lagoon. Behind the jeep, four uncovered trucks, each carrying thirty battle-hardened troopers dressed in olive-drab fatigues, followed Macias's vehicle at a high rate of speed.

As Macias settled back in the jumpseat of the jeep, his olive-drab fatigue cap pulled low over his eyes, the big cigar clamped in his teeth, he looked like his hero, Fidel Castro. Because of this strong resemblance, the men in his command called him Fidelito, Little Fidel, behind his back.

The colonel had risen through the ranks because of his dedication, but mainly because of his friendship with Castro. He knew now that if he could kill or capture these invaders without assistance, it would enhance his career militarily and politically.

The large living room of the ranch was now blazing with light. Major Pieter Kuznetsov and his Cuban mistress, Concetta, now fully clothed, sat next to each other on a large brown leather couch. Rafe and Vinnie stood covering them with their M16s.

In one corner of the room the four Russian guards lay bound and gagged. Their eyes were wide with terror.

Kyle stood next to Palmer near the couch, while Ordile and Lopez worked just outside the open French doors, prying up pieces of slate from the patio with the entrenching tools they had carried in their rucks.

"Tell me," Kuznetsov addressed Kyle in broken English. "Are you commandos? Or are you in the pay of the CIA and come to assassinate me?"

"Don't worry your head, Major," Kyle reassured him. "We're neither."

"Les' jes' say we're on a *treasure hunt,*" Rafe said lightly.

Vinnie chuckled, then crossed to the French doors and looked out to where Cliff and Manny were working.

"They almost got all the slate off the patio, Doc," he said to Kyle, using the nickname Kyle hated.

"We're only goin' to be here a short time," Kyle said to Kuznetsov. "If you cooperate, nobody'll get hurt."

The major gave Kyle a skeptical sneer, his thick lips barely parting. The woman, Concetta, tried to smile, but it only came through as a terror-stricken grimace on her pretty face.

"We've got a little excavatin' that shouldn't take too long," said Vinnie, laughing again.

"Rafe, Vincent," said Kyle, moving to the open doors, "break out the E.T.s from your rucks." He turned to Palmer. "Captain, you keep the major and his girlfriend company while we dig."

Rafe looked at Palmer and gave him his best "shit-eating" grin. "Sort of makes it like the Officers' Club, don't it, Captain Palmer?"

Macias's jeep pounded along the two-lane blacktop Kyle and the others had used an hour before. The men in the four trucks sat grim-faced and silent, clutching their weapons. Some of them smoked, but on the whole they sat quietly and stared at nothing.

Fidelito shouted at his driver and pointed to a small dirt road that opened up on the right.

The driver slowed the jeep and cut the wheel, careening into a dark tunnel cut through the mangrove forest. The trucks followed the jeep, their headlamps illuminating the dark road and jungle on each side.

In a matter of minutes they had covered the mile to the clearing that bordered the small lagoon. The jeep and trucks ground to a halt as the searchlights from the patrol boats picked them up.

On a command from Macias, the soldiers in the trucks leapt from the vehicles and formed up in four platoons, three deep by the side of the trucks. Each man carried a Kalashnikov AK-47 assault rifle and a machete. Two men in each platoon were armed with a Katusha rocket launcher, and each trooper carried an extra rocket for the gunner.

The mound of black dirt next to the patio was over three feet high. Down in the large hole, Rafe and Vinnie, their shirts off, chopped and dug at the stubborn earth with their entrenching tools.

Light from the living room streamed through the open doors on the patio, illuminating the men as they dug. Manny Lopez and Cliff Ordile rested on a pile of slate near the doors, watching Kyle Youngblood, who was staring down into the ever deepening hole.

"Anything yet, Rafe?" asked Kyle as the black man hoisted another shovelful of dirt onto the pile.

"Nothin', Blood," Rafe answered, wiping at the sweat running down his face and chest. "You sure that dude said the patio?"

In the brightly lit living room, Carl Palmer sat watching the Russian missile adviser and his pretty Cuban mistress with his cold blue eyes. The Browning High-Power 9-mm dangled from his hand, the blue steel conical-shaped silencer protruding from its muzzle like an obscene joke.

In the spacious cabin of the 181, Colonel Ramon Macias bit the end off a large cigar and spit it into an empty coffee can on the table. He removed a lighter from the breast pocket of his shirt and ran his thumb over the wheel. The silver lighter flamed. Macias placed it to the tip of the cigar and sucked inward. Then he blew a cloud of acrid gray smoke into the air.

Across the table, Guillermo Ortega watched the bearded colonel intently as he picked up the water-logged *Playboy* magazine that had been retrieved from the old fishing boat. Macias glanced at it and dropped it back on the table.

"I do not feel these Yankees are equipped for a lengthy stay," he said, blowing another cloud of smoke in the air.

"In any event, they will have to return to this lagoon." Ortega replied, nodding. "The 176 is their only way off the island. Should we call for an air search?"

"No," Macias said firmly. He leaned forward to emphasize his point. "They are only a small force. If we capture or annihilate them, it would be a feather in our caps."

"I agree, Colonel," Ortega said, smiling. "Our superiors would look favorably on us."

Fidelito stood, pushing his chair back. His head almost touched the overhead in the cabin.

"I will deploy my men for twenty-four hours in an ambush around the clearing near the 176," Macias said, stroking his beard. "We will wait for the Yankee bastards to return."

"Agreed," said Ortega, putting out his hand. "I will draw off to the mouth of the lagoon and block it. They will not be able to see us from the shore." The two Cuban officers shook hands across the table. "I will also put four of my seamen aboard the 176 to man her guns."

Macias smiled and pushed the big cigar into his mouth. Then he turned and mounted the ladder to the deck.

Ortega watched as the colonel's feet cleared the last rung. He shook his head and sat down. It was amazing how much the man resembled Fidel.

Chapter 37

The mound of black dirt had now grown on both sides of the patio. Kyle had stripped off the loose-fitting white shirt and joined Rafe in the hole. The light from the living room cast odd shadows on the two men, making the sweat on their muscular torsos glisten. The various shrapnel scars and bullet wounds the rancher had acquired over his twenty years of military service were clearly visible.

Ordile and Manny Lopez were sitting quietly, looking at the large Grecian pool, while Vinnie ran his hand over one of the cat statues. Rafe Phillips drove his shovel blade into the packed earth at the bottom of the hole.

There was the harsh scraping sound of metal on metal. Rafe and Kyle both stopped digging. Vinnie turned and looked at the men in the hole as Cliff and Manny rose and crossed to where Kyle stood staring at Rafe.

It was as if time stood still under the dark Cuban sky. No insects chirped, no dogs barked. It was a sound that heralded the answer to all their dreams and fantasies.

"Oh, shit," said Rafe softly, turning to Kyle. "I hit somethin' with my E.T."

He threw his tool out of the hole and dropped to his knees, clawing at the clammy earth with his hands. Kyle crowded in behind him, trying to see what it was he had found.

As Vinnie, Manny and Cliff watched Rafe, they could see his hands smooth the dirt away from what looked like the top of a large metal box. The black man outlined the rectangular lid with his fingers and then brushed the loose earth away with the palms of his hands. He leaned back from the waist up so that his buttocks rested on the heels of both feet.

The black metal rectangle in front of him was inscribed in gold letters that read:

CASINO
VILLA DE CAPRI
HAVANA, CUBA

Kyle peered over his shoulder.

"That's it, Rafe!" he said, the excitement creeping into his voice. "That's it! Get it the hell out of there."

Vinnie jumped into the opposite side of the hole and helped Rafe dig away the earth on both sides of the metal box. When there was room to reach in, he and Rafe grasped the metal rings attached to each side of the box.

With a great deal of effort they tore the chest from the imprisoning earth and hoisted it over the side of the hole onto the loose dirt at the side of the patio. The five men stared at the object they had come so far to find. It seemed as if none of them wanted to make the first move toward the footlocker-size chest.

"Open it up!" Surprisingly, Lopez was the first to speak.

His voice seemed to work as a catalyst on the others. Rafe and Kyle scrambled out of the hole, followed by Vinnie. All five men crowded around the chest, looking down at it. A large padlock hung from the hasp on the front of the box; it was all that barred their way to the dream.

No one moved. It was as if they were afraid to open it.

"Gimme the crowbar!" Rafe demanded. Ordile reached down and picked up the short metal bar. He handed it to Rafe, who dropped to his knees in front of the chest.

Rafe slid the straight beveled end of the crowbar under the hasp and applied pressure. There was a loud crack as the welded joint that held the hasp in place ripped out of the chest.

Kyle stepped forward and placed his hand on the lid. With a quick movement he flipped it back. The hinges made a squeaking sound.

There, in the stark, bright light of the living room, lay rack upon rack of black one-hundred-dollar casino chips, gleaming up at them mockingly from the open box. Each tray held a thousand dollars' worth of chips. In 1959, at the Capri, the contents of the chest was worth millions, but now they were worthless pieces of plastic.

Each man reacted in his own way. Manny Lopez seemed to sag visibly. Cliff Ordile turned away and walked to the pile of slate and sat down. Vinnie Troiano kicked at the dirt sullenly as Kyle stood with a stunned expression on his face.

Suddenly Rafe reached out and violently snatched a tray of the black chips from the top layer. There were more trays of chips underneath.

The black man leapt to his feet, his shiny face contorted with rage. He drew back his arm and fired the tray he was holding into the box with such force that they scattered over the ground.

"*Chips . . . chips!*" he roared. "Un-fuckin'-believable!"

In the living room, Carl Palmer, unaware of what had happened out on the patio, sat looking morosely at Kuznetsov and his Cuban mistress. As Rafe threw the tray of chips into the chest, it had made a clacking sound as it hit, causing the ex-captain to turn and look through the open doors.

The Russian officer, seeing his chance, bolted for the doorway that led into the hall. Palmer heard the swift movement behind him. He turned to see the bald man almost across the room.

"Son of a bitch!" shouted Palmer, snapping two shots at the fleeing Kuznetsov. The Browning made a peculiar zipping sound as both slugs found their mark.

The first shot struck the major in the upper back, lodging near his heart and causing a massive internal hemorrhage. The second bullet struck higher, severing the spine near the fifth vertebrae, causing immediate paralysis. The Russian officer felt his legs disappear, and then he was driven forward into the wall. He bounced off it, then fell facedown on the inlaid wooden floor.

Concetta saw the bright blossoms of blood appear on the back of her lover's white shirt. She leapt to her feet in panic and started toward the open patio doors.

"*Madre de Dios!*" She screamed as she ran.

Palmer spun and fired point-blank at the screaming woman. The slug hit her between the shoulder blades and drove her through the doors, onto the patio at the feet of Kyle and the others.

Ordile looked down at the woman who had fallen at his feet. He knelt and turned her over. Then he put two fingers on the pulse in her neck. There was none.

Kyle was the first to reach Palmer as he was bending over Kuznetsov's body.

"What happened?" Kyle demanded.

"He made a break for it," said Palmer, rising. "I shot him."

Before any of the other men could move, Kyle hit Palmer with a devastating right-hand punch that lifted the ex-captain off the floor and deposited him next to his victim.

"We don't need a goddamn body count here, Palmer!" railed Kyle, a terrifying black look on his face. "I don't know what this one is going to cost."

Palmer looked at Kyle sullenly, rubbing the side of his face where Kyle's fist had struck him. A thin trickle of blood ran from the corner of the ex-captain's mouth.

On the other side of the room, the four Russian guards looked on in wide-eyed terror, not knowing what their fate was going to be now that their major had been killed.

"All for a bunch of worthless fuckin' chips," said Rafe, dropping onto the couch.

"Forget it," Ordile said loudly. "We'd better haul our asses out of here before daylight. We're runnin' late."

"You're right," said Kyle, turning as Palmer got to his feet. "Rafe, you and Vinnie dig that hole a little deeper. We got three bodies to bury now . . . thanks to the captain."

"Why bury 'em?" said Ordile, moving to Kyle's side as Rafe and Vinnie exited the patio. "We could just leave 'em and beat it."

Kyle walked over to Kuznetsov's body and lifted it to his shoulder.

"I want everything back the way we found it," he grunted. "If they have to search for the major . . . that takes time."

"What about them?" asked Cliff, jerking his thumb in the direction of Russian guards.

"Hide 'em, so it'll take a while to find 'em," answered Kyle. "By that time we'll be long gone." He turned to Palmer, who was still rubbing his jaw. "Unless the *captain* wants to use 'em for target practice."

Rafe and Vinnie were in the large hole working furiously to make it deep enough to accommodate the bodies of Palmer's two victims and the sentry Ordile had shot. Manny Lopez knelt by the body of Concetta, praying softly. He had put her on her back and crossed her arms across her chest. She looked as if she were asleep.

Vinnie drove the blade of his shovel deep into the bottom of the hole. There was another sound of metal striking metal as he hit something.

"What the fuck was that?" said Rafe, who stopped chopping at the black dirt.

"Another box?" said Vinnie, dropping to his knees and clawing at the dirt.

"Kyle! Kyle!" Rafe shouted toward the open doors. *"We found another box!"*

Kyle, followed by Ordile and Palmer, came through the doors onto the patio. Manny Lopez rose from where he had been keeping a vigil next to the body of Concetta. The men surrounded the hole and watched as Vinnie and Rafe freed the black metal chest from the earth and handed it up to them. The same inscription, in gold, was on the lid.

Vinnie drove the blade of his E.T. into the soft earth that had been under the second box. Again there was the scrape of metal on metal.

"There's another one down here!" he said, his voice high with excitement. Rafe dropped down next to him, and together they dug the box out of the ground with their hands.

Kyle and Cliff Ordile took the chest from them and set it next to the first two. They were identical in size, shape and color.

Rafe and Vinnie pulled themselves out of the hole and joined the others around the new find.

"Gimme the crowbar," Rafe said resignedly. "I'll try it again."

Lopez handed him the metal bar. Rafe dropped to his knees in front of the chest, inserted the end and popped off the hasp and padlock.

"Probably more chips," Palmer said sarcastically.

Rafe stood and flipped the metal lid back with the toe of his boot. The top flipped over with a creaking noise, and there it was: stacks of twenties, fifties, hundreds, five hundreds, even thousands, lying in neat little bundles. They were all wrapped with orange paper bands, citing the amount of money each packet held.

The black man stood staring down at the bonanza. His mouth worked but nothing came out. His eyes filled and tears streamed down his dark cheeks.

Nobody moved. It was as if they were afraid the money would disappear if they touched it.

Cliff Ordile was the first to react. He reached into the chest and took out three bundles of bills and started to toss them like a juggler.

Manny Lopez and Vinnie hooked arms and did a crude version of the Mexican hat dance on the packed dirt of the patio while Carl Palmer looked hungrily at the rest of the bundles in the box.

Kyle took the short crowbar out of Rafe's hand and knelt in front of the chest that was still padlocked. He inserted the end of the bar and popped off the hasp and lock. The rancher set the end of the crowbar under the lid and flipped it back.

The results were the same: neat stacks of bills lying row upon green row, framed by the metal rectangle. It was as pretty a picture as any of them would ever see.

"*Payday!*" shouted Rafe. "Pay-mothafuckin'-day!" he said again softly as he dropped to his knees and grabbed bundles of bills and hugged them to his chest and face. Some of them fell to the ground and broke open, scattering like expensive green leaves on the dark earth.

Kyle rose and turned toward Palmer, who was staring almost glassy-eyed at the two chests full of money.

"How much do you think?" Kyle asked dazedly.

"Twenty-five, thirty million," Palmer speculated with a trace of a smile on his bruised lips.

"God bless Señor Palermo . . . wherever he may be," intoned Manny, running his hand over the stacks of bills in the second chest.

"I doubt if Big Tony's with God," said Ordile, his voice full of meaning. "But our asses may be . . . if we don't get out of here soon."

Chapter 38

Macias had placed his men well. Half of his command had set up in the mangroves along the outer edge of the clearing and dock where the 176 was still tied up. A man from Ortega's boat was in each of the .50-caliber gun rings. Two more were manning the .76-mm cannon on the foredeck.

The other half of Macias's men were dispersed around the other side of the lagoon, so that they would have cross fields of fire. Anyone caught in the deadly killing zone would be cut to pieces.

Ortega's boat had pulled back to the mouth of the lagoon, as he had suggested, but his guns were still within easy range of the perimeter in the jungle glade. Macias had placed his jeep, with its .50-caliber machine gun, in an advantageous position on the edge of the clearing. They had a clear field of fire at anyone coming from the road.

Macias sat in the jumpseat of the vehicle, contemplating the glowing tip of his ever present cigar. He dreamed of the glory this victory would bring him . . . possibly another medal from Fidel, or a change of command. He placed the cigar between his lips and drew inward. The tip glowed cherry-red in the pitch black before dawn. He removed the cigar and blew a large cloud of gray smoke into the moist night air.

The bodies of Kuznetsov, Concetta and the Russian sentry had been buried beneath the black slate of the patio. Rafe, Vinnie, Ordile and Lopez had just put the last slate in place and were tamping it down with the heels of their boots as Kyle swept the excess dirt off the black surface.

"Jefe," Lopez said, turning to Kyle, "the bodies are buried. The guards have been locked in the old smokehouse. All is back in place."

"Okay . . . thanks, Manny," said Kyle. He tapped Vinnie on

the arm. "Vincent, get me the two big duffel bags. They're in my rucksack." He looked at Rafe. "Rafer, arm the Claymoors and put two in each bag after we load the money."

As Kyle stepped into the brightly lit living room Carl Palmer looked up from the long wooden table, where he had stacked the packets of bills. The rancher blinked. He had not seen so much money in one place at any time in his life. The riches did not concern him, nor what the money could buy him personally. What it did mean was that it would give him a better-than-average chance to get the man who had wiped out his family.

"What's the count?" asked Kyle as Palmer turned back to the table.

"A little under thirty million," the ex-officer said coolly. "About twenty-eight six, to be exact."

Kyle whistled as Rafe and the others came through the open doors.

"Load half the money into each bag and place one Claymoor in the middle and one on top," said Kyle as Vinnie removed two rectangular M.A.s and the det cord from the duffel bag he was holding.

"Be careful with those sumbitches," said Ordile.

"No sweat," Vinnie answered as he and Rafe began to stuff the money in the watertight bags. "They're not set for the remote . . . yet."

"What does it say on the mine?" Lopez asked as he watched Rafe and Vinnie load the money into the large bags.

"Front . . . toward enemy." Kyle said in a voice a student might use in reciting a rehearsed speech in class.

"You bet your boody . . . *toward enemy,*" said Vinnie, placing the second Claymoor inside the filled bag. "Whoever's in front of one of these babies when they detonate gets seven hundred little steel balls shoved up his ass."

Palmer stood, shrugged into his rucksack and slung his Uzi onto his shoulder. He looked directly at Kyle.

"What's the purpose of putting the mines with the money, Youngblood?" he asked, heading for the door.

Kyle picked up his rucksack and slid his arms through the straps.

"It's an insurance policy, Palmer," he said evenly. "If we don't get the money, then nobody's goin' to get it."

Chapter 39

The sun had risen on the eastern horizon when Kyle and Manny Lopez turned their bikes off the two-lane blacktop into the thick mangrove forest near the hidden lagoon. The others were huddled in a small circle around the two bags of money, waiting for them.

As the two arrivals dumped their mopeds into the thick undergrowth with the other bikes, the men rose and waited for Manny and Kyle to join them.

"God!" said Ordile. "I can't believe how smooth this thing has gone."

"It's not over yet," said Kyle. "Not till we're back in Key West."

Manny Lopez took the point, with Kyle directly behind him. The others strung out on the trail, some with their weapons slung, the rest holding them loosely in their hands.

Rafe and Vinnie each carried one of the large duffel bags over their shoulders. The rear part of the bag sat on their rucksacks. As they moved through the heavy forest Manny Lopez turned to Kyle.

"This is a beautiful land, is it not?" the Cuban said.

"I haven't seen many prettier," Kyle answered, looking around.

"I love this island," Manny said, pushing forward. "I don't want to leave. This is my Cuba."

"Maybe you'll be able to come back someday," Kyle mused. He shifted the straps of his rucksack where they were cutting into his shoulders.

It had all gone pretty easily, he thought, except for the skirmish with the patrol boat and the Russian major. In the end it would work out better, using the faster vessel to get back to the *Pet-o-Gold*.

Bright sunlight was trying to cut through the interlaced mangrove branches when they reached the tree where Kyle had cached the six-man raft and outboard motor. The party stopped at the base of the large tree. Ordile reached out and started to untie the rope lashed to the trunk.

"Leave it," said Kyle. "There's no need for it now. No sense carryin' extra weight."

They left the tree and pushed on behind Manny toward the patrol boat, the lagoon and home.

A few minutes later Manny Lopez, followed by Kyle, broke out of the mangrove forest at the edge of the clearing. The squat Cuban stepped into the open and stopped. He stared at the 176, still tied to the old dock. Everything seemed in place, yet there was something that didn't seem right.

Kyle felt it too. There was something that made the hairs at the base of his neck prickle. He had felt it in 'Nam, when a V.C. attack on his position was imminent.

As Vinnie pushed out of the jungle behind him, Kyle's face took on the dark look of war, and he started to drop into a crouch as Lopez turned and saw him slip the safety off his Uzi.

"Is anything wrong?" Manny asked, the alarm evident in his voice.

Before Kyle could answer, the distinctive stutter of a dozen AK-47s rent the early-morning quiet. The .50-calibers on the 176 joined in with a staccato popping sound.

Manny Lopez grimaced, then looked at Kyle with a surprised expression on his face as the first rounds from the 7.62-mm automatic rifles stitched across his chest and stomach. Bright red blood gushed from his nose and mouth, staining the white campesino shirt he was wearing.

The Cuban dropped the Uzi he was holding and crumpled to the ground as the fire from the jungle's edge intensified. Bullets clipped leaves, and pieces of wood and bark chipped off the mangroves as the other men in Macias's command poured heavy fire in on the Americans.

Kyle crawled to Manny, who was lying on his face in the dirt. Rafe and Vinnie opened up, pumping grenades from the M-203s into the line of trees on the far side of the clearing. There were small explosions of orange flame, followed by black smoke.

The fire from the line of trees seemed to slacken a bit, then intensified once more. Ordile crawled to Kyle's side. He got his Uzi into firing position behind a log and opened up on the two men at the exposed 76-mm cannon on the foredeck of the 176.

One of the men took a shot to the head. He screamed and toppled backward into the brackish water of the lagoon. The other man tried to feed the gun and fire it by himself. The Uzi's fierce fusillade of lead cut him down before he could bring the gun to bear.

Kyle felt for a pulse in Manny's neck. It was very faint, but it was there. He turned the wounded man on his side as a Katusha rocket splintered a tree twenty yards to their right.

Manny groaned as Kyle moved him. Blood was still running from his nose and mouth. The Cuban tried to speak, but only bubbles of frothy blood appeared on his lips. He raised one hand and pointed back through the forest.

"Beach . . ." he said, gasping, "Not far . . . you can make it."

"Easy, Manny, easy . . ." said Kyle softly as he slipped a couple of grenades out of the Cuban's rucksack. The wounded man reached out and picked up a handful of the moist soil.

"It is okay, Jefe." He smiled. "It is okay . . ."

A gurgling sound issued from his throat, and he rolled back on his face, dead. Kyle rose to one knee as Palmer slipped out of the jungle and joined the small knot of men behind the log.

Kyle pulled the pins on the grenades he was holding and hurled them at the invisible enemy at the jungle's edge. Then he dropped down behind the log.

"Nice of you to join us, Captain," he said to Palmer, who was now firing his Uzi in the general direction of the 176.

Vinnie and Rafe were laying down heavy fire with their M16s, the snap of the rifles mixed with the stutter of the Kalashnikovs to make a deadly cacophony of sound. Ordile kept raising up and spraying the line of trees with his Uzi, trying to suppress the heavy fire that was chewing the jungle around them to pieces.

Macias crouched behind his jeep. His driver and gunner had been killed by one of the grenades from Rafe's M-203. The colonel cursed the dumb luck of the Yankees. He would have had them all, but his men on the other side of the clearing had started to fire too soon. He had seen one of the invaders go down, but the others had regrouped and kept up a heavy fire with automatic weapons and grenades.

The tall colonel knew that he could not annihilate the Americans in the position they held at the present time, even with his superior firepower. He would have to attack and overrun the Yankee's location. Macias looked up and down the line of trees, where his men were pouring hot fire on the intruders.

He stood behind his jeep and put the metal whistle to his lips. Fidelito blew one shrill blast, and the men in his command stood as one and started to move forward, firing their weapons as they crossed into the clearing.

"What the fuck happened?" yelled Rafe as he fired his M16 at the advancing Cubans.

"Lopez is dead," Kyle answered, swinging the Uzi and squeezing the trigger. He watched as two men in olive-drab fatigues fell on the marshy ground. "They must have found the boat."

Vinnie was pumping grenades from his M-203 as the Cubans came out of the mangroves. The *crump crump* of the metal cylinders as they hit were paralleled by geysers of smoke and flame.

Men were dying as they advanced across the clearing toward the stubborn fire that was decimating them from behind the fallen log.

"Kyle," shouted Vinnie, his M16 snapping like an angry dog at the men in the clearing, "they're gettin' closer. I wish we had brought one of those M-60s with us."

Kyle was firing his Uzi with one hand, taking time out to pull the pin on a grenade and toss it almost point-blank into the advancing Cubans. He smiled as one of the smooth-skinned canisters blew two men into the air. Then he rolled on his back to slap a new magazine into his snub-nosed submachine gun.

"If we can slow them up . . ." Kyle gasped. "Manny said there's a beach through there." He jerked his thumb up the trail they had just come through. "We may be able to launch the raft."

The Fidelistas, urged on by Macias, were inching closer to the Americans. Many of them were down, either dead or dying, but still they came on. A heavy pall of smoke hung over the lagoon, giving it an eerie appearance.

"How are we goin' to hold 'em, Youngblood?" screamed Ordile. "Them fucker's are comin' in."

Kyle pulled one of the duffel bags full of money toward him. Swiftly he unstrapped the bag as a Katusha rocket hit high in a tree ten yards from them. Pieces of burning branches fell on the defenders. Black smoke billowed as the mangrove forest started to burn.

Kyle reached into the bag and pulled out the Claymoor mine and detonator cord. The clacker was taped to the cord. Kyle handed the first mine to Vinnie. Then he plunged his hand into the bag again and felt around the packets of bills. His fingers wrapped around the second M.A. and pulled it out.

"Vinnie," he said quickly, "you and Cliff set the M.A.s up by the log and pull back. Palmer will cover you with his Uzi."

"Where are you going to be?" asked the ex-captain, firing his submachine gun at the advancing Cubans.

"Rafe and I will get the raft and motor," said Kyle, firing at a group of Cubans to his left. "When I send Rafe back for you, set off the Claymoors and get your asses back down the trail."

Both Cliff and Vinnie nodded and kept firing at the slowly advancing Cubans, who were now seeking cover in the open field.

Rafe picked up both duffel bags and took off at a trot down the trail. Kyle gave Palmer a thumbs-up and took off after the black vet. The ex-captain waited a couple of seconds, then slipped into the jungle and followed the two men down the trail.

Vinnie spread the short metal legs on the Claymoors and set one on each side of the log. He knew that the seven hundred steel balls in each one would fire out in a fan-shaped pattern, hitting anyone in the target area.

Cliff Ordile was keeping up a heavy fire with his Uzi, trying to keep the Cubans at bay, but as the fire slackened, the tough veterans under Macias's command took heart and came on again.

Vinnie ran the det cord from both mines back into the jungle. He looked around for the first time and was surprised to see that he and Ordile were alone. The stocky Italian was sure Kyle had told Palmer to stay and give them supporting fire.

He looked back at the clearing. There were eighty to a hundred men moving toward them. He prayed he had positioned the Claymoors right.

Vinnie reached down and picked up a short stick. He threw it at Ordile, who was slipping a new magazine into his Uzi.

The stick struck the ex-CIA man in the back, and he turned. Vinnie waved him toward the opening in the mangroves with the hand that held the clacker.

Cliff got to his feet and started to move toward Vinnie in a hunched-over, running gait. A quick, stuttering volley from an Ak-47 stitched across his back. He threw up his arms and fell sprawling in the marshy soil. One of the rounds had pierced his heart. He was dead before he hit the ground.

Vinnie watched the gray crew-cut man for an instant. There was no movement in his arms and legs. He remembered what Kyle had said on the boat. Even if he was wounded, they would have to leave him.

He held the clacker tightly in his hand as he watched the advancing men in the killing ground. Vinnie had set many M.A.s in Vietnam with trip wires but had never used one on "command detonate."

He took a deep breath and activated the clacker. The electronic spark ignited the pound of C-4 explosive in each Claymoor, and fourteen hundred steel balls were propelled toward the advancing enemy in a deadly fan-shaped pattern.

There were two sharp, loud explosions, followed by a whirring sound as the balls flew through the air at tremendous velocity. Most of the men in the fan-shaped area were struck in the legs and stomach because the M.A.s had been set at a low angle.

Vinnie stared at the carnage the mines had wrought. Many of the Cubans were down, their legs and torsos shredded by the metal pellets. The wounded men screamed and groaned in agony, reaching supplicating hands toward the sky.

About thirty of Macias's command were left on their feet, too stunned to fire their weapons. They stood frozen in place, looking down at their dead and dying comrades.

The tall colonel had been one of the lucky ones, moving forward on the far right of the killing ground. When the mines had gone off in the faces of his men, Macias had thrown himself flat, clawing into the marshy earth.

Now he got stiffly to his feet and surveyed his dazed and bloody troops. Somehow he knew that he would have to rally the men he had remaining, and he started to move toward them.

Both Rafe and Kyle heard the blast as the two Claymoors decimated the Cuban soldiers in the clearing. The sound of hurried footsteps made them turn.

Carl Palmer was moving up the trail toward them at a rapid rate. He carried his Uzi across his chest.

"I told you to stay with Cliff and Vinnie," said Kyle coldly. "They needed covering fire."

"They're okay," snapped Palmer, breathing hard. "Where's your raft?"

Kyle turned his back on the ex-captain and looked at Rafe. "Go back and get Vinnie and Cliff," he said. "Be careful."

"Gotcha, Blood," said Rafe, setting down the duffel bags and giving Kyle a dap handshake. Then he turned to Palmer.

"You still doin' the same ol' shit, Captain? I guess the leopard don't change his spots."

He unslung his M-203 and took off down the trail toward the lagoon at a fast trot.

When the survivors of Macias's four platoons realized there was no one firing at them from behind the log, they regrouped and started to advance again, at a much slower pace this time. Some of them raised their weapons and fired sporadically at the invisible enemy near the trail's opening.

Vinnie, from his vantage point near Cliff Ordile's body, saw them coming. He pumped five rounds in quick succession from his grenade launcher at the oncoming ranks of Cubans. He heard the satisfying crump as the grenades exploded. Then he picked up his rucksack and started for the opening in the mangroves.

The seaman on the .50-caliber gun aboard the 176 caught a flash of white in the dense green and brown of the jungle. He swung the barrel of the heavy weapon toward the point, pulled the cocking lever, and squeezed the trigger.

A stream of white-hot tracers spewed from the gun's muzzle. The distinctive chirp and pop could be heard above the stutter of the AK-47s, like a familiar dog's bark in a pack of hounds.

As Vinnie reached the line of trees he stopped to shrug into his rucksack. The pause was fatal. It was then that the stream of tracers found him.

The impact of the .50-caliber slugs knocked Vinnie flat on his face. He felt a searing, burning pain in the center of his back. The handsome Italian coughed weakly, and a gout of blood issued from his mouth and stained the dark earth beneath him.

He had dropped the rucksack when he was hit, but he still clung to the M-203 with his other hand. His whole left side felt numb. He tried to raise his left hand and couldn't.

A cold fear clutched his innards. He was going to die . . . here in this strange place. He would never be rich, never have the things he wanted. Kyle's words rang in his ears: "Any wounded will be left behind. We'll be movin' fast . . . wounded slow us down."

Again the fear swept over him like a wave. He heard the sound of footsteps. He tried to see who it was, but his eyes wouldn't focus. Then he was looking into Rafe's shiny black face.

"Hey, wop," Rafe said softly. "What'd you do to yourself, man?"

Vinnie tried to speak, but the blood in his throat garbled the words. Some rounds from the AK-47s clipped the foliage over their heads.

The Cubans were inching closer. Rafe could hear them calling to each other in Spanish as they came nearer.

"*Cuidado!*" one of them yelled in alarm. Then there was a short burst of automatic fire.

Rafe knelt next to the critically wounded Vinnie.

"I'm goin' to take you with me, bro," he said, grasping the young mate under the arms and lifting him onto his shoulders. As he did so, Vinnie groaned in pain and dropped the M-203. Immediately Rafe's white campesino shirt was drenched with blood from Vinnie's gaping wounds.

The black vet rose to his feet and hefted the inert body, to better seat it on his shoulders. Then he took off up the trail toward where he hoped Kyle and Palmer would be waiting.

The six-man raft and motor were where they had left them. Kyle untied the rope and lowered the bulky package to the ground. He removed his rucksack and tied the small, powerful outboard motor across the top of it. Then he shrugged back into the straps. The self-inflating raft was in a large carrying bag with handles.

Carl Palmer stood watching him. The two big duffel bags full of money were at his feet.

"As soon as Vinnie and Rafe get here with Ordile," Kyle said, hefting the raft/bag in one hand and his Uzi in the other. "The two younger guys can carry the dough. You can cover the rear."

"Where do you figure this beach is?" asked Palmer, fingering the trigger of his Uzi.

Kyle put the raft down and pointed at a spot to the left of the trail facing the lagoon.

"Manny pointed in that direction," he said. "I figure it's got to be up the shoreline from the spot where we docked the boat . . . maybe a quarter of a mile."

There was a crashing sound down the trail. Both men raised their submachine guns as Rafe, carrying the nearly unconscious Vinnie, came into view.

"What happened?" said Kyle, rushing to him as he lay the young mate gently on the ground.

"Ordile's dead," said Rafe breathlessly. "So are a lot of Cubans." He paused. "Vinnie's hit pretty bad."

Kyle felt for a pulse in Vinnie's neck. It was weak.

"Rafe, it's no good, he said, shaking his head. "We've got to leave him. We all agreed."

Vinnie opened his glazed eyes and looked at Rafe's sweat-streaked face. He shook his head weakly from side to side and mumbled incoherently.

Rafe stood and looked at Kyle beseechingly.

"Blood," he said in a tone that held a world of meaning. "You know I never went against you. . . ."

Palmer slipped the 9-mm, sans the silencer, out of his waistband, and offered it to Kyle.

"Kill the kid and let's go," he said with an air of finality.

The rancher looked at him for a beat, his black eyes glaring into Palmer's malevolent blue stare. A crashing noise and the sound of bodies moving through the forest made both men turn back toward the lagoon.

"Not this time, *Captain*!" said Kyle. He turned to the black vet. "Pick him up, Rafe."

Chapter 40

The surviving members of Colonel Ramon Macias's command moved cautiously up the trail toward the raft/tree. The men at the point of the column slipped from tree to tree, watching for any movement that might signify an ambush.

One of the men, in the center of the trail, spotted something on the ground. He approached it carefully. It was olive drab in color and had straps attached to it. The man stood his ground, fearing the Yankees had set a booby trap with a satchel charge.

The two other men joined him. One of them picked up a heavy stick and threw it at Carl Palmer's discarded rucksack. The stick struck it with enough force to set it off, had it been booby-trapped.

The other troopers came up and stood around it. One of them poked it with his machete. Another used the muzzle of his AK-47 to turn it over. Satisfied that it was okay, the man with the machete hacked it open. Palmer's extra C-rations, toilet paper, socks, and spare ammunition was all that they found.

Palmer had dropped the rucksack so that he could sling one of the big money bags across his back. He carried the other duffel in his left hand, and the Uzi in his right.

Rafe had placed the unconscious Vinnie over his left shoulder and grasped his M-203 by the handle in front of the trigger guard. Kyle lugged the bag holding the six-man raft as if it were a heavy suitcase. He held the Uzi tightly in his right hand.

They had broken into the forest at a spot in back of the raft/tree, taking the direction Manny Lopez had indicated. Kyle was at the point, using his body to break through the heavy undergrowth. Palmer was next in line, struggling under the weight of the two duffel bags.

Rafe brought up the rear, listening to Vinnie's uneven breathing as he struggled through the jungle. The black man tried to keep his gait as smooth as possible so as not to injure his wounded comrade any further. It was nearly impossible in the heavy brush.

A short distance behind them, Macias had gathered around him the thirty-three able-bodied men left from his four platoons. One of the men, who had tracked wild pigs in the Zapata Peninsula, was brought forward.

"See if you can locate the direction the bastards took," he said to the soldier.

The man started to circle the tree, looking into the tangle of moss, tree limbs, and vines. He had not gone ten steps when he found the spot where Kyle had broken into the jungle.

The soldier knelt and picked up some broken vines and branches. He looked at them closely and put them to his nose.

"Colonel," he said brusquely, pointing toward the trampled area, "this way!"

Macias waved his arm at the men on his right.

"Vamanos, muchachos!" he shouted. *"Rapido!"* The men melted quickly into the jungle. The tall colonel waved an arm at the remaining troops. *"Rapido, muchachos!"* He shouted again and followed his men as they slipped silently into the jungle to the left of the torn area Kyle and the others had used.

Once in the heavy undergrowth, the Fidelistas moved swiftly, using their machetes to good advantage. The first column headed toward the right, trying to get ahead of the fleeing Americans. The second column was cutting its way above the Yankees, in order to close in behind them.

A short distance ahead of the encircling columns, Kyle was bulling his way through the heavy brush. Palmer, directly behind him, was laboring badly and gasping for breath. Rafe was not in as bad a way, but he was staggering under Vinnie's one hundred and eighty pounds of dead weight.

"Youngblood . . ." The ex-captain gasped. "Got to stop . . . can't go on."

Kyle swung the raft/bag, clearing away some vines.

"If we stop, we're dead," he said, gasping for air himself.

Palmer threw down one of the duffel bags and fell on it. Rafe nearly tripped over him. He dropped on one knee.

"Les' take a minute, Blood," he said with a wheeze, slipping Vinnie off his shoulders and looking at him. "We could use it."

Kyle stopped and turned. He was perspiring profusely. The rancher dropped the canvas bag with the raft and sat on it.

"How is he, Rafe?" he asked softly.

The black man wiped some of the blood off the corner of Vinnie's mouth with the sleeve of his shirt.

"Not good," Rafe said, shaking his head.

"He's a dead man," Palmer whined. "What good does it do to carry a dead man? He only slows us down. You could carry one of the duffel bags."

"Shut the fuck up!" Rafe hissed, his face contorted with rage.

"We don't even know if we're going in the right direction," Palmer whined again, the panic evident in his voice.

Before either Kyle or Rafe could answer the man, there was a slight sound and movement in the forest ahead of Kyle. He spun and crouched behind the large canvas bag, bringing his Uzi up and pointing it in that direction.

About ten feet in front of Kyle, one of the Cuban soldiers appeared out of the jungle. He was about to swing his machete at an overhanging vine when a burst from the rancher's Uzi cut him down.

Immediately another Fidelista took his place, leveling his AK-47 at the three men crouching in front of him. Before he could pull the trigger, Rafe dropped him with a round from his M16.

There was more movement on either side of them. Rafe gently lifted Vinnie's unconscious body to his shoulder and got to his feet. Palmer grabbed the duffel bags; at the same time he turned his Uzi on a thrashing sound in the brush on his right. The wood and creepers splintered as they were struck by the rounds from the submachine gun, and the thrashing stopped.

"Les' get the hell outa here!" shouted Kyle, picking up the raft/bag as he smashed into the jungle a bit to the right of where the dead Cuban soldier lay.

The rancher swung the big canvas bag, trying to clear a path through the heavy undergrowth. He could hear movement in the jungle all around them now.

A Fidelista appeared magically out of the dense green foliage. He fired his Kalishnikov point-blank at Palmer. Fortunately the rounds struck the big duffel bag strapped to the ex-captain's back. The stacks of greenbacks absorbed the impact of the slugs and did not reach Palmer's body.

Kyle wheeled and shot the man with a short burst from his Uzi. The Cuban screamed once and threw up his arms. Then he disappeared into the verdant green carpet of the jungle floor.

Another soldier leapt out of a clump of mangroves as Kyle passed. He brought his machete down heavily on Kyle's back, slicing into the rancher's rucksack. Kyle turned and struck the man across the face with his Uzi, breaking his cheekbone and jaw and knocking him unconscious.

Not far behind them, Ramon Macias could hear the short bursts of gunfire. He knew his men had made contact with the Americans, and that soon he would have them.

In a nightmare battle, fighting the jungle as much as the Cuban soldiers who were trying to cut them off, Kyle, Rafe and Palmer struggled steadily toward the shoreline. Behind them they left a string of dead and dying Fidelistas.

Kyle, at point, thought he saw a flash of blue through the matted mangroves and vines. The next minute he had broken out of the line of trees and onto a short crescent of golden sand, edged by the greenish-blue waters of the Gulf of Batabano.

Kyle sprawled on the sand, gasping for air, as Palmer staggered onto the beach and fell beside him. Kyle had been nicked twice in the side and shoulder by rounds from the AK-47s.

Palmer had not been hit, but his face and arms had been deeply gashed by sharp branches and thorns. His campesino shirt and trousers, as well as Kyle's, had been torn to shreds by the heavy plant growth.

There was movement to their right, and both men pointed their Uzis in that direction. Rafe, who was bleeding heavily from a machete slash across his right forearm, wobbled onto the sand and fell to his knees. He set Vinnie gently on his back, then collapsed beside him, breathing heavily, his white shirt and trousers soaked with the blood of the man he had been carrying.

Bright sunlight bathed the beach and made the three men squint after the dim passage through the mangrove forest. Kyle was the first to move. He sat up and looked at the gulf, shimmering in the early-morning sunlight.

Kyle turned to Palmer and Rafe, but before he could speak, the stutter of an AK-47 echoed from the jungle, and a row of neat little explosions of sand stitched across the top of the dune behind which they were lying.

Rafe and Kyle crawled to the top of the ridge of sand and started shooting into the thick growth of trees. Palmer crawled toward them firing his Uzi.

The fusillade from the line of trees became heavier. Little geysers of sand spurted up around them and across the top of the dune.

Kyle turned to Rafe, who was pumping the last of his grenades from the M-203 launcher into the massed mangroves.

"Cover me," he shouted. "I'm goin' to inflate the raft."

The rancher crawled back to the raft/bag and pulled it to him. He glanced over at Vinnie, who was lying on his back with his eyes closed. He didn't look good.

Kyle turned from the sorely wounded man and peered at the blue-green gulf lapping the beach. It looked to be about seventy-five yards away.

He grasped the large canvas bag by its handles and inhaled deeply. Then he rose and took off in a zigzagging sprint toward the water. The rucksack and outboard motor pounded crazily against his back and neck as he ran through the sand.

The Cubans in the jungle saw Kyle stand and started to fire their weapons, bracketing him with little spurts of sand as he moved toward the water. Kyle dropped to the beach and crawled the last ten yards to the water.

Rafe had pumped the last of his grenades into the jungle and was firing his M16 at the invisible enemy.

"Palmer," he shouted at the silver-haired man, "you got any grenades?"

"Negative," Palmer called back, firing another short burst from his Uzi. "They were in my rucksack."

"We got to do somethin'." Rafe shook his head. "Which bag got the Claymoors?"

"Back there." Palmer jerked his thumb at the duffel lying next to Vinnie.

Rafe crawled to it under the lip of the dune. Quickly he undid the strap, reached in and removed the mine, det cord and clacker. He fastened the strap and crawled back to Palmer.

"Captain," he said, "I'm goin' to set this widowmaker for when we make our move. Cover me."

Palmer opened up, firing sporadic bursts with his Uzi as Rafe slithered over the top of the dune.

Down at the water's edge, Kyle had inflated the large bluish-gray raft. He shrugged out of his rucksack and untied the outboard, clamping it in place at the rear of the rubber boat. Then he threw his Uzi and pack into the inflatable and pushed the boat into the water.

Rafe set the M.A. on its short retractable legs and crawled back over the dune, trailing the det cord behind.

"She's all set," said Rafe, slipping off his rucksack and crawling toward Vinnie. He glanced up and looked at Kyle, who was gesturing to him to make a run for the raft.

"Blow the thing!" Palmer yelled at Rafe. "Let's get the hell out of here."

The black man stared at Vinnie's inert form lying on the sand.

He placed two fingers on the pulse in the wounded man's neck. There was none.

"Oh, no, man. Oh, no . . ." The horrified Rafe moaned.

As the black man knelt by Vinnie's body Palmer crawled to him.

"Come on, come on!" He screamed. *"They're coming. Blow the goddamn M.A. and let's get the hell out of here!"*

Bullets were pockmarking the sand around them as Rafe raised the clacker. There was a roar and the same whirring sound as the C-4 ignited and propelled the seven hundred steel balls into the Cubans coming toward the beach.

As soon as the Claymoor went off, Palmer climbed to his feet and sprinted down the beach toward Kyle and the raft. Rafe lingered a beat and stared down at Vinnie's body. Then he picked up his M-203 and the other duffel bag and followed Palmer toward the water's edge.

In the line of trees, what was left of Macias's command came out of the thick mangroves onto the beach. Some of them had been wounded by the deadly steel balls. Others had been dazed by the explosion. All that were left on their feet were fourteen of the original one hundred and twenty who had left the base camp.

Palmer had reached the water as Macias, who had been behind his men, came onto the beach. The tall colonel saw the rubber boat in the water, and the American wading toward it, as Kyle held it steady.

Rafe was halfway to the water, sprinting like a halfback heading for the end zone, when the Cubans opened fire. He was bracketed by pockmarks as the rounds from the AK-47s struck the sand. He started to zigzag . . . another twenty yards and he would be in the water and to the safety of the raft.

Suddenly he felt a searing, burning sensation in his left shoulder, and he was knocked sprawling in the sand. The duffel bag rolled a couple yards in front of him and stopped. Rafe looked up and saw it. He crawled to the bag and started to drag it the last few feet toward the water.

Kyle watched in horror as Rafe was hit. When the Fidelistas saw the black man go down, they intensified their fire, trying to finish the Yankee off. Little explosions of sand were erupting around Rafe as he crawled toward the water.

Kyle reached into the raft and retrieved his Uzi as Palmer waded to him.

"Stay right here!" he shouted at his former captain. *"I'll be back!"*

Firing his Uzi at the Cubans as he moved through the waist-deep water toward the beach, he could hear Palmer yelling behind him.

"Youngblood . . . don't be a hero!" the man screamed. *"We got half the money . . ."*

Kyle turned for an instant and leveled the Uzi at Palmer.

"Stay there or I'll kill you!" he shouted, then continued on toward Rafe.

The black man had just reached the water's edge when he looked up and saw Kyle kneeling over him.

"Hey, Blood," he said weakly, "nice to see ya."

The remaining soldiers, urged on by Macias, were starting to move down the beach, firing as they came.

Kyle brought the Uzi up and got off a quick burst before the hammer struck on an empty chamber. He dropped the machine gun and grabbed Rafe with one hand, and the big duffel bag with the other, and dragged both of them into the water.

Once they were in the light surf, Kyle was able to handle Rafe and the watertight bag much more easily because of their buoyancy, but the small geysers of water were erupting on the surface around them as the Cubans moved closer.

"Palmer!" Kyle shouted, pushing Rafe and the bag ahead of him. *"Cover us!"*

The former captain had slipped out of the duffel bag and thrown it into the big raft next to Kyle's rucksack. He still held the Uzi in his right hand. Palmer hooked an arm through the rope that encircled the rubber boat and started to fire his submachine gun at the soldiers on the beach. The suppressing fire took effect immediately as the Fidelistas dropped facedown on the sand and stopped firing.

Kyle half pushed, half swam the remaining ten feet to the raft. He tossed in the money bag, then he put an arm under Rafe's legs and slipped him into the unsteady boat. The black man groaned as he landed on his wounded shoulder.

"Thanks, Blood," he said to Kyle. "I needed that."

"Don't mention it," Kyle said. "But I'm gettin' tired of savin' your ass."

Palmer scrambled into the bouncing boat as Kyle held it steady. Then the rancher hoisted himself over the rubber gunwale near the outboard motor.

As soon as Palmer stopped firing, the men on the beach rose and started advancing cautiously toward the water again. Macias stood behind them, cursing and kicking the soldiers nearest to him who lagged behind.

Kyle bent over the small outboard motor. The raft was drifting slowly away from the shore, but no more than fifty yards of open water separated the men in the vulnerable raft and the Cubans, who were now at the water's edge, firing their assault rifles.

Kyle primed the motor and pulled the cord. The small motor sputtered and died. He pulled the cord again with the same result.

"C'mon, baby," said Kyle softly to the temperamental outboard. He reached for the cord and pulled it again. As if the piece of machinery had listened to him, it sputtered to life with a buzz-saw sound. The rancher pushed the lever forward, and the raft spurted away from the shore like a frightened animal.

On the beach, the remnants of Macias's men took heart and rushed knee-deep into the surf, firing their AK-47s at the fast-disappearing inflatable. Fidelito stood on the beach shaking his fist in rage as the Yankees dwindled in the distance.

Kyle was at the control handle, his head resting on a money bag. Palmer sat in the bow, cradling the Uzi, the other money bag at his feet.

Kyle looked at the two men. For the first time he realized Vinnie was not with them. He reached out a hand and tapped Rafe, who opened his eyes.

"Vinnie . . . ?" Kyle's eyes finished the question. Rafe shook his head sadly and looked away. Kyle patted the black man's knee, then headed the rubber boat out into the Gulf of Batabano.

The blue-gray raft had been moving on a southwesterly line toward the rendezvous point with the *Pet-o-Gold* for about forty-five minutes when it happened.

Rafe was resting, eyes closed in the middle of the raft. Palmer was still in the bow, lying on his back, his head propped against the gunwale.

The hot tropical sun burned down, reflecting off the shimmering water, searing Kyle's eyeballs as he scanned the horizon for a sign of the *Pet*. The monotonous buzz of the outboard was comforting to him as Kyle held the control handle and felt the vibration run through his hand and into his arm and shoulder.

He glanced at the bag of money under Rafe's head. It had cost the lives of three good men, but if it helped him get to Marty Fallon, so be it. Images of Marian and the children came in waves and faded away as he looked off in the distance. Men like Marty Fallon ran the world, because of their wealth and power. No one could punish them unless they were as wealthy and powerful.

The rumble of big diesel engines floated to Kyle across the open water. He turned, half expecting to see the friendly lines of the big

Hatteras fishing boat coming toward them. Instead, a half mile away and closing fast, was the sleek gray shape of the 181 patrol boat.

Ortega had two men on the .50s and two on the 76-mm cannon on the foredeck. He was at the helm, because two of his men had been killed in the fierce firefight at the lagoon.

Rafe and Palmer both raised their heads at the sound of the heavy engines.

"Oh, shit!" exclaimed Rafe as Palmer aimed his Uzi at the patrol boat that was speeding toward them.

"Save it," Kyle shouted at him. "It's like tryin' to kill an elephant with a peashooter."

"What do you intend to do?" Palmer yelled back at him as the gunner on the 181 began to open fire. The raft was still out of range, but the Cuban vessel was closing the gap.

Small geysers of water began to appear near the raft as the patrol boat's machine guns chattered from her sides, punctuated by the *chunk chunk* of the cannon on her foredeck.

"Palmer, take off your shirt and wave it before they hit us," shouted Kyle, cutting the outboard and leaving the little boat drifting helplessly.

"Blood!" said Rafe incredulously. "You givin' up?"

Kyle did not answer. Instead he dropped into the bottom of the raft and started to unstrap the three-foot cylinder he had attached to his rucksack. The rancher popped the top off the watertight container and removed the olive-drab tube inside. He held the LAWs rocket in both hands as Palmer removed his shirt and started to wave it over his head.

The rancher knew that the M-72, 66-mm light antitank weapon he held in his hands had a shaped charge that would pierce armor. All he had to do was get a chance to fire it.

When Ortega saw Palmer waving the white shirt, he barked a terse order at his men to stop firing. The bearded captain had mixed emotions. He felt a murderous rage toward the Americans, and yet he was curious to find out what their mission had been. Perhaps, after he had captured and interrogated them, they could meet with an accident at sea.

The 181 was now only a thousand yards from the raft. The gunners still were at their posts, wary of any suspicious moves the Yankees might make.

Kyle sat with his back toward the fast-approaching patrol boat. He had extended the tube that held the rocket to its full length and flipped up the sight. The M-72 was ready.

"Palmer, keep wavin' and smilin'," he said to the former captain. "Rafe, count off the yards by hundreds, so I'll know where she is. Both of you stay low so you don't get hit by the back blast. I'll try to fire it away from you . . . but stay low."

"Six hundred yards . . ." said Rafe, peering over the side of the raft. "Five hundred . . . four hundred . . . three hundred . . ." Rafe's voice was tinged with anxiety. "Two hundred . . . one hundred . . ."

Kyle could hear the twenty-seven-footer's engines drop from a rumble to a steady throb as the 181 throttled back. His finger tightened on the trigger of the weapon in his hands.

The ex–Green Beret turned quickly and raised the tube to his shoulder. Palmer flipped off the gunwale of the rubber boat into the water and grabbed onto the encircling rope. Rafe clawed into the bottom of the raft as if he were trying to dig a hole through it.

The 181 had closed to within seventy-five yards of the raft. Too late, the men on the foredeck saw the dark man in the rubber boat raise the tube and point it at them.

Kyle could see the terror on the men's faces as he squeezed the trigger. There was a whooshing sound, and the olive-drab cylinder bucked in his hands as the projectile, trailing sparks, sped toward the patrol boat.

On the bridge, Ortega saw the rocket coming. He tried to spin the wheel in an evasive maneuver, but it only tended to turn his craft into the path of the missle. The rocket hit the hull, just aft of the gun crew on the foredeck. It pierced the hull and continued on a diagonal line before exploding in the magazine.

There was a thunderous roar, and the 181 seemed to lift out of the water in a geyser of smoke and flame. Pieces of wreckage from the doomed boat flew high into the sky and then dropped lazily back into the waters of the gulf.

Kyle was stunned by the force of the explosion. He was blown backward and toppled over the gunwale into the water. The rancher went under and came up gasping for air. Then he reached and grasped the rope trailing from the crazily bobbing raft.

Rafe lay in the bottom of the inflatable as flaming wreckage fell around him. He had been slightly singed by the back blast of the LAWs, but other than that he had suffered no other injuries.

Palmer pulled himself into the boat and surveyed the flotsam on the water that had been the Cuban boat. The aft section of the hull was still afloat but was burning badly and starting to sink. There were no signs of life.

Kyle came dripping into the rubber boat and dropped heavily

into the stern section. He lay there looking up at the clear blue sky, thinking how close they had come to death.

"Nice goin', brother," said Rafe, giving him a thumbs-up gesture. Kyle nodded and looked past him toward Palmer.

"Very resourceful, Youngblood," the former captain said. "Very resourceful."

Two miles south of the confrontation between the 181 and the six-man raft, the *Pet-o-Gold* was cruising lazily through the placid waters of the gulf. Pet was using the outriggers so it would look as if they were fishing.

The attractive blond and Denise were seated at the control console on the bridge when the rumbling explosion of Ortega's patrol craft blowing up rolled across the water at them. Both women looked in the direction of the sound and saw a long plume of black smoke tracing into the sky.

"That has to be them," said Pet, throwing both throttles into high gear. "I'm heading for the smoke. They may need help."

"I knew it," Denise said, straining her eyes toward the column of smoke. "I had a feeling they'd run into trouble."

Pet spun the wheel, and the big Hatteras's bow rose in the blue-green water as she sped toward the smoke, leaving a wide, frothy wake behind her.

Kyle watched from the stern of the rubber boat as the *Pet-o-Gold* made her way toward them. Palmer sat in the bow of the raft waving his white campesino shirt so that the women on board would see them. The rancher noted how pasty white the man's back looked in direct contrast to the deep tan of his neck and arms.

The powerboat slowly drew alongside as Kyle and Palmer maneuvered the raft around to the stern, where Denise waited with a line. She dropped it down to Palmer, who tied it to a rubber ring on the bow of the raft.

Kyle lifted the duffel bag nearest to him and flipped it over the transom, while Palmer did the same thing with the other bag. Kyle then moved to Rafe and helped him mount the short boarding ladder hooked over the transom.

Palmer went up the ladder, still carrying his Uzi. Kyle picked up his rucksack and followed the former captain into the cockpit.

Rafe leaned back against the padded coaming of the bench on which he was sitting. There were tears in his eyes as he held his wounded shoulder.

''We made it,'' he said, caressing the bench with his hand. ''We made it.''

''Where are the others?'' Denise said to Kyle as he picked up Palmer's Uzi and leaned over the transom.

''Dead!'' Kyle said, untying the line and firing a short burst into the inflatable.

There was a pop and a hissing sound as the rubber boat deflated and settled beneath the surface of the bluish-green water. Pet Palmer gave the big boat full throttle as her husband climbed the ladder to the flying bridge.

The lithe blond turned as she heard Palmer behind her.

''Miss me?'' he asked, sliding on to the padded seat in front of the console.

''How did it go?'' she asked softly, kissing his cheek.

''A bit rough.'' Palmer sighed deeply. ''But there is around thirty million in those green bags . . . and there are only three of *them* left.''

Pet nodded knowingly as her husband gave her a thin-lipped smile. She turned the wheel slightly to the right and set a course for Pinar Del Rio at the western tip of Cuba.

Chapter 41

For three hours the *Pet-o-Gold* had headed due west, past the Isle of Pines, aiming for the Yucatan Channel once more. They had passed a couple of small fishing boats and once a plane had buzzed them, but overall the traffic had been fairly light.

Pet Palmer had gone below into the main cabin to prepare coffee and sandwiches in the galley, leaving her husband at the wheel. The delicious smell of the freshly brewed coffee drifted up from the galley like the scent of an old girlfriend's perfume.

In the spacious cockpit Rafe lay back against the padded coaming as Denise Palermo removed the gauze pad and adhesive tape on his shoulder wound and looked at it.

"It's not bad," she said, applying a new pad. "You're lucky. The bullet went through the fleshy part of the shoulder."

Kyle sat across from them sipping a half-dead beer.

"That's a pretty expensive footrest you got there, Rafe," said Kyle, pointing his bottle toward the duffel bag on which Rafe had propped his feet. "I'm glad you ain't hurt bad. I'm goin' to need help dumpin' the Recoilless and the M-60s before we get back to Key West."

Rafe looked at him and smiled, his even, white teeth standing out in his black face.

"Hey, Blood," he said softly, above the rumble of the diesels. "Thanks for pullin' me off that beach."

"I only went back for the money," said Kyle, laughing and draining the bottle.

Denise put two strips of adhesive tape from the first-aid kit across the gauze pad.

"I feel bad about Vinnie," the attractive brunette said, stooping and running her hand over the bag at Rafe's feet. "I liked him."

Kyle's and Rafe's eyes met for a beat, then both men looked down at the deck.

"There's a lot of money in those bags," said Kyle, obviously changing the subject.

"Can I see it?" Denise blurted out, the excitement shining in her dark eyes. "Can I touch it?"

Rafe leaned over and started to loosen the straps on the duffel bag.

"Not *that* one, Rafe!" said Kyle sharply. The black man stopped and gave Kyle an odd look. He pulled the other bag over and loosened the buckles.

"Help yourself, lady!" He held the open bag out to Denise.

She reached in and withdrew four packets of green bills, banded by orange money wrappers. The dancer pressed the money to her ample breasts and closed her eyes as if she were embracing an old friend.

"I hate to bother you while you're havin' so much fun," said Kyle, holding out his empty bottle. "Would you mind gettin' us a couple of brews?"

Denise slipped the money back in the bag and stood up.

"Anything for the man who just made me a millionaire, sir," she said, curtsying before she went down the ladder into the cabin.

"How come you didn't want her to look in the other bag?" Rafe asked curiously.

"The last M.A. is in there," said Kyle, lowering his voice. "I don't trust anyone but you. If somethin' happened, I want the damned money to blow up."

"Why?"

"We broke our butts to get it," Kyle said softly. "No one else deserves it."

Rafe nodded slowly as Denise came up the ladder with two cold beers. She handed one to each of the men in the cabin.

"Thank you, ma'am," Rafe said, raising the bottle to her. Kyle just nodded and took a short sip of his beer.

The black man put the brown bottle to his lips and was about to drink when a tremendous explosion shook the *Pet-o-Gold*. Denise was thrown to her knees, and Rafe was knocked off the padded bench. Kyle rushed to them and started to help them up as smoke billowed out of the companionway into the cockpit.

Carl Palmer leaned over the bench seat, his face contorted with fear.

"We're under attack from another patrol boat!" he screamed. *"She hit us!"*

Kyle and Rafe scrambled for the ladder to the bridge. The rancher was halfway up when he turned to Denise.

"There's an extinguisher inside the door. See if you can get that fire out." He continued up the ladder with Rafe on his heels.

When they reached the bridge, Palmer pointed to a spot at about ten o'clock off their port side. Coming out of the setting sun like an avenging angel was the 176. Colonel Ramon Macias was on the bridge, a cigar clamped in his teeth. One of now dead Ortega's crewmen was at the helm, but the survivors of Fidelito's command were manning the .50-calibers and the cannon on the foredeck.

Kyle went for the M-60 on the starboard side. Rafe dived for the gun on the port side. Both he and Kyle set the weapons on their bipods and brought them to bear on the charging patrol boat.

Kyle started firing short bursts at the 176, hanging the belts over his shoulder and arms. On the other side of the bridge, Rafe was directing a fusillade of lead at the fast-moving twenty-seven-footer.

Still the Cuban boat came on with the .50s chattering from her flanks like angry dogs and the cannon spewing fire from its muzzle. The 176 was only fifteen hundred yards from the *Pet,* and closing fast.

Palmer spun the wheel to the right, and the Hatteras turned and tried to open some distance between itself and the pursuing vessel. As they turned, Rafe's gun raked the starboard side of the Cuban boat, chewing up the superstructure and killing one of Macias's men in the .50-caliber gun ring.

Down below, Denise Palermo had found the big CO_2 fire extinguisher and turned it on the blaze in the cabin. Within minutes the white powder had smothered the flames and smoke that had been sparked by the cannon round. As the smoke cleared, the brunette could see the gaping hole above the waterline on the port side, where the shell had entered the cabin.

The plush salon was a shambles of charred wood and smoldering cloth. Splintered furniture lay everywhere.

Denise slowly made her way to the galley, which was forward of the mangled cabin. As she stepped into the moderately sized alcove, she saw Pet Palmer.

The lithe blonde was lying on her back near the sink. The coffee urn had been punctured by the explosion, and the brown liquid was leaking out onto the counter and dripping into the dead woman's face.

Above deck Palmer had the *Pet-o-Gold* wide-open, but the Cuban boat had closed the distance to one thousand yards. It would not be long until the *Pet* would be at point-blank range. The fire from the M-60s was having very little effect on the Cuban craft.

Kyle lowered his gun to change belts. As he did, he spotted the tarpaulin-covered Recoilless rifle he and Rafe had mounted on the foredeck. It was a long shot, but they were up against it. What was the word Palmer had used? Resourceful.

Kyle tapped Palmer, who turned around.

"Rafe and I are goin' to try to fire the Recoilless," he shouted. "Wait until we give you the sign, and then bring her about."

"Pet was down below," said Palmer, giving them the thumbs-up. "Have you seen her?"

Kyle shook his head and tapped Rafe's arm.

"Let's go," he said, sliding down the ladder into the cabin.

Kyle climbed onto the gunwale and made his way to the side deck, followed by Rafe. The spray and wind were whipping at their bodies as they made their way along the slippery deck, holding on to the handrail fastened to the bulkhead of the cabin.

Once they reached the foredeck, Kyle made his way to the tarp-covered weapon. Rafe started to pull the cover off the M-40, 106-mm gun. Kyle grabbed his arm.

"Let's load her," he shouted, "before we show what we've got."

Rafe nodded and unsheathed his Ka-Bar. He pried open the case of shells lying next to the gun's tripod.

"Hey, Blood," he said excitedly, "we got HEAT."

"High-explosive antitank rounds?"

"Yep," said Rafe, nodding. "Them boys thought of everything."

Kyle knelt on the slippery foredeck and opened the breech of the M-40. Rafe handed him one of the HEAT rounds. Kyle slammed it home and closed the breech. Then he turned and gave Palmer a circling motion with his right forefinger.

Palmer spun the chrome wheel sharply, and the big boat tacked hard to starboard as it went into the turn. Kyle and Rafe had to grab on to the legs of the Recoilless rifle to keep from falling overboard.

As the *Pet-o-Gold* circled, she was raked by fire from the .50-caliber machine gun on the 176. They could hear the sound of glass breaking as the side windows shattered.

Kyle looked across and could see the patrol boat's broadside, now barely two hundred yards from them. Both boats were running parallel to each other.

Rafe whipped the tarp off the M-40, and Kyle swiveled the gun into position. It was practically a point-blank shot.

On the bridge of the 176, Macias saw the black man unveil the Recoilless rifle, but he did not believe his eyes. Pleasure boats did not carry such weapons. He watched incredulously as the dark, hawk-faced man at the gun fired.

The HEAT round struck the bridge of the Cuban boat, killing Macias and the helmsman at once. The 176 veered crazily as Kyle slammed another shell into the breech. He lowered the barrel of the gun slightly and fired at the patrol boat, which had now edged closer.

The shell struck the Cuban boat amidships at the waterline. The shaped charge in the round exploded as it entered the cabin, and the 176 broke in two with a rending, screeching sound that sounded like an animal dying. Debris from the stricken boat fell on the water in a large circle as both halves of the vessel slid beneath the waves.

Rafe and Kyle were stunned. They collapsed to the foredeck and lay there looking up at the cloudless blue sky. From where Kyle lay, he had a clear view of the flying bridge and Palmer, who had been joined by Denise Palermo.

The pair were talking animatedly, then Palmer quickly left the bridge and headed down the ladder to the main cabin. Denise took over the wheel.

Kyle rolled over and rose to his knees.

"Come on, Rafe," he said. "Somethin's up."

The two men made their way around the slippery side decks to the cabin and then up the ladder to the bridge. Denise was steering the stricken Hatteras as best she could. None of the engines or the cables to the rudders had been hit. She had taken some .50-caliber rounds below the waterline and was taking on seawater in the bilge that was causing her to handle sluggishly.

"What's wrong?" asked Kyle, joining Denise at the wheel. She looked at him and then turned back to the helm.

"Pet's dead," she said in a low voice. "The first shot killed her."

"Rafe, go below and see if you can help Palmer," Kyle said without emotion. "I'll check out the damage up here."

Rafe cautiously pushed open the hatch to the main cabin. He stood in the companionway and surveyed the wreckage, shaking his head.

"Captain Palmer . . ." he called softly. "Captain Palmer . . ." There was no answer, and no one was in the cabin.

The black man came down the ladder and moved slowly around the smashed and charred pieces of furniture. He edged toward the forward alcove, where the galley was located, and spotted Pet's feet, shod in white tennis shoes. They were sticking out from behind the galley's side bulkhead.

Quickly he stepped inside and knelt beside Pet's body.

"What a shame," Rafe said softly, feeling for a pulse in her neck. There was none. He looked at his fingers. They were slippery with blood. She must have taken a piece of shrapnel in the back of the head, he thought.

Rafe turned to rise. As he did, Palmer, who had been hiding behind an open closet door in the galley, lunged out at him with a large bread knife.

The black vet tried to fend off the crazed man, but he could not raise his arm high enough because of the shoulder wound. Palmer sank the knife high in Rafe's right pectoral. The blade glanced off the collarbone and buried itself in the muscles of the chest.

Rafe emitted a strangled cry and toppled violently backward across Pet's body. As he fell, the knife stuck and was wrenched from Palmer's hand.

On the bridge, Kyle and Denise heard Rafe's abbreviated cry for help. Kyle looked at her questioningly.

"Stay here," said Kyle. "I'll check things out below."

"Be careful," she said as Kyle hoisted himself over the Venturi windshield. "Palmer didn't look too rational when I told him about Pet."

Kyle hung on to the windshield and lowered himself to the foredeck. From there he could look through the forward windows into the galley. The decorative curtains were slightly awry, and he could see Pet's body with Rafe sprawled across it, the bread knife sticking out of his chest. There was no sign of Palmer.

"Damn . . ." Kyle cursed as he made his way around the slippery side deck, holding on to the handrail.

When he reached the cabin, Kyle stepped softly on the cushioned seat and down onto the deck. He edged toward the open hatch and took the ladder steps one at a time.

The rancher moved through the smoldering ruin of the main cabin toward the alcove, warily looking for his former captain. He slipped the Browning 9-mm out of his belt. Kyle had removed the silencer when they had left the ranch so that it would be easier to handle.

From where he stood, he could see Rafe and part of Pet Palmer's body. The black man moved his arm and groaned. He wrapped his fingers around the bread knife sticking in his chest and vainly tried to pull it out.

Kyle moved forward quickly, holding the high-powered automatic out in front of him. As he passed the water closet the door flew open, and Palmer, who had been lying in wait, swung a wicked-looking gaffing hook at Kyle's head.

The ex–Green Beret ducked, but the hook continued downward and crashed into his forearm, jarring it and knocking the gun to the deck.

Palmer raised the hook again, a crazed look in his eye as Kyle fell backward over a smashed chair.

"Palmer, what's wrong?" Kyle managed to say before the crazed man brought the hook crashing down again. This time the point caught in the edge of the large table and stuck.

Palmer let the handle of the hook go and went after Kyle's Browning on the deck at his feet. As he raised the gun Kyle scrambled toward the ladder to the cockpit as a round from the 9-mm splintered a panel of imported teak near his head.

Kyle hit the ladder to the bridge and went up it like a cat up a tree. He dived for the M-60 nearest him and picked it up, then glanced down to see if the belt was seated properly and draped it over his arm. Then he stepped to the top rung of the ladder.

Palmer burst out of the cabin, into the cockpit, gun in hand. He hit the ladder and started up as Kyle took his position at the top, the big gun cradled in his sinewy arms.

Carl Palmer stopped on the steps, raised the automatic, and aimed it at the hawk-faced man straddling the entrance to the bridge. It was his last conscious act.

Kyle saw the 9-mm come up. He swung the sleek muzzle of the M-60 and bisected Palmer with the front sight. The ex–Green Beret squeezed the trigger, and the gun jumped in his hand, spewing leaden death at point-blank range.

The ex-captain's chest and stomach disappeared in a welter of blood and tissue as the brass-jacketed slugs struck home. He was driven backward down the ladder, as if some giant hand had picked him up and dropped him in the cockpit.

Carl Palmer lay where he fell, between the two olive-drab duffel bags full of money, his glazed blue eyes staring up at the cloudless sky, the Browning 9-mm still gripped tightly in his hand.

Chapter 42

It was late that night when the *Pet-o-Gold* dropped anchor in the Gulf of Mexico off Key West. They were still too far out to see the lights of the city, but they had passed a number of charter boats heading away from the resort town for some night fishing.

Kyle had disposed of the M-60s and ammo, as well as the Recoilless rifle in the Yucatan Channel. He had used the guns as ballast and tied them to the bodies of Palmer and his wife, then dumped them over the side.

The job had been repugnant to him, but it had to be done. They couldn't go sailing back into the Florida Keys with two dead bodies and enough weapons to start another world war.

He had hidden the money bags in the bilge. When Kyle had opened the hatch to the lower compartment to hide the bags, he found them almost filled with seawater, which accounted for the *Pet*'s sluggish handling. The rancher started the bilge pumps to try to keep the Hatteras from settling deeper in the water.

Rafe was asleep in one of the usable bunks in the main cabin. Kyle had removed the knife and packed the deep wound with gauze pads from the first-aid kit to stem the flow of blood. Palmer's knife had not hit any vital organs, and the black man was in no danger. He would still have to see a doctor when they reached Key West.

As another charter boat passed them in the dark, Kyle watched the fisherman's running lights disappear into the night as he sat in the cockpit sipping a beer. Denise Palermo sat on the padded bench across from him, her feet tucked under her.

"I'm tired," he said, tilting the bottle back and taking a long swig of the bitter brew. He let it run down his throat before continuing. "There's over twenty-eight million in those bags. I'm goin' to give a full share to Manny's wife and kids. I'll split what's left with you and Rafe.

"That's seven million apiece!" Her surprised voice floated to him in the dark. "Share and share alike?"

Kyle leaned back and took another swig of his beer before answering.

"Equal share for equal danger," he said easily. "You handled yourself real well under pressure."

"Thanks," said the brunette, shifting her position on the seat.

"What the hell is money?" continued Kyle. "It's just so much paper after a million. I've got enough for what I have to do."

"Kyle . . ." There was silence for what seemed like a minute. "You're going after Fallon?"

Kyle stood and looked out at the dark gulf. The cold fire burned within him as he spoke.

"Yeah," he said harshly. The hot sting of tears flooded his eyes as he thought of Marian and the children. "There's no power on earth that can keep me from him now."

She could barely make out his back in the darkness as the *Pet* rocked gently on the swells.

"Rafe told me what happened," she said softly. "Sometimes life deals you a shitty hand . . . I'm sorry."

Kyle turned toward her. He could make out her profile against the running lights of another charter boat.

"You gotta play what you're dealt or fold," Kyle said coldly. "I ain't foldin'."

Denise felt uneasy talking about Kyle's tragedy. She wondered if it was guilt she felt because her father had been a man like Marty Fallon.

"I'm glad Rafe's going to be okay," she said, changing the subject. "He'll have to see a doctor when we hit Key West."

"Look, I don't want to go ashore just yet," he said. "I want to think about a place to cache this money for a while."

"Why do we have to hide it?"

"God," he answered, "we'd have the IRS and Treasury people all over us if we spent big sums of money or tried to bank it. You got to do it a little bit at a time . . . hide it for years."

At the mention of the Treasury, Denise felt a sharp stab of conscience.

"What about your plan for Fallon?" She said. "You'll be spending money."

"That's different," Kyle said, crossing over to her side of the cockpit and sitting down. "I'll be dealin' with people who wouldn't go near the government."

There was a long silence as Denise again felt the sting of

conscience. She wanted to tell this dark man who was sitting next to her.

"K-Kyle," she said, stammering, "sometimes people make mistakes. They're forced to do things they don't want to do."

He turned toward her in the darkness. Her voice sounded strange, almost as if it were another person speaking.

"That's true," he said, missing her meaning entirely. "I'm goin' below. I want to check some of those charts to see where we can land without bein' seen."

He stood up and stretched. Then he quickly crossed to the companionway that led to the cabin.

Denise sat in the dark for a long time, staring out at the quiet waters. Her mind struggled with her conscience as she thought about what she had to do.

Big Tony's attractive daughter put her hand to her cheek. When she took it away, she was surprised to find it was wet with tears.

Chapter 43

The sound of a .45 being cocked next to his head woke Kyle from a deep sleep. He rolled on his side, blinking in the early-morning sunlight, trying to remember where he was and why the round black eye of a gun was being stuck in his face.

The rancher swung his legs over the side of the bunk and sat up. As he focused his eyes he made out a tall, burly, crew-cut man aiming a blue-black automatic at a spot between his eyes. Behind the crew-cut man stood a silver-haired man in a three-piece suit.

"Good morning, Mr. Youngblood," Chet Allen said sweetly. "It's a good thing you're such a sound sleeper."

"Who the hell are you?" Kyle asked curtly.

"None of your fuckin' business," McGregor said sharply, menacing Kyle with the .45.

Chet Allen patted his partner on the arm.

"That's not polite talk to someone who just made us millionaires," the silver-haired man said smoothly. They both laughed as Denise sat up on the bunk next to Rafe's. She blinked the sleep out of her eyes and stared at the two men blankly.

"What do you want?" asked Kyle, standing up and pulling a T-shirt on over his head.

"Don't be naïve, Youngblood," Allen answered in a smooth, oily tone. "Let's just say we're on *government* business."

Kyle looked across at Denise, who was still staring at the two T-men.

"I don't know what you're talkin' about," Kyle said, switching his gaze to McGregor's gun hand.

"From the look of things, you had a rough time of it," Allen said as he glanced around the ruined cabin. "Where are the others?"

Kyle was silent. His entire body was taut, like an animal waiting to spring. Allen turned to Denise.

"They're all dead," she said, not looking at Kyle.

"Pity," the silver-haired T-man reflected. "But worth it . . . *if* you came up with the money."

"It was a waste," interjected Kyle, looking directly at Denise. "We didn't find a penny."

Allen turned a malevolent stare on Kyle, who stood hanging on to a shelf near his head. Then he looked at the lithe brunette, who was still sitting on her bunk.

"Is that right, Denise?" he said mockingly. "You didn't find any of your father's money?" She rose from the bunk and moved away from Kyle, who was still staring at her. "You remember our little deal?" Allen continued.

There was a long beat, like when a heart skips in its rhythm.

"We got it all," she said hoarsely, not looking at Kyle. "Over twenty-eight million."

Kyle glared at her, and Allen smiled like a father whose offspring had just presented him with an outstanding report card.

The ex–Green Beret sighed deeply and shifted his position.

"You ever notice how piles of crap stick together?" he said, looking directly at Allen.

Phil McGregor, who was standing next to Kyle, lifted his arm and swung the .45 in an arc at Kyle's face. Kyle blocked the blow with his left forearm and brought his right knee up hard into the T-man's groin. McGregor grunted and started to double over, but Kyle straightened him up with a smashing right hand to the face, breaking the big man's jaw. He dropped the automatic to the deck and fell backward on the bunk Kyle had used.

Chet Allen scrambled backward and reached for the revolver inside his jacket. Kyle slammed two speared-right hands into the man's aorta and left cheek.

Allen screamed as his cheek fractured and the big artery ruptured. Kyle spun him around and put him in a classic choke hold: one arm across the windpipe, tightly grasping the opposite forearm, as the other hand gripped the back of the victim's neck in a half nelson.

Kyle applied tremendous pressure with his powerful arms. Chet Allen growled incoherently and kicked his legs as his windpipe and larynx were slowly crushed. His eyes rolled up in his head, and he went limp in Kyle's arms.

Denise Palermo gave a little scream as Kyle released the T-man, who fell to the deck. Kyle turned and saw Phil McGregor reaching for his .45 at the brunette's feet.

Kyle lunged for the gun. If McGregor reached it first, he would have Kyle dead to rights. As the big man's fingers stretched for the weapon, Denise's foot shot out and kicked the .45 toward Kyle, who snatched it from the floor.

Kyle tried to bring the gun to bear, but McGregor closed with him before he could aim, and the two men struggled against each other for control of the weapon. There was a muffled report as the .45 went off, and the tall man staggered backward, a widening red stain on his vest and jacket. He looked down and tried to reach for Kyle's neck with his big hands. Kyle stepped back, and the T-man crashed to the deck across his dead partner.

As Kyle turned to Denise, the .45 still in his hand, the sound of heavy footsteps on the deck above made him look toward the open companionway. A burly man appeared carrying a compact MAC-10 semiautomatic pistol. The man started down the ladder.

Kyle brought up McGregor's automatic and snapped a shot at the burly man. The slug hit the intruder in the center of the chest and exited in a gaping wound under his left clavicle.

As the man toppled down the ladder into the cabin, Denise screamed and crossed to the bunk where Rafe lay moaning. She was now in Kyle's line of fire.

Kyle grabbed her by the arm and pulled her down as another man, armed with the same weapon, filled the companionway. The second gunman fired a burst from his Ingram MAC-10 and sprayed the cabin. Chips of wood flew in all directions as the 9-mm slugs imbedded themselves in the expensive teak.

Kyle snapped a hurried shot at the man on the ladder, and the gunman started to retreat, firing as he backed up. Kyle squeezed off another round as the man backed into the cockpit.

The ex–Green Beret rolled agilely across to the bunk in which he had slept. He reached under it and pulled out the rucksack he had carried off the beach at Punta Mora. Kyle reached into the olive-drab pack and wrapped his hand around a smooth-skinned one-pound hand grenade. He withdrew the "baseball" and made for the ladder.

Denise lay where he had pushed her. She looked at the terrifying expression on Kyle's face. To her, he looked like an animal fighting for its life.

When Kyle reached the cockpit, the second gunman had already leapt from the gunwale of the Hatteras into the twenty-one-foot sportfisherman the now dead T-men had used to intercept the *Pet-o-Gold*.

As Kyle's head appeared above the gunwale, the man with the MAC-10 opened up, firing a whole magazine at Kyle. The gunman turned to his partner, who had just untied the stern line.

"*Let's get the hell outa here!*" he yelled at the other man, who started for the control console as the boats drifted apart.

As the hired gunman with the MAC-10 slipped another magazine into his weapon, Kyle pulled the pin on the "baseball" and lobbed it into the cockpit of the twenty-one-footer. The killer saw the oval-shaped sphere land near him and scrambled after it.

He was too late. The grenade detonated with a roar. A thousand tiny metal pieces spread out over a ten-meter radius. Some of them imbedded themselves in the body of the hired gunman, causing him to cry out in pain.

The rest of the hot metal shrapnel, driven by the force of the explosion, pierced the fuel tank, and the small boat went up in a ball of flame and smoke, showering the *Pet-o-Gold* and the surrounding water with flaming debris.

Kyle ducked behind the gunwale, when the sportfisherman blew. Then he rolled over on his back and lay looking up at the billowing cloud of smoke, not even realizing he still had McGregor's automatic in his left hand.

Denise came tentatively up the ladder into the cockpit. She saw Kyle lying on the deck and came toward him.

Slowly he raised the .45 and aimed it at her trim abdomen. The attractive brunette stopped and waited.

"Go ahead," she said softly. "I deserve it."

"Why . . . why the double cross?" he asked, lowering the muzzle of the gun. "We cut you in—over seven million dollars."

Denise stood there, her dark eyes glistening with tears.

"Allen grabbed me after the fight at the Caribe," she said almost inaudibly. "He threatened me. I felt you guys were going to cut me out . . . it's my father's money."

Kyle raised up on his elbows and stared at her.

"By the time we were in Key West, you knew different," he said, getting to his feet.

"It was too late," she said, fear in her voice. "I was scared. Allen told me I would go to jail."

Kyle turned his back on her and looked over the transom at the hulk of the burning boat as it settled in the green water of the gulf.

"Why'd you help me down in the cabin?" he said, not looking at her.

"Instinct." Denise shrugged. "I made a mistake in Miami. By the time I knew you guys were straight with me, I was up to my ass in T-men."

Kyle turned and sighed heavily. He started for the cabin.

"Makes no never mind, anyhow," he said, looking back at her. "They would have killed the three of us after they got their hands on the money." He stuck the .45 in the waistband of his jeans. "Start the engines while I get rid of your pals. We'd better get out of here before somebody comes to see what's burnin'."

He started down the ladder. She stood looking at him.

"Kyle . . ." she started to say.

He stopped on the second step, his head and shoulders visible above the deck. He fixed her with a look that made her blush.

"I guess you are your father's daughter," he said softly as he descended the ladder into the main cabin.

Chapter 44

About twenty miles north of Key West, Sugarloaf Key sat like a broken horseshoe astride the Overseas Highway. Kyle had picked the key off a chart he'd found in the main cabin. The gulf side of the small island appeared to be an isolated, intricate series of coves and inlets.

Kyle had weighted the bodies of the dead T-men and their hired gunmen with whatever heavy ballast he could find and slipped them over the side. Then he headed the battered Hatteras toward the desolate western side of Sugarloaf Key.

They had found a small isolated cove and anchored the boat near shore. Kyle removed a couple thousand dollars in mixed bills from one of the bags and took off on foot across the key, leaving Denise and Rafe aboard the *Pet-o-Gold.*

On the more populated ocean side of Sugarloaf, he found a gas station, a motel and a small airstrip. There was an old sun-bleached Ford service van parked outside the motel office.

Kyle found the owner of the truck, a thin, balding man, behind the motel registration desk, where he worked as a day clerk. He offered the clerk a thousand dollars for the use of the vehicle with no questions asked. Kyle told the clerk he'd be able to pick up the van the following day in the parking lot of the Garrison Bight Marina in Key West. The thin man, who was used to all sorts of bizzare offers and odd characters because of the smuggling and drug-running activity in the area, nodded and smiled. He handed Kyle the keys as the rancher counted out ten one-hundred-dollar bills on the desk.

Kyle drove the old Ford as close to the isolated cove as the dirt road would permit, then hiked the short distance to the boat. From there he waded into the water and swam out to the *Pet* and climbed aboard.

Denise was asleep in the bunk next to Rafe. Kyle woke her and told her to get Rafe ready. Then he rummaged through a forward locker, found an inflatable three-man raft and dragged it to the cabin as Denise got Rafe to sit up.

Kyle quickly inflated the raft and dropped it over the stern, tying it off to one of the cleats in the gunwale. He then went below and retrieved the two duffel bags and carried them up on deck.

Denise brought Rafe to the ladder, and Kyle helped him into the small rubber boat. Then he gave her a hand over the transom. When she was seated, he dropped the bags full of money down to her.

There were a set of oars in the boat. Denise picked up one as Kyle untied the raft from the stern. Then she paddled toward shore with Rafe and the money.

Kyle quickly went below and opened all the gas jets on the galley stove. Then he took the remaining smooth-skinned grenades from his rucksack and placed them on a pile of debris in the center of the main cabin.

He went back to the locker where he had found the raft and removed a five-gallon can of kerosene. Kyle unscrewed the lid and doused the pile with the contents of the container.

When he had finished in the cabin, Kyle made his way to the flying bridge and seated himself in front of the control console. He punched the starter, and the big diesels rumbled to life. He eased in the starboard engine clutch and pushed the throttle forward. The big boat turned slowly around in the small cove.

Once her bow was headed in a direct line out into the gulf, Kyle engaged the other engine and the *Pet* moved forward. The rancher secured the chrome wheel with a bungi cord to insure she would stay on course, then he dropped into the cabin and removed the flare pistol he had stuck in the waistband of his jeans.

Kyle looked through the open hatch, aimed at the pile of debris and fired the flare. There was a whooshing sound as the kerosene ignited and the debris started to burn. Flame and smoke appeared and were fanned by the breeze that blew through the holes in the hull.

Satisfied, Kyle mounted the gunwale and dove off the transom into the clear green waters of the small cove. Slowly he started to swim toward the beach where Denise and Rafe waited for him with the two large duffel bags full of money.

The next morning at 11:00 A.M., Kyle sat across from Rafe's bed in a white, antiseptic hospital room in Key West. The black man had a gauze bandage around the machete wound in his forearm. Rafe's bed was in the up position, and a small color television was playing an inane giveaway show.

Rafe smiled broadly as he squeezed Kyle's hand.

"We did it, Blood . . . we did it," he said ecstatically, grinning from ear to ear.

"Have you called Betty yet?" Kyle asked gently.

"Nope. Afraid to." Rafe laughed. "Figure she'll give me the usual sack of shit."

Kyle leaned closer and whispered, "Wait till she sees what you brought her. I think the crap will stop."

"I sure hope so," the black man said softly.

"I told you how I want to split the money," Kyle said. "Full share for Manny's wife and kids. Vinnie and Cliff had no close kin—"

"What about Denise?" the black man cut in.

Kyle sat back and sighed. He stared at the television for a beat, where a fat woman, dressed as a lobster, had just won a new car.

"I don't know, Rafe," he said softly, turning back to the bed. "After the deal she pulled with those Treasury guys, I don't trust her."

"She was scared, Blood."

"If she stays alive, she's a threat to me and what I have to do," Kyle continued.

"I like her," the black man said sincerely. "She came through for us . . . I think we can trust her now."

Before Kyle could answer, a young intern pushed open the heavy wooden door and entered the room. He was an owlish-looking man with thick glasses. He carried a white clipboard with some official-looking papers on it.

"How are you feeling this morning?" he chirped cheerily as Kyle and Rafe eyeballed him.

"Fine, Doc," Rafe answered as the doctor came to the bed. "I only got one complaint."

"What's that?" said Owl-eyes attentively.

Rafe gave Kyle a sidelong glance and grinned.

"It's these gowns," he said, plucking at the light blue smock he had on. "Every time I get out of bed, everybody gets a look at my black ass."

Rafe guffawed loudly, and Kyle grinned as the young doctor looked around the room uncomfortably.

"Ah, yes . . . I see," the intern said. "Mr. Phillips, you

sustained a gunshot wound, as well as a severe laceration and puncture wound. We have to file a report with the local authorities."

"The cops?" Rafe shot a look at Kyle.

"Yes, the police." The owl-eyed doctor stood with his pen poised above the clipboard. "Now, how did you receive these wounds?" Rafe looked at the doctor, then at Kyle with a questioning look on his face.

Kyle stood up and walked around the bed to where the doctor stood.

"Doc," he said quietly, "this man has a mean wife."

"Did *she* do this to him?" The intern blinked.

"No," said Kyle. "He was playin' cards with some nasty people, and they didn't think a deck should have five aces."

"What does his wife have to do with it?"

Kyle's tone became more confidential as he continued.

"She don't like him to gamble. If she found out . . . well, she might do worse to him." Kyle put his hand in his jeans pocket and slipped out two one-hundred-dollar bills. "You wouldn't want to be responsible for this man's death?"

Kyle dropped the two bills on the clipboard, and the doctor's eyes bugged behind his thick lenses. He looked at Rafe and then turned to Kyle.

"The wounds really aren't that serious," he said, pocketing his sudden windfall. "They won't have to be reported." He adjusted his glasses and quickly exited the room.

"Good move, Blood," said Rafe, lying back on the bed. "That dude didn' know whether to shit or go blind."

"You take it easy," Kyle said, patting him on the shoulder. "I'll be back. I got some stuff to do."

Rafe looked at him oddly. He couldn't quite figure out the look on Kyle's face.

"You goin' to meet Denise?" he asked.

"I don't know where she is, Rafe," said Kyle. "After we got Manny's van at the marina and dropped you here at the hospital, she took off . . . said she had to think."

"Look, Blood," the black man said softly, gripping his arm, "don't do nothin' foolish. Wait for me."

"You hurry up and get the hell out of here," Kyle said reassuringly. "I won't do nothin' without you . . . besides, I want you to know where I stashed our share of the money."

Rafe laughed and sat up, his black face brightening.

"Knowin' you, it's probably buried in some jungle around here."

Kyle leaned close to him. He lowered his voice till it was barely audible.

"It's buried, all right," he said. "In an abandoned missile silo on Boca Chica Key. M-35 is now worth fourteen million."

"M-35," mused Rafe. "What'd you do with the rest?"

"Manny and Denise's share are in the van with the last 'widow maker,'" said Kyle. "I still don't trust her. I set the mine on remote. Just in case."

Before Rafe could answer, a picture flashed on the small television screen. Both men stopped and stared. It was a film clip of Carl and Pet Palmer arriving in Key West earlier in the week. They cut to a shot of the *Pet-o-Gold* in the slip at Garrison Bight, and then a chopper shot of a burned-out hulk floating on the surface of the gulf.

Rafe reached out and turned up the volume. The announcer's rich voice filled the room.

"In what appears to be a tragic boating accident, it is feared that sportsman T. Carl Palmer, and his chain-store heiress wife, Petula Goodman Palmer, of West Palm Beach, Florida, died in a fire and explosion aboard their fifty-three-foot Hatteras, the *Pet-o-Gold*.

"The burned-out hull was found floating in the Gulf of Mexico four miles west of Sugarloaf Key. The Coast Guard has said that no bodies have been recovered as of yet.

"A search will continue for the next four days."

Rafe and Kyle stared at each other for a long beat. Then Kyle reached out and punched the on/off button on the set, causing the screen to go black.

Chapter 45

Later that day Kyle was sitting on one of the double beds at the South Beach Motel. The second green duffel bag lay at his feet, about two-thirds full. On the bed around him lay stacks of bills bound neatly with orange paper wrappers.

The rancher picked up a couple packs and stuffed them into the bag. He repeated the same process until there were only a few of the small green bundles left.

He looked at the other bed where a number of newspapers and magazines lay scattered about. The front page of the local news caught his eye. There were large pictures of Carl and Pet Palmer, and a shot of the *Pet-o-Gold* before it had burned.

Kyle shook his head and continued to stuff the money into the duffel. There was a slight tapping on the door that caused him to look up quickly.

Kyle rose and slipped a hand between the mattress and boxspring. When he withdrew it, he had McGregor's .45 clutched in his fist. He pulled the slide back and let it snap into place. Now there were four rounds in the clip, and one in the chamber.

Cautiously he eased to the door and put his ear against it.

"Yeah," he said softly, "can I help you?"

There was a beat, and a nervous voice he could barely hear came through the door.

"It's Denise."

"Are you alone?"

"Yes."

Kyle opened the door and admitted the attractive brunette. She was wearing a flower-print sundress and a pair of fashionable dark sunglasses.

As Kyle crossed back to the bed she closed the door quietly behind her but did not lock it.

"Where were you?" he asked, uncocking the .45 and slipping it back under the mattress.

She came over to the bed and looked down at the money still lying on it. Then she looked up at Kyle, who sat down again. He had his shirt off, and Denise marveled at the number of scars that traced his arms and muscular torso.

"I had some things to do," she said nervously.

"What are you doing with the money?"

Kyle stuffed a few more packs down into the bag before answering.

"This is yours and Manny's shares," he said. "I'm just storing it for you . . . can't carry this much money around in a gym bag."

"Anything new about the Palmers?" she asked, sitting in a chair near the door as Kyle buckled the straps on the duffel bag.

"Paper said they were lookin' for some people who were seen boardin' the boat at the marina," Kyle said, throwing the bag on the bed. "They figure they were killed when the fire and explosion took place."

"Lucky us," she said, laughing.

Before he could answer, the sound of a large engine and the squeal of tires penetrated the room. Denise and Kyle stared at each other as three car doors slammed outside. There was the sound of footsteps and a hard knock on the door.

Before he could stop her, Denise was out of her chair and at the door. She opened it, and three burly men in ludicrous Hawaiian shirts pushed past her into the room.

Kyle was off the bed quickly and reaching for the .45, but one of the men leveled a sawed-off 12-gauge at him, and he straightened up and raised his hands.

"More friends of yours?" Kyle sarcastically asked Denise as she closed the door.

"Friends of my father's and *mine*," she said, turning to him. "That money belongs to them and to me. We're only taking what's ours."

"What's this 'we're' shit," one of the men near her said, slipping a .357 Magnum from the belt around his bulging waist. "This is family money."

"Whatever happened to finders keepers?" said Kyle, his hands still in the air.

The man with the 12-gauge jerked it at Kyle meaningfully. "Watch your mouth, wiseass," he said. Then he turned to Denise. "All the dough in that bag?"

She nodded.

"Open it," the man with the Magnum said, waving the gun at Kyle.

The rancher pulled the big duffel bag toward him and unbuckled the straps at the top. He made the opening wider, pulled out a couple packs of bills and dropped them on the bed.

The third man walked over and picked up one of the packs. He pulled off one of the bills and looked at it closely.

He turned and said to the others, "It's the real McCoy." Then he looked back at Kyle. "Pack it up," he said curtly.

Kyle put the money back in the duffel, strapped it closed and placed it on the floor. The swarthy man with the Magnum stuck the pistol in his belt and lifted the bag by its canvas handle.

"Take me with you," Denise pleaded, rushing to him. "I called you and told you about the money. I'm Big Tony's daughter."

The man pushed her away with his forearm and started toward the door with the bag.

"Listen, sister," he said harshly. "You and your boyfriend are lucky we're leavin' you alive. It's only 'cause you *are* Big Tony's daughter. We woulda found out about the money sooner or later. We been watchin' your old man for years, waitin' for him to make his move."

"What about the others?" she asked.

"We're the only ones left alive who worked with him at the Capri," said the man with the Magnum. "Everyone else who knew about the money your old man stashed is dead." He pushed her out of the way and opened the door. The man without the gun exited, followed by the thug with the 12-gauge shotgun. "Both of you keep your mouths shut and count your blessings. Ciao." He left, closing the door softly behind him.

Kyle put his finger to his lips, cautioning Denise not to speak. He slipped to the window and peered out the side of the venetian blinds.

Kyle watched as the man with the bag opened the trunk of the light-colored sedan and flipped the big bag inside. He slammed down the lid, and the three thugs climbed into the late-model vehicle. The man behind the wheel started the engine, and the sedan started to back out of the parking space.

Kyle raced to the night table and opened the drawer. His fingers closed on the clacker for the Claymoor he had placed in the duffel bag.

The ex–Green Beret slipped back to the window in time to see the sedan at the entrance to the parking lot. There were no other cars or people near the vehicle.

He squeezed the electronic device, and the entire back of the automobile exploded in a sheet of flame and smoke as seven hundred steel balls powered by a pound of C-4 went ripping through the car and its occupants.

As the gas tank blew, the hood of the car rose in the air and landed on the motel office roof, leaving the car burning furiously in the driveway.

Denise stood in the corner by the door where the burly man with the bag had pushed her.

Kyle turned from the window. "It worked," he said softly. "It's a good thing you remembered those guys from Cuba, or they would have been all over us as soon as they found out we had the money."

She came toward him with a strange smile on her face.

"How much did you blow up?" she asked as he went to the closet.

"About two million. I had to make it look good, just in case they looked in the bag."

"Not a bad price to pay to get those guys off our backs," she said as she crossed to the bed and sat down.

"Yeah," he said, opening the closet door. "The rest of the bag was filled with newspapers and magazines."

There were two large valises in the closet. He reached in and took one out.

"What's that?" Denise said, standing up.

"Your share," Kyle said, pushing it toward her. "You earned it today."

Denise Palermo looked at this strange man, and an overwhelming feeling of compassion gripped her. Tears shone brightly, and then, unbelievably, she was across the room embracing him.

After an awkward moment Kyle patted her shoulder, then broke apart.

"I'm sorry," she said tearfully. "I don't know what came over me."

"A simple thank-you would have been enough," Kyle quipped, and they both laughed as sirens screamed in the distance.

"I wish I could go with you to get this Fallon," Denise said earnestly.

"Thanks for the offer," he said, "but this is something I have to do alone. I've got the money to bring him down."

He offered her his hand. She took it and kissed his cheek.

"Thanks for everything—and good luck," she said, picking up the valise. "Say good-bye to Rafe for me."

"Can you handle that?" he said, opening the door for her. "I can take it to your car."

"I'm okay." The attractive brunette stopped and put down the bag. "You didn't put a mine in this one, did you?"

They both laughed, and Denise picked up the bag and walked to the small compact car she had rented. As she put it into the trunk she turned and smiled at Kyle, who was standing shirtless in the doorway of the room.

Behind her, at the entrance to the motel, he could see a maze of police cars and fire trucks surrounding the smoking hulk that was the remains of a tan, late-model sedan.

Chapter 46

Two days later Rafe and Kyle were headed north in a nondescript pickup they had rented from an agency in Key West. Manny's van had been disposed of in a salt pond on Boca Chica Key. It was a desolate spot they hoped wouldn't be visited by anyone for years to come.

As the truck ate up the miles, Kyle was already formulating a plan that would enable him to get to Marty Fallon.

The two men rode along in silence for twenty minutes.

"You're thinkin' about Fallon," Rafe said lightly. "I can tell by your tone of voice."

Kyle looked at him and smiled.

"Sorry, Rafe," he said. "I guess I was doin' some plannin'. Now that we got the money, it's all I can think of."

"Blood, you can't go after that dude alone," Rafe said, "not after what Big Tony told you he got on that island. You'll need me."

Kyle looked at him and smiled.

"That's all I need." Kyle said. "You got a wife and kids. If Fallon don't get me, Betty will, for takin' you away again."

They both laughed.

"Kyle," Rafe said sincerely. "Ever since you saved this poor boy's ass in 'Nam, I been wantin' to do somethin' for you. Let me do this."

"I don't know, Rafe," Kyle said slowly, tightly gripping the wheel of the truck. "Let me see how I feel . . . I don't want you to die doin' my job."

Rafe looked at him and shook his head.

"Your old code of honor," the black man said, looking at him.

"I guess so," Kyle replied, and pushed the truck a bit faster toward Miami.

• • •

They had reached the Magic City after dark and headed for Little Havana. Kyle had found Manny Lopez's address on the van's registration in the glove compartment of the vehicle.

They found the house on a small, well-kept side street. It had been freshly painted and had a small wooden porch.

Kyle parked the truck in front of the house, and both he and Rafe got out. Kyle took the large valise out of the truck bed, and the two men walked up to the door.

Rafe rang the bell. After a few seconds a small brown face with Manny's eyes peered out from behind the curtains and looked at them.

"Is your mom at home?" Rafe asked.

The face disappeared, and after a short wait the door opened, and Clara Lopez, a small-boned, dark woman with a pretty face, stood in the doorway.

"Yes," she said softly, "can I help you?"

"Mrs. Lopez," Kyle said gently, "we're friends of Manny's. Can we come in?"

She ushered them into an immaculately kept living room and asked them to sit. Kyle and Rafe both sat on the couch with the valise facing them. Clara sat in an easy chair in front of them.

"Is anything wrong?" she asked quietly.

"Señora," Kyle began, "we have some bad news." Her hand went to her throat in a gesture reminiscent of Marian when she was frightened.

"Is it Manuel?" she asked, looking at them with sad eyes.

"I'm afraid so," Rafe answered as four small children entered the room. They ranged in age from ten to four. The little ones looked at the strangers with large brown eyes. "He gave his life to help free Cuba." The black man looked across at Kyle, who nodded.

"Madre de Dios!" Clara Lopez said, crossing herself. The two smaller children came to her and huddled close.

"You and the children can be very proud of him," Kyle said, rising and taking the suitcase to where she sat.

"What is this?" she asked, looking at the large bag.

"This is Manny's share of what we were doing," said Kyle, setting the bag on its side in front of her. "He sent it to you."

Kyle knelt and opened the bag. As he lifted the lid her brown eyes took in the rows of stacked bills that filled the valise.

"There's almost seven million dollars in there for you and the children," said Rafe as he watched the tears spill down Clara Lopez's cheeks.

They drove from Little Havana to the Liberty section of Miami. Before they had left the Keys, Kyle had taken Rafe to Missile Silo M-35, on Boca Chica Key, to show him where he had cached their share of the money. They had both agreed to take two hundred thousand apiece and come back for the rest, as it was needed.

As they came down Palmetto Drive and Rafe saw his house, he asked Kyle to stop the truck and turn off the lights.

"Blood," he said nervously, "you got to do me a favor."

"Anything, brother," said Kyle.

"You got to go up there and talk to her first. If she sees me with all these bandages, she's goin' to tear into me."

They left the truck and walked up to the house together. Kyle went up the steps while Rafe waited in the shadows on the sparse lawn.

There was a light on inside the house. Kyle knocked on the porch door. He could see Betty rise from her chair in front of the television set and make her way to the door.

She shaded her eyes with her hand and peered out. When she recognized Kyle, she opened the door.

"Where's Rafe?" she said, looking past him toward the street.

"Betty, I . . ." Kyle started to say.

"*I knew it!*" she screamed at him. "*I knew you'd kill him.*"

Rafe stepped out of the shadows and looked at her. She gave another little scream, ran down the steps and embraced the black man, who was grinning broadly. "*You damn jackass!*" she screamed again as she hit him on his wounded shoulder. "Why'd you worry me like that?"

"Arghhhh!" Rafe yelped in pain, grabbing his shoulder. As he did, most of the two hundred thousand fell to the ground, like a lazy shower of leaves from a tree.

Betty stared down. In the dim light from the house she could see the bills lying on her lawn.

"Oh, Rafe," she said, crooning. "Oh, Rafe, honey, ya did it . . . ya really did it."

The black man grinned like a big cat and looked up at Kyle on the step. Then he glanced back at Betty, who was picking up the money and stuffing it into the bosom of her robe as if she were picking cotton in an Alabama field.

• • •

Later, in the house, long after Betty had gone to sleep on a pillowcase full of one-hundred-dollar bills, the two men, one black, one white, both sharing a common bond, sat in Rafe's living room sipping beers.

"How long you plannin' to wait, Blood?" said Rafe, tapping the bottle against his even, white teeth.

"I want to start as soon as possible," said Kyle, closing his eyes. "The longer I wait, the stronger that bastard gets."

"You gonna be able to get at him . . . with all that shit he got?"

"I'll get to him or die tryin' " Kyle said coldly.

Rafe took another swig on his bottle.

"Is it worth dyin' for, Blood?" said Rafe, knowing he could make a statement to his comrade because of what they had shared over the years.

Kyle turned to him and smiled.

"You know somethin', Rafe," he said softly, "you're startin' to sound more like Marian every day."

EPILOGUE

The silver-haired man sat in his wheelchair, watching as the blood-red sun dipped toward the green sea. He popped the end off the plastic tube in his hand and slid a large, expensive cigar into his palm.

He bit the tip off the cigar and spit it onto the stone floor of the long balcony of his cliff house. Behind him, a tanned, muscular blond man in a tight bikini hoisted himself out of the large pool and stepped, dripping wet, to the crippled man's side.

He took a large towel from one of the handles on the wheelchair and toweled himself off. He hung the towel over his shoulder and took a silver lighter from the metal tray on the chair. He flicked the wheel with his thumb and held the flame to the crippled man's cigar.

The man in the chair sucked greedily inward till the tip of the cigar glowed cherry-red. Then he blew a plume of acrid, gray smoke into the pristine air. The muscular man behind him began to massage the silver-haired man's neck and shoulders as he looked out at the white crescent of beach below them.

Armed men with automatic weapons and vicious guard dogs patrolled the sand, while above them on the fortresslike house searchlights and radar dishes were constantly scanning the sea and sky.

"What do ya think, Terry?" Marty Fallon said as he looked at the end of his glowing cigar. "Ya think he'll be able to get to me?"

"No way, Mr. Fallon," said the muscular blond, massaging Marty's neck and shoulders. "You got a hundred guys protecting you . . . guard dogs up the ass . . . radar . . . alarm systems . . ."

"Yeah, I know all that crap," Marty said, flicking the ash off his cigar. "But there's somethin' about this guy . . . there's somethin' about him. . . ."

Terry dug his thumbs into his boss's taut shoulder muscles.

"You ain't got a thing to worry about, Mr. Fallon," he said, smiling, "not a thing."